BY PAMELA TERRY

The Sweet Taste of Muscadines
When the Moon Turns Blue

WHEN THE MOON TURNS BLUE

WHEN THE MOON TURNS BLUE

A Novel

Pamela Terry

BALLANTINE BOOKS

NEW YORK

Published in the United States by Ballantine Books, an imprint of Random House, a division of Penguin Random House LLC, New York.

BALLANTINE is a registered trademark and the colophon is a trademark of Penguin Random House LLC.

Library of Congress Cataloging-in-Publication Data
Names: Terry, Pamela, 1956– author.
Title: When the moon turns blue: a novel / Pamela Terry.
Description: First Edition. | New York: Ballantine Books, [2023]
Identifiers: LCCN 2022030069 (print) | LCCN 2022030070 (ebook) |
ISBN 9780593359204 (hardcover) | ISBN 9780593359211 (ebook)
Subjects: LCGFT: Novels.
Classification: LCC PS3620.E7726 W48 2023 (print) |
LCC PS3620.E7726 (ebook) | DDC 813/.6—dc23/eng/20220623
LC record available at https://lccn.loc.gov/2022030069
LC ebook record available at https://lccn.loc.gov/2022030070

Printed in the United States of America on acid-free paper

randomhousebooks.com

2 4 6 8 9 7 5 3 1

First Edition

Book design by Jo Anne Metsch

For Sandee

. . . But how can you have a sense of wonder if you're prepared for everything? Prepared for the sunset. Prepared for the moonrise. Prepared for the ice storm. What a flat existence that would be.

—MARGARET ATWOOD

Ah, me!—not dies—no more than spirit dies;
But in a change like death is clothed with wings;
A serious angel, with entranced eyes,
Looking to far-off and celestial things.

—HENRY TIMROD

WHEN THE MOON TURNS BLUE

Through a slit in the green curtain he could just see the garden, asleep in the wintertime sun. A thin stripe of morning light occasionally touched his shoulder like a knighthood.

Let her open the window, he thought.

You won't require an open window, the voice replied.

He didn't try to turn his head this time. He knew no one was there.

How much longer?

Not long now, I shouldn't think.

He wished he could tell her what he knew. She seemed so pale now sleeping there beside him, almost invisible.

As the morning got closer he could once again hear the paper-soft flutter of wings. He closed his eyes to see them. Feathers. Feathers of white, blue-black, and gray. Falling and flying like snow. Coming down from the ceiling, drifting in through the window glass.

He secretly wished for the black.

Soaring up on the wind currents, flying out over the oceans. He had coveted that casual liberty since his boyhood. To run and run, to lift away. An unspoken longing buried deep in his soul.

You can go now.

I can? Where should I go?

Anywhere that you wish.

The silhouette of a raven cast a violet-hued shadow into the dimly lit room. The bird briefly hovered outside the window, then spread its black feathers, lifted over the treetops, and was gone.

To glide on the winds of winter.

I

—

BUTTER
AND
MARIETTA

Butter Swann sat listening to the eulogy from a pew five rows back from the front. She could see the side of Marietta's face clearly. She saw her reach a black-gloved hand up to her neck and rub it hard in a little circular motion that left a bright red blotch on the whiteness of her skin. Marietta still had perfect skin, even after all these years. Butter couldn't help but notice. Hardly any gray in her hair, either. Still as auburn as it had been when they'd first met in kindergarten. Butter could tell when it was natural and when it wasn't. She watched as Marietta shifted in her seat on the front row of the church, bending her head sideways, stretching her neck. Butter knew what this meant; she'd seen it happen to Marietta many times before, though not, she realized now, in a long, long time. Age had its small concessions; migraines usually went for younger prey.

Yes, she was sick, Butter thought, as she watched Marietta open her purse and pull out a flowered handkerchief—an old one from her mother, probably, still smelling of that lilac perfume

Caroline had always worn—and hold it to her mouth. Even from here you could see how pale she'd suddenly gone. Butter felt a needle prick of panic for her once close friend. They'd not had a conversation of any consequence in years, not since Marietta had called Butter—Butter would never forget the word—"crass." Crass! All because Butter had complained about those emergency room doctors seeing that Mexican boy before her grandson, Peter, when he broke his leg skiing on their family vacation in Park City. No insurance, you could tell they weren't even *American,* for God's sake, and Peter having to wait on a gurney in the hallway of that little hospital for two whole hours while they went before him. If she thought about it now, the anger could still come before the guilt. Well, she'd been upset. Couldn't Marietta have understood that?

"Harry Cline was one of the last of the great gentle men . . ." Reese Pearson was speaking now, his eyes glued to the typed-out speech in his slightly shaking hands. Butter's eyes traveled back down to the front row. There was Marietta's brother, Macon, sitting beside her, his wife, Glinda, in a forest green suit and hat. Who wears a hat anymore, Butter asked herself. She crossed her legs, smoothing down her dress. Even though she'd told herself she wouldn't do it, she couldn't help but remember her own husband's funeral. It had taken place right here, nine years earlier come May; and she'd been sitting right there where Marietta was now. Lord, the stress. Everybody staring, watching her, just like she was watching Marietta.

Of course, that funeral hadn't been the same for Butter as this one was for Marietta, what with her and Joe practically divorced when he fell off the roof and died. Butter shook her head a little at the memory. He'd never pay the money to hire that towheaded neighbor boy to clean his gutters like the rest of the men on the street. She'd told him. Well, at least it was quick. His head hit the corner of the window box on the way down and that was that. There'd been a wren's nest in that window box. Not one of the tiny blue eggs had broken.

Her son, Christo, had wanted her to have Joe's funeral at his church; they'd had a row about it. Christo and Jen went to Sanctorium, one of those modern churches that eschewed denominational labels, preferring, Butter supposed, to make things up as they went along. She and Joe had visited with them there one Easter. She'd bought a new suit for the occasion, just as she'd done every Easter of her life, and walked into the dark, windowless place only to be met with people in jeans and T-shirts. The music sounded like the stuff she heard on the radio, and the ministers, all wearing robes—the one part of religious tradition they seemed to approve of—bobbed and bounced around the stage like car salesmen. She'd left that day, squinting in the noontime sun, feeling like she'd just sat through some sort of spiritual action movie. There was no way on earth she'd have launched Joe on his final journey from that place, no matter how much Christo wanted her to.

Joe's fifteen-year-old cat, Marvel-Ann, had dropped dead two weeks before her master. Of old age, the vet said. Privately, Butter had always thought the thing simply wanted a head start. That cat hated her. Marvel-Ann would've had no intention of living with Butter in her new condo in Windward Oaks, which was where she moved after Joe died. Thank goodness they hadn't signed the divorce papers before he went. Not having to split everything down the middle meant she could afford to upgrade to a bigger unit, right by the pool. All things work together for good, Butter thought, which was, she supposed with an inward smirk, another opinion that Marietta Cline would've called "crass."

That one conversation over chicken salad down at Mama's Way Cafe five years ago had effectively ended their friendship. Butter could never find a way to start it up again, and Lord knows, Marietta had never even tried. Still, they'd known each other since childhood, and Butter wouldn't have wished a sick headache to fall on the woman right in the middle of her husband's funeral, no matter how Butter's face still burned at that memory of their last lunch together. As Reese finished his eulogy, she saw Richard Kyle get up from his seat on the second row and walk toward the pulpit. He bowed his head, and everybody else followed suit. Butter watched as Marietta dug her fingers into her neck again. You can't pray away a migraine, she thought, with a sympathy that surprised even her.

A shadowless glare pierced Marietta's left eye like a drill as she sat at the end of the front row pew. Already the flowers were fading—red into mauve, yellow to beige, green to a papery gray. Soon every wreath, bouquet, and spray would look like a black-and-white photograph, all color erased by the pain that was, even now, beginning to creep down from the crown of her head like hot lava, settling hard behind her eye. Then the nausea would come. As sure as she was sitting here now—back stiff and straight, legs crossed at the ankle—Marietta knew a wave of sheer sickness was going to douse her in cold sweat and knock her sideways. Experience told her she had about fifteen minutes.

And I saw a new heaven and a new earth: for the first heaven and the first earth were passed away; and there was no more sea . . . Harry's old friend from college, Richard, was reading from Revelation now, his voice faltering only a little when he looked out over the crowd. The church was full, even the balcony. Marietta wouldn't have expected anything less; Harry had been one of the nicest men anywhere near Wesleyan, a lot nicer than she was, she thought to herself. She'd lived with him for thirty-six years, so she ought to know. Harry Cline treated everybody like he'd known them forever, would help anybody with anything, anytime. He allowed people second, even third, chances. Marietta had learned early on to never leave him alone in the shop; he'd practically give stuff away. It still rankled a bit every time she passed by that mahogany highboy that sat in Richard and Becky's foyer. Harry had sold it to them for about thirty dollars more than he paid for it. The thing was worth a fortune. "Now, Marietta, we'll never miss that money," he'd told her. And he was right, as usual. They hadn't. Marietta placed a gloved hand over her closed eyes.

He'd always said her headaches could more accurately predict the weather than the barometer that hung on the porch. At this early hour the forecasted winter storm was still advancing across Alabama, an inexorable line of pink on the meteorologist's map that promised ice would fall in Wesleyan at dusk. Couriers of dense white clouds covered the January sun, flooding the church with a bright, bloodless light. She put her handkerchief to her mouth and tried to relax the muscle in her neck that felt as rigid as the handle of a hammer. She searched for something to take her mind off the pain. She searched for Harry.

His alabaster urn sat on a wooden pedestal in front of the altar, looking like the one warm place in the church. Roman in design, its stone the color of honey, the urn was a treasure Harry found at a London auction twenty years before, when death seemed like something that always happened to other people. They'd laughed when he told her he wanted to make sure she'd always have someplace pretty to live. Turned out he'd been house hunting for himself and didn't know it.

Pancreatic cancer wastes no time. The doctor told him nine months in April, and nine months it had been. Harry hadn't wanted to tell anybody he was sick, a decision that suited them both, and he'd gotten away with it, too; they'd taken two trips to the beach; he didn't even start to look ill till the final few weeks. But Marietta hated that he'd died in winter; she'd wanted him to see another spring. She also knew some people might never forgive her for keeping them in the dark, and one of them was sitting right beside her.

Most people didn't have marriages like hers and Harry's anymore, Marietta thought. She'd listened to enough women talk about their husbands; countless Chardonnay lunches—when she used to go to them—inevitably careened into competitions of sorts: whose husband was the most unenlightened, the most insensitive, or simply the dumbest. She never joined in; she *liked* Harry, and this made her feel separated from the rest of her girlfriends, so much so that, years ago, she'd stopped accepting invitations, preferring to close the shop for an hour or two and go to lunch with her husband instead. She and Harry still talked, still laughed—they'd been friends before they were lovers, maybe that made a difference—they worked together, played together, and along the way they'd become family, closer than blood kin could probably ever be. Seeing Harry through to this cold January morning was the hardest thing Marietta had ever done. Whether or not she'd survive it, she wasn't prepared to say.

Like wisps of smoke, her thoughts traveled back home, slipped through the front door and up the stairs to their bedroom, over to the table by Harry's side of the bed, and inside the top drawer, where there sat—she could see the white-topped orange plastic as clearly as if she held it in her hand—the bottle of pills, full and unopened. Harry hadn't needed them in the end. But perhaps, just maybe, she would. She didn't know yet. Sitting here now, she felt a profane degree of comfort in knowing that escape, if she really wanted it, was possible.

And I saw the holy city, new Jerusalem, coming down from God out of heaven . . . The words washed over Macon Hargis unheard, as insignificant to him as a tinkling cymbal. He stretched his arm on the back of the pew, sending a little cloud of Jockey Club after-shave floating past his sister. He'd splashed this same scent on his cheeks since high school—ever since he'd learned it was JFK's favorite—and it was so much a part of him now he couldn't even smell it anymore. But Marietta could, and it sent her stomach another inch closer to her throat. Her heart started to race. She knew that either she was going to have to leave, smack-dab in the middle of her husband's funeral, or she was going to vomit all over her black suede boots.

The little white swinging door sat no more than a dozen feet away from her, just past the baby grand piano where Lurlene Pearson was sitting in her navy wool dress, pink polished fingers atop the ivory keys, ready to play "Shall We Gather at the River?" as soon as Richard was done with his scripture reading. Three steps and Marietta could be out. If she was lucky, she might even make it to the bathroom before she threw up, though how she'd get home she had no idea. Macon had driven her here; she couldn't just ask for his car keys, and she couldn't grab him up by the lapels and drag him out without an explanation she felt too sick to give. It was useless to look for Gordon; she knew he wouldn't be here. She suddenly thought of her father, gone for a quarter of a century, and wished for all the world he was sitting beside her. If his daughter were sick, Logan Hargis would have instinctively known. He'd have picked her up and carried her out that door no matter how old she was or what was going on around him.

Waiting for her turn in the program, Lurlene studied the song in front of her. It was an odd choice for an Episcopalian funeral, but Marietta had told her Harry requested it especially because it reminded him of his great-aunt, and having known Nina Cline herself, Lurlene could see the sense of that. No better woman in Wesleyan when she'd been alive, even if she had been a Baptist. From her spot on the piano bench Lurlene had been sneaking glances over at Marietta throughout the service, and the woman didn't look good. She'd always been pale—redheads usually are—but in the past ten minutes she'd gone whiter than blackboard chalk. Lurlene played for most of the funerals at St. Cyprian's and she'd pretty much seen it all, from fainting to fits. Any minute now, Marietta Cline was going to fall over into one of those categories, she'd bet anything. She just hoped Macon was paying attention. But right now, that big black crow sitting on the windowsill seemed much more focused on Marietta than her own brother was.

. . . and the city had no need of the sun, neither of the moon . . . Richard's words were muffled by the throbbing pain in Marietta's head. They came toward her as no more than rhythm, the singsong cadence of someone reading aloud. Her hands had turned to ice inside her leather gloves. As Richard left the pulpit, his reading completed, she teetered wildly at the crossroads of choice. Go, or stay. It was going to be humiliation, no matter what she did. So sick now she could barely sit up, Marietta suddenly rose.

Shall we gather at the river . . . the first strains of the hymn began and, mercifully, the crowd all stood up to sing. *Where bright angel feet have trod* . . . Marietta took a step forward. *With its crystal tide forever* . . . In three swift steps she was at the door. *Flowing by the throne of God* . . . Marietta pushed it open and was gone.

2

BUTTER

Gather with the saints at the river that flows by the throne of God. The hymn was just ending when Butter opened the door to the ladies' room. Inside, the once sunny yellow walls had long ago dulled to a dingy beige, a color made worse by the fly-filled fluorescent light that flickered from the ceiling. The smell of old perfume and disinfectant clung to the air like a bad memory.

"Well, if you're going to throw up, this is sure the room to do it in," Butter said.

A weak sound, somewhere between a laugh and a retch, came from the last cubicle. Inside, Marietta was bent over at the waist, her hands on her knees. Butter picked up Marietta's black clutch bag, which lay forgotten on the discolored linoleum floor, brushed it off, and waited. After a few moments, Marietta sighed, stood up, and leaned sideways against the metal wall.

"Come on. Let's get out of here," Butter said. "My car's near the side door. I'll drive you home."

"Where'd you come from?" Marietta asked, turning slowly

around, the visage of Butter Swann swimming before her squinted eyes.

"I saw you leave. Knew you had a migraine. I'd been watching you for the past twenty minutes. God, you were white as a ghost. I figured this was where you were heading so I went out the back and around. Come on now. Let's leave before everybody gets out."

"I can't just leave my own husband's funeral, Butter." Marietta's eyes were filling with tears.

"Well, Mare, I don't really think you have much of a choice." Butter took Marietta by the shoulders and turned her around to face the mirror. Deathly pale, with two wavy black lines of mascara vertically striping her face, she looked every bit as bad as she felt. Butter's eyes met hers in the reflection. "You're telling me you can go back in there?" she said. "You're telling me you can ride, sitting up, in the car with Macon and Glinda, then stand in a receiving line at that restaurant for a couple of hours, shaking hands and nodding, without falling flat on your face? Is that what you're saying?"

Marietta stared at Butter in the mirror and slowly shook her head.

"No, I didn't think so." Pulling down some paper towels from the dispenser, Butter wet them with cold water and handed them to Marietta. "Here, wipe your face with these and let's go. With any luck we'll have you in bed before too many people even notice you're gone."

They could hear Reverend Vaught speaking as they left. Raw winter air hit Marietta the minute Butter opened the door to the parking lot, and she breathed it in, feeling the chill deep down in her lungs. The cold made the pain in her head almost bearable, but she knew it was only a momentary relief. She pulled her dark sunglasses out of her coat pocket and put them on.

"Come on, my car's over there. God, it's gotten colder in the past thirty minutes." Butter buttoned up her coat's fur collar tight around her neck and headed down the stone steps. "Yep, those are snow clouds. No doubt about it. I don't mind snow so much, but I sure hope they're wrong about us getting ice. I'd hate to lose that pear tree right outside my window."

Marietta looked up. Thick and white, the clouds were so low she felt she could reach out and grab a handful only to watch it freeze in her palm. She could taste the coming ice in the air. She followed Butter to where her white Range Rover was parked. Butter unlocked the doors and opened the back one, pushing the box of glossy real estate brochures from the seat to the floor.

"Here, get in and lie down. I won't talk, I promise. I'll take the curves easy and no sudden stops. Put your purse under your head and close your eyes. I'll get you home as fast as I can."

Marietta climbed in and did as she was told, trying to breathe away the urge to be sick again all over Butter's camel leather seats. She felt the car start, back up, and pull out onto Meridian Street. They stopped at the light on the corner, then went straight. It was about five miles to her home from here and with the Saturday morning traffic, it could easily take fifteen minutes or more. She covered her closed eyes with her hand; even the pale peach-colored light seeping through her eyelids was too much.

Butter drove in silence, which, as anyone who knew her could attest, was an unusual thing when she had someone else in the car. Her thirty-year career as a realtor had taught her that it was best to fill up the corners of quiet spaces with circuitous and continuous conversation. Prospective home buyers made quicker decisions when left with less room to formulate thought. Butter had learned to answer questions before they were asked, to whisk away possible concerns with torrents of rosy-hued sentences that focused only on the positive aspects of any matter at hand. What was originally a sales tactic had long ago bled over into her daily life, and sometimes, on the rare chance Butter stopped to listen to herself, she thought she sounded like a walking advertisement for just about everything. But one look at Marietta's ashen face told Butter that conversation, no matter how innocuous or one-sided, would not be well received right now.

She wasn't exactly sure why she'd left the service to rescue Marietta. But as soon as she'd caught the glimpse of Marietta's dark maroon coat disappearing out that white swinging door she'd known how sick she must have been. Marietta would never have left Harry's funeral otherwise. Never. Butter had immediately turned from her seat and hurried up the aisle without a second thought. With a sharp little shake of her head, she gripped the steering wheel a bit tighter, telling herself that Marietta probably wouldn't have done the same thing for her. This of course gave her a clear lane on the moral high road, and the air was good up there. Crass, my eye.

Traffic was much heavier than usual, no doubt the result of the weather forecast. This ritualistic running of the Southerners took place every time there was the merest hint of the smallest flake of winter precipitation. Gripped by an irrational fear of being trapped in their houses—snow over the windows and nothing to eat—everybody south of the Mason-Dixon Line was propelled to the grocery store like hordes of hungry locusts by any prediction of ice or snow. By noon the citizens of Wesleyan would have stripped every shelf bare of items that under normal circumstances they rarely ate and sometimes didn't even like. Loaves of white bread were gathered up by the armload. Buttermilk, bought by the gallon. The occasional ham hock was sold. Cars were circling the Piggly Wiggly as Butter drove past, each one looking in vain for an empty parking space.

Wesleyan Square was a frozen study in gray. The live oaks appeared paralyzed by the cold; their bent, divaricated branches still draped with spidery moss; it hung like timeworn tinsel on erstwhile Christmas trees. No one was out on the sidewalks; the shops were already closed in anticipation of the storm. Butter rolled to a slow stop at the corner, turning to look at the front of Cline's Antiques. Someone had placed a wreath of white roses on the door and wrapped wide black ribbons around the necks of the two bronze stags that stood sentry, one on either side. Glancing in her rearview mirror Butter could see Marietta lying in the backseat, her hand over her eyes, as silent and still as stone.

At the stop sign just past the bank Butter looked up to see her own face staring down at her from the billboard Poteete and Lee Realtors had recently installed to celebrate her number one status in sales. There she was, at least ten feet high and grinning like a possum, each gleaming white tooth as tall as a two-year-old child. Butter had feigned embarrassment at such a public, and gargantuan, display of her success but deep down felt like it was way past time. She'd driven over here to stare up at this sign at least five times now. Having worked her fanny off for years to get where she was, she didn't mind one bit if every single citizen in her hometown knew how successful she'd been. Her only regret was the timing. No matter how much airbrushing had been done to her photo—and there'd been a lot, she could tell—even Butter couldn't pretend she looked as good as she once had. It had been a long time since she'd heard someone remark about the resemblance between herself and Olivia Newton-John, something that used to happen frequently in her twenties. Well, it's hard to pull off that sort of beauty after sixty, she thought with a defensive little grin that faded as soon as she realized Ms. Newton-John had done a pretty good job of it herself. But still. The billboard was a big deal, and it made her proud. She felt a little guilty, wishing Marietta was sitting up to see it, and mad at herself for still wanting to impress the one person she couldn't.

Butter turned on Second Avenue, speeding up some now that the traffic was thinning. She passed Tillman Elementary School, deserted and quiet on a Saturday morning. If this ice storm really did materialize as predicted, those kids wouldn't be at school Monday. Southern school buses didn't roll with ice on the ground. Second Avenue Baptist Church sat on the corner, the gray headstones in its cemetery next door looking strangely expectant under the lowering clouds. Just a couple of miles to go and Marietta would be home. "We're almost there," Butter whispered.

Marietta and Harry lived in the oldest part of Wesleyan, in an area informally known as The Glade, where the trees were big, and the houses were passed down through families like Bibles. Tradition would have been served had Macon Hargis moved in here after the death of his and Marietta's mother, Caroline. He was the firstborn, after all. But Macon had always had his eye on the fabled Southern plantation house that hid behind a tall wooden fence a couple of miles east of Wesleyan Square, and when he was thirty that house unexpectedly came up for sale. He'd bought it immediately, despite knowing the purchase meant he and his new wife, Glinda, would now have to wait longer than they'd planned to afford the two children they would eventually have. So the two-story brick cottage with the tall ceilings and small bathrooms went to Marietta instead.

Butter saw the pair of giant oak trees that flanked the entrance to The Glade and turned in. She drove slowly. She'd forgotten how pretty it was in here, each house and garden like an illustration in a fairy tale. She had the freedom to gawk with abandon; everybody who lived here was at Harry Cline's funeral.

Every neighborhood has a personality that speaks louder than words and Butter knew the language of each. She could match a person to the perfect house at thirty paces. People who chose to live in gated communities liked to be thought of as separate, maybe even special, whereas those who moved into townhomes often craved the community close quarters provide. The ones who flocked to subdivisions where each house was indistinguishable from the next and the overlords of homeowners' associations threatened legal action at the first manifestation of individuality, well . . . those were the people concerned with fitting in, the ones most comfortable being part of a herd. Butter understood. She passed no judgment. Real estate was like a giant puzzle to her, and when she found the right people for the right house she always felt like squealing. Her talent—and she thought of it as talent—came from years of experience, of course, but neighborhoods always told you who they were looking for; you just had to know the signs.

The Glade was no different. These streets called out to Wesleyan's square pegs, those people for whom other neighborhoods in this conservative Southern town were nothing more than ill-fitting round holes. Diversity was more than a buzzword in here. Behind the glowing windows of the houses in The Glade lived iconoclasts and curmudgeons, the gregarious and the gay—the old, the young, the black, and the white. People here wrote letters to the editor, listened to NPR for fun, and believed fur always looked better on an animal than on a person. This was a neighborhood of chalk-painted sidewalks and garden tours, fall festivals and voting drives, lemonade stands and trick-or-treaters.

Tree-lined streets curved around the sorts of brick cottages and wide-porched bungalows that were common in old black-and-white movies. They'd been built in defiance of the dictates of contemporary design and looked today much as they had when their oaks were just saplings and their gardens were new. Beyond repairs and repainting, the homeowners here were loath to alter the modest charm of their houses in the slightest degree. They liked their creaky floors and sticky windows. It had been a while since Butter had driven through The Glade; hardly anything ever came up for sale here.

She slowed down to a crawl, looking past the frozen lawns and silver shrubbery for the Pinehurst Street sign. There it was, up ahead on the left, a big black bird perched atop it, dark feathers shining in the winter light. Turning in, Butter could see Marietta's house clearly, its rose-colored brick covered in the ivy that Butter would advise her to remove if she ever intended to sell.

Butter turned in her seat. "We're here, Mare," she whispered.

3

MACON
AND GLINDA

She had embarrassed him, again. Macon slammed the car door and yanked his seatbelt across his chest, his jaw set like a vise. Glinda got into the car quietly on her side, knowing better than to say a word, and after a long minute, Macon took a deep breath and turned the key. Backing out and pulling in behind the others lined up to make their way to the reception, he pretended not to see his paralegal, Larry Motter, and his wife, Sue, as they attempted a sorrowful little nod in his direction, Sue standing on her tiptoes to get a better look. Larry had been angling for years to be included in one of Macon's annual boat trips up the coast, too eager to ever be asked.

Macon was used to the stares. He expected them, even. Today at the funeral he'd sensed people straining to catch any hint of emotion they'd never before seen him display, some chink in his armor of professional detachment, and he'd been determined not to give them a scrap. He'd felt eyes on him for as long as he could remember, like invisible, insistent pulls at his coat sleeves, a constant scrutinization to see just how much he'd inherited from his father, a father who remained, by those who remembered, nearly equally celebrated and reviled.

Though he shunned introspection as a matter of principle, Macon knew the main reason he'd stayed in Wesleyan to make his reputation as one of the top defense attorneys in the Southeast was simply to show that he could. It was now said around town that if Macon Hargis took your case it meant two things: one, that you were guilty, and two, that you'd never spend a night in jail. People were friendly to Macon, much in the way one is friendly to an animal nobody wants to provoke, but he didn't have many close friends. Those already gathering at Micheline's for the reception awaited his arrival with more than the usual trepidation; his sister had walked out of her own husband's funeral, and nobody knew quite what to say. Most fervently hoped they could avoid saying anything at all.

He didn't quite believe his eyes when he saw Marietta leave the service. He hadn't known the words to the hymn everybody had started singing, so he was already feeling awkward, and then he felt a movement beside him and there she went, the door swinging behind her, once, then twice, so that everybody could see. And now, for the rest of the damn day, he was going to be asked, over and over, what had happened, what was wrong, where was Marietta? He'd punched her number into his phone as he walked to the car, but the call went straight to voicemail, and he was too mad to leave a message.

He should have been the one to do the eulogy. He wouldn't have wanted to, but it should have been him, the logical choice, the expected person to represent the family. He knew people were wondering why he hadn't. But my God. Not only hadn't she asked him, she hadn't even told him Harry was sick. Him, her only brother. Just how did she think that would make him look? It didn't help, of course, that Glinda had started bawling like a baby in the middle of the service. She'd never been that close to Harry. What was wrong with the woman? He kept his eyes straight ahead, glued to the car in front of him. He could almost hear Glinda's thoughts pinging around in her head, searching for words. Macon ignored her.

He wasn't sure the exact moment his sister had given up on their relationship, but he was sure it had happened. Her phone calls had been consistent for years—birthdays, Thanksgiving, Christmas. She'd phoned every time she and Harry had gone on one of those buying trips to England or France, just so he'd know they were out of the country if he happened to need her for anything. She even used to call him for advice sometimes, or just out of the blue to see how his family was doing. Macon never reciprocated; he could never think of a reason to get in touch, and besides, he knew he'd talk to her sooner or later. Then one Thanksgiving about six years ago, Marietta's call hadn't come. He didn't even notice it till they were putting up the tree a week later. He sloughed it off. If anything was wrong, he would've heard, he told himself. But then Christmas came and went, and all was silent from his sister. Hers and Harry's presents sat under the tree till it came down on New Year's Day, then lay on a bookshelf in the den for three more months.

One morning in late March there was a knock on the front door. When Glinda opened it, Marietta was standing there with their Christmas presents, still beautifully wrapped, in her arms, the shiny red and green paper looking so odd with her spring outfit. Harry was waiting in the car. While Glinda ran to retrieve their gifts, Macon came to the door to say hello. He was as friendly as he knew how to be, but his sister's expression had remained as unreadable as a sphinx, and though the birthday and Christmas cards still came every year, there had been no more presents, and she hadn't phoned him since.

Macon wanted to feel bad about the apparent loss of his sister's affection, but in truth, he was mostly relieved. They'd never been what anyone would call close, and Macon pointed to the nine-year gap in their ages as the cause; Marietta might as well have been a different generation altogether. But mostly, she was a reminder of all the things he'd chosen to forget.

It had never been easy to be the son of Logan Hargis. Certain things had been expected of Macon from the time he was old enough to realize who his father was and what the man stood for. By the time he was ten he'd come to anticipate teachers' raised eyebrows when they called out his name on the first day of a new class, and he knew they were sizing him up to see just how closely he'd been cut to the pattern of the controversial editor.

Early on, like most small boys, Macon had idolized his dad. He'd wanted to dress like him, talk like him; he'd jump to place his feet inside Logan's footprints whenever they walked on the beach. Logan liked cornbread and buttermilk, so Macon liked it, too. Logan admired the junior senator from Massachusetts, so Macon had a Kennedy campaign poster hanging on his bedroom wall. Country music, Weejun loafers, *The Red Skelton Show* on Tuesday nights . . . all were favorites of Macon Hargis because his father liked them first.

But before he'd gotten too far along in school he'd come to feel that Logan's willingness to spark controversy and take stands only brought trouble. It does something to a kid when he's walking with his buddies and they pass signs labeling his father a traitor—or worse—stapled to telephone poles every twenty-five feet. Macon had been spat on, had his clothes stolen in gym class, had been "accidentally" forgotten by the team bus driver, who left him at a neighboring school after a football game one particularly rainy night. He still felt humiliation color his face when those memories surfaced.

When the cross was burned on his family's front lawn, Macon had been in his first year at college, already on a different path, one that would garner both financial security and respect. He had more than enough of both from the people who mattered long before Logan Hargis passed away.

Marietta had been different, of course. She'd always been their father's shadow, and as far as Macon could see she was every bit as uncompromising and quixotic as Logan, slicing a ramrod-straight path through life, her view forever sketched in shining black and white.

As he drove past the corner where Latham Drugs once stood,

Macon remembered the night, years ago, when they'd taken their mother, Caroline, out for dinner for her birthday. All five of them in one car with Harry driving. They were out on Highway 4 when it had started to rain, pouring buckets, and nobody had thought to bring an umbrella. Fortunately, a Walmart was up ahead, but Marietta had flatly refused to stop there. Made Harry drive all the way back to Randall Latham's little drugstore downtown. "Walmart is destroying places like Wesleyan," she'd said. "I've never been inside one, and I won't be starting today." They barely made the dinner reservation it had taken him months to get.

He'd become used to seeing his sister's name beneath a particularly blistering op-ed in the morning paper, used to seeing her photograph, and Harry's, too, for God's sake, *both* of them in pink knitted hats, under headlines that read, LOCAL COUPLE TRAVELS TO WOMEN'S MARCH IN WASHINGTON. His colleagues had long since learned not to mention Marietta's exploits to Macon. But this latest one—walking out on her own husband's funeral—would be mentioned today, you could bet your boots it would. What had possessed her? And what was he supposed to say? His knuckles turned white on the steering wheel.

Glinda stole a glance over at her husband as the traffic crawled through town. He radiated a tension that was as keen as sound; it · filled the space between them, constricting her throat so completely that had she been able to think of something to say she doubted the words could be heard.

Lately it was difficult for her to imagine Macon as the man he was when they married. Though his appearance had to have been changing throughout their years together, as everyone's does, she hadn't really started to notice it until recently. He'd turned seventy in November, and she wasn't far behind. She'd hardly escaped the evidence of time's passing, she knew, but decades of staring at herself in the mirror every single morning and night, tending to her lines and wrinkles as one would a perennial garden, had inured her to the changes in her own appearance. The alterations had come on so gradually, the few extra pounds, the age spots, that irritating little jiggle in the middle of her neck. Macon, on the other hand, had just all of a sudden looked old. Overnight it seemed, his once red hair had become striated with silver and his wide shoulders had ceded their brawn to bone, making his shirts look bigger and his arms look longer. He reminded Glinda of one of those old lions in National Geographic specials on TV, still prowling through the pride as they'd always done, but diminished somehow, betrayed by their own bodies as they weakened around them.

When couples have been together long enough to grow old, shouldn't they feel a sweet sort of affection for each other whenever they see the extra lines and gray hair? Shouldn't those things serve as visible prompts for gratitude, a wistful moment to indulge in the memories of a long, happy life? She'd always figured that would be the case; she'd counted on it. But now that it was here, all Glinda felt was anger, and she didn't know what to do with that. How can you be angry at someone for just getting old? And if there were other reasons, she hadn't wished to excavate her psyche to find out what they were.

When faced with a situation devoid of a bright side, Glinda usually ignored it as best she could. Problems had to be explained within the code she'd followed for the whole of her life: an amalgam of personal wisdom gleaned from her parents, the Bible, and the various and sundry self-help books she kept in steady rotation on her bedside table. She liked things to be nice. She wanted people to get along. Above all she needed the reliability of goodness, whether real or perceived. This was a requirement she extended all the way to fiction, consequently shunning almost anything penned after Dickens. Sensing a trend, she'd quietly left her book club when they chose to read *White Teeth*. She'd read *Pride and Prejudice* seventeen times.

But recently, her changing feelings toward Macon kept crashing through her carefully constructed narrative like rogue waves. They bubbled up in her brain, unbidden and demanding, filling her with a worry she'd never before known, one that felt almost physical, like a weight she'd never counted on carrying and was increasingly being asked to lift. Sometimes she couldn't stand to look at him, and that scared her half to death.

Glinda turned to stare out the window. They were passing the park, as if on cue, and the stone statue stood as it always did, impassive and defiant, at the nexus of a network of red-brick sidewalks lined with azaleas. This morning it was the same color as the air.

She blamed the statue. It had sat in Griffin Park for so long most of the people in town hardly saw it anymore. At least the white people didn't, and being white, Glinda had barely looked at it, ever. It might as well have been one of the oak trees that shared the same plot of land. She could honestly say she hadn't even known the name of the man sitting on the horse at the top of that stone plinth before all this started a year ago. But now she did, and so did most of the people in Wesleyan, many falling like landslide rocks on either side of a dividing line of opinion that, though invisible, was as sharp as a soldier's sword.

The statue belonged to Old Man Griffin, so really, he was the one she should blame. Everyone called him that. Now that he was approaching the homestretch of his eighties, the appellation fit a bit better than it had in decades past, but then, it had always had more to do with personality than with age. His house sat atop a hill directly across the street from the park that bore his family name, behind the coal black fingers of a Gothic iron fence, hidden by a thicket of loblolly pine.

It had been raining that night in 1916 when the county voted to put the road through the Griffin property, and the group of county commissioners who ventured out to the house after the decisive meeting had done so with great reluctance, not knowing exactly what Old Man Griffin's father, Lucius, would say, or do, about the decision, but each willing to bet it wouldn't be good. The rain had knotted itself into a thunderstorm by the time Mary Griffin ushered them into the study where her husband sat at his carved oak desk, staring at them evenly from behind long, tented fingers. The air was violet with the smoke curling up from his cigar.

Not daring to drip rainwater on any of Mary's silk damask sofas or chairs, the men had stood awkwardly around the dimly lit room, trying hard not to let their eyes wander to the small door at the left of the fireplace where, as some of them had heard—and a few of them knew—the clean white accoutrements of the Klan were carefully folded.

The men explained their case to Lucius—"The town is growing and the road is essential." "We've really no other choice." "We'll be able to pay you a little of course."—but Lucius remained silent, rain battering the windows all the while, and Mary in the hall with her ear to the door. When they'd finished their news, it had been underscored with a clap of thunder that rattled the Limoges in the dining room next door.

In the end, they all wondered how they'd gotten off so easy. All Lucius Griffin wanted in exchange for his land was to build a park on the remaining field on the other side of the new road, a park he would create, and his family would maintain, and in which he would erect a statue to the Confederate general Henry Benning, a former judge on Georgia's Supreme Court and an old friend of Lucius's much revered father, Hiram. Well, nobody had a problem with that. The brick sidewalks were laid around the oaks while Meridian Street was being extended, and Griffin Park opened to balloon-filled skies on the Fourth of July 1918.

It had taken only a century for people to realize who Henry Benning really was, and now that they knew, over half of them wanted him gone, and they wanted him gone before the one-hundred-year celebration that Old Man Griffin was planning for this summer.

When Macon had decided to take the case, Glinda hoped it would be like all the others: something she could easily ignore. She'd never delved beneath the surface of his work; attorney-client privilege had proven a convenient reason for remaining ignorant about the men who so often sat, smugly unruffled, beside her husband in the courtroom downtown. But this case was different. People were talking about the statue everywhere—from the Piggly Wiggly to the Junior League—and they were asking Glinda what she thought. So far, she'd managed to avoid giving her opinion, which was fortunate, as she hadn't yet been able to articulate one in her head.

Macon was confident the case would be decided quickly, and in his client's favor. Old Man Griffin owned the land, he said. His family had put the statue up. It was, therefore, private property and nobody's business but his. The lawsuit was frivolous, the case was open and shut. But Glinda wasn't so certain. There was money behind the group of people who called themselves Monument Removals Encourage Development (a name that provided their opponents with an unfortunate acronym, MRED, which was gleefully used at every opportunity by those who remembered the talking horse from the sixties), and she had an uncomfortable feeling that they were ready to employ every ounce of publicity this case could engender to their favor. Macon had been on the six o'clock news four times already.

And she knew what people were saying; "friends" always had to tell you. She'd gotten the inferences, felt the sidelong looks. A sizable portion of the population now saw her husband as the protector of some sort of historic racism that had pockmarked the town generations ago, and whose scars had merely been sloppily spackled over with excuses throughout the ensuing years. Had she been squarely cornered and forced to defend Macon, Glinda told herself she would have done so, but so far, by ducking out of meetings early, and checking out the parking lot for familiar cars before she entered the grocery store, she'd managed to avoid any direct confrontations, and she hadn't yet admitted, even to herself, how much the whole thing bothered her.

So great was her skill in avoiding personal scrutiny, Glinda had never allowed these worries to swarm in her head for too long, but this morning as she sat in Harry's funeral, still trying to believe her brother-in-law was gone, they had risen to the surface and burst free into the air around her, shadowy thoughts turning into emotions she didn't quite understand; the more she tried to tamp them down, the more they seemed to break off from the center to circle around her husband like crows over corn.

She could see his jaw working back and forth in frustration. "Macon," she said, hating the pleading tone of her voice as it left her body. "Try not to be mad. You understand, don't you, how awful this is for her. Everybody grieves differently."

"Nobody runs out of their own husband's funeral, Glinda. Who does *that*?" Macon felt another surge of irritation as he asked the question out loud. When you got right down to it, funerals were performances, he thought, and the show must always go on, no matter what. Everyone could hold it together for an hour, at least. Everyone, it seemed, but his sister.

Glinda tried another tack. "I just hate that Maggie and the girls couldn't be here." She leaned forward and looked up through the windshield at the low, gray sky. "I can't tell if those are snow clouds or not. Can you?"

Macon kept his eyes on the car ahead of him, its NOT MY PRESIDENT bumper sticker adding fuel to his anger with each passing mile. "I don't know what kind of clouds they are, Glinda. But if Bob has to be back at work on Monday, they can't risk getting stuck here for days." Personally, Macon thought an ice storm was likely. He could feel it in the air.

He'd told their daughter, Maggie, not to worry if she couldn't make the funeral. The impending winter storm was already canceling flights to the west of them, and it would probably get worse as the day wore on. Plus, since they were newly minted teenagers, he knew his grandchildren, the too-plump twins, Martha and Bea, would much rather stay home in Virginia than travel with their parents down to Georgia for the funeral of their uncle, a man they hardly knew. No one had expected his son and his wife to make it. Josh and Lizzie had been living in France for the past year. His teeth clenched when he thought about that, too, still remembering the reasons the couple had left the country in late 2016, preferring, Josh said, to live someplace that hadn't just elected a fascist. The row with his son had been spectacular. Glinda still didn't know the real reason they'd left, and if Macon had anything to do with it, she never would.

They were nearing the square now and he could see his hopes of finding a parking place close to the restaurant rapidly dwindling; all the cars in front of him were going to the same place, he knew. Abruptly, he made a sharp right turn that caused Glinda to grip the sides of her seat. He pulled over to the curb in front of McEntyre's Bakery and stopped the car. "We'll just walk from here," he said, undoing his seatbelt and opening his door.

Frowning, Glinda adjusted her hat and got out. As Macon put the coins in the meter, she buttoned her suit jacket up to the neck. She'd left her heavy coat at home. Macon took her by the elbow and together they crossed the street, but there was no way she could match his stride. She'd shaken off his arm by the time they reached the sidewalk.

4

BUTTER

Number 17 Pinehurst Street looked the same as it always had. Its wooden front door was as heavy as the door of a church, with a round window at the top that was laced with the lead lines of a spiderweb and filled in with bits of stained glass. Butter remembered the parallelograms of colored light that would fall on the dark wood floor of the small entry hall in the late afternoon.

On this windless winter morning empty gray hands of a dozen hydrangeas reached up through the ground beneath the arched casement windows, and along the side garden a row of old hemlocks loomed over a long, serpentine bed of sleeping gardenias, like basses on the top riser of a choir. The bricks of the driveway were set in a curious pattern, undecipherable to anyone save the bricklayer himself, and they added another layer of whimsy and charm to a house already brimming with both. Butter loved this place. With its tall, pointed roof and ivy-covered brick, it looked like the home of a benevolent witch, a place where nothing bad could ever happen. That is, until you saw the blotch of black in the center of the lawn.

As flagrant as a wound, the spot drew the eye like a magnet. A four-foot circle where grass was never allowed to grow, covered over every season—first by Marietta's father, Logan, and later by Marietta herself—with cold, dark mulch. It was ringed with old river rocks, and a jagged piece of stone rose up from the center, its face engraved with these words:

On the night of September 14th, 1966, a cross was desecrated here by cowards in white hoods. This spot shall remain as dark as the hearts of the men who committed this act for as long as racism prowls our world.

May it serve as a reminder that men are remembered for the evil that they do.

LOGAN HARGIS

The sign had been a compromise. Logan had originally planned to leave the charred cross standing in the center of the yard, but Caroline wouldn't have it. She rarely put her foot down about anything but when she did you couldn't budge her.

Marietta and Butter had been only nine when it happened, but Butter still remembered how wide Marietta's eyes had been when she told her friend about it the next day in the school cafeteria. Caroline had kept Marietta away from the windows, so she never saw the flames, but she heard the men yelling outside in the dark and Butter thought that had to have been just as bad. Her own parents were strangely quiet about it when she told them later that afternoon, but she overheard them whispering in the kitchen after she'd gone to bed, her father saying, "Well, after what that fool wrote this time, I'm surprised it wasn't any worse."

Butter was pulled from her memory by the sight of Marietta's ashen face filling the rearview mirror as she slowly sat upright. She looked, if possible, even worse than she had when they left the church. Butter got out and opened Marietta's door. She stood and leaned back against the car as she dug in her purse for her house key. "You don't have to come in, Butter. I'm fine, really. I'll be okay."

"Nonsense," Butter said. "I'll see you in and settled, lock up when I leave. Then I'll head over to the reception and let everybody know what happened."

Marietta cringed inwardly at the thought of all those questioning faces, wondering where she was. But there was nothing she could do about that now. As if to underline that fact, her stomach seesawed again and she moved toward the door, Butter following close behind.

Stepping inside, Marietta placed a hand on the head of one of the most enormous dogs Butter had ever seen to stop him jumping. "It's okay, Smudge," Marietta said. The big white, fluffy dog looked around Marietta and sized up Butter.

"Smudge?" Butter asked, hesitating a little before following Marietta in.

Marietta tossed her black handbag onto the table by the door and began to slowly climb the stairs, one hand on the railing, the large dog at her heels. "He had a tiny black mark on his forehead when we got him, the only bit of color in his coat. But he was just a puppy. It disappeared by the time he grew up," she said. She and Smudge vanished into the second-floor hallway. "I'll bring you something to drink," Butter called up after her.

Butter often thought her real estate career had given her all the training required should she ever decide to become a detective. She could stroll through a house about to go on the market and come out with enough information on the people who lived there to write their biographies. Though hardly a fanciful thinker, through the years she'd come to believe that houses have memories, that it is possible for rooms to absorb the spirits of those who lived within them, in much the same way a favorite perfume still clings to the fibers of an oft-washed shirt.

She never would have shared this feeling with anyone, of course—she'd have been laughed out of her office—but it had happened too often for her to ignore. That peculiar bleakness in the houses of unhappiness, the finespun frisson of cheer where laughter and love had flourished and grown. She couldn't deny she'd felt both. Once, in an upstairs bedroom in which a child had mysteriously died generations before, she'd been so overcome with an inexplicable dread that she'd refused the listing and gone to the beach for a long weekend.

Standing alone in this familiar entry hall only reaffirmed her privately held belief, for even on this sad morning, Marietta's house was as it had always been: as welcoming as a hug. Love had lived in these rooms; Butter could feel it. She couldn't recall the last time she'd been here but the memory of her first visit remained as limpid as a mirror. She'd felt welcomed then. It had also been her introduction to self-consciousness and, not coincidentally, the first time she'd eaten, or even seen, an artichoke.

They had been in the second-grade coat closet when Marietta told her that her parents were inviting them all over for dinner. It was two weeks before Christmas, the last day of school until the new year, and everything seemed dipped in magic. Glittered paper bunting hung all around the classroom, and there was a Christmas tree taller than Principal Lowry in the main hall of the school. A dinner at her best friend's home, with her parents, no less, seemed like a party on a scale Butter could hardly even fathom. Both girls giggled with excitement the rest of the week. Butter only hoped her dad would behave.

For as long as she could remember, Butter's father had kept one eye out for anybody who thought they were better than he was. Just like their old dog, Axel, who bared his teeth at some of his kind while letting others pass without so much as a sidelong glance, Jimmy Lockwood had a set of criteria for offense that were baffling, and those who fell into this dreaded category were as varied as the reasons that landed them there. The rich were always suspect, of course, but so were some of Butter's schoolteachers, a couple of preachers, the old man who owned Vinyl Pie Records on the back side of the square, and that waiter with the freckles at Betty's Meat and Three out on Highway 4. Butter used to entertain herself on family vacations by trying to predict just who would be labeled "cocky," her father's euphemism for any behavior that skated too close to the shores of perceived condescension for him to abide.

She really had few worries about her parents meeting Marietta's, however. She knew they weren't rich; she and Marietta had talked about it. Marietta hadn't been allowed to get the new Easy-Bake oven either. Her parents thought it was way too expensive, just like her own. And Butter had met Caroline Hargis several times when she picked up Marietta from school; she had laughing eyes and an open smile that you couldn't help but return. She'd seen Logan Hargis only once, at the Halloween carnival, but he'd shaken her hand and called her "kiddo." Butter liked him a lot; she liked them both, and was sure her parents would, too.

On the night of the dinner, they all dressed up. Her mother, Sandra, wore her Christmas dress, the name that always came to mind when Butter saw the red damask sheath with the black velvet collar and cuffs make its appearance each and every December. Her dad wore his green plaid tie and shined his shoes.

Butter's tummy clenched a little when the three of them pulled up at Marietta's house to see scores of tiny white lights covering a row of hemlocks along the left side of the yard. Jimmy Lockwood had a definite opinion about white lights at Christmas, equating their fairly recent appearance on the holiday decorating landscape with a faux sophistication that was, even now, he said, beginning to creep insidiously into the houses of Wesleyan. White Christmas lights landed someone in her dad's "snooty" category, right down there with the men who wore those pastel shirts with the little green alligators on the pockets or the women who pronounced the word "foyer" as "foy-yay." But before Jimmy could utter a word of disdain, Sandra had said, "Oh, look at that pretty tree!" and they'd all turned as one to see a huge Christmas tree filling the front window of the house, triumphantly aglow with the comfortably familiar multicolored lights. Feeling like she'd dodged a bullet, Butter breathed a sigh of relief and they all trooped up to the door.

Logan Hargis had thrown it open before they could knock,

clapping a hand on Jimmy's shoulder and leading them into the house. There was a great laughing commotion of removing coats and shaking hands before they all went into the candlelit sitting room, and everybody found a seat. That night the house had smelled like cinnamon and pine, with top notes of roast chicken that made Butter's mouth water. Wrapped presents tumbled out onto the floor from underneath the tree and Nat King Cole's velvety voice lifted off the record playing in the corner, filling the air with carols.

Spying the Hargises' collection of records, Jimmy said, "I see you've been listening to Johnny Cash. Now, there's a good singer."

"You could not be more correct," Logan replied, picking up Cash's *Orange Blossom Special* LP, which had played over and over in Butter's house since its release earlier that year. "The songs on this are something else, aren't they? I love those Bob Dylan ones. Are you familiar with Dylan?" Jimmy said he wasn't really, and the two of them began a long discussion of music that continued until Caroline called them to the table for dinner.

The dining room windows were hung with garlands of magnolia leaves—Butter had never seen anything like it—and there were two large red poinsettias in white china pots on the table. Everything seemed to glitter and glow, including her parents' faces, as they sat down to a feast of celebratory proportions. Roast chicken, green beans wrapped in bacon, sweet potatoes and oranges, and a platter full of something Butter had never seen before in her life. They looked like little green pineapples, and for a minute she wasn't exactly sure if they were food or decoration. But then the plate was passed around. Marietta took one, Caroline took one, so when it became her turn, Butter took one, too, even though she didn't have any idea how to eat it.

Hungry for instruction, she glanced down the table at her parents. She saw her father, who was still deep in the conversation about music, look at the strange little food with a quizzical expression, then pull a green leaf off the thing and stick it, whole, into his mouth. Caroline and Sandra were talking recipes; Marietta was telling her brother, Macon—tall, a teenager, and very grown up—to stop kicking her foot beneath the table. Butter watched Macon pull off one of the leaves, dip it in the bowl of butter sitting by his water glass, and drag it between his teeth, returning the stripped leaf to his plate before grabbing another. Down the table, her father was still chewing the leaf he'd taken, making a bit of a face at how tough the thing was, and Butter suddenly knew he'd eaten it wrong.

If they'd noticed, and how could they not have, not one of the Hargises let on in the slightest; she'd been so grateful for that. On the way home after the evening was over, Jimmy had said to Sandra, "Well, now, that was one of the best dinners I've been to in a good long while. But I'm here to tell you, those little green pine cones were the toughest things I've ever had to eat in my whole life." Even now, all these years later, Butter could feel little embers of embarrassment flicker on the edge of flame.

Who knows why we choose the friends we do when we're children? The Lockwoods and the Hargises had little in common, anyone could've seen it. Jimmy Lockwood worked at Harlan's Hardware store till the day he died; Logan Hargis was the editor of the *Wesleyan Journal,* known throughout the country for his searing editorials on race and civil rights at a time when those kinds of things got you noticed, especially in the South. But the two of them went fishing together every other weekend for years after they met that December night. Jimmy was a pallbearer at Logan's funeral in 1993.

Butter looked around her. The walls in the small entry hall were the color of a new persimmon, and the carved wooden coatrack that had held her winter coat on that first holiday visit still sat behind the door, dotted now with a collection of Harry's flat caps and Marietta's wide-brimmed sun hats. Harry's long gray overcoat hung there. Butter remembered seeing him wearing that less than two weeks ago as he walked slowly toward the shop on a cold, sunny afternoon, a small stack of Christmas presents held in his arms. She wished Marietta had told her he was sick.

Butter's curiosity about houses was insurmountable, even in the worst of times, so, though she knew her way to the kitchen, she turned in the opposite direction to stick her head into the sitting room. She hadn't been in Marietta's house in more than five years, and she was curious to see what had changed.

The lamps were all on and wood neatly stacked in the fireplace. Everywhere she looked there were subtle arrangements of flowers, a few fat yellow roses in a blue-and-white china cup, more in a tall purple vase. A lone white orchid in a painted tin cachepot. The furniture was polished, tapestry cushions were plumped, brand-new magazines were fanned out on ottomans.

She continued on into what was now the library. The largest room in the house, this had once been the bedroom of Marietta's parents, but when she and Harry moved in, they had painted the walls a glossy green and filled them floor to ceiling with bookshelves. As a realtor, Butter was used to using the term "library" euphemistically; most new houses were advertised as having them these days, grand spaces lined with mahogany shelves that were so often destined to hold more football trophies and family photos than anything remotely literary. But these bookshelves were full of books, with more in teetering stacks all over the room—by every overstuffed chair, on every antique table—the effect more cozy than cluttered. Along the top shelf, rows of identical blue glass vases held feathers, all different kinds, all different colors, a beautiful effect that ran the length of the room, the blue glass catching the faint afternoon light.

Like the sitting room, the library looked ready for a photo shoot. New Diptyque candles sat on side tables, a tiny box of matches beside each one. Butter counted five pots of sweet-smelling narcissus tucked around the room. The tall fireplace was, like its smaller counterpart next door, full of wood and newspaper kindling, ready to light. When had Marietta had time for all this? Her husband had just died.

Butter walked into the big, open kitchen and took a glass from the cabinet next to the sink. As is to be expected when somebody dies in the South, neighbors had brought enough food to feed the five thousand. Plastic-wrapped platters and plates covered the counters like toadstools after a summertime rain.

She opened the refrigerator, finding it just as crowded as the counters, and removed a Diet Coke, then looked in the freezer for something cold for Marietta's head. Spying a bag of frozen peas, she knew instantly what they were for. Marietta hated peas, always had, so these were here for one reason only. Butter grabbed them, headed back through the dining room and into the foyer. A slanted row of Hargis faces watched from dark wooden frames as she climbed the stairs.

The bedroom door was already ajar, so Butter pushed it open with her shoulder. The fragrance of tuberose, Marietta's favorite flower, filled the room, emanating from a large bouquet of the spiky white blossoms sitting atop a painted blue table next to the bed. A card sat beside the flowers, Marietta's name neatly printed across it in bright purple ink.

Butter remembered this room well, though it looked much different now. Gone were the twin four-posters. Flipping back through her memories, Butter could easily find herself and Marietta on a long-ago hot September afternoon, windows open, the toast-colored blades of the ceiling fan moving the thick, humid air around and around while they sat cross-legged, still in summer shorts, atop the white trapunto bedspreads, with thick textbooks on their laps, doing homework. If she thought about it, she bet she could still draw the pattern those bedspreads always etched on the backs of her bare thighs.

The bone structure of the room was the same: its high, pitched ceiling still outlined by a spine of oak beams, and a ceiling fan— the same ceiling fan?—still hanging from the longest beam in the center.

The posters had vanished, of course. Butter had watched those thumbtacked images change through the decades—from Hayley Mills and Paul McCartney to Gloria Steinem and Kate Bush. Now several large Brady Goode paintings hung on walls that wore a soft floral paper the color of seawater, and the round braided rugs she remembered had been replaced by a large sisal that lay on the dark hardwood floor like sand on a shore. A trail of discarded clothes now led to the bathroom door, where

Smudge sat in full guardian posture. Butter picked up the maroon coat and black dress and laid them on the chair by the window.

She could see the back garden from here. The Clines were modestly famous for this garden; it had earned a stop on the Wesleyan Garden Tour every May for years. As she looked down on it now, the normally lush half acre resembled a vintage photograph, all silver, gray, and brown, the only movement provided by the birds crowding on and around the Victorian bird feeder in the center of a circle of topiaries shaped like baby elephants. The largest crow Butter had ever seen sat atop the feeder like an ornament. As she watched, it slowly turned its head to look up at the window, almost as though it knew someone was staring back down.

Just as it was downstairs, everything was picture perfect in the bedroom. Even the sheets looked ironed. Butter set the cold drink down beside the flowers and went over to pull the green curtains closed. "No, please leave them open," Marietta said as she turned out the light in the bathroom and came toward the bed, the big dog following on her heels. "If the storm comes, I want to be able to see it. I'll put a washcloth over my eyes if the light is too much."

"All right," said Butter, turning around to see Marietta, clad in an extra-large pair of red flannel pajamas that almost made her look frail. "Here, I've got you a cold drink and a bag of frozen peas for your head. I bet if you go to sleep, the headache will leave."

Marietta pulled back the thick white duvet, smiling weakly. "God, I hope so," she whispered as she crawled into bed and pulled the covers up to her chin.

Handing her the cold package of peas, Butter couldn't stop herself from saying, "Boy, Marietta. This house looks like a magazine layout. Everything is just perfect."

Marietta slowly smiled. "It was Gordon. Must have been. Such a sweetheart, that man."

Of course. Butter looked at the note leaning up against the vase of tuberoses. That had to be who it was from. Turning her head, Butter indulged in an extravagant eye roll. Well, that made sense. Gordon Lovett owned Epiphanies, the only bookstore in Wesleyan and one so carefully curated it might as well have been his home library. He wore a yellow rose in his lapel, lived in a pink house, had a tricolored corgi named Trilby, and was forever peppering his conversation with literary references no one ever caught. He and Marietta had been friends since they all were kids. Butter liked that odd little man no better than she'd liked the odd little boy he'd once been (remembering the nickname he'd saddled her with in Tillman Elementary School still rankled; it had taken years to get rid of the thing), and she would have bet anything the feeling was completely reciprocal.

Since he'd moved back home twenty-five years ago, Gordon and Marietta were often together, just as they'd been growing up. He even went with Marietta and Harry to England every other season on those trips they took to find old furniture and what-nots. Nice for some, Butter thought. She kept telling herself she ought to take a trip overseas, but she never seemed to figure out who to take along with her, and if she was honest, she'd never been entirely sure how comfortable she'd feel around all those foreigners.

"Yes, well, it certainly looks like he's left nothing undone here today," she said, keeping the snide edge out of her voice with effort. "Okay now, I'm going to lock up and head back. People will be getting to the restaurant soon. Don't worry. They'll all understand." As she looked at Marietta lying there, her face as white as the sheets, the overwhelming loss her old friend had just suffered washed over Butter, bringing unexpected tears to her eyes. "I'm so sorry, Mare," she said. "I know this has to be a horrible day for you."

"It's not the worst day, Butter. Not hardly the worst day."

In a reflex she resisted with difficulty, Butter almost reached out and touched Marietta's forehead, but she turned to leave instead. Smudge followed her out the door. The dog stood on the landing and watched as Butter went down the stairs, paused, looked around her, and breathed a heavy sigh. He saw the shiny silver box sitting on the table catch her eye. An obvious antique, no bigger than a playing card, with a small letter "H" engraved on the lid. The big dog watched the woman pick up the box and open it to find nothing inside but a cracked leather lining. He saw her turn it over in her hand—once, twice—then silently slip it into the pocket of her coat before walking out of the house and closing the door behind her with a soft click. Smudge heard her start her car, then turned and went back to his place by Marietta's side.

5

GLINDA

The walls of Micheline's Italian Restaurant were covered in a red damask fabric that cushioned the crowd's conversation to a reverential level and against which Glinda's green suit stood out like an emperor's emerald. The hat had been a mistake, she knew that now. She'd take it off if she wasn't afraid her hair would be a mess underneath. In her desire to be inconspicuous, the minute Macon disappeared from her side she slipped into the food line, accepted a plate of lasagna, and head down, slid behind the cluster of people gathered near the serving table to a quiet, chilly corner of the room beside the frosted front window. She pulled out a chair with her foot and sat down, crossing her feet at the ankle, the plate of lasagna warm in her lap.

Glinda let her gaze wander the room, lingering here and there on people she knew, careful to meet no one's eye. When the pinging sound of knife on glass silenced the voices, she, along with everyone else, turned to see Butter Swann, cheeks pink from the cold outside, deliver her news about Marietta.

"She's got a migraine. Just heartbroken not to be here, but really, she's so sick she could barely sit up. I told her y'all would understand. I put her to bed and hopefully she'll be able to just sleep it off. She's had these things for years, you know. Awful that it should happen today, of all days." Butter smiled apologetically and everyone murmured in commiseration, though Glinda could sense a slight lifting of the respectful melancholy that had filled the room when the arrival of the widow was still considered a possibility. The conversation seemed a bit livelier after Butter had spoken.

Without warning, Glinda felt tears salt her eyes. She couldn't imagine too many things worse for her sister-in-law. Glinda had never known another couple like Marietta and Harry. Over the years, she'd see them occasionally, having lunch together at that outdoor café down the street from their shop, bent toward each other in conversation, or once, when she'd been behind them at a traffic light on a summer's day, she'd watched as they laughed at something—loudly, heads thrown back—their giggles and howls spilling out of their open car windows and into Glinda's, the sound filling her with a green-tinged curiosity that made her suddenly sad. Thinking of Marietta now, at home sick in bed, missing Harry's funeral, Glinda realized that happy endings really didn't exist, no matter what she read in books. Sooner or later, one way or another, we all end up losing the people we love.

She caught the tear before it spilled over her lashes and quickly turned her head, pretending to look out through the window at the gray afternoon. How was it possible that time moved so fast? Already there was valentine candy on the shelves of the drugstore, the heart-shaped boxes so red she'd thought they were leftover Christmas decorations when she first saw them last week. Easter rabbits seemed to become jack-o'-lanterns overnight, and tartan-bowed wreaths appeared on front doors with a celerity that stunned, then depressed her, every single year. She could no longer rely on a sensible progression of seasons; they flew past with such mocking speed, taking her youth right in front of her eyes and leaving her wondering just what had happened. She didn't suppose they'd ever slow down now. Harry had been four years younger than she was, and he was already gone.

Glinda picked at her lasagna with indifference, her appetite not pricked in the slightest. When the conversations around her dipped in volume, she caught her husband's voice, scanned the room, and found him holding court in the middle of a circle of dark-suited men, his Pecksniffian laugh rising above the din of conversation like a bray. She couldn't remember the last time she'd heard Macon really laugh; when he laughed in her memory, he had a young face.

"Well, I'll tell you one thing," she heard him say, "those MRED folks . . . or 'Mr. Ed,' as I like to call them"—this was met with snickers and grins—"they have gone and bitten off more than they can chew. They're trying to appeal to the business-minded people here in Wesleyan by suggesting that the statue will impede further development in town, but I'm not so sure all this attention they're stirring up just won't bring more development in. And the kind of development we'd all welcome, if you know what I mean."

Balding heads nodded, spurring Macon onward. "The thing is, there's an awful lot of people who miscalculated the amount of veneration we have for our heritage around here. They act like we should be ashamed of our own ancestors. Well now, fortunately I don't have to litigate all that. This case doesn't require it. It's an open-and-shut deal, what with the statue being privately owned and all. I mean, suing to have it removed on account of it being some kind of threat to public safety? Just a bid for publicity. I'll have them packed up and gone in a heartbeat.

"But I'll tell you what, this kind of stuff is happening all over the country right now, and while I know we've lost a few of these battles recently—that statue of Lee coming down in New Orleans still makes my blood boil—I can tell you one thing for certain: we won't lose old Henry Benning here in Wesleyan, Georgia. You can take that to the bank, boys."

It wasn't as if she hadn't heard him talk like this before; Macon's oft-used word "heritage" had long been a euphemism for something Glinda had never wanted to examine too closely. But for him to speak so openly, the assumption of accordance clearly evident in his tone as well as his words, at the funeral of his sister's husband, a man who'd made his own feelings about the Benning statue crystal clear long before there'd ever been any serious talk of its removal, well, it was almost profanatory.

From her seat in the corner Glinda's eyes narrowed as she watched Macon's little conclave break up with backslaps and grins, the men scanning the room for their wives, and moving toward them like homing pigeons. She could see Macon making his way across the room to her almost as though he were trudging through mud, each step taking a minute or more in her mind. Glinda felt strangely dizzy, the various voices in the room co-alescing into one huge sound that became a roar the closer Macon got, and just as his bottom was nearing the red leatherette seat beside her, Glinda slid her large uneaten plate of lasagna be-neath it.

6

MARIETTA

Time gives us all a gift upon waking. For the briefest of moments, it hangs suspended, not moving forward or back, not yet committed to sadness or joy, free from anticipation or regret. In those few vague seconds, you could be anywhere, any age. It's an infinitesimal twinkling before reality laughs in your ear, taking your heart in its fist and squeezing it tight, and for Marietta today, it was a cruel trick that gave her, if only for an instant, a flash of counterfeit comfort before her eyes flew open and she suddenly felt Harry leave her again. The room was nearly dark. She'd been asleep for more than five hours.

It took her a minute to realize the migraine was gone. The parts of her head that had throbbed with pain felt lighter now, as though heavy, hot stones had been replaced with clean, cool air. Grateful for the comforting weight of a big dog's head lying across her ankles, she reached down and dug her fingers into Smudge's thick white fur. Though she'd done nothing more than open her eyes, the dog had known, and had lifted his head to look at her.

Remembering the forecast, she got up and went to the window. A misty drizzle had started, and the wind was up; she could see the lacy branches of bare trees clawing at the clouds. "Come on, Smudgy. You need to go out before it turns bad." The dog hopped down from the bed and stretched. As Marietta breathed in the fragrance of the tuberoses on the table by her bed, she saw Gordon's note, easily identifiable by the neat block lettering and purple ink, and picked it up. Taking her fleecy robe from the back of the door, she placed the note in her pocket, and together she and Smudge headed downstairs.

Butter had been right. The rooms were flower-filled, polished, and consoling in their beauty, as Gordon would have known they would be. It was easy to see that he'd been here; the living room was full of yellow roses, and there were new issues of *Country Life* and *Tattler*, his two favorite magazines, lying atop the ottomans.

Gordon Lovett didn't do funerals. He'd lived in New York City during the eighties and early nineties, and had attended enough of them to last till the end of his days, at which point—he'd made this very clear—he wasn't having one of the things himself. Harry wouldn't have expected him to be at St. Cyprian's this morning. Marietta certainly hadn't.

She unlocked the two large doors that opened out from the library, and Smudge stuck a hesitant nose into the cold, wet air. The cold he didn't mind, but the wet was another matter entirely.

"Now, come on, boy. You've been inside all day." She looked up at the lowering sky. "And this drizzle is going to change to something much worse. Get on out there." Marietta gave Smudge's back end a little push with her knee. The big dog threw her a look of resignation, then padded onto the stone porch and down the stairs. She watched him as he went out into the dusk, looking for all the world like the light from an oversize firefly as he bobbed along the crooked paths, vanishing now and then behind some low-hanging limbs, only to reappear deeper into the gray landscape.

Marietta turned on the back light for Ivy, the eight-year-old girl who lived next door, whose bedroom overlooked the garden. Harry had been great friends with Ivy Harper, just as Marietta was with her mother, Enid. Enid and her husband, John, had been two of the very few people who'd been aware of Harry's illness through its whole duration, and early on Ivy had devised a way for Marietta and Harry to let her know if they needed anything in the night: if all was okay, they were to turn on their porch light at dusk and leave it on till morning. If Marietta needed anything, all she had to do was turn it off.

"Won't the light shine in your window and keep you awake?" Marietta had asked the little girl when she approached them with the idea. "Why don't we say we'll turn it *on* if we need you?"

"Oh no, it'll be better to look out and see it shining and know everything's all right," Ivy had said. And somehow Marietta had known what she meant. It was a ritual she intended to continue, knowing, without being told, that Ivy would find just as much comfort in seeing that light as Marietta would have in turning it on.

Walking into the kitchen she took out a bag of kibble and filled Smudge's empty bowl. Looking around, she shook her head again at the amount of food that covered the long, freshly scrubbed table. Enough for a family of bears. She wouldn't have to cook for a month. As soon as they'd heard about Harry, people who'd known Marietta from childhood had pointed their cars toward The Glade to bring her food. Throughout this long, strange week, she'd received each kind offering with gratitude, even though, in truth, every thoughtfully home-cooked meal now filling her refrigerator and overflowing onto her counters was in itself but another odd reminder that Harry's death had indeed taken place.

Marietta had meant it when she told Butter that today wasn't the worst. Even that horrible morning when poor Dr. Mackey—his voice thin, his face ashen, his eyes never quite locking onto theirs—had given them the test results identifying the source of the new, nagging pain in Harry's back, results that choked Marietta's breath and caused her to slide out of her seat in a faint . . . even that hadn't been the worst day.

No, the worst day had come a couple of months later, on a sunny summer morning when she'd sat knitting by the bedroom window, watching Harry down in the garden. He'd been on his hands and knees, meticulously clipping the row of topiary elephants on which he'd labored for more than two decades. She'd laughed at his vision the day he planted them; tiny little boxwoods, no taller than ducklings, that he planned to coax and coddle into an octet of elephants as the focal point for their garden. Now lush and large, they marched around the old bird feeder, holding trunks and tails, like an illustration from a children's book. She'd smiled as she watched him work, his face shielded by his faded red hat, and then out of nowhere, Marietta could have sworn she'd heard a loud rumble of thunder, so loud she'd felt it in her chest, though there hadn't been a cloud in the sky. And it had come over her like a fever. The inescapable fact, the unavoidable horror. That this would be Harry's last summer in the garden. Harry was going to die.

We all know this; we all have to know this. It's written in our contract on the day we are born. But the imminence of death is buried so deep beneath the marrow of our bones, we seem to be hardwired to ignore it as long as we can. That ancient knowledge is sometimes disturbed by the strange lump or odd twinge, and the moment we feel it awaken, our minds tear out into lands we've never traveled, where the roads are unmarked, the shadows are deep, and the darkness is occult. But then the crisis passes—the lump is benign; the twinge is just something we ate—and the door that almost opened slams shut tight once again.

Even when the doctors said "terminal," it didn't seem real. Harry had joked that it sounded like he was headed off to a grand, cavernous station where he'd catch a train to someplace he'd never been before. He said he'd always wanted to see Kathmandu. They'd even laughed. *Laughed.*

But on that morning, in those seconds she'd watched as Harry worked happily away at the most quotidian of tasks, Marietta had felt the dark, impending knowledge rise up from all its hiding places inside her, felt fear itself pull her into a soul-crushing hug that left no room for hope or denial, no second chances, no possibility of turning back the clock to one of the now too-few days they'd had together. No. No. Harry was going to die. And she knew it now. That. That was the worst day.

From that morning on, Marietta had walked down the street bewildered to see people functioning as normal. Still in line at the coffee shop, still bouncing babies on their knees in the park, still walking dogs, still sitting in traffic, still laughing, still arguing, still . . . living.

It had been his choice, but she'd been relieved that Harry hadn't wanted anyone to know, preferring to go on living normally, without the inevitable looks of pity or worry—or, worse, embarrassment—without the explanations he'd continually have to give. He'd declined any kind of treatment. The doctors had explained the chances of success were minuscule, and the chemo would have to be so strong he'd most likely not feel like doing much of anything, none of which was acceptable to Harry. They'd given him something for pain and he'd walked out of the office with plans.

They needed a new refrigerator, he said. So, he'd bought one and had it installed the next week. The roof, the hot water heater, the central heating and air . . . all were checked and serviced. The arborist came and made sure all the tall trees were healthy and able to withstand summer storms. Harry tried to make Marietta sit down and go over their finances, but she'd burst into tears and refused to do so, running upstairs and slamming the bedroom door, something that shamed her when she recalled it now. Later that night, when they'd gone to bed, he'd whispered to her that she'd be all right. "There's enough, hon. And with the life insurance that'll be coming, you'll be set. You won't have to worry at all. You can buy you some of those red-soled high heels if you want to." She'd turned over and placed her head on his chest, matching her breath to his.

Just as they'd always done in late summer, they'd spent several weeks in the cottage they always rented on Dog Island, both of them trying to behave as though everything was normal. It was the only time Marietta could ever remember shading her feelings from Harry, and she knew he was doing the same for her. Neither wanted to break the other's heart, so they'd talked about the usual things: the books they were reading, what to cook for dinner, the latest atrocities emanating from the nation's capital. Eventually they hired the Harpers' older daughter, Thea, to watch the shop in the afternoons. They suspended the paper and stopped watching the news. And their world became smaller and smaller until all they could see was each other.

She'd been enormously grateful for Gordon, for her sake as well as for Harry's. Gordon was the one person with whom she'd always felt complete freedom to express her darkest fears. He never judged, never served up platitudes, never behaved as though she wasn't going through hell. And, miraculously, Gordon always found a way to make her laugh. Unexpected, belly-shaking, disinfecting laughs that left her oddly hopeful long after they faded. She knew he'd provided the same support to Harry; knew she'd never be able to repay him for that.

Occasionally during those painful months Marietta would stay awake just to watch Harry sleep, counting his breaths, her hand on his chest as it rose and fell in peaceful rhythm. On those nights, the feelings of jealousy that nibbled around the edges of her fear unsettled her. She knew what was coming, and she knew which one of them she'd much rather be.

Thanks to her father, Marietta had never been afraid of death, having made its acquaintance after her young aunt Kathleen had died suddenly in a car crash out on Old Cherokee Road when Marietta was still a small child. Everyone had gathered at the house and the enormity of family grief had scared her, so she'd disappeared upstairs to her room. Logan found her there, sitting on the floor between the twin beds, with her knees pulled up to her chest and her dog, Trixie, lying protectively by her side. He'd pulled her onto his lap, called her Sugarfoot, and told her not to be afraid. He'd said the people who are left behind are always sad when someone they love is gone, but that death itself is nothing to fear. For the person who's died, he'd said, a grand adventure is just beginning.

"You know those big balloons you wait every year to see come down Fifth Avenue on Thanksgiving morning?" he'd said. She'd nodded. "Well, you may not notice it, but next time, if you look, you'll see there are a bunch of people holding on to heavy ropes that hold those things to the ground. If they didn't hang on tight, those balloons would just take off up into the sky. And they're trying to do just that, you can tell by how hard those people are pulling on those ropes.

"Well, just like those balloons, there are a lot of ropes holding you to the ground. People, places, things that you love. Even Trixie here has got a bit of one in her mouth." The dog looked at him earnestly, as if she understood exactly what was being said. "You can even be unaware of some of the people holding them. But as you go on through your life you'll start to feel each one of those ropes letting go, one by one, until finally, the last one will drop and you'll just simply float away on a breeze, right on up to the heavens, like a bird."

Marietta wondered how many ropes she had left now. She was only sixty-one, hardly done with her life. But it was difficult to picture the years up ahead without Harry; he'd held her fast and steady for so very long. The shop, this house, her dog, her friends. How strong were her ropes? How long would they hold? Did she even want them to anymore?

Marietta's roster of friends had shuffled in recent years—with a lot of people plummeting to the bottom, and Gordon landing solidly on top—ever since Harry had suggested they start a Facebook page for the shop. "Look here, hon," he'd said one rainy afternoon as they sat in the office eating their lunch. "I think we should do this." He'd swung his laptop around to face her. "See? Here's a shop kinda like ours up in North Carolina. They post photos of new things when they come in, and I swear, they seem to sell within a day or two. We could do that. Especially with that new shipment about to get here. We went a little overboard last trip, after all. I don't know where we're going to put everything."

Marietta had put her glasses on and stared down at the screen. "Well . . . maybe. Tell you what, I'll take the pictures and write up the copy, if you handle everything else. All that fiddly stuff on computers bores me to death." Harry had theatrically rubbed his hands together and spent the rest of the day setting up the page for Cline's Antiques. They'd had thirty followers by the time they locked up at five.

Marietta remembered the very day she'd taken a look at the thing. Harry was taking Smudge for a walk and she'd stayed behind to do a bit of housecleaning. In between polishing the tables and vacuuming the rugs, she'd stopped to answer some email and glance at the news, eventually landing on Facebook. She had no idea so many people she knew were participating on this site, but once she'd clicked on one familiar face, dozens more started popping up, and before she knew it, she'd fallen down a rabbit hole into a world every bit as unsettling as Alice's.

Growing up the daughter of Logan Hargis, Marietta was used to ideological disagreements around her very own family dinner table. Due to her father's penchant for accumulating friends of wildly divergent personalities and beliefs, she was also used to those disagreements reaching fever pitch long before dessert was served. But what she found on Facebook was something entirely different. When had this happened? It seemed as though while she'd been looking the other way an ugliness had been let loose and was now running rampant among the very people she thought she knew.

It was as if she'd been given the burdensome power to read minds. The words people wrote, alone in their rooms, pierced their everyday disguises and ripped off the masks they wore for the world. It didn't take long before Marietta no longer trusted the outstretched hands and open smiles of those who displayed such entirely different personas online. It was hard not to picture the paintings they hid in their attics, the Dorian Gray truths of their souls. She felt pushed into a judgmental position she'd never wanted or expected, one that made it hard to discern between anger and grief.

Harry told her to ignore it. Gordon just made snarky jokes about the dearth of intelligence in the modern-day South. "'When we are born, we cry that we are come to this great stage of fools!'" he'd said, holding the back of his hand to his forehead. But she'd felt changed by what she'd seen. When Nancy LeCraw came into the shop one morning to look for an antique lamp, all Marietta could see was the paragraph the woman had written on the refugee problem at the border, words of such vitriol and invective that Marietta had to double-check the photo at the top of the page to make certain this was indeed the same woman who held weekly Bible studies around her pool in summer. Old customers, high school friends, pillars of the Wesleyan community—so many wrote such hateful and ignorant things. Even her great-aunt Evelyn, living in a retirement home in Montgomery, and eighty-five if she was a day, applauded the sort of blatantly racist statements that, had she been asked, Marietta would have sworn the old lady certainly deplored. But nothing hit her harder than seeing her brother's page, full of praise and support for political candidates who horrified her; Macon's comments and opinions had almost made her sick. It was as though she'd never really known anyone at all. She had felt her circle narrowing.

It had been around this time that she and Enid had been making blackberry jelly on a hot August morning, and Marietta asked her friend if she was on Facebook herself.

"Yeah, I've got a page. But just for the family. To keep up with everybody's kids, you know. I do some snooping now and then, and I know what you mean. It's pretty bleak out there."

"I just wish I'd never seen it all."

"Not me," said Enid, wetting the corner of a tea towel and blotting some of the dark purple jelly from her shirt. "I say, take your hood off and let me see who you are."

Marietta winced. "Yeah, I guess. It's all just kind of broken my heart."

Enid put her spoon down and stared hard at her friend. "Let

me ask you something," she said. "What did you think when Obama was elected president?"

Marietta kept stirring the boiling blackberries. When she spoke, her voice was serrated with something so close to bitterness it surprised her. "Well, I thought it meant we'd changed a little, finally, I guess. That we'd grown, moved past something. I remember I went to J. P. Allen's the next day to buy a few Christmas presents and the lady who waited on me was black, and I started to cry right in front of her. She thought I was crazy; I know she did."

"Yeah, I thought so." Enid started measuring out more sugar. "You wanna know what John and I thought that night?"

"What?"

"We thought, 'Lord, this is gonna cause a backlash like nothing we've ever seen before.'" Marietta looked up at Enid, who continued, "All these people you've seen on Facebook? You think this new president created them? Honey, they've been here all along. He just picked up the rock and waved it around in the air so they could all slither out into the light. He's managed to validate ugliness and bigotry. It won't be going away anytime soon."

Marietta had slammed berries into the strainer with more force than was necessary, sending blackberry juice up onto her sleeve. "Damn. And now my own brother is out there defending that stupid statue in Griffin Park, so it's all going to start up again." She stuck her arm under the faucet and turned on the cold water.

"Start up again?" Enid laughed. "Hell, Marietta. You think it ever stopped? Pass me those lemons. Just because white people are finally noticing some of these things and realizing just what they were meant to communicate to people like me doesn't mean *we* hadn't gotten that message a long time ago. You don't think every time my daddy rode past that statue of old Henry Benning he didn't feel like crap?" She began cutting the lemons in two and Marietta had felt an embarrassment that was easy at that moment to blame on her brother.

That night on the phone, Marietta had mentioned the conversation to Gordon, and his response had made her laugh, even as it resonated like a truth she'd been loath to admit. "You've been thrown for a loop because you expected something more, something better." His laugh was edgy and wry. "And that, right there, is where you made your first mistake. You want too much of humanity, Marietta, you always have. You set yourself up for disappointment thinking that way, and eventually, if you're not careful, for disillusionment, too. Then you cut people loose, can't forgive them because you can't make peace with who you think they really are. Now me . . ." She imagined Gordon, on the other end of the phone, bowing his head theatrically, putting his hand over his heart. "I *expect* people to be dumb, tribal assholes every time I walk out my door, and I can tell you that I am rarely disappointed. But when I am, when someone's kind or compassionate or, God help me, has an IQ that allows them to think past the tip of their nose, well, I gotta say, it just makes my day. Those are the moments I live for. Marietta, 'expectation is the root of all heartache,' and you, my dear"—she heard him muffle a sigh—"please do forgive me, but I know for a fact that you've always gone out *your* door every day expecting people to do the right thing, to feel as you do about what's good and what's bad, to always choose the righteous path because, in your mind, that path is just so clear. And what do you get? Grief and sorrow, yes . . . grief and sorrow, every damn day. One of these days you're going to have to stop that and realize that the only soul you're responsible for is your own. Just let people be who they are and don't worry about it."

As usual after talking with Gordon, she'd hung up feeling better, but only marginally so.

She realized now that she'd been used to seeing people collectively, unconsciously collating them into groups in her head. Here were the scholars. There were the kooks. Here was good. There was bad. But what she'd seen on Facebook had ripped those categories from her mind like the useless pages of an old calendar, and she'd been left feeling cheated somehow, and sorrowful at the loss of a certain kind of innocence she'd enjoyed for years.

She'd been defensive when Gordon told her she "cut people loose," his casual observation making her uncomfortable because she knew, deep down, he was right. She knew she should try to look past people's words, to dig all the way down to their intentions instead. Her father had taught her that. But continuing on as normal with someone after reading their vicious comments made her feel complicit in the attitudes she deplored. At least that's what she told herself. Was this what had happened with Butter five years ago? She remembered that afternoon over lunch, listening to Butter's dramatic complaint about the hospital making her grandson wait in the hallway with a broken ankle while the doctors attended to an immigrant family, and feeling like she wanted to scream. Come to think about it, she *had* raised her voice when she called Butter "crass"—several people had turned around to stare. Afterward it had been too hard to apologize for something she truly felt, so she never did. But erasing Butter from her life had never really been her intention.

She'd been on her way to the cleaners the day she saw Butter's billboard for the first time, and she'd laughed out loud in her car. It seemed so fitting; someone like Butter should have been up on a billboard for years. Butter had always been such a vivid person; with the golden hair, the bright blue eyes, she could've been dressed in black from head to toe and would've still walked through the world in a fluffy cloud of Technicolor. The nickname Gordon bestowed upon her in third grade had stuck, not because it was particularly funny, but because it was so true. But there was more to Butter than fluff, and Marietta felt a wave of shame that she'd seen her own part of the relationship as the only one that mattered. She should have called Butter the day that billboard went up.

Friendship had been so easy when they were little. Any differences were simply gathered up and kneaded into the relationship, making it more elastic and interesting, while any disagreements

were dealt with on the spot, erupting like waterspouts and dissi-
pating just as quickly. But time apart can magnify those peculiar
parts of people that go unnoticed when we're young, and with
the years comes another code of conduct: a reticence disguised as
politeness and, in Marietta's case, a judgment that could too often
masquerade as personal conviction. She never told Butter what
had happened in Atlanta. Maybe that was part of the problem.
Holding back something that frightening, that real, made every
other part of their friendship seem trivial.

Now, standing alone in the kitchen, Marietta let her mind wander back to those yellowed walls in the bathroom at St. Cyprian's
and the awful moment when she'd stepped out of that cubicle
feeling worse than she could have imagined, and she knew in her
heart there was no other person alive she'd rather have seen than
Butter Swann. Regret and embarrassment colored her face.

Unable to face all the rich food that filled her counters, Marietta looked in the refrigerator for a carton of cold yogurt and a
Coke. Finding those, she sat down at the table and pulled Gordon's note from her pocket. Propping her feet up on a chair, she
took a spoonful of yogurt and opened the little envelope, pulling
out a gilt-edged notecard with Gordon's name embossed at the
top.

> *Hello, my dear. I guess you can tell I paid you a visit. Hope my
> little bit of sprucing up made for a warm welcome home. Keep an
> eye to the skies. If the ice storm comes, hopefully you won't lose
> power. If you do, the fires are all ready to light. And if I'm the
> one to lose power, Trilby and I will be on our way to your house
> lickety-split. I love you. Call me. x G*

Marietta rose, went into the entry hall for her handbag, fished
out the phone she'd had muted since morning, and sat down on
the stairs. Twenty-nine messages, eight of them from Gordon.
Most of these had come in before Butter could have made it back
to the reception, so she assumed people had just been wondering
what happened. Well, Butter would've told them; no need to call

them back now. But Gordon was another matter. He'd be expecting to hear from her. She decided to text him instead.

I'm home now. You might have heard; I got a migraine at the funeral. When it rains, no? Butter drove me home and I've slept most of the day. The house is a marvel, Gordon. Thank you so much. Fingers crossed the power will stay on. I'm just eating something now, and I think I'll go straight back to bed when I'm done. I'm okay, really. I'll phone you in the morning. Love you more than words.

Now that she'd texted it, she realized that all she really did want to do was go straight back to bed. Remembering Smudge out in the garden, she went to the library doors. She could see him clearly, standing just beside the topiary elephants, his big shaggy head lifted up to where a huge black bird sat on the feeder finial. Hearing the door open, both dog and bird turned slowly to look at her.

The drizzle changed to ice just then, falling like a million frozen teardrops, hitting every naked branch, every leaf-covered flower bed, with a sound like a crackling fire.

7

GORDON
AND BUTTER

All through the night, as quietly as a cat, ice slid down from the skies over Wesleyan, covering the town with a coating of molten silver that snapped weak limbs from pine trees and pulled power lines down from their tall wooden poles. In the hours before dawn it drifted across town to the little woodland garden that encircled Gordon Lovett's lakeside cottage, swaddling his boxwoods and birdhouses in inarticulate white.

It was the silence that woke him. Deep and impenetrable, almost a sound unto itself, it pushed against his windowpanes, crept into his room, and covered his ears like a pair of gloved hands. Gordon woke with a start and lay stone still in the metallic light, lost to himself for more than a minute, hands closed tight on the border of a starched linen sheet, eyes darting around the room on a heart-pounding search for something familiar.

Bit by bit, friendly shapes began to materialize out of the pearly air. A tufted leather armchair said good morning from the corner, its sizable seat dotted with evidential cookie crumbs from the previous night. A book-covered desk nodded in front of the window, its polished walnut top rolled back to reveal the barely organized chaos of a busy man. And over by the fireplace, a round, tartan-covered dog bed lay empty, with a corgi-shaped indentation hollowed out in its center, left cold by the abandonment of its warmth-seeking owner, who now rested comfortably at the foot of Gordon's well–blanketed bed.

Wishing to remain in this most agreeable of positions, the dog lay as still as he possibly could, his brown eyes shut tight against the dawn. But as usual, he found himself betrayed by his furry metronome of a tail, which had begun to wave madly at the sound of Gordon's first stirring. The dog had never understood, nor at all appreciated, how little control he seemed to have over the emotions expressed by that traitorous appendage.

Gordon's eyes latched onto that wagging tail and he smiled. "It's no use, Trilby. I know you're awake," he said.

At the sound of his voice, Trilby the corgi rose, stretched, and began to navigate the hills and valleys of the bedcovers to plop his head onto Gordon's chest. Truth be told, Gordon was grateful for the company. It had taken him forever to fall asleep. Between worrying about Marietta and listening to the gunshot crack of tree limbs breaking off in the woods all around him, Gordon had stayed awake for most of the night. None of the trees had hit the cottage, as far as he could tell, but he hadn't yet taken a look at the garden. He'd lived here for more than two decades, and this was the first ice storm he'd experienced. There'd been one once when he'd been a teenager, though, and he remembered the power was out for a week.

Lying there under the covers, absentmindedly scratching the grateful Trilby's ears, Gordon recalled that long-ago conversation when Marietta had convinced him to move back to Wesleyan after his years in New York City. He could still hear her voice over the phone.

"Oh, come on, Gordy," she'd said in that beguiling way that always meant he'd end up doing whatever it was she wanted despite his feeble protestations. "You know you need to get out of that city. Shuffling around every day, staring at the pavement, everything you see reminding you of Alan. How can you stand that anymore? Just come back down here for a little while. Rent a place for the fall, it'll be beautiful then. If you want to you can be back in New York in three or four hours, anytime you wish. The old bookshop on the square is closing. You know the one just three doors down from our shop? You could buy it; keep doing what you've been doing, only it would all belong to you. And you never know, you might just like being back home. Miss Hepburn's cottage? The one we always loved at Bobbin Lake? It's up for sale. You know those houses are never available. There's only five of them. You remember how pretty it is over there. The place is a little run-down now, but it just needs your touch to be spectacular. What do you say?"

Of course Gordon had remembered Bobbin Lake. It seemed only yesterday that the two of them, loosed from the confines of Tillman Elementary School, had cut through the woods on their way to visit Jasper, the truculent, dun-colored pony that old Miss Hepburn kept in a grassy little field out behind her house. Marietta, always convinced that Jasper's peevishness was merely a well-rehearsed act brought on by feelings of inferiority over his diminutive size, would feed the fat pony alms of carrots and peppermints, while Gordon, more realistic about Jasper's dark nature, busied himself in finding new holes in the holly hedge through which he could better view Miss Hepburn's magical little house. With his bespectacled face sticking out through a halo of holly berries, he would stare in amazement at its pale pink stone, its plethora of climbing roses, its vegetable garden full of watermelons.

Frederick Hepburn, Miss Hepburn's artist father, had built the cottage in the twenties and, perhaps under the influence of that riotous age, had actually had the stone painted pink, an action that, although no doubt of questionable beauty when first done, had resulted in a most appealing sight in the century to come. The years had worked their magic and faded the color to nothing more than a hint of its former self, the consequence being that in every season, in every sort of weather, the house just seemed to glow. Gordon remembered seeing it in spring, when its western wall was covered in a tangle of Lady Banks' roses. The pink cottage had appeared to him then almost bewitched, as though its radiance grew up from some magical source deep in the ground, the same source responsible for piglets and peonies.

To think that there was even a remote possibility that he could find himself living there had been almost overwhelming to Gordon. So naturally he'd said yes, as they'd both known he would, and despite his many years in New York, he found it surprisingly easy to return to Wesleyan. The people there didn't so much welcome him home as behave as though he'd never left in the first place. This might have been a blow to the carefully constructed image he'd fashioned for himself as a sophisticated New Yorker—one who'd actually been, for one night, on the Broadway stage—but instead, Gordon found it enormously refreshing. Once again, he was back to just being Gordon Lovett, Margo and Jack Lovett's only son, Wanda and Wendy's little brother, the chubby little boy with the quick wit and oversize personality who, when he wasn't tap-dancing in the halls, or buried in a book, was forever tagging along after Logan Hargis's redheaded daughter.

He'd renamed the bookshop Epiphanies, and it took only a couple of years for people to stop asking him why. Carefully curated, with old wooden floors, cushy armchairs, and a tiny café in the back, it had once been listed by *Southern Living* as a destination bookshop, which didn't increase his customer base nearly as much as the weekly book club he started fifteen years ago. Every Friday morning, often long before Gordon flipped the front door sign over from CLOSED to OPEN, Wesleyans of various backgrounds and ages lined up in anticipation of warm croissants, coffee, and the chance to give their opinions on the book of the week. These titles were all chosen by Gordon—nobody possessed the temerity to suggest otherwise—and though it had been Marietta's idea to christen these weekly gatherings "Breakfast at Epiphanies," she'd insisted Gordon claim credit for the name.

They'd been friends from that very first day they'd met in the cotton candy line at St. Cyprian's fall festival when they'd been, what? Four? Five? Certainly too young for school, for by the time they'd marched into that venerable institution they'd already formed a union of friendship that was tighter than skin onto bone. Being a year older, Gordon was never in the same class as Marietta, but he'd wait for her every day after school and they'd walk home together, each telling the other stories of their day, his always exaggerated and embellished for maximum comedic effect. He adored her. Not even the arrival of Harry had been able to alter their bond. In fact, Gordon had loved Harry nearly as much as Marietta did, and after he'd moved back home, some of his fondest memories were of the times they'd all spent together. His grief at Harry's passing was nearly as strong as hers, though he did all his crying in private.

He interrupted his reverie to reach for the old-fashioned alarm clock on his bedside table. It had been his mother's, and Gordon, who detested the sound of the thing, consistently depended on his ability to wake up five minutes before it went off each morning to silence its wails before they even began. He switched the thing off now without looking it in the face.

"*Up, Trilby!*" he said as he nudged the dog off his chest and threw back the Pendleton blankets. With a wounded look, Trilby reluctantly rose to his feet and attempted a halfhearted stretch atop the bedcovers, one that concluded with a belly flop and a sigh, signaling the corgi's intention to stay precisely where he was until the fragrance of sausages began climbing the stairs to tickle his nose.

But there would be no such luxuries today. The power was out. Gordon switched the bedside light on and off several times, the bulb remaining stubbornly dark, and let out a loud and heartfelt "Damn." The room was so cold he could see his breath drifting across it in a cloud. Swinging his legs over the side of the bed, he stuck his toes into the navy velvet slippers lined up precisely where his feet hit the floor, walked to the window, and peered outside.

The garden looked stunned, as though caught in the act of

running away. Hemlock branches hung down to the ground, and the pine trees, bent into hieroglyphically contorted shapes, leaned on one another for support. The holes in the rutted dirt road that encircled the lake were frozen; they stared up at him like unblinking old eyes, their muddy irises bleary with cataracts of gray ice. The lake was as still as a painting.

Staring out at the macabre whiteness, Gordon reached over for the desk lamp, turning it on and off a couple of times before convincing himself that he was, really and truly, in the dark. He was. And if experience was any indication, he would remain so for at least a week. With so few houses around Bobbin Lake, they tended to sit on the lowest rung of priority for the local power company. Three were owned by families from Atlanta, and used only in summer. Old Mr. Stieglitz lived in the last one and would have gone to his daughter's in Seabrook at the first suggestion of bad weather. Gordon was the only person here. He shivered a little and looked over at Trilby, still snuggled down in the warmth of the bed. "Damn," he whispered.

Butter had fallen asleep on her sofa. An hour after delivering her news about Marietta to the people gathered at Harry's reception, she'd left the restaurant with the phone numbers of three potential clients in her purse, and a large serving of chicken tetrazzini in an aluminum take-out box.

After she'd turned off Quarles Avenue into the long willow-lined drive that led up to the imposing white mansion at Windward Oaks, she'd felt the usual thrill when the lady in the guardhouse saw her resident sticker and waved her through with a welcoming smile. Butter belonged here, and as usual, she indulged herself in the brief fantasy that she was pulling up to her very own estate, not just to one of the newly added condos in the back.

She loved her address, loved seeing it on her mailing labels, loved writing it in the upper left-hand corner of every Christmas card she sent. She loved pretending the lushly green lawns and immaculately tended tennis courts were hers alone, that the people who splashed in the pool outside her back door were merely guests she'd graciously admitted into her private realm.

Butter had hungered to live here from the time she first heard the old Bruce mansion was going to be converted into condominiums. Oh, she knew she'd never be able to afford one of the units in the main house. There were only six of them, and with their tall carved ceilings and cool marble fireplaces, the price for even the smallest one was well beyond her reach, and always would be. But when construction began on the U-shaped addition that would eventually surround a kidney-shaped pool, Butter began squirreling away cash.

She knew now that her divorce from Joe had been inevitable from the moment she'd taken her vows. But there'd been three of them at the altar that September morning, and she'd felt she owed Christo a father, for at least as long as it took for him to grow up. In the end, she waited till he was thirty-two.

We make the most important decisions of our lives when we're least equipped to do so. If Butter had known the passionate, insatiable boy she was having sex with in his baby blue Mercury Cougar would, in such a few short years, become a mentally torpid tax accountant, would she have so readily climbed into that backseat? As the years slipped away it became harder and harder to extricate herself from the marriage her teenage self had so readily, so giddily, leapt inside. Joe wasn't a bad person, after all; he just turned out to be so achingly dull. Butter felt she'd wasted so much of her life futilely searching for topics they could talk about with equal enthusiasm or, in Joe's case, any enthusiasm at all.

In the end he'd taken her request for a divorce with all the animation of a stuffed owl, displaying the same sort of placid acquiescence he did when his favorite brand of pickle relish was sold out at the store. "Huh. You sure?" had been his response. Such was Butter's guilt over the prospect of leaving him, she'd failed to notice that Joe wasn't particularly devoted to the marriage himself. She seriously doubted he'd miss her at all.

But she never had a good chance to find that out, what with Joe hurtling off the roof with a fistful of wet leaves from the gutter he'd been cleaning before the papers had even been signed. Butter then had all the money she needed to move into Windward, and she'd wasted no time in doing so.

She'd hired Bailey Weeks, the hottest, blondest decorator in Wesleyan, to create the trendiest interiors she could imagine. Everything white, straight-lined, and sleek, with "pops" of bright color in pillows and throws. The house had been photographed for the Style section of the Sunday paper the month it was finished, garnering a good three years of fruitful promotion for both Butter and Bailey Weeks.

But yesterday afternoon when she'd parked her car beneath the pear tree and walked up the narrow path to her door, for the first time ever she'd felt a ripple of dissatisfaction before the key even turned in the lock. Having indulged in what her mother had always called "the sin of comparison," Butter couldn't now wash the images of Marietta's warm, colorful home from her mind. She had sensed nearly tangible traces of love and laughter in every corner of that house, and as she stood in her own foyer, taking in all its cool perfection, she'd felt, once again, painfully, embarrassingly jealous. Yes, she'd just left Marietta's husband's funeral. Yes, Marietta was a grieving widow. But still, as always, Butter would have changed places with her in a heartbeat. The silver box hiding in the bottom of her coat pocket had felt as heavy as shame.

It wasn't Marietta's beauty that she envied; Butter had always been the prettier one, and she knew it. Marietta had those strange eyes, too large for her face and green as those of a cat. She could pin people to the wall with those eyes; Butter had seen her do it. Still, when Marietta was in the room, nobody really paid much attention to anybody else, and Butter knew that, too. For years, she'd told herself that this was because Marietta was taller than most women—you couldn't help but notice her—but Butter knew, deep down, that it had to do with something else, something inexplicable that Marietta had possessed since childhood, some sort of empathy that read as wisdom and drew people to her like sinners to a confessional.

People told Marietta things. Something about her made them spill secrets and problems all over her as though she were some kind of oracle, like she'd perhaps give them a clue, or hint, or prescription that would change their lives for the better. Thus unburdened, these people would walk away thinking what a perceptive conversation they'd just had, and it wouldn't be until later that they'd realize it had been almost completely one-sided. Marietta so often did nothing but nod. After Butter had fallen out of line with her, she realized those had been the sorts of conversations she'd been having with Marietta for years and couldn't help but wonder whether Marietta's silences had sprung from empathy or judgment. It was often so difficult to tell.

Always fearful of dropping food on the white furniture, Butter had eaten the tepid tetrazzini standing over the kitchen sink before grabbing a blanket and curling up on the sofa for a night of old movies and chilled Beaujolais. Around ten, she'd reached for the bottle to pour herself another glass, more disappointed than surprised to see it was empty. Needles of ice were scratching the windows when she drifted off to sleep with the television still on, throwing dancing black shadows across the white room.

. . . *but it doesn't take much to see that the problems of three little people don't amount to a hill of beans in this crazy world* . . . Butter woke to the sound of Humphrey Bogart saying goodbye to Ingrid Bergman in the pouring rain. She listened until the plane carrying Ingrid lifted into the air, the torrential rain competing with the sound of the whirring propellers. Then her eyes flew open. It never rained during that scene in *Casablanca*. Butter reached for the remote and turned off the television. The sound of the rain continued unabated. She kicked back the blanket, swung her feet off the sofa, and stepped down into a good two inches of cold water. "*Damn!*" she yelled, in a voice shrill enough to cut glass.

.　　　.　　　.

Gordon took his wool robe off the bedpost and pulled the collar up around his ears. "Come on, Trilby. Let's go see what's what." The corgi hopped down from the bed and followed his master out across the tiny landing and down the back stairs to the kitchen. Gordon could feel the icy cold of the stone floor through his slippers. He looked at the thermostat on the kitchen wall. Forty-nine degrees.

"Well, boy, 'better three hours too soon than a minute too late.' We can't stay here. We'll freeze to death before brunch." Gordon looked down at the dog, who had climbed into his bed by the oven, anxious to get his paws off the cold floor.

Gordon might well have been the only man in Wesleyan who owned a set of car chains. He patted himself on the back now as he recalled his decision not to leave them behind in New York. Yesterday afternoon, in anticipation of this very situation, he'd had the boys at Carlisle's BP put them on his little green Fiat and was now able to leave his cold house for a warmer situation, unlike the rest of his hometown's housebound, powerless residents. Nodding to himself, he went upstairs to pack a bag.

When he was done, Gordon picked up a corner of Trilby's red tartan bed and dragged it behind him down the short flight of stairs and out to the car. Then, having secured their essentials, and with a tight hold on the steering wheel, he pulled out onto the dirt road, ice cracking beneath the tire chains and Trilby sitting up straight as a judge in the passenger seat. Gordon pointed the Fiat toward The Glade.

When the maintenance man arrived at Butter's condo, he found precisely what Butter had, at very loud volume, described to him on the phone. Water was indeed streaming down through "a hole as big as a Volkswagen Bug" in her kitchen ceiling, and though he was no expert on décor, the bottom floor did look "completely ruined," and a good three inches of gray water was climbing up every white sofa and chair. He turned off the water to the house and the gushing stopped, but the damage had already been done.

"Didn't you leave your faucet dripping last night, ma'am?" he asked.

He had a low voice that Butter might have found comforting in any other situation.

But the question, brimming as it was with perceived recrimination, did not go over well. "How was I supposed to know to leave my faucets dripping?" Butter asked, each word rising in volume and bite.

"Well, they put those little signs out in the parking lot. You didn't see them?"

"No . . . *Fred-die.*" Butter leaned forward a little and made an exaggerated point of reading the name embroidered in black on the pocket of his shirt, both syllables stretched to their limits by sarcasm. "I did *not* see any little signs in the parking lot telling me that my home was about to be destroyed in the middle of the night."

The poor man correctly assessed the risk of continuing in this vein, and abruptly turned to head down a more encouraging path. "Well, don't worry . . . all this can be cleaned up, they'll vacuum the water out, get the plumbers in to fix the pipes. But now, I'm not going to lie, it'll take a while. With it all iced over this morning, it'll be hard to get a lot done today. Most of the guys couldn't make it in." He paused, waiting for this information to sink in. "Have you got someplace you can go stay for a week or so?" he asked. "I'll be happy to drive you. It's pretty slick out there. I can wait while you pack some stuff, if you like."

There are few feelings worse than impotent anger. Butter stood, her bare feet freezing in the cold water, looking around at the ruination of her home. In the microsecond before she burst into tears, she asked, "Can you drive me to The Glade?"

8

GLINDA

The house had been built in 1839, so the four fat white columns that held up its gabled front porch were not merely
the affectation of an architect anxious to appeal to nostalgic
Southerners. This was no mere facsimile of the Greek Revival
era; it was the real thing. Passersby got only brief glimpses of
white as they drove past, so tall was the ivy-covered fence that
encircled the three lush acres surrounding the house. The pointed
roofline of the stable was just visible if you were coming from the
west, and occasionally, if you were lucky, you could catch a
glimpse of the large roan-colored horse, Red Rascal, who spent
his summer afternoons in the green meadow closest to the road.
From the time he was old enough to think for himself, Macon
Hargis had wanted to live here, and for the last forty years he'd
done just that.

On this frozen morning the big old house blended seamlessly
into a landscape of white. Frost veined the fanlight in the gable,

and icicles hung from the roofline like melted sugar dripping off a wedding cake. Behind a second-floor window at the back of the house, overlooking a garden of slumbering roses, Macon's wife of forty-six years was wide awake.

Glinda's nose was cold. It was the only part of her body exposed to a room whose temperature, she was certain, had fallen to freezing, or below. Obviously, nothing about the last twenty-four hours had altered her husband's ingrained habit of turning the heat off at night, not even an impending ice storm. *Damn the man.*

Funny, she realized with a start, she'd grown so used to that last thought being closely followed by a swift, sharp inner recrimination—usually delivered, she'd noticed, in her mother's voice—that on this morning when it sailed through her head unhindered she regarded it as further proof that she'd simply lost the thread. As if she needed further proof after yesterday afternoon. Burrowed under the blankets of the guest room bed, Glinda had thought all night and still didn't know exactly why she'd done it.

The laughter had been the worst. She supposed it had been Macon's look of surprise that caused it: such a startled expression, and one she couldn't recall ever seeing cross her husband's face. Or it could have been the sound of that four-layer lasagna meeting expensive black wool, a sickening sort of squish that had both appalled and delighted her in equal measure. If only she'd pretended it had been an accident. But instead, she'd taken one look at Macon's bug-wide eyes and let out a laugh like a peahen, a piercing sound that had silenced every voice and turned every head in their direction.

So many faces, all staring at her, and all she could do was laugh. She'd laughed a laugh she'd never heard before—staccato and shrill—till tears melted her mascara and painted lines on her cheeks. She'd laughed as she picked up her purse, laughed as she pushed her way through the stupefied crowd, each open-mouthed stare only making her laugh all the harder. She hadn't turned for a second look at Macon but opened the big glass door and walked out, suddenly finding herself alone on the sidewalk, the temperature a good ten degrees colder than when she'd walked in.

She'd teetered to the car like a drunkard—fishing in her purse for the keys, laughing all the while—and it hadn't been until she pulled around to the garage at the back of their house a good twenty minutes later that the full weight of what she'd done landed on her shoulders like bird droppings.

The rest of the afternoon had been lost in a mist of humiliation and confusion. She'd flown first into the bedroom closet, pulling down sweaters and shirts and throwing them into a suitcase that was full before she even realized what she was doing. Then she'd sat down heavily on the bed, staring into space for what could have been minutes or hours, she didn't know.

Eventually she wound up in the guest room down the hall, buried beneath the cedar-scented blankets she'd dragged from rarely opened drawers, and there she'd lain, waiting for whatever it was that was coming next.

Unaccustomed as she was to deciphering the workings of her own heart, Glinda lacked the internal vocabulary to explain herself, even to herself. Bereft of any sort of justification, she knew facing Macon was unthinkable, so when she heard a taxi pull up outside, and his distinct step on the front porch, she simply lay there, still as the grave, behind the locked door of a bedroom in which she'd never spent a single night.

She'd heard him down in the kitchen around dusk, heard the muted timbre of television voices just after dark, then, long after the drizzle outside the guest room window had hardened to ice, heard him climbing the stairs. She'd held her breath as his footsteps passed outside her door without stopping. The click of their bedroom door as it closed sounded like something final. She'd spent the night feeling lost.

Now in the pale blue light of the morning, she lay with the blankets up to her nose, considering her options. Confronting Macon face-to-face didn't seem to be one of them at the moment, though even she knew that was inevitable. Her confusion over her behavior didn't seem to have worked its way out of her system in the slightest, and try as she might, she simply couldn't picture herself providing her husband with a believable explanation, not to mention a credible apology. She felt all rational thought washed cleanly away by a panic she'd never known before.

She sat up as suddenly as if her pillow had caught fire and looked around the room. There was her suitcase, right where she'd left it, already packed with everything she'd need. Glinda got up and dressed as quietly as she could, leaving the bed unmade. She crept downstairs without pause, silently opening the closet in the entry hall to retrieve her warmest coat before heading for the side door at the rear of the kitchen.

Macon's black Hummer sat sullenly in the cold garage, almost daring her to open the driver's side door and hoist herself in. She'd never driven this thing; it was Macon's vehicle exclusively, its trunk crammed so full of the many accoutrements of his two greatest loves—his horse and his boat—that she'd have to put her suitcase on the backseat. But she didn't know how much ice was on the roads this morning, and though Glinda wasn't entirely sure where she was heading or where she'd end up, she at least had the presence of mind to make certain she got there in one piece.

Pulling out of the garage, she looked around at an altered world of silver. Even her surroundings were no longer what she expected; the winter trees and frozen boxwoods had become oddly unfamiliar during the night, as if the whole world was trying to transform itself into something alien, much as she herself seemed to have done. She shivered and sat up as tall as she could in Macon's seat, her feet barely reaching the pedals.

The slick driveway was no match for the weight of the big black vehicle; ice cracked and crunched beneath its wheels like crickets on hot asphalt as Glinda pointed it toward the road, turning right and heading, without really realizing it, in the direction of her sister-in-law's house in The Glade.

9

WILL, BUTTER, GORDON, AND MARIETTA

Will Cochran hated to see women cry. Especially the way this particular one was crying in the seat next to him right now, quietly sniffling with her head leaning against the palm of her hand. It'd be better if she'd been a wailer, he thought, easier to deal with somehow if you knew even a small part of it was performance. This pitiful little weeping was making him wish he'd never agreed to help Freddie out this morning.

But he couldn't have said no; what with his daughter-in-law in bed with the flu and his two grandkids at home from Sunday school because of the ice. He was lucky his son's shirt had fit him.

"Come on now," he said, as Butter let out a particularly pitiful sigh. "I told you. It's really not all that bad. Happens all the time in the winter, you know. Pipes just sometimes freeze in the cold and when they do, they can split wide open. I've seen worse, believe you me. Why, just imagine if you'd been out of town and come back home two weeks later to a house not only wet but stinking to high heaven. You wanna talk about a mess? Now, that's a mess, let me tell you."

He was talking too much and he knew it. If she'd just say something, *anything* . . . then he'd feel okay about shutting up. He liked to think he was a pretty good listener; Ellen had always told him he was.

In truth, Butter only halfway heard him. She was just barely aware of the large man sitting beside her in the cab of the Windward Oaks maintenance truck, deftly negotiating the icy stretches on the long driveway out. Her head was swirling with the images of her once pristine house now awash in dirty, dingy water. Insurance, time, money: all were flashing in her mind like fortunes floating up on a Magic 8 Ball. Her tears were a wholly inadequate measure of how sorry she truly felt for herself.

She couldn't think exactly why she'd told this man to drive her to Marietta's. Maybe it was because her old friend was the last person she'd thought about last night before sleep. But she didn't want to go to Christo's, she knew that much by instinct. Her son had an unconscious way of making her feel like every misfortune that befell her, from a flat tire to a bad cold, was in some inexplicable way her fault. Showing up at her son's door in dire straits was something she never intended to do if she could possibly help it. Of course, appearing at Marietta's in a similar state was merely a lateral move. She needed to pull herself together. She sat up a bit and looked out the window at the white sheets of frosted lawn falling away on both sides of the drive out of Windward Oaks.

Ice storms were so rare in this part of the country that even as they frantically prepared for the forecast, the citizens of Wesleyan really believed, down deep in their souls, that the weatherman was just crying wolf. Summer's heat was so intense here, every growing thing seemed to store it up in memory and marrow as defense against the slightest idea of a real winter, the kind accompanied by ice and snow, the kind other parts of the country might reasonably fear. She'd seen weather like this only once before, the year she'd turned seventeen, and with this sudden recollection,

Butter remembered she'd gone to stay at Marietta's way back then, too. In the shock of her current situation some little part of her brain must have taken it upon itself to reach back into her past, and direct her down the same road she'd followed the last time ice covered Wesleyan, back to her best friend's house.

The electricity had gone off at the Lockwoods' the second day of that long-ago storm, when an ambitious pine tree by the side porch, grown too tall for its roots, had fallen under the weight of its icy needles, yanking down every power line on the street. Jimmy had to be at the hardware store—so many people were needing things to help fix their ripped roofs and busted pipes— and Sandra was going to her sister's in Seabrook, where the ice had met a wall of warmer air and fizzled into rain. Neither of those options had appealed to Butter in the slightest so when Caroline Hargis had called to ask her over to stay with Marietta for the duration, she'd grabbed at the chance with both hands.

Seventeen is an age when girls are making plans, and Butter and Marietta were no different than most. For three whole days in that blessedly warm house, the two friends had discussed and dissected their wildly divergent dreams for the future. Butter was besotted with the new quarterback on the Wesleyan High School football team. Joe Swann had arrived at Wesleyan in his junior year—tall, blue-eyed, and blond—with an arm that could throw a football farther than any Wesleyan Hornet had ever done before him. In a town where everybody had grown up together, Joe Swann was an unknown quantity; he ambled down the school corridors with mystery trailing behind him like the aroma of Sunday dinner.

Marietta, on the other hand, was heading to the University of Georgia with the intention of becoming a journalist just like her father. Butter had thought she was out of her mind, and she'd told Marietta just that. But Marietta had said she wanted to see the world and report back on all its darkness and light. She'd been at that paper in Atlanta for less than two years, though, before she was back home again in Wesleyan. Butter smiled to herself (and to her credit, felt bad for doing so), remembering she'd been proven just a little bit right for once.

The wheels of the truck skidded sharply left as Will tried to stop at the red light on the square, bringing Butter back to the present and causing her to reflexively reach out for his arm. They slid a good five feet, narrowly missing a parking meter, before Will was able to right the truck again.

"Whoa! That was a ride. Better take it slower."

Smudge knew Gordon was about to pull into the driveway a good four minutes before he did so. The Fiat had a uniquely pitched whine whenever it reached third gear, a sound neither Gordon nor his mechanic would hear for another two years, but one which Smudge recognized as soon as the car turned off Meridian Street and into The Glade. The big dog hopped down from his place beside the sleeping Marietta and padded silently out of the room and down the stairs to wait.

Gordon was careful not to slam the car door. There were many reasons not to wake Marietta this morning, and the fact that she'd had a migraine yesterday was but one of them. Those things could come on suddenly, he knew, having been with her on a buying trip to New Orleans several years ago when she suddenly turned the color of old fruit right in the middle of a lamp shop on Magazine Street. She was pale as a baby for three days afterward. It had been a long time since he'd seen her that sick.

He turned his key in the lock as quietly as he could, wincing in anticipation of unwanted noise that mercifully did not come. Even Trilby, thrilled to see Smudge as much as Smudge was to see him, seemed to understand the need for silence, and quietly followed his big friend through the dining room and into the kitchen, their nails making little clicks on the hardwood floors as they went.

Gordon could tell within seconds the heat was still on in the house, and he thanked God for small favors. He'd been prepared, had it been cold and dark, to pack up Marietta and point the Fiat south toward the most luxurious hotel Tripadvisor recommended. Putting his suitcase down by the stairs, he headed into the library, where he congratulated himself for having laid that fire in the grate during Harry's funeral. Tightly rolled sections of the *Wesleyan Journal* tucked beneath perfectly stacked logs. It had been Alan, the boy from New Hampshire, who'd taught him the technique, and he never struck a match to wood without remembering. It had been years since he'd stopped trying to forget; the pastel memories colored every day of his life and he knew they always would. He would never know why he'd been spared.

During those years in New York, he'd felt as though the plane he'd been too late to catch had crashed out over the ocean, cutting every person on board into fragments too small to be marked, and leaving him alone with an unused ticket in his hand, proof that he should have been one of their number. Week after week, then day after day: the car kept swerving just in time, the bullet barely missed, the lightning bolts hit the earth just beside him, close enough to knock him down, over and over and over, obliterating almost everyone he knew, and burning black holes in the fabric of his life. Understanding wasn't so important to him anymore. How could it be, in a world where so much went unexplained?

Closing the fire screen Gordon watched as scintillas of Halloween orange inched slowly upward, whispering to one another as they rose—a sizzle here, a sputter there—like gossip traveling through a dull morning. In less than a minute the fire was blazing, knocking the cold morning back to the corners of the room. Then, smiling, he tiptoed into the kitchen to make himself a pot of coffee, the aroma of which, far more potent than sound, drifted out of the kitchen and up the stairs to Marietta's bedroom door.

It was a good two years after her mother's death that Marietta could have sworn she'd seen her drive through Wesleyan Square in a red Corvette convertible. She'd been walking down the sidewalk on a summer day when her eyes had drifted over to the line of cars set loose by a green light, and there was her mother, in a navy-and-white polka-dot dress and pink lipstick, red nails draped over a white steering wheel, the wind blowing her blond hair back from her face. Marietta had stopped stock-still right in front of Harlan's Hardware and watched the car go all around the square till it flew straight down Meridian Street on its way . . . where? She couldn't possibly imagine.

The whole thing had sat her right down in one of those plastic Adirondack chairs the hardware store kept out front, the letters and bills she was on her way to mail crumpling inside her closed fists. Her mother had been laughing—one of those head-rocking, teeth-displaying kinds of laughs—something Marietta wasn't sure she'd ever once seen her do while she walked among the living. A polite little giggle, a twinkle in the eye, a genial smile—those were the bows in her quiver when she needed to respond to anything in the humor or amusement range. Raucous laughter just wasn't in there. Caroline Hargis had been gracious and steady, good in a crisis and hard to rattle, but impossible to picture in the scene Marietta had just witnessed.

And of course, she was dead. Marietta had been the one to close her coffin after the family had had their last look, Caroline having threatened to curse both her children mercilessly if they allowed the citizens of Wesleyan any opportunity for a long, hard, and unreciprocated gander at her as she lay in the most undignified and vulnerable state of her life. "I don't care what you dress me up in or how much lipstick that Landers boy slaps on me at the funeral home, I'll still be dead, and I don't want the Junior League filing through giving reviews on my appearance. So, a closed casket, you two hear me?" Marietta and Macon had dutifully nodded together in the hospital room, but when it came time to actually close the thing, Macon wouldn't come near it, so Marietta had to do it.

Now as the fragrance of freshly made coffee curled under her nose her first thought was, naturally, of Harry. He'd always been the first one up, always the one to put the coffee on. Was it really so strange for him to be doing it this morning? She'd already put her slippers on before she remembered.

Acting on a hunch, Marietta looked out the window and saw

what she thought she might see: Gordon's little green car in her drive. Surprised to feel no annoyance, she reached for her robe and went downstairs.

Her old friend was sitting at the kitchen table by the window, a copy of *Vanity Fair* open before him, his arms crossed over his chest as he rubbed his palms up and down his arms. "Oh! Well, hello there," he said, as she walked into the room. "I swear, I don't think I'll ever get warm. Thank God your heat stayed on or we'd both be huddled down there in the middle school gym with the rest of the great unwashed. Lord, honey, you look like a big ol' unmade bed. Here, sit down." He stood up and pulled out a chair, eyeing Marietta surreptitiously to try to ascertain how she really was, but Marietta walked past him and went to stand by the window.

"It's so beautiful out there," she said, watching as Trilby and Smudge chased each other through the still, white garden.

"Beautiful, and colder than spite." He stood beside her and handed over a hot cup of coffee. "So, how are you?"

Marietta shook her head slowly, still staring out to the garden, where a gathering of cardinals, and one large black bird, were taking turns at the feeder. The huge dark bird turned to look in her direction, then flew to the tree branch closest to the window, its claws gripping the silver ice. "I'm all right, I guess. A little numb. I keep thinking I should be crying, but I just don't seem to have anything left inside to help me do that."

Gordon put his arm around her. "Well, Lord knows you've done more than your share in the past year. Numbness is probably the best we can hope for today. Come over here and sit down." Just then a discordant duet of barks rose up from the side of the backyard. Through the kitchen window Smudge and Trilby could be seen taking turns leaping up to get a better look at the front drive, a competition the short-legged Trilby was losing.

"Somebody's here?" Marietta said, looking up at Gordon in dismay.

Gordon turned and headed into the dining room to peer out the front window, Marietta close on his heels. They watched as

an unfamiliar white truck came to a sliding stop in the street outside. A big man got out and went around to open the passenger
door for a small, blond woman who appeared to have been crying.

"Uh-oh. By the pricking of my thumbs, it's Fluffy."

"Don't call her that, Gordon. She hates it," Marietta whispered, hiding behind Gordon so as not to be seen.

"That's why I do it," he whispered back. "Good Lord, what
on earth is *she* doing here at seven o'clock in the morning in the
middle of a goddamn ice storm?"

They watched from behind the dining room curtain as the
man led Butter up the driveway, his right hand cupped under her
elbow, his left around the handle of a Gucci suitcase. She slipped
once and that right hand shot around Butter's waist quicker than
thought. The large man half-carried her the rest of the way to the
porch.

"He looks like a cartoon bear," Gordon whispered, causing
Marietta to giggle in spite of herself. The two of them stood back
from the front door, pushing each other forward, each seeing
their own confounded expression reflected in the other's face.
The knock, when it came, was solid and loud. It was Gordon
who opened the door.

There was a brief moment of confused silence, which was
broken by Butter, who looked past Gordon as though he wasn't
there. "My house flooded," she said. "I don't know why I came
here. I guess I just remembered the last ice storm." Her puffy eyes
seemed at least two sizes larger than normal as she stared at Marietta.

"Well, come on in out of the cold," said Marietta, ignoring
Gordon's theatrical sigh as he stepped aside and put his hand out
to the man no one seemed to know.

"Hello, I'm Gordon Lovett."

"Will. Will Cochran." Will was making a point of wiping his
skillet-size shoes on the door rug.

"No. That's not right," said Butter, turning around. "Your
name's Freddie. You told me."

"No, ma'am. I didn't. You just read it on my shirt. This belongs to my son. I'm helping him out today." Looking to the others, he continued, "His wife, my daughter-in-law, she's sick. Freddie needed to watch the kids. And Windward likes everybody to wear a uniform. I had the day off, so I thought I'd give him a hand. Lucky we're both the same size."

Gordon made a little sound that Marietta promptly interrupted. "Can I get you a cup of coffee? Gordon's just made a pot."

"No. Thank you. I need to get on back." Then, turning to Butter, he said, "The Windward guys will be in touch, Mrs. Swann, about your place. They'll know more by tomorrow, I'm sure."

"Well, okay," said Butter. This was the first time she'd really noticed the man, and she held his gaze a tiny bit longer than she meant to. "I, I really appreciate it. And I'm sorry if I was, well, you know."

"Oh, don't you worry about it. You were just fine. I know waking up like that had to have been a real shock. You take care now."

The three of them moved as one to the window to watch him go down the drive, steady as a rock.

"Fluffy's got a boyfriend," Gordon whispered in a singsong voice.

"You shut up," Butter shot back.

IO

GLINDA, MARIETTA, OLD MAN GRIFFIN, AND SPOT

If anyone had been standing by the side of the road when the huge black Hummer roared past, kicking up ice like sawdust, they could have easily attributed its swinging, swerving path to too much speed on frozen ground. In truth, a direct line could be drawn between the precarious road conditions and the unstable driver, a combination that has never been known to come to any good. Glinda Hargis would have been hard-pressed to give an account of any of the miles she'd gone in the past ten minutes. She could have been anywhere for all she knew.

As though they were falling through pinpricks in a sunshade, little shafts of memory were hitting Glinda as she drove, each one sharp enough to make her flinch: the way Macon's mouth had formed a perfect O when he sat down on her lasagna, the shock on everyone's faces when she'd laughed (oh, how she'd laughed) all the way out the restaurant door.

She'd made a fool of him, something he'd never be able to forgive, and something—she knew this as well as she knew her own name—he'd tried to avoid for the whole of his life. How could she possibly explain why she'd done it? Did she even know herself? In her rush to leave the house this morning, she'd left her phone at home, so that even if Macon had tried to call her, she wouldn't know it, and for that she thanked God. Right now, she couldn't imagine talking to him ever again.

The need for justification being at least as strong as guilt, it wasn't long before Glinda's humiliation had worked its way around to something much better tolerated, and something that only increased the speed of her car: anger. She remembered seeing Macon surrounded by those disdainful old men, remembered their sneers when they talked about the group of people working to get the statue of Henry Benning out of Griffin Park. Macon didn't know it, but she'd read one of the leaflets those people had placed on her car one day at the library and thought about it for days and days afterward. She'd even looked up Henry Benning online and been appalled at what she'd read. Why, no wonder black people didn't want him staring down at them every time they walked past. And now for Macon to make *fun* of those people, to call them "Mr. Ed"! Yes, they should have chosen their name more carefully. But how could they have known people would be so cruel as to tie the acronym to a talking horse from the sixties. She felt bad for all of them.

Some necessary part of herself had broken. Without even a tap on her brakes, Glinda ran straight through the light at Second Avenue, barely registering relief at the lack of other cars on the road. She saw her behavior as one sees the faint diagonal line of a riptide drawn across a calm ocean; all the things she'd willfully ignored for the whole of her life were roiling beneath her, grasping at her ankles, mutinous and threatening. This must be what it felt like to drown.

"Were you really so afraid of what I might do when you left that you sent these two over here?"

Marietta asked the question to the air around her, hoping

Harry would hear. She sat on the edge of her rumpled bed, having closed the door on the bickering downstairs, and thought, not for the first time, how quickly adults can slide back into the behavior of childhood. Butter and Gordon had never gotten along. There had always been a rivalry for Marietta's favor, something she herself had been oblivious to as a child, but that became uncomfortably clearer as the years went by. It had always been better to keep them apart. And now, on the morning after Harry's funeral of all days, they were both downstairs in her kitchen, making her breakfast. This was not how she'd planned to spend the next few days. Marietta put her head in her hands and laughed out loud, the sound slapping at the strange quiet of the room.

It's the sight of an ice storm that gets all the attention down South. Frozen trees bent over at the waist, all that blinding white—it's like waking on another planet. Folks notice the silence later, when they step out of their houses or sit in an oddly bright room all alone, and it comes as a shock to the system. When a blanket of ice is thrown over the Southern landscape and a world normally full of wind chimes and wren song freezes solid, the drops that slip from a melting icicle can hit the ground like drumbeats. Perhaps this is why Marietta heard the Hummer barreling into The Glade long before she would have on an ordinary day. The thing shattered that eerie silence like a coal train. She went to the window and stared.

When she saw it pull up outside, she expected to spot Macon in the driver's seat but was surprised to see her sister-in-law's white hair falling over the steering wheel, her forehead on her hands. Glinda had gone gray the way most women hope to but rarely do, her once jet-black tresses first turning a striking salt and pepper before giving way to snow white. Her hair seemed more lustrous and impressive now than it ever had in her youth. She usually wore it in the sort of perfect chignon women practice on for hours alone in their bathroom mirrors but never actually master; there was never a hair out of place. Today it fell over her face like a sheepdog's.

Marietta watched, transfixed, as Glinda sat for a good two

minutes, never moving to open the car door. Then she heard the quartet of footsteps chasing each other up the stairs, the muffled knock on her bedroom door.

"Mare?" Butter had won the race. "I think your sister-in-law's here."

Marietta opened the door and went past them down the stairs, both Butter and Gordon close behind. The three of them stopped at the window, looking out as Glinda began to clamber down from the Hummer's front seat as though negotiating her way out of a ride at the fair.

"Lord, what's happened to her?" Gordon whispered. "She looks like she's been pulled backward through a hedge."

Glinda stopped and stood for a moment in the driveway before moving onto the lawn for better footing. The three at the window moved back in anticipation of her approach but she veered out into the yard and stopped in front of the dark spot where the little monument stood, staring down at it with an expression of what could only be described as grief on her stricken face.

"Is she crying?" whispered Butter.

"This can't be good," said Gordon.

Porter Griffin always slept like a rock, a fact he felt was indicative of a clear conscience and not the coffee cup of Jack Daniel's he took to bed with him every night of his life. He was a man of solidified habits, and the bedtime whiskey had long ago become as much a part of his routine as the shiny linen suit he'd worn to the First Baptist Church every Easter Sunday since the Truman administration or the series of identical beagles he'd owned since his childhood, the current one being named, rather unoriginally, Spot.

He knew the people of Wesleyan called him Old Man Griffin and had done so long before his chronological age had warranted it. He didn't care. In his mind the moniker afforded him a certain gravitas that transcended his given name. It carried with it a bit of respect, a bit of history, and—the best part—a bit of fear. People didn't attempt to cross him, just as they hadn't his father, a man who unfortunately wasn't allowed to live long enough to be called Old Man Griffin himself, having died of tuberculosis when Porter was four years old.

He'd been the much-wanted son of Lucius and Mary, the only child of two only children, and it took them sixteen years to have him. Lucius was already sick when the boy was born so Mary was prepared for her life as a widow when it came, having vowed to her husband that she'd keep his memory forever painted in primary colors for their son. She'd done just that, refusing to throw away a single shoe, shirt, or suit coat, and setting a place at the dinner table for the man every night. She'd kept a framed five-by-seven photo of Lucius in her big red purse until the day she died.

When Porter was little, Mary had eschewed the usual bedtime stories, instead telling her son tales of Lucius's greatness, and pointing so often to the statue of Henry Benning standing tall in Griffin Park across the road, clearly visible from Porter's upstairs window, that the boy soon came to feel it to be nothing less than a statue of his father himself.

He'd dated girls in college but never found one to equal his mother, and so, at the brutal, brittle age of eighty-eight and a half, Porter Griffin was still sleeping in the bedroom of his childhood, the view from his window as unchanged as his view of the world, well and truly the last of his kind.

His only preparation for the ice storm had been to throw another blanket onto Spot's dog bed downstairs, an act rendered unnecessary by the fact that the beagle had no intention of staying there on a night as cold as this one, or any other night, truth be told. The dog was at least as set in his ways as his owner, and one of his habits was to wait outside Porter's door every night, listening for a certain rhythmic breathing that told Spot the old man was finally asleep, and that now was the time to nudge open the door and climb up into the bed alongside him. Both man and dog pretended not to notice this blatant disregard of hierarchy the same way all those with pliable consciences ignore the rules when they feel a mutual benefit. Spot had comfort, Porter had companionship, and neither was complaining.

Porter hadn't listened to the weather before bed, having long ago stopped watching the local news due to a lack of trust in anything they had to say, including the forecast, so he'd gone to bed knowing only that the sky was hanging too heavy and low to bode well. When he woke in the morning, he could tell by the oddly bright light in the high-ceilinged room that something had happened outside.

Sticking his bony legs out from underneath the handsewn quilts piled atop his double bed, Old Man Griffin got up and slowly walked to the window, the same place he headed to first thing every morning, to gaze out at the same view he'd counted on being there for the whole of his life, knowing that, through sunny days and rainy ones, occasional snow and, rarely, ice, the statue his father had erected in the park across the street, the park that bore his family name, would always be there to greet him.

He saw the shock in his own reflected face when he looked down across the hill toward the park and found nothing to stop his eyes till they reached the oak trees on the far side of the fence. Nothing but cold air in the place where the statue should be. The plinth on which it had stood was wiped clean as his beagle's conscience.

If his life flashed before Porter's eyes there wouldn't have been much to see. He just felt a little like he slipped, and then the world went black.

Spot glanced up, rolled over, and went back to sleep.

11

LURLENE, LARRY, PETER, AND THEA

When something good happens in a small town, people remember it for a little while. When something bad happens, they remember it forever, or at least until something worse comes along to take its place.

All through the cold night, news of the scene at Micheline's restaurant between Glinda and Macon Hargis had traveled through the cellphones and landlines of Wesleyan with far greater speed than the ice that shrouded the city come morning. In fact, given that everybody had stayed home that night in anticipation of the bad weather, it provided a much-needed entertainment, one no mere ice storm could ever hope to match. Taking a degree of pleasure in seeing one's betters brought low is widely considered to be a characteristic of the less noble side of human nature, but a scant few went to bed feeling guilty for their private amusement at the news that Macon Hargis had been so publicly humiliated by his wife. Everyone wanted to know more, and no sleeping soul suspected that this headline would be superseded by another come morning, one with far greater implications and consequences for them all.

The second person to discover the statue was missing was the first one to phone the police. Worried about her camellias, Lurlene Pearson had risen early, tiptoeing quietly to her guest room window to check whether the eaves of her white Colonial had protected the pretty red flowers from a coffin of ice. Her gaze never made it that far.

You could stretch a trapeze line from her guest room window all the way across the park to Porter Griffin's bedroom and it would stay straight as a pointed finger, so, like him, Lurlene noticed the statue was gone the second she looked out. But the pine trees that lined the old man's front yard prevented Porter from seeing what was so clearly obvious to Lurlene: not only was the statue gone but what remained of General Henry Benning and his faithful steed lay shattered and strewn across the brick pathways that crisscrossed around the empty plinth; no piece remaining was larger than a horse's hoof. Lurlene went to find her phone.

The Wesleyan Police Station was new. The old one, which had stood for the last half century beside Dunaway Drugs, had finally become an embarrassment; there was only so much the city council could do with its concrete-block walls and flat roof. Three years earlier, when a candidate for mayor decried its appearance during a campaign debate at the high school—saying that Petey's Check-Cashin' Place on the highway out of town looked far better—Mayor Mac Baker had suddenly found the funds to erect a brand-new building, complete with Pottery Barn chairs, laptop computers, and a fountain right outside the front door. Consequently, Sergeant Larry Crowder didn't much mind the night shift anymore.

He'd arrived before the ice, expecting a quiet night, and that was just what he'd gotten—though he was sure, if first light revealed fallen trees and blocked roads, he'd start getting calls. People always called the police first, even if what they really needed was the power company or a tow truck, and sure enough, as the black faded into gray and the ice-covered parking lot began to slowly materialize out of the darkness, the phone on his desk rang out loud as a yell, causing him to drop his toast, jam side down, on the front page of yesterday's paper. Larry reached around the side of the phone and turned the ringer down before he answered, wishing, not for the first time, that the cleaning lady would stop turning it up every time she dusted. He didn't know of a single officer in this precinct who was hard of hearing.

"Wesleyan Police Station." His voice sounded loud in the quiet.

"Larry? That you?"

He hated people being so familiar. "This is *Sergeant Crowder*," he replied. "Can I help you?"

"Larry, this is Lurlene Pearson. I'm calling you from home. Something's happened. You better gird your loins, son. Somebody's pulled that statue down. It's lying all over the park like a sackful of spilled groceries. Y'all better get down here."

Larry Crowder's stomach dropped. It had been his mother's belief that every child, no matter their gender, could benefit from the artistic discipline provided by piano lessons, so for one and a half long years Larry had sat under the tutelage of Mrs. Pearson—his little hands with their dirty fingernails poised just so over the keys, a metronome relentlessly tick-tocking beside him—as he tried and failed, again and again, to master "Für Elise." When futility was finally faced and Larry was allowed to quit the lessons, he couldn't say for sure who was happier, himself or Mrs. Pearson. He was thirty-five years old now, with three kids of his own, and the woman would always strike a certain type of dread in his heart. He asked her now if she was sure and wished immediately that he hadn't.

"Of course, I'm *sure,* Larry. I can still see a lot better than you ever could."

Larry pushed his glasses up his nose and frowned. "I mean, did you . . . do you . . . see anything else?"

"What more do you want? I'm telling you, the thing is lying out all over the ground. And I seriously doubt the hand of God pushed it over. Though that's always a possibility, I guess. But my money's on somebody getting rid of it last night when no one was out. You and I both know that Old Man Griffin's not going to take this well at all. You better figure out what you're going to do before he gets up and sees it. And you better figure it out fast."

Larry hung up the phone and stared at it for a long minute, his mind full of expletives he would have said out loud if anyone had been there to hear him. As it was, he stared at the frozen fountain outside the front door, slowly sipping the coffee that had already begun to go cold. Then he looked in the drawer for Detective Cochran's number.

Peter Swann had just turned the corner of Duncan and First Streets. He was walking this morning, a bagful of *Wesleyan Journals* slung over his shoulder, just like the old-fashioned paper boy that his mother probably thought he was. All he needed was a tweed cap and an innocent grin and he could have stepped right out of a Norman Rockwell painting. She'd been the one who thought it was such a good idea for him to take the job when Mr. Addison offered it up one morning after church. "Do the boy good," Sonny Addison had said, his Bible clasped to his chest and his round, florid face ablaze in the October sunshine. "I delivered papers when I was his age. Got me up early and made me a bit of spending money, too. Helped teach me the value of a dollar, something kids today need to learn, Lord knows."

Peter had been skeptical at first; the few dollars he stood to make would hardly pay for a dinner out once a week for him and Thea, but at least he wouldn't have to ask his folks for the money. They didn't know about Thea yet, and he wasn't ready to tell them. So he'd accepted the job, and for the last two months he'd delivered the paper to all the people living on the tree-lined streets that spread like a sunburst out from Griffin Park.

On a normal day he would've been in his ancient Park Avenue

with his hands around the Hula-Hoop-size steering wheel, pitching papers out the open window and taking mile-wide corners in that big, old, baby blue boat of a Buick that had been his grandfather's last car. Driving it, he knew, caused him to appear both courageous and ridiculous simultaneously, but his parents had him by the short hairs: he'd hardly saved enough to afford a tricycle, much less a car—so when Christo offered him the keys, Peter held his head high and took them with the most sincere smile he could muster, the prospect of vehicular independence trumping any vanity he might have possessed at sixteen.

And of course, this wasn't a normal day. There was ice all over the roads and he didn't fancy the idea of hitting some of the stuff in that Buick. So he'd put on his hiking boots in the pitch dark, walked the two miles to Mr. Addison's warehouse to pick up the papers for his route, and started off on foot. He knew he'd get credit for showing up at all. A lot of the other guys hadn't.

He would never have admitted it to his parents, but Peter actually looked forward to the couple of hours each morning when he had these neighborhood streets all to himself. Being the only person awake often felt like being the only person alive. His grandmother always said you could never stay mad at someone when you saw them sleeping, and as he passed the silent houses, he imagined all those people inside snuggled down in their beds—covers pulled up against the cold, or legs dangling off mattresses in the summertime heat—and he felt like he knew what she meant.

For the past few years, it had seemed to him that everybody in town had separated like you did in dodgeball, right down the middle, across an expanse much wider than a gymnasium floor. Worse, it felt like that's what you were *supposed* to do, choose a side, and defend it against all comers. Maybe it had always been this way and he just hadn't noticed when he was little. But it seemed silly when he came through these streets at dawn, thinking about everybody sound asleep in their houses, all of them waiting to wake up and go at it again. He liked Wesleyan better before the sun came up.

Peter made his way down Duncan Street, throwing the papers and giving himself two points each time he hit a porch cleanly. His score was pretty high as he turned the corner across from the park and reached in his bag for the Pearsons' paper. He was just about to let it sail when he stopped. Something was different. He couldn't say what exactly. Had a tree fallen? He'd seen several down since he left, pines and poplars pulled over by the weight of the ice, power lines tangled around them like cold spaghetti. He turned a circle and stared. Then he saw it.

The statue was gone. The plinth where it had stood looked obscenely naked; he felt almost guilty for staring. Bits and pieces of the Confederate general lay scattered all over the frozen ground, his venerated countenance reduced to dust. Peter dropped the paper he was getting ready to throw and reached into his pocket for his phone.

Floors creak in older houses. There's just not that much you can do about it. With her bedroom directly beneath her baby sister's, it was easy for Thea Harper to work out exactly what Ivy was doing most of the time. She'd heard her jump down from her bed, heard her walk to her window seat and back again at least four times in the past hour. She knew Ivy was checking on Mrs. Cline and that light signal they had, and this morning of all mornings, Thea didn't blame her.

Thea liked Marietta Cline almost as much as her sister did, and she had liked Harry Cline even more. He and Marietta always came to her dressage shows and could be heard cheering almost as loud as her parents whenever she won a blue ribbon. Thea had even talked to Harry about working for the group trying to take down that statue, and he'd told her he thought it was an excellent idea. He'd written her a good-size check in support of the organization. Harry was too sick to come to the protest they'd had last September, but that'd probably been for the best as it happened to coincide with the arrival of Hurricane Irma, flicking her angry tail end through Wesleyan and sending hail and hard rain down on everybody who'd been brave enough to defy her threats and attend. Some of the hail had actually dented the roof of Peter's blue car, and that thing was built like a tank.

All the two of them had been allowed to do so far was put stamps on mailers and leaflets on car windshields at the Piggly Wiggly on Saturdays, but both Thea and Peter felt good about doing what they could. There was so much they couldn't do; at least they could do that.

Thea smiled when she thought about Peter. She'd never known a boy so sweet. Her parents even liked him, she could tell, although they didn't really want to, and she could tell that, too. She knew what they were thinking but it just wasn't like it had been when they were her age. Having a white boyfriend wasn't a big deal anymore; none of her friends thought a thing about it. Still, she hadn't yet met his folks, and couldn't say she was really looking forward to it. Not just because they were white but also because they were so religious. These days, really religious white people made her nervous.

Thea burrowed down farther in bed. She'd bet anything her riding lesson was going to be canceled; in bad weather people called off everything down here. She caught the phone before the first ring was done; Peter's face was looking up at her from the screen in full grin. "Hey," she whispered.

"You awake?"

"Yeah. Where are you?"

"I'm out delivering papers, and you won't believe it. Somebody's knocked it down, Thea. The statue's gone."

Thea sat up straight as a board. "You're kidding. You sure?"

"Of course I'm sure. I'm standing right in front of it. It's all broken up all over the park."

"Peter, you better get out of there. I'm serious, don't you be standing in front of that thing when people find it."

Peter, who until that moment had observed the scene the way he'd have done if it had been on television, removed from the reality of the thing, suddenly realized she was right. He shouldn't be seen here. He slung the Pearsons' paper toward their porch like a Frisbee and ran as fast as he could without slipping on the ice lying ready to trip him up. He never noticed the hand holding back the lace curtain from the window on the second floor.

12

LURLENE, REESE, AND WILL

Lurlene let the curtain fall. She'd stared over at Porter Griffin's window for a good five minutes, waiting to see movement or light, but nothing had given her an inkling that the old man was awake. As much as she didn't want to venture out in the cold, she knew she was the only person who'd check on him, and this morning, of all mornings, he'd need checking on.

She knew nobody liked Old Man Griffin. She didn't really like him herself. But she'd noticed that it was when she hoped he would change that she liked him the least, so over the years she'd chosen to expect his disagreeable nature the same way she expected grass to be green. It just was. She'd been raised to pay attention to her neighbors—to call, to look in, to cook for whomever she could whenever she thought they might need it—so every now and then she walked up the hill to knock on Porter Griffin's door. It wasn't clear to her whether he welcomed her visits—he was never particularly pleasant—but she did it for her soul, not his.

Down the hall Lurlene's husband, Reese, was buried up to the neck in blankets, his fat down pillow halfway over his balding head. Harry's funeral had depressed him more than he wanted Lurlene to know, and truth be told, he welcomed the ice storm; its gray bleakness felt like a sympathetic friend. He'd left the faucets dripping, covered up the gardenias, and stacked a load of firewood by the back door, all necessary chores done in anticipation of the escape that sleeping late provides. There'd been a few loud cracks and thuds in the night—oak limbs falling from the trees in the park, he figured—but he'd just ignored them, rolling over closer to Lurlene's warm body before drifting back down into the ignorance of sleep. His plans for hibernation dissolved when she reentered the bedroom, sat down with mattress-bending force, and began to put on her socks.

"What are you doing?" he asked, without opening his eyes.

"You need to come look, Reese. Somebody's got rid of that statue once and for all."

"What? What are you talking about?"

"Just what I said." She poked him hard with her elbow as she pulled on her shoe. "Somebody's knocked the thing down. Or pulled it down, I don't know. In the night sometime. I'm going over to Porter's. He'll be fit to be tied."

"Take those shoes off, Leeny." Reese had already swung his legs off the bed, his bare feet recoiling from the cold of the hardwood floor. "You're not going over there in this weather. You fall down when it's dry as dust outside—God knows where I'll find you if it's icy. Why you won't use that cane I got you, I'll never know."

While it was true Lurlene fell more than most people, it was something she'd always done, something that had more to do with not paying attention than it had to do with age. Reese was used to seeing her head disappear from across the roof of the car when she got out on her side, like a Muppet whose skit had just finished. He'd been witness to her coming down concert stairs on her butt, somersaulting midsentence over that crack in the sidewalk in front of St. Cyprian's. He knew that cane was an insult to a woman who, as she was frequently fond of pointing out, had only just entered her seventies and could still touch her toes without effort, but he couldn't help worrying that one day she wouldn't bounce up as quickly as she'd always done in the past.

Lurlene was poised to argue but stopped herself. It was icy outside, and sometimes getting up after splaying out took a little longer and looked a lot less dignified than she liked, though she'd never admit this to Reese.

"Well, you're probably right. You go on ahead. The key to Porter's place is in the kitchen drawer. Take it with you just in case you can't get him to the door. He can't hear squat these days."

"I hope that old geezer won't shoot me when I waltz into that house." Reese was buttoning up a flannel shirt, and despite the teasing look in his eye, Lurlene knew he was at least halfway serious.

"Well, we both better go." She stood up and pulled on a cardigan.

Reese opened his mouth to protest but stopped when he saw the set of her jaw. "Porter's used to me coming in to see him," she said, "and I'm the only soul in town that beagle won't bark at. The thing'll yell like a banshee if you show up by yourself. Come on, I'll hold on to your arm. You can be my escort." She grinned up at him and he sighed.

The cold air bit their faces when they opened the back door. The eaves had protected the porch stairs from the ice, but sure enough, Lurlene's feet went akimbo when she stepped out onto the drive. Reese held her upright and she took a firmer grasp on his arm. It was so quiet outside her laugh sounded louder than it was.

Dawn was painting a diagonal stroke of pink across the park and soon the sun would challenge the ice to see who would rule the day. The magnolia tree at the end of the Pearsons' drive looked made of glass, poised to shatter if they touched a single leaf. Crossing the street, they walked carefully alongside the wrought-iron fence surrounding the park and could see tiny bits of stone on the ground, stone that until last night had made up the body of general and horse, each small, jagged piece now as indistinct as smoke.

For the first twenty years they'd lived across from Griffin Park, Reese and Lurlene had barely noticed the statue of Henry Benning; it was one of those things you just didn't pay much attention to, like a lamppost or telephone pole. But once you *did* notice it—or perhaps more accurately, once it was pointed out to you—you could never look at it the same way again. Over the last year the thing had stirred people up into a bad stew. It didn't seem like a week had gone by when the park was empty of trouble. People were either draping signs over the thing itself or hanging them all up and down the fence. One Monday morning last summer they'd awakened to find a rather fitting obscenity sprayed across the horse's gray rump. Taken together, these occurrences had decisively changed their habit of sitting out on the front porch after dinner. They'd moved their rocking chairs around to the back.

"Maybe this will be the end of it," Lurlene said.

"The hell it will," said Reese.

They stayed off Porter's glazed driveway, choosing instead to use the side door by way of the lawn, a wafer-thin sheet of ice cracking beneath their feet as they climbed the steep hill. No light was on, and as Lurlene had predicted, Spot the beagle stayed quiet, though they could hear him snuffling behind the door when they reached it. Lurlene pressed her nose to the glass and looked in. The dog jumped as high as he could to let her know he was there.

"Well, Spot's awake. But I don't see hide nor hair of Porter," she said. Letting go of Reese's arm, she put her hand in her coat pocket and pulled out the key. "You stay here. I'll go see if he's up. I want to tell him about that thing before he sees it. I'll call you if I need you."

"Okay," Reese replied, banging his arms against his sides in an effort to warm himself up. "I'll be right here."

. . .

Detective Will Cochran had changed his clothes, locked up Butter's condo, and returned the key to the Windward maintenance office with the instruction that she be contacted on the repairs as soon as possible. He'd hesitated a few seconds with his hand on the doorknob, before asking the guy at the desk for her number, ignoring as best he could the sly smile that played around the fellow's mouth as he handed over the scrap of paper with the number scrawled across it in pencil.

It had been five years since Ellen died, and those years had been long. He'd spent the first one in a haze of grief, the next three twisted with self-pity, and the last fighting down feelings of guilt over the hope that had begun to nip and gnaw at the edges of his belief that no matter how long he had left to live, his life was really over. He'd begun to enjoy himself again, and there were days Will felt almost embarrassed about that.

He'd surprised himself with his reaction to Butter Swann. When he first heard her voice on the phone, he'd stuck her squarely in the box labeled "hysterical females," a category he avoided like bad food. But as he drove home now, taking it slow on the slick roads, he realized he'd been wrong, for even in the midst of tears—and who wouldn't be upset at the destruction of such a carefully ordered home—she had met his eyes with a chutzpah and spunk he'd found damn attractive in spite of himself. He laughed now remembering the way she'd called him *Fred-die,* angrily drawling the name out for maximum effect. Of course, those blue eyes hadn't hurt a thing, either. He'd had a predilection for blondes when he was younger only to see it disappear when brown-haired Ellen stole his heart, but obviously the fondness still flamed somewhere inside him. Maybe he'd call her, maybe he wouldn't. But he couldn't seem to shake the feeling that he might.

He was just turning back onto Meridian Street when his cell-phone rang. He picked it up and cradled it against his shoulder.

"Will Cochran."

"Detective Cochran, this is Sergeant Crowder down at the station. I know you're supposed to be off today, but we've got a situation. That Confederate statue in Griffin Park, the one everybody's all het up over? Well, I got a call a little while ago that somebody knocked it down last night. I had Corky Bacon drive by, and well, it's true, the thing's all over the ground. Technically of course it belongs to Old Man Griffin, so I'm not real sure what we're supposed to do. He hasn't called us or anything, but he will, you can bet on it. I just wanted to check in with you and see what you think we should do."

"Good Lord." Will stopped his car at a red light in an empty intersection. He hadn't seen this coming; he doubted anyone had. "I'll drive over there and take a look. I guess we're lucky everybody's staying in this morning. You just sit tight. If anybody calls you just say we're checking into it. Whatever you do, don't make assumptions that'll set folks off. I'll be in touch." He did a U-turn in the middle of the road and headed back the other way.

Lurlene had seen a dead body once before. She'd been twelve and playing center field for the Hubert Stanley Middle School softball team on one of those late spring afternoons that felt more like summer. Brenda Cox had been at the plate, and since it was accepted as fact that Brenda couldn't hit anything smaller than a beach ball, Lurlene had been letting her mind wander in the soporific glare of the sun. She could still hear the unexpected crack of the bat, still see the flash of white in her left eye as the ball flew low across the field, fast as a dart, straight into the forehead of Katie Quattlebaum.

You could tell Katie was dead the moment she hit the ground. It wasn't the wound, or the mile-long stare in her open eyes. It was the stillness. Whether on intake or sigh, when breath takes its leave, a body might as well be made of wood.

So she knew immediately that Old Man Griffin was gone. Not by the unnatural way his legs were bent beneath him, or the look of, what was it . . . fright? . . . rage? . . . still shining from his fixed and faded blue eyes. No, it was the stillness. Just like Katie. Lurlene backed out of the room, shooing Spot behind her, closed the door, and left.

Out in Porter's backyard a two-toned turkey buzzard was putting forth a great deal of effort to take flight, with a lot of hopping and flapping of wings, but had yet to lift off the ground.

13

MARIETTA, IVY, BUTTER, GLINDA, AND BRADY

As yet unaware of the events occurring simultaneously around the city, Marietta stood in the doorway of her guest room trying to decide whether or not to wake her sister-in-law. She was caught in a snare of emotions, each vying for prominence, and each as unpleasant as the others. All she had wanted was to be alone. Yet here she was, juggling three people as disparate and incompatible as any God ever created.

One would think that grief would dull the senses, that the loss of someone who felt like a part of your own body would strip away your ability to see color or hear rain on the roof. Instead, Marietta was finding the opposite to be true; the coffee she'd brought up for Glinda smelled so strong it almost made her sick. Every consonant and vowel coming from Gordon and Butter's conversation downstairs reached her like noise itself.

Once they'd gotten her inside, Glinda had allowed herself to be ushered up to this room without saying a word, climbing into the small bed under the eaves and falling asleep faster than if she'd been hit on the head. Looking down at the thin outline of the woman she'd known for more than forty years, Marietta remembered what she'd been reminded of the first time she met Glinda and smiled in spite of herself.

The summer she turned six, Marietta's great-aunt Evelyn had taken a vacation to Colonial Williamsburg and enlisted the family in caring for her mynah bird, Mr. Smith, installing his large brass cage in the dining room, and leaving with no more than a wave.

Sleek and dark, with eyes like ebony beads, Mr. Smith had sat by the window for a week, observing the family with a quietly quizzical air. When he chose to speak, which wasn't often, his voice was high-pitched and colorless, like one you'd expect of a clown. Marietta had hated passing by that bird, though Macon seemed to spend an inordinate amount of time with the thing, which everybody thought was actually quite kind as his had been the loudest dissenting voice when Mr. Smith's impending visit had been announced.

They all found out the reason for Macon's inexplicable devotion one hot afternoon when Mr. Smith began yelling out unspeakable words during Sunday dinner, each expletive worse than the last, and each uttered in Macon's unmistakable Southern drawl. Mr. Smith was gone the next day, but unfortunately the bird kept those words in constant rotation till the day before his twenty-first birthday, which also happened to be the day he fell off his perch and died.

The first time Macon brought Glinda home to introduce her to the family, Marietta had felt she was in the presence of that mynah bird once again. She could feel herself being watched by two bright dark eyes peering out from a face that was familiarly tiny and bright. Glinda's hair was as darkly perfect as that mynah bird's feathers, and she already displayed an evident habit of echoing Macon's every word as though he alone could operate an invisible string at the back of her neck, one that generated not only her speech but the smiling nods that came with it. Marietta had found it astonishing that her brother hadn't noticed the resemblance himself.

Now as she watched her sister-in-law sleeping, Marietta was ashamed to admit to herself that she'd never really paid much attention to Glinda as the years had gone by. She simply saw her as she imagined everyone else did: as an auxiliary of Marietta's dominating brother. Seemingly content to stay in the background as he orchestrated their lives—choosing the church they attended, the cars they drove, their summertime vacations, the schools for the kids—Glinda had faded in Marietta's mind into nothing more than a grisaille version of Macon. She'd always assumed Glinda traveled alongside Macon in harmony, flourishing in the financial and societal success his career provided. What if she'd been wrong? What could have happened, so suddenly, to crack them in two? Sitting beside them yesterday on the front pew of St. Cyprian's, she'd thought everything was the same as always.

The family photographs that lined the hallway around her showed the Hargis family at their best, group shots in which no one blinked, school photos after the braces came off. It was here you could so clearly see generational resemblance: Marietta's eyes so much like Aunt Kathleen's, Macon the mirror image of Logan when both had turned eighteen. Almost as though it had tapped her on the shoulder, Marietta turned around to stare at a picture of her brother that hung three feet from where she now stood. Macon grinned back at her from a face barely twelve years old, one full of laughter and optimism so easily lost with the years, a face Marietta couldn't even remember. By the time she'd reached the age Macon was in this picture, her brother had become a different person. At least that's how it had always seemed to her.

"*Well!* The Frenchman was right. Hell really *is* other people." Marietta jumped as Gordon whispered loudly in her ear, peering around her shoulder at Glinda. "I didn't foresee these two showing up, God help us. But come on down and let her sleep. Fluffy and I have almost got breakfast on the table, and I managed to do it all without stabbing her with a bread knife, so you should be proud. You need to eat something, and then we'll decide what to do with them."

"I don't know, Gordon," Marietta whispered. "Something bad

must have happened over at Macon's for Glinda to turn up here. I don't remember a single time during all the years they've been married that she's come to this house by herself. I guess I should call him."

"I wouldn't if I were you. Not right now. Not till you know more. She'll wake up, eventually, and you can talk to her then." He snickered as he steered Marietta toward the stairs. "Maybe she just finally had enough of that pompous ass."

"He *is* my brother."

"And nobody knows better than you what a pompous ass he is."

You're the one that I want.

You, ooh, ooh, honey . . . The soundtrack of *Grease* was thrown into the house like a grenade, causing the two of them to stop still on the bottom stair. They heard Butter answer her phone in the kitchen.

"Of course, that's her ringtone," hissed Gordon. "Nobody else in the whole wide world would have that one. How long is she going to stay?"

"I have no idea. But her house is flooded and I'm not going to kick her out in the street."

Gordon made a face. " 'When sorrows come, they come not single spies. But in battalions!' Why didn't she go to her son's place?"

"I don't think they get along all that well."

"Hmmm. I guess she's too much for him as well." Gordon's voice dripped with sarcasm, and it was Marietta's turn to make a face.

"Well! You will never guess. Not in a million years." Butter rounded the corner and met them in the entry hall, holding her phone in the air like a town crier holds a scroll, her face alight with the sort of excitement only really juicy news can engender. "It all happened after I left. I missed the whole thing." She looked from Marietta to Gordon as though watching a rapid volley at a tennis game.

Gordon pushed past her and headed for the kitchen, Butter

right behind him. "So?" he said. "My dear, 'smatter with your gossips, go.'"

"Huh?" said Butter.

"Tell us," Gordon replied, over his shoulder. He kept his back to her as he placed his second cup of coffee in the microwave to reheat it.

With escalating feeling Butter related the story she'd just gotten from a friend who'd witnessed the scene between Glinda and Macon at Micheline's restaurant, complete with sound effects of the lasagna as it met Macon's suit-clad bottom, and the screeching laughter that came out of Glinda as she went through the crowd on her way out the door. While she poured the orange juice, Butter told how Macon had sat there for the longest time, a look of confusion on his face that had spun slowly toward embarrassment before finally settling on a sort of anger that stopped the women who'd been heading his way to help dead in their tracks.

"He didn't say anything to anybody. Just got up and left. Headed out of Micheline's with all that mess on his britches and went straight down the square and out of sight. Nobody followed him. Too scared to, I guess. If only I'd stayed a little bit longer! I missed the whole thing."

Gordon looked up to the ceiling, beyond which Glinda lay sound asleep. "Apparently, 'though she be but little, she is fierce,'" he said, then turned to Marietta and asked, "Has she said anything? At all?"

"No." The syllable came out in a croak. Marietta's throat had tightened like a fist and breakfast suddenly felt like the last thing in the world she wanted.

Next door, Ivy Harper sat cross-legged in her window seat, watching the big black bird perched on the ledge outside Marietta's bedroom window. She could see the creature more clearly now. As it sat still and alone in this strange world of white, its dark feathers captured her gaze like a crack in a clean mirror. The bird had been there every time Ivy had gotten up in the night to watch the ice slinking down from the sky. She would've sworn it had looked straight at her three times.

When her mother had told her an ice storm was coming, Ivy hadn't known what to expect. She liked storms, but this one—so quiet, nearly invisible—had been unlike any she'd known. No torrential rain gushing through the gutters and running off the roof. No flame throws of lightning, no sky-cracking thunder. This storm had been as silent as moonlight.

Though it had been a consolation prize when baby Sergio came along to claim her bedroom under the eaves for his nursery, this attic room was really the best in the house, and Ivy knew it. When the windows were open, and the wind was blowing, it was sometimes difficult to remember you were actually inside. There were wooden floors that creaked when you walked over them, and best of all, on the far side of the room, down two half-moon steps, was a small alcove with a wide window that was blessed with an uninterrupted view of Harry Cline's garden.

Harry had been the first person she'd met when they moved into The Glade. Ivy had been only four and hadn't known that many adults outside of her own family, but one day she walked past the Clines' while Harry was out in the front yard planting tulip bulbs. She'd seen the black spot on the lawn and wondered what it was, so she marched up the drive to ask him.

Harry had pushed his hat back on his forehead and looked at the child, wondering how much to say. "Well, I tell you, this happened a long time ago, long before you were born, so the men who did this aren't around anymore, and we don't need to be scared of them. But one night they came up here and set something on fire in this yard, and—"

"Why'd they do that?" Ivy had interrupted.

"Because they were mad about something the man who lived here wrote in the paper. But mostly because they were scared."

"What'd he write, that man who lived here?"

"He wrote that we should all respect one another."

"Why'd they get mad about *that*?"

"Well, pretty much because they thought they should get all the respect because they were better than some other people."

"Why don't you plant some grass here so it's not all burnt lookin'?"

"Because we want people to always remember how ugly it is to think like those men thought."

Ivy had nodded gravely and said, "My daddy says we're all the same before God."

"And your daddy's quite right." He'd taken off his hat, looked up at Ivy, and grinned. "Wanna see something fun? Did you know there are green elephants in my backyard? Come on, I'll show you."

From that morning on, Ivy was in and out of Marietta and Harry's house all the time. Under Harry's watchful gaze she carefully pruned the boxwoods so that they looked more and more like elephants every day, Marietta let her lick the beaters whenever she baked a cake, and she was teaching both Ivy and Thea to knit. When the Clines brought Smudge home it was love at first sight; it had been Ivy who'd walked the big dog all around The Glade when Harry got too weak to do it himself those last months. It was through Ivy that Marietta and Harry became close friends with Enid and John, and it was Ivy who'd probably miss Harry the most out of everyone in her family.

She'd seen Smudge and Trilby in the garden around dawn and realized Mr. Lovett from the bookstore must be there. But it had still been too early to knock on Marietta's door, so she'd gone back to bed awhile to get warm. Now she was up again, watching the sun light up the ice so bright she had to shield her eyes from the glare. It shone into Marietta's kitchen window and Ivy could now clearly see her, sitting at the table with Peter's grandmother, buttering a piece of toast. Ivy hurriedly dressed.

Running down the stairs, she paused at Thea's bedroom door, hearing the rapid tick-tick-tick of her sister's fingers as they typed out a text. It was a familiar sound. Ivy opened the door and looked in. Sure enough, Thea was sitting up in bed, thumbs flying across the surface of her phone. She looked up and motioned Ivy inside.

"What's going on?" Ivy asked.

Thea held up a finger, hit a few emojis for emphasis, and laid the phone down on the bed beside her. "Somebody's torn that statue down," she said, her eyes widened with significance.

"Who?"

"*I* don't know. Peter called me a few minutes ago. He saw it."

"Was it somebody you know? Somebody from that group you're working with?"

"No, Ivy! None of them would just go and tear the thing down."

"Well, I bet they're gonna get blamed for it. Who else would've done it? Unless it just fell over or something. It's really old."

"Yeah, it's old. But I don't think those things just fall down on their own."

The two sisters looked at each other, each one understanding the implications of this event in different degrees. Thea hadn't told her parents she and Peter had been helping out at MRED. The only person who knew was Peter's grandmother, and she'd promised not to tell his parents. The secret was even more important to keep now.

Ivy broke the silence. "I'm going over to Marietta's. I'll see if she knows anything. Your boyfriend's grandmother is over there. The lady from the billboard? I saw her through the window."

"No, Ivy. *You* don't know anything. You remember that. Just keep your mouth shut. We're staying out of this."

They were halfway through breakfast when Ivy's face peeked in at the back door glass. Gordon got up to let her inside and she made a beeline for Marietta's outstretched arms. Both Butter and Gordon felt the need to look away as Marietta silently held the child to her for a long minute, her head resting on Ivy's, before holding her back and looking into her eyes. "How're you doing, Ivy?" She pushed a chair out with her foot and Ivy sat down.

The little girl told them about the statue before they could pour her juice.

"I just can't believe it," said Marietta. "Just like that? It's gone? Who on earth did it?"

"Whoa, boy," said Gordon. "Now, this is going to hit the fan in ol' Wesleyan, big-time. The fight was just getting good, and now somebody's declawed the cat."

Butter was quiet, slowly moving her eggs around her plate with her fork. She knew Peter had been working with MRED for a good while now, but the faintest possibility that he could be involved with anything like this just didn't bear thinking about. She was close to her grandson, closer than she'd ever been to Christo. She knew Peter told her things he'd never tell his parents—they didn't even know about Thea—and she felt a warmth about this that eclipsed any other good thing she'd ever felt in her life. It was the one relationship that mattered most to her. She'd protect it with her life.

Peter was her second chance. It pained Butter to think of it that way, but with his fervent adoration of her he'd lifted the curtain on the way things had always been with her son: stilted, almost formal, the result, she supposed, of him arriving long before she'd figured out anything important at all. She'd been so young. Christo had caught her off guard—hell, he'd been the reason she married Joe, and it had taken her years to even halfway admit that to herself.

Peter's trust in her had been transformative. When he'd told her about Thea, his eyes shining with the unabashed glow of a first crush—she could still remember the way those felt—she'd seen it as some sort of gift. Who'd have thought she'd be the one person in the family her grandson would trust to welcome his black girlfriend without reservation? Butter adored Thea and felt just as protective of her as she did of Peter.

Ivy continued telling her tale, directing it now toward Butter as though they were old friends. "Yes, ma'am, Peter called Thea this morning when he was out delivering the paper. He saw it."

Marietta raised her eyebrows, and Butter, her openness a surprise to both of them, spoke up. "Thea and Peter are friends," she said. "In fact, they're dating. You know, they're boyfriend and girlfriend." Ivy continued eating, with Gordon looking from face to face, waiting for further comment that never came.

Upstairs, Glinda had opened her eyes, seeing nothing she recognized for a good thirty seconds. When she remembered where she was, exhaustion and embarrassment fell over her, almost pushing her back down into sleep. Instead, she slowly rose and went to the door; the mere prospect of staying by herself for one more minute was more than she could take.

She followed the sound of voices down the stairs and into the kitchen, where all conversation ceased the moment she entered the room. The smile she attempted was nowhere near successful and she knew it. She sat down at the end of the long wooden table and looked at her hands.

"Do you think you can eat something?" Marietta asked, acutely aware that sometimes, no matter how much well-meaning people think it's something you should do, eating is the least palatable activity a person can imagine. Her own breakfast remained untouched.

"I'm not really hungry. Thank you." Glinda's voice sounded thin and unused, even to herself. She looked around the table, seeing Ivy for the first time, the girl's face as innocent and accepting as only a child's can be. "I don't know why I came here. Harry's funeral, and well, I just . . ." Looking back down at her hands, she said, in a whisper, "You know what? I think I've just left my husband."

The everyday sounds of the house took over. The hum of the refrigerator, the crackling of the fire, the clicking of the coffeemaker—sounds that go unheard when the world spins normally. The four adults sat still, and Ivy, looking from face to face, suddenly knew she should go out in the garden to play with the dogs.

Brady Goode slipped on the ice at the edge of his drive, clumsily righting himself by grabbing hold of a branch on the old magnolia tree that concealed his house from the street. The big tree shuddered, sending slivers of ice down on his shoulders and hair. When he was steady on his feet again, he pulled a cap from his coat pocket, put it on, and glanced up Pinehurst Street to find the monotony of January shattered. He grinned.

Brady hated winter in the South. It always surprised him how quickly all the prismatic pageantry of autumn just dried up and tumbled to the ground, where it succumbed to the rake and the leaf blower with not so much as a whimper. The lemony springtime for which this land was so famous was still weeks away, and this was usually the time of year when, to his artist's eye, everything looked blurred, the land and sky so often the same color, neither the usual browns, blues, or greens but a muddy amalgamation of those three that rubbed out the difference between morning and dusk. The ice storm was a novelty Brady hadn't expected, and for all the inconvenience it brought, he couldn't help but be astonished at its ability to pull The Glade out from under the flat, dull paw of winter. The severity of the whiteness startled him; the pale gray clouds lay so weighty and low, he almost felt the need to duck. His spirits lifted as he started to walk up the street.

He had left the consistently pleasant weather of Los Angeles ten years ago, anxious to experience the changing of seasons, thinking that alone might serve as a partial cure for the languor that had settled in his spirit the day he walked out of Lompoc Penitentiary. He could hardly remember the man he'd once been. A few bad investments, a few shady decisions, and the advertising agency he'd worked so hard to build had slipped from his grasp like the reins of a runaway horse. His wife left him, he served six months for insider trading—a crime he still wasn't exactly sure how he'd managed to commit—and when it was all over, he could barely recognize his own reflection in the mirror. Despite warnings from the few friends he had left, Brady made the most drastic change he could think of: he packed up all the things he really cared about—a bit stunned to find there were so few—and moved to the South, the home of his mother's ancestors and a place he'd never even visited, to do what he'd always wanted to do. Thanks in large part to Marietta and Harry Cline, he'd succeeded. They'd loved his work at first sight, and when the first three paintings they hung in their shop sold within days, they'd asked him for more. So, without planning or premonition, he was making a good living now as an artist, well known nationwide as something he'd wanted to be since childhood.

People in Wesleyan viewed Brady Goode like an exotic variety of tree that bloomed profusely in total indifference to the soil in which it was planted. They'd never see him as a Southerner—he was viewed as the prototypical Californian, though nobody knew what that was—but they proudly claimed him as a city son whenever he was featured in a national magazine or newspaper, and, gowned and tuxedoed, they flocked to the opening nights of his gallery shows like iron filings to a magnet. If one of them was lucky enough to own one of his paintings, it was usually hung in the entry hall so nobody could possibly miss it. Brady had few truly close friends, but after his experiences in Los Angeles, he rather liked it that way.

The ice muffled every sound save the crunch of his boots on the sidewalk. The air was sharp as glass, his breath a visible hood above his head. Looking out over the bent silver trees he could see the dormer at Marietta's bedroom carving a triangle in the cotton wool sky and wondered if she was feeling better. He pulled his collar up higher, wishing, not for the first time, that God would put a little more thought into the people he chose to take versus the ones he left behind. Harry Cline should still be here.

As the street curved, he saw John Harper slipping and sliding back up his drive. Brady called out, "No paper yet?"

John planted his feet side by side for stability and turned his head toward Brady. "Hey! No, don't really know what I was thinking. Maybe it'll get here later, but I kinda doubt it. This stuff doesn't look likely to melt much today."

Brady nodded toward the Hummer in front of Marietta's house. "That's some vehicle. Wonder who it belongs to?"

John turned his head without moving his feet, then looked back at Brady. "Yeah, something, isn't it? Belongs to Macon Hargis, Marietta's brother. Used to make me laugh to see him driving that thing around town like a little Napoleon."

Brady grinned. "Takes a special kind of guy to pull that off, I guess. Well, at least he's over there taking care of her. I couldn't get her off my mind last night. Hope she's all right after yesterday."

"Oh, Macon's not there," said John, shaking his head. "His wife is. I suppose you saw their little incident yesterday at Harry's reception? Enid and I heard her pull up just after dawn. Sounded like a herd of elephants. I had to get up and look. Can't imagine she's too used to being behind the wheel—she looked pretty shook up when she climbed out. You be careful out here now. I'm going inside where it's warm."

Brady threw up his hand as John went cautiously back up the drive. He'd just reached the Hummer when he saw Marietta's front door open. She stepped outside. Brady recognized his friend Gordon Lovett behind her, and remembered the two other women from yesterday, the one with the white hair especially. In the gelid silence their words were clear, bright, and easily heard.

"I told you I'd get it, Marietta." Gordon sounded irritated.

"And what makes you any better equipped to make it down the driveway than I am?"

"It's *my* suitcase. I'll get it." The white-haired woman, Macon Hargis's wife.

"Don't y'all be silly. We'll all go." The blonde.

Brady stepped out from the shadow of the hemlocks and called out. "Marietta? It's me, Brady. You all need some help over there?"

Marietta put her hand up to her eyes, looking toward the corner of the front yard. "Oh, Brady! Hello! Well"—she looked around her—"yes . . . we do, if you're offering. My sister-in-law's suitcase is there in that"—she hesitated—"that . . . car. The door's unlocked. If you could grab it, we'll meet you halfway."

Brady opened the door to the Hummer and pulled the suitcase out. "You all stay where you are. I've got boots on; I'll bring it up to you."

The four of them stood huddled together under the eaves of the house, watching Brady negotiate the icy driveway with as much skill as he could manage, everyone relieved when he made it safely to the top. He walked past them to the open door and set the case down in the entry hall before turning to Marietta.

Standing somewhat back, Glinda and Butter politely looked away as Brady took Marietta's hand and placed it to his flannel-covered heart. "You doing all right?" he asked her. "Need anything?"

"I'm just fine, Brady," Marietta answered, smiling. "Here now, let me introduce you." She turned to face the others, keeping Brady's hand in hers. "This is my sister-in-law, Glinda Hargis, whose suitcase you just so valiantly retrieved." Brady nodded to Glinda, who held his eyes as she gave him a small smile of thanks for his effort. Marietta continued, "And this is my friend Butter Swann. And Gordon, of course."

Brady cleared his throat and took off his cap to run a hand through his dark gray hair, clearly uncomfortable. There was blue paint on his fingers. "It's good to meet you both. And good to see you, Gordy. You owe me a dinner, you know." He clapped Gordon a little too heartily on the back, causing Gordon to take a few hurried steps forward. "You order those McCarthys for me yet?"

"They're probably sitting down at the shop," said Gordon. "I've been closed for the past few days. I'll drive over to check as soon as I can. The Border Trilogy, right?"

"That's it. Just let me know. And you are on notice. I expect one of those to be a book club pick before long. Too many women's books lately."

"I've told you, Brady. Just because it's written by a woman doesn't mean it's a woman's book. You need to branch out anyway."

Brady laughed, and a silence fell. "Well, I'd better be going," he said hesitantly. He was avoiding looking directly at Glinda Hargis and feeling embarrassed anyway. "Rummy will be wanting his breakfast. You all better settle in here. I'll be surprised if this stuff doesn't refreeze tonight. You got enough food?"

Butter and Gordon laughed. "Enough food?" said Marietta. "We've got enough for the whole neighborhood. In fact, why don't you come up for dinner one night this week?"

"You just tell me when, and I'll be here," said Brady, moving past Glinda and catching a hint of jasmine perfume.

"I'll call you," said Marietta, and Brady waved over his shoulder as he went back down the drive.

It took some effort for Butter to turn away from the sight of the retreating back of Brady Goode. Despite being three inches shorter than she would have preferred, he was a handsome man. "You are so lucky to have some of his paintings," she said as she watched him go.

"We are," said Marietta. "But he gave them to us, you know. Years ago. We could never afford them now. Come on, let's get in out of the cold."

By the time Brady made it safely to his drive he could clearly see the light in his window, flickering through the magnolia tree like a lantern. He'd left the radio on as a distraction for Rummy, his black Maine coon cat, who wasn't too keen on this weather, so the lyrical notes of a Chopin étude greeted him when he walked inside. It could be worse, Brady thought. Rummy was curled up on the table by the living room window, studiously watching the cardinals who were jockeying for prime positions on the bird feeder outside.

"If it just wasn't for that glass, you'd have 'em, wouldn't you, Rum?"

The cat slowly turned his head and considered his owner critically for a moment before gracefully leaping from the table. Rummy's tail swept behind him like the train of a cape, and he sauntered slowly into the kitchen, his impending meal appearing to be the very last thing on his mind.

Brady picked up a clean china bowl from the drying board, filling it with a mixture of kibble and canned food just like his vet had told him to do. "And to think I was always a dog person," he said as he set the bowl down in front of the huge cat, who twitched his tail in unconscious appreciation.

Brady poured himself another cup of coffee and wandered out into the glass-lined studio. Thoughts floated through his head without intention, halting here and there at points of pleasure or amusement—Butter Swann's blue eyes or Gordon Lovett's round face—before settling, rather comfortably, on Glinda Hargis's pretty, sad smile. They lingered there the longest. He'd watched her push her way through the crowd at the reception yesterday—her wild laughter, that forest green suit. That woman has secrets, he thought. And secrets interested Brady.

The light that fell through the windows seemed to come from some other source than the sun. It was strange light, sharper than he'd ever seen it, cold, bright, and impossible to ignore. It was as if the room had been picked up in the night and placed in an entirely different landscape.

He stood back from the painting currently occupying the large easel—squinting at it, cocking his head. Seeing it in this new light made him critical, unsure just what it lacked, but knowing he wasn't yet pleased. Then, taken with an inspiration so sudden it felt like impulse, he picked up the half-finished canvas and set it aside, replacing it with a new one, clean and untouched. With a bit of charcoal, he quickly began sketching the face of a woman, one with shiny white hair and bright dark eyes, almost like a bird's.

14

BUTTER, GLINDA, GORDON, AND MARIETTA

Butter threw her suitcase up onto the same twin bed she'd slept in whenever she stayed with Marietta in those long-ago years, then looked around the guest room and smiled. She was feeling better. The crowded house made it seem like her troubles were shared, as though whatever had happened to her this morning was something she could handle. It was a feeling she was keeping hidden at the moment, what with Marietta and Glinda sitting downstairs, each with greater problems than her own. This is not a vacation, she told herself, even though deep down she felt like it was.

She hated being alone. If anything happened to her without someone to share it with, Butter felt it really hadn't happened at all. Most of the time she spun too fast to think much about her solitary state, but there were times, more frequent than she'd like to admit, when an old lonesomeness would creep over her, a holdover from those still Sunday afternoons when she'd been a girl, lying across her bed after church in that melancholy purgatory when the weekend was almost over, and school was coming fast on its heels. After Joe died, she started running to chase that feeling away. She was now in the best shape of her life. As she opened her suitcase, she caught a glimpse of the tiny silver box so recently lifted from Marietta's hall table and stuffed it into the sleeve of a sweater.

Downstairs Glinda sat alone in the library trying to picture Macon back at home, wondering whether he'd yet looked into the guest room to see if she was there or if, as she suspected, he'd gotten up, showered, and dressed before going downstairs for breakfast, the way he always did. He was rattled; she'd lived with him long enough to know that much. But when Old Man Griffin called, screaming to high heaven about his beloved statue being gone, she also knew her absence would slip down to second place on her husband's list of priorities. Anger rose up to color her face once again. It was such a new feeling, but one she was beginning to get used to. Little by little it was melting into the crevices of her body like a hot drink, one that, on first sip, had numbed and frightened her but now only made her feel clearer, more alive.

She went to the window to look out to where Marietta and Gordon were standing side by side, watching Smudge and Trilby chase each other around the garden, and she thought how awful it was to be given a glimpse of how far you've come from the person you intended to be, or planned to be, or, worst of all, *could* have been, especially when the time is too short to rectify anything. But Glinda knew that was what she had seen, sitting on that pew at Harry's funeral in an invisible light as bright as the one that knocked St. Paul to his knees on that road to Damascus. All of a sudden, she could see herself—once bright as a new penny, as her daddy used to say, but getting smaller and quieter with each passing year, taking the easy way, avoiding the hard things, safe, taken care of—until, now . . . what?

But then, of course, she thought . . . there's Maggie and Josh. Of course, yes. She'd put two wonderful people out there in the world. Maybe that's why God gives people children, so it's harder for them to feel that they've wasted their lives. With kids, you make so many choices without really choosing. And no one blames you. But then you look up, and they're gone, and you're left with something you don't even recognize, your life a creation you don't remember making and, in some cases, don't even want. And I guess that's when you focus on grandchildren, Glinda thought. Then great-grandchildren. Then you die without ever thinking too hard . . .

Memories are often stored in a place you don't visit until trouble pushes open the door. Glinda hadn't thought of her grandmother's cellar in decades but could now see it clearly: the tiny window level with the ground, the cool, damp dirt of the floor, and herself, standing there as a child with an old, grimy packet of hollyhock seeds in her hand. She had asked if she could plant them, and the old lady had given her permission along with the warning that they might not all come up. "Some will be fine," she'd said, peering into the packet and shaking it. "Some won't. But you'll see, oftentimes these old seeds I've had forever end up looking better than the ones I bought yesterday. Just give it a try."

Glinda turned from the window and walked over to the bookshelves that lined the green walls. Cocking her head, she read the colorful spines to herself in a whisper. Some classics—she'd read them all before—some Kate Atkinson, a Donna Tartt, and . . . wait, she remembered this book, its stark cover and block letters. *White Teeth* . . . the one she hadn't wanted to read eighteen years before. She pulled it off the shelf and took it to the chair by the window. She'd read the first two pages when Butter burst into the room, her eyes wide.

"I forgot my pills," she said. "I've got to go back to the condo and get them."

When displeasure is cloaked in sarcasm and wit, you can manage to say whatever you want and only a few really know how you feel. Gordon had learned this early on. With twin sisters euphemistically labeled "stocky" and fond of dressing in ruffles, he'd had to. If Glinda and Butter had even an inkling of how much he'd been irritated by their unanticipated arrivals, he'd be very surprised. But irritated he most certainly was. He stuffed the high-thread-count sheet into the crevices of Marietta's sunroom sofa, determined to make it as comfortable for himself as he possibly could, all the while attempting to disguise the feeling that he should rightly be sleeping in one of the guest rooms upstairs. But with Glinda now ensconced in the single, his only choice would be sharing the twin-bedded room with Butter, something he couldn't have imagined if you'd paid him.

"Well, can't she just stay off them till she can get back home?" he asked Marietta in a whisper that somehow managed to be louder than his usual voice.

"Be quiet." Marietta grabbed the other end of the sheet and pulled it tight. "They're antidepressants. I don't think you're supposed to just stop taking them cold."

"Can you honestly tell me if Fluffy has some sort of psychotic break, either one of us would be able to tell?"

Marietta pretended not to hear the question. "Glinda has offered that Hummer thing for us to drive. I seriously doubt we'll even notice the ice on the roads."

"Well, why do you and me have to go?"

"We can't let those two go by themselves, Gordon. Not in the state they're in. Only two people fit in your car. You can drive Fluf—Butter—by yourself if you want to." She stood up and looked at his face. "No, I didn't think so. Now, come on."

Gordon sighed theatrically but Marietta pretended not to hear and left the room to get changed. He plopped down heavily on the newly made-up sofa and crossed his arms over his chest like a disgruntled child. "Misery acquaints a man with strange bedfellows, Trilby," he said, and the corgi looked, as always, as though he completely understood.

Marietta kept her cards close, always had, and though Butter's and Glinda's presence made it more difficult, Gordon was watching his old friend with a rapier eye. Their history had taught him to do so. He remembered all those years ago when she'd first told

him her plans to write like her father, to travel the world and
report on it all, the ugliness, the beauty, the hope, the despair.
Logan had instilled in his daughter the unwavering belief that life
would always improve, that despite setbacks of unimaginable
length, we are always moving forward, that history is something
to learn from and never repeat. Gordon had always had serious
doubts about that worldview. But off Marietta went to the University of Georgia to pursue a journalism degree, while he over-
shot her on his way to New York City with no plans ever to
return to the South.

Nineteen-eighty found them living the lives they'd imagined.
Marietta was a junior reporter for the *Atlanta Constitution,* and
Gordon was working in tiny theaters so far off Broadway they
were barely still in New York, a city he gleefully told her was akin
to the place the Donkey Boys took Pinocchio. His nights were
swirls of sybaritic color the likes of which he'd only dreamed of
as a little boy in Wesleyan, while her days were filled with chance
after chance to finally do the sort of work she'd been raised to
believe made things better. Who could have guessed the realities
that lay ahead for them both?

In late winter, Marietta was assigned to help cover a new case.
The previous year, four black children had been found dead in
the city. On March tenth, the fifth one was discovered. By July
that number had risen to eight. With every new victim's family
she interviewed, Marietta fell deeper and deeper inside the fear
and despair that shone from their eyes. On August twenty-second,
the day after the ninth body was found behind a shopping center
dumpster, Logan and Caroline drove up from Wesleyan and
checked Marietta into a hospital, where she stayed until the day
before Christmas.

Gordon was the only one who knew. He came to see her at
Thanksgiving but didn't tell her of the rumors just beginning to
rattle through the clubs and cafés of New York. It wasn't that he
didn't believe them, just that they were too frightening to even
consider. By the end of the decade most of the people he loved
were dead.

He heard the jangling of keys and rustling of coats coming from the entry hall. "Come on, Gordon!" called Marietta. "We're leaving." With a grimace seen by only Trilby and Smudge, Gordon hoisted himself off the sofa and stomped off toward the front door.

15

LURLENE, WILL, AND MACON

It was hard to tell if Lurlene was upset just by looking at her. Reese had always figured this was partly because of the many times she'd had to play piano at funerals and weddings of people she didn't really know, or particularly like. She'd learned to keep her expressions unreadable. It was in her voice where her feelings were clear. On the phone he could instantly tell if she was tired or worried, happy, or just plain mad.

So she came out of Old Man Griffin's side door looking much the same as when she went in. No fright or shock had modified her features in the slightest. It was only when she spoke that Reese knew something was wrong. There was a quiver in her voice, each syllable unconnected to the last, rising and falling faster than raindrops on waves. He reached for her arm when she uttered the very first word.

"Well . . . he's dead. All crumpled up in front of the window." A rope leash was around her right wrist like a camp bracelet;

Reese's eyes followed it down to where it ended in a circle around the neck of an overweight beagle. The dog regarded him calmly, as though privy to information Reese was not. "And it looks like we've got us a dog," said Lurlene. "There'll be nobody else to take him." Reese could've sworn the beagle grinned.

The three of them made a comical sight coming back down the drive, Reese trying to keep Lurlene upright as her feet threatened to slide out from under her with every step, and Spot pulling against his leash in anticipation of an adventure he'd hoped for but never truly expected. When they reached the flat surface of the road only two of them were pleased to stop.

They saw Will's car before its driver saw them. "Wave!" Lurlene urged her husband, and Reese did as he was told. Will pulled up alongside them and rolled the window down.

"Thanks for stopping," Reese said. "Could you do us a favor and phone the police? Our phones are at home and I'm afraid there's been a tragedy here at Mr. Griffin's house. He's passed away. Upstairs in his bedroom. My wife saw him." He looked down at Lurlene for confirmation.

"Yes," she said, bending to look in the car. "I'm Lurlene Pearson and this is my husband, Reese. I try to look in on Porter Griffin every now and then. I guess you can see his statue's been pulled down. When I saw that this morning, I knew he'd be upset. I didn't want him coming down here with it as icy as it was, so I . . . we . . . came over to see about him. I let myself in— I've got a key—and found him. In his bedroom, slumped down in a heap by the window. He's as dead as can be."

"You sure he's dead?" asked Will.

If there was anything she detested more than someone asking if she was sure right after she'd just told them a fact, Lurlene couldn't think what it was; there was no mistaking the edge in her voice. "Completely sure, son." The man didn't look all that much younger than either her or Reese, so the "son" was said to better even out the situation to her liking.

"Well, I'm sure sorry to hear that. But, Mrs. Pearson, as it so happens, I *am* the police. Detective Will Cochran, and I was just on my way out here to the park to see this statue for myself. I believe you talked to my desk sergeant earlier this morning?"

"Larry's a sergeant now? Well, good for him. Yes, that was me. I phoned up as soon as I saw what had happened." She cocked her head at Will, her eyes squinted. "You're new, aren't you? I don't recall meeting you before."

"Well, ma'am, I've been with the force for about six months now. Moved here from Virginia last summer. Thought I'd left this kind of weather behind. And you didn't see or hear anything in the night, is that right?"

"We heard some limbs cracking, some trees falling," said Reese, pointing his thumb back over his shoulder. "A big old poplar came down just back there on Fuchsia Drive. Missed the power lines, but from what I can see, it really messed up the Hollifields' front yard. If we'd heard that statue fall, we'd have probably just figured it to be another tree. Wouldn't have made any difference to get up and look. Couldn't have done anything about it in the middle of the night."

"Yeah, I suppose you're right about that. And now, about Mr. Griffin. You said . . ."

They heard it coming a good ten seconds before they saw it. Spot stood up to his full height of thirteen inches, released a series of operatic barks, and they all turned to see the big black Hummer coming down Duncan Street, its slow-moving presence just as menacing a sight as its designer must have intended it to be when it rolled off the assembly line back in 2006. As it turned in front of the park, Will gave a low whistle. "That's an H1 Alpha. Lord, I haven't seen one of those things in years. Wonder who that belongs to."

"It's Macon Hargis's," said Reese. "You know, the lawyer? Used to see him driving that thing around here all the time. I hear he still takes it to Beaufort once a year. Fills it with a bunch of his buddies and heads up there where he keeps his boat. Takes them all down the ICW every spring." He watched the thing take the corner and laughed. "He must have to stop for gas every twenty miles." He leaned around his wife to get a better look. "That's not Macon driving, though."

"Most ridiculous thing I've ever seen in my life," said Lurlene. As the Hummer went past, she could have sworn she saw Gordon Lovett sitting behind the wheel, then figured she must have been mistaken.

But Will, whose eyes were trained to notice details, saw Marietta Cline in the backseat, and the bright blond hair of Butter Swann shining from her place in the front.

Macon had felt her presence as he came up the stairs, long before he saw the always open guest room door was closed. He'd known she was in there, listening, expecting him to knock, to push the door open and demand an explanation for her bizarre, idiotic behavior. Well, let her wait, he'd thought, as he walked past that door without slowing his pace in the slightest. Let her wait. Let her wonder.

But he was the one who had waited. All night, he'd lain on his side of the bed, twisted by a witch's brew of toxic emotions. He didn't know which one was worse: shock, humiliation, or rage. They'd come in such rapid succession, bubbling and churning inside him all night as he lay on his back, clenching his fists. Sleep had been out of the question.

If Glinda had looked up at the house when she pulled out that morning, she would've seen Macon's face in the window, incandescent with the anger his ironclad control normally kept at bay. But she hadn't looked up; she hadn't looked back. He'd watched as his Hummer rolled down the driveway, never stopping, never slowing, until it disappeared.

He'd showered and dressed in a suit, just like every other day of his life, before he remembered it was Sunday and he had nowhere to go. Now he sat at his kitchen table with his eyes squinted shut, trying his best to figure out what to do.

They'd wanted him to run for mayor. A fitting and flattering cap to the career he'd fashioned for himself over all these long years. He hadn't told Glinda yet, and the fact that he hadn't let him know he'd been unsure of her enthusiasm for the prospect. After his humiliation at the restaurant yesterday, would they still be as ready to back him in a campaign to beat Harrison Gray, a man who, despite his liberal record on the school board, was popular enough to make it a tight race? There wouldn't be room for missteps, and what happened yesterday, especially if Macon didn't play it right from here on out, could be a serious one. A candidate can be hated, disagreed with, or mistrusted, and still win in a landslide. But laugh at him and he's cold dead in the water.

He supposed he could tell everyone that Glinda was "having problems," the accepted euphemism employed when any political couple crosses swords. She could straighten out, join him at a few campaign stops, and the gossip might possibly be quenched. But Macon had never seen his wife behave as she had yesterday, and "having problems" didn't really work when the problems were actually real.

When his phone rang, he reached for it so fast he knocked his coffee cup over. Dabbing at the mess with a paper towel, he answered loudly, "*Hell,* hello?"

"Mr. Hargis? You up?"

He'd always hated this most rhetorical of rhetorical questions. "I answered, didn't I?" he snapped. "Who is this?"

"Name's Will Cochran. I'm with the Wesleyan police force. I'm over here at Porter Griffin's place. Wasn't sure who else to call."

16

GORDON, JEN, PETER, AND GLINDA

From her place high up in the passenger seat beside him, Butter was watching Gordon's every move with something akin to alarm. He could feel her stare, but was far too terrified to snap at her. Keeping the Hummer between the lines in the road occupied every working brain cell he had. He wasn't exactly sure why he'd been tapped to drive the thing, other than the simple fact that he was male. Glinda had handed him the keys in much the same way he'd imagine Mrs. Claus handing Santa the reins on Christmas Eve, all three women staring at him with the sort of placid expectation that made it impossible to wriggle out of the predicament in which he now found himself, pressing down on the gas pedal with the tips of his toes. If it'd been anybody else, he would have laughed his socks off. As it was, he didn't find the situation comedic in the least.

He shifted in his seat and wondered how ballet dancers do it. How long you can point your toes before your foot begins to cramp? Surely there was a way to lower the seat in this thing, he thought . . . I'll pull over when we're well and truly away from any slick spots on the road and see. Of course, it'd be just my luck if there's some sort of height requirement for driving one of these monsters. I'm probably breaking some kind of law . . .

"Looks like they didn't get much ice out this way," said Marietta, sticking her head between the seats. "You think so, Gordon?"

"I'm not looking for ice, Marietta. I'm just trying to keep this black fire engine in the road. Why anybody would want one of these things, I don't know."

"Well, you know what they say about the men who drive them," Butter said, biting her thumbnail and not thinking. "Big car, little—"

"Butter!" Marietta's voice cut through Butter's last word and Gordon glanced over to see Butter's face turn red.

"Oh. I'm sorry, Glinda!" Butter said. "I tend to blurt things out without thinking."

Glinda, who'd been turned toward her window, watching the white, contorted pine trees flow past, gave a small snort, which the rest of them thought a promising sign.

"I can't believe that old statue's really gone," said Butter, leaving her previous inappropriate remark dissolving in the air, and turning around in her seat to look at the empty park disappearing in the back window. "I mean, just like that."

"Gone with the wind," Gordon muttered, gripping the steering wheel a little tighter as he felt the heavy vehicle go over a patch of ice. "How fitting."

"Wind couldn't have done that, dummy," said Butter, missing the joke entirely.

Jen Swann had already been out to the front porch three times, wrapping her new Christmas robe a bit tighter with each visit, and craning her neck to see as far as she could around the corner. She was hoping to catch sight of Peter coming back home. He wasn't late, not yet, and he was on foot, so the chances of all this ice putting him in any sort of peril were admittedly small, but still, she wished he'd begged off his shift just this once. She'd bet the other boys had. People would have understood. Who reads the paper anymore anyway?

This job was supposed to have been a learning experience for her son; she'd never expected him to actually enjoy it. But no matter the weather, Peter was up and out the door every morning before she even woke, returning after his shift was over—cheeks flushed with the cold or sweaty from the heat—happy as a lark, and ready to go to school. Jen felt slightly disappointed about this, though she couldn't have told anyone why.

They'd been as prepared for a teenager as any parents could be. Determined to keep the evils of modern education as far away from their son as possible, they'd homeschooled him during his middle school years, which everyone said was when most kids began to go off the rails. But when Christo changed jobs two years ago, they'd needed her to go back to work, so homeschooling was no longer an option. They'd enrolled Peter immediately in the school their church was starting (the rolls of Sanctorium Academy were filled long before they even broke ground), but with a completion date still a year and a half away, and despite her misgivings, Peter was going to Wesleyan High. Jen had to admit— and she was hesitant to the point of denial about doing so—that Peter was thriving there. His grades were high, he had more friends than she could ever properly investigate on social media, and by all appearances her son was a cheerful, well-adjusted sixteen-year-old boy. Privately, Jen found his happiness suspicious.

She shut the door and went back into the warm kitchen, where Christo was turning the last of the pancakes in total disregard for the new diet she'd told him repeatedly had been her only New Year's resolution. How would she ever lose the fifteen pounds that stood between her and the buttons on that pink linen suit she'd bought—and paid way too much for—if he made her pancakes for breakfast? Eat those, and the whole day would be shot. Might as well tear into that shortbread still left over from Christmas. She went to the table in silence.

"Here you go," said Christo, setting a full plate before her. "Perfect morning for pancakes. I've even warmed up the syrup." When combined with obliviousness, his enthusiasm was as irritating as a whine. Jen picked up her fork and started to eat.

Christo sat down, placing his napkin on his lap with an exaggerated flourish. "Man, I love this weather. Nobody expects you to do a thing. Everybody's stuck inside, can't go anywhere, nothing's open. You can go back to bed if you want to, watch TV all day long, and it's perfectly fine."

Jen poured more maple syrup onto her pancakes. "Maybe I'll feel that way when Peter gets back. I don't like him out there in this."

"Oh, come on. He's loving it. The kid's never seen weather like this in his life. I bet he's having a ball out there. I would've been at his age."

"Have you called your mother?" Jen said this on purpose, a guileful response to the calorie-laden plate in front of her. She resented being the one to remind him, but knew if she didn't, Christo would forget, then he'd put it off even longer because he felt bad about forgetting, and by the time he actually did get around to calling Butter his own guilt would cause him to hear an accusatory tone in his mother's voice that was as familiar as it so often was imaginary. One thing Jen did not want in her life was a relationship with her son that in any way resembled the one her mother-in-law had with hers.

"Uh, well, no. Not yet. You know Mom sleeps late on Sundays. I'm sure she's fine, or I would have heard. I'll call her later."

The back door banged open before Jen could respond. They heard Peter in the laundry room taking off his boots, and soon the sound of him racing down the hall toward the kitchen. As he went past, Christo called out, "Hey, Pete! Pancakes! Fresh off the griddle. Come in here and sit down."

There was a slight pause, and Peter stuck his head around the door. His face was pink from running as fast as he could manage without slipping on the ice, and his blue eyes were round with an excitement that raised the flag of Jen's interest to full staff.

"What's the matter?" she asked.

"Huh?" Peter had quickly rearranged his expression to a more commonplace one but was still too slow for his mother.

"I said, what's the matter? What's happened?"

Peter's shoulders fell and he knew he was beaten. If his mother found out about the statue later in the day, which she most certainly would, she'd be aware that he'd passed by it earlier, would know he'd seen and known it was missing, then she'd want to know why he hadn't told them. His mind jumped ahead to all the questions that would follow, and in an instant he saw how much better it would be if he just told them everything now. Plus, there were pancakes on the table, and he was hungry.

"That Confederate statue's gone in the park," he said, sitting down and reaching for the platter of pancakes. "Somebody knocked it over last night. Or pulled it down, you know? I mean, I don't know how, but it's gone. Smashed. All over the park in front of the Pearsons' house. I saw it."

The look that passed between his parents was one Peter couldn't read. It wasn't the look of elation that he would have wished for, but never expected. Nor was it anger, regret, or even surprise. No, if he'd been forced to name it, Peter would have said that Christo and Jen looked, just for a second, more frightened than anything else. That momentary flash of fear told him, much louder than speech could have done, that he must keep his involvement with MRED secret for as long as he possibly could.

Gordon had just taken a deep cleansing breath when a noise like a cannon shot sounded and he felt the Hummer lurch to the right. He jumped down on the brake with all of his weight and jerked the wheel toward the side of the road, which is an action ill-advised on the ice. The big vehicle slid about thirty feet before finally stopping cold. All three women cursed, with varying degrees of skill, and everyone fell forward, each of them hanging over their seatbelt like a trout on a hook.

"What'd you *do*, Gordon?" Butter said.

"Me? What'd *I* do? *I* didn't do anything, Fluffy, dear! I was just trying to keep this thing on my side of the yellow line when all of a sudden, I don't know, it had a stroke, or something."

"I think we've had a blowout," Marietta said.

"Oh well now, that's just great," said Gordon. "That's just peachy." He unhooked his seatbelt and opened his door, his loafers dangling over the asphalt until he felt ready to jump. The other three followed him and together they stood on the side of Meridian Street in the cold, staring down at a twenty-inch tire that was flatter than a handprint. Their breath like smoke circles around their heads, the four turned as one to look up and down the empty road. Rawboned pine trees lined either side, ice-bent toward the street like palm fronds at Easter. There wasn't another car to be seen.

"We need a *man*," said Butter.

"Well, what in the hell am I?" asked Gordon.

"Can *you* fix this thing?" asked Butter.

"I cannot," said Gordon.

Unexpectedly, it was Glinda who started to laugh first.

Not a soul passed by during the long hour they spent changing the tire. Through a combination of YouTube videos that Butter found on her phone and a twelve-year-old owner's manual that by luck still remained in the glove compartment, the four of them managed to complete the job without injury or anger. Gordon and Marietta stood side by side with their arms around each other, bouncing on the handle of the jack to lift the thing up while Butter and Glinda hoisted the heavy spare into place. When they were finished, they stood back, staring down at the tire in amazement, at least two of them halfway expecting it to pop off and roll down the highway like a ten-cent doughnut. But it didn't. Butter clapped Gordon on the back, saying, "Good job!" and this time everybody laughed.

There was a general lifting of spirits when they were once again moving, and by the time they pulled up to Butter's door at Windward Oaks, Gordon's right toe had gone totally numb, which made driving the Hummer infinitely more comfortable.

17

—

ERNEST, WILL,
AND MACON

The office of Monument Removals Encourage Development was in what used to be the Zabbo's Diner on the southern edge of town. Chip Dibbits had been trying to sell the place ever since the brand-new Sonic Drive-In had gone up next door, pulling all his customers to the right like a stiff wind. Tater Tots and milkshakes, and you didn't even have to get out of your car. Chip couldn't compete with that. Zabbo's had sat for three long years with a For Sale sign in the weeds by the road, so he was happy to take MRED's four hundred a month for rent.

Ernest Adcock knew this wasn't the ideal location—particularly as it still looked just like the diner it'd once been, with teal-and-white-striped awnings and a big letter "Z" up on top of the roof. It had taken him two weeks to figure out how to turn that thing off. But he also knew it was the only place MRED could afford. It'd been remarkable how fast rents had risen downtown as soon as landlords heard who they were and what they were trying to do.

Ernest had graduated last summer from Duke with a major in public policy and a new propensity toward activism that worried his parents and confounded his friends. When, that same summer, the university's president had the statue of Robert E. Lee removed from the college chapel, all Ernest could think about was the Confederate statue that had stood in his hometown's park for the whole of his life. He decided to take a year off, stay home, and work to get it removed. Those things have been coming down all over the country, he thought. Why, Mayor Landrieu had already been able to get four down in New Orleans alone— *four!*—and Louisiana was at least as obdurate as Georgia. Ernest was hopeful, as most twenty-one-year-olds are.

Oh, he'd known it'd be hard going, he'd told his volunteers that, but to his surprise word got out and donations started coming in, more than enough to pay for the monthly rent and printing up some flyers. But it had been the media coverage that had really taken the lid off the pot. One snippet on the local ten o'clock news had been picked up statewide, then regionwide, then before Ernest knew it, there he was, being interviewed for a national PBS program on the ever-evolving reckoning of racial issues in the South. His parents hadn't known whether to be proud or embarrassed.

Of course, if he'd been more experienced in the beginning, he'd never have chosen that name. Being born a long thirty-one years after Mr. Ed trotted across the TV screens of America, Ernest had never even heard of the horse or his sitcom, so when the older generation of Wesleyan began to utilize the acronym for laughs, his confusion only seemed to add to their hilarity. But it hadn't been until the morning Old Man Griffin walked into Zabbo's (Ernest still had a hard time seeing the building as anything else) that he'd fully realized just what he was up against. This was an unusual case, as Porter Griffin made crystal clear to him while he stood in MRED's makeshift office, staring a hole straight through Ernest, all the while never raising his voice above a whisper.

"I've dedicated my life to keeping that statue up, son. It belongs to me. The whole damn park belongs to me. And it ain't going nowhere. Hell, my daddy must have been some kind of wizard, seeing way into the future like he did. He must've known there'd come a day when city governments would turn traitor and decide to pull these monuments to history down around our ears. Bunch of cowards. That's why he didn't let 'em have it. Kept it in the family, so you liberal types couldn't tell us what's best.

"Now, I ain't got nothing against you personally, boy. I know you probably see me as just some old man who don't know his butt from a hole in the ground, and that's fine by me. But you listen here. I know this one thing, and you'd do good to remember it. I know if you don't protect your culture, they'll take it right out from under you. You'll look around one day and you won't even know who you are anymore. You'll look like everybody else, act like everybody else. We'll all just be the same."

"We are all the same, Mr. Griffin. That's the whole point."

The conversation, if it could accurately be called such, ended there. Porter Griffin walked out the door and spat on the ground. In less than an hour Ernest Adcock heard from the old man's lawyer, and before Ernest really knew what was happening, the entire town of Wesleyan seemed to have taken sides and drawn swords. It was enough to make you doubt yourself, not to mention other people.

At ten in the morning, Ernest's black Honda slid sideways into Zabbo's parking lot with all the grace of a rooster. He'd worried about the leak in the back of the building, unsure if the old roof would be able to hold up both that big letter "Z" and a blanket of ice, but as soon as Mrs. Pearson had called to tell his mother about the statue being down and Porter Griffin being dead, Ernest knew he had much bigger worries than a leak in the roof.

He'd just completed a quick tour and, relieved to find everything dry and intact, had plugged in the coffeemaker and turned on the heat, when he heard an almighty crash. Sticking his head around the storeroom door, he was just in time to see a faded blue pickup truck charge out of the parking lot, its back wheels pulling hard to the right as it tried to stay in the road. Amid all the glass that covered the checkerboard floor lay a brick as big as Ernest Adcock's forearm.

Will sat at Porter Griffin's kitchen table watching a turkey buzzard stomp along the old brick wall that surrounded what was left of the rose garden, putting one three-toed foot in front of the other, and bobbing its chapped red head as though in agreement with itself.

He was waiting on the EMT guys to get there. He'd called them as a matter of procedure, but Lurlene Pearson had been right: Old Man Griffin was about as dead as anybody could be. She'd told him to call Macon Hargis, and he had, though Hargis's reaction hadn't exactly been brimming with compassion.

"Good God. Today? He had to die *today*?"

"Well, Mr. Hargis, I'm sure he didn't plan his departure to inconvenience you, or me. You don't have to come if you don't want to. As I told you, I just didn't know who else to call. Lurlene Pearson was here with her husband, and they said they'd never heard tell of him having any family in town. Or any friends either, at least none that they knew of. Seems Mrs. Pearson checks in on the old man every now and then. She told me to call you."

"Lurlene Pearson." Will heard Macon curse in barnyard fashion. "Well, it'll be all over town by now. I better get over there. Give me thirty minutes. My wife's got my truck, and I don't know what my driveway's like." He hung up without saying goodbye, which was exactly what Will had expected.

If he had thirty minutes, Will figured, he might as well take a look across the street, and see if he could find anything that might point the way to discovering what exactly had gone on in the night. Pulling on his gloves, he slipped and slid down the icy drive and into the silent cold of the park, pretending not to see Mayor Mac Baker's red pickup slide sideways through the stop sign at the corner, discreetly turning his head as Mac veered past him with a pained, slightly panicked, look on his face. If the mayor was heading to his office on a Sunday morning, Will thought, then the news was getting out.

He stared at the rubble around his feet, kicking a few clods of old marble with his boot. There were no tire tracks to be seen—not that any car could wedge itself between the opening in that wrought-iron gate anyway—and it was so shady in here, the ice hadn't stuck to the brick pathways, so no footprints were visible anywhere. He squatted and stared at a few bits here and there, picked up a few things, measured a few things. What a mess, he thought. Despite himself, Will couldn't help but feel a bit of relief that old Porter Griffin had seen fit to pop his clogs before he was able to cause the God-a'mighty ruckus he would have caused about this. It was when he was leaving that he saw it. A rope, raggedly cut and still tied in a fat knot around what remained of a stone horse's hoof. He picked it up and put it in the trunk of his car as he made his way back up to the house.

He was in the kitchen warming his hands over a burner on the stove when he heard Macon Hargis bang on the back door.

"He's upstairs?" Macon said, as he laid his briefcase on the table and headed down the hall.

"He is," Will replied, calling after him. "The EMT guys are still up there, but you go on ahead it you want. I'll wait here."

Macon returned in less than five minutes and Will was gratified to see the paleness on his face. There's nothing like death to lower you down to everyone else's level, he thought.

"You want a drink of water?" Will asked.

"Yeah, if you've got one."

Will found a juice glass in the cabinet, ran it full of tap water, and handed it to Macon. The two men sat down across from each other at the kitchen table.

"I guess you noticed that statue's been knocked down last night," Will said.

"What?" Macon set his glass down sharp. "Well, that probably explains it, I guess. Him falling out dead right in front of that window. One look, and . . . Good God."

"Well, we don't know what happened. Time of death, or nothing like that. Not yet."

"You want to take a bet on what killed him?"

"Not allowed to, sir. Not in my line of work."

Will stood up and walked to the window. Still trying to lift off into the air, the turkey buzzard had made it as far as the first limb of a dogwood. "So was Mrs. Pearson correct?" he asked. "The old man's got no family?"

"Not a soul that I know of. Of course, I'll go to the office and look through everything to make sure, but he's never mentioned anybody. He's got a will, I think, we drew it up years ago, but I don't remember . . ." Macon's voice trailed off, his mind on a journey back to the rainy morning when he'd watched Old Man Griffin sign that particular document.

The things we forget are so often more important than those we remember. Macon could've told you what he was wearing the first time his father took him fishing, could still see the little red-and-white plaid shirt as clearly as the flowers on the juice glass he'd just set down on the table. But a twenty-minute meeting thirty years ago had been completely erased from his mind, leaving not even a tracing of detail, in spite of its obvious significance. Outside, chunks of ice were letting go of the tree limbs. They hit the driveway like dropped china cups, and as Macon listened to them fall his heart did the same thing, right straight down to his shoes.

18

MARIETTA
AND HARRY

"Oh, hell! My pear tree!" Butter's wail erupted before Gordon put the Hummer into park. The limbs of the Bradford pear that stood by Butter's door were bent toward the ground under the weight of the ice, leaving only one standing tall in the middle.

"God, Fluffy," said Gordon. "It looks like a peeled banana."

"You." Butter turned and pointed a red-nailed finger in Gordon's face. "You get out and help me. Since I'm here there might be a few more things I need to get, and you're going to carry them."

"Me? Why? I don't know how you expect—"

"Yes, you," Butter cut him off cleanly. "Get out. Now."

Gordon didn't bother to turn around and plead his case to Marietta but managed to make a show of climbing out of the Hummer with a lot of groans and sighs. Marietta and Glinda watched from the warmth of the car as Butter and Gordon stepped cautiously up the sidewalk. Butter took out her key, and the two of them disappeared inside.

The Hummer was silent. Next to Marietta, Glinda's head was rested on the back of the seat, her eyes closed, a clear signal that conversation was not something she wanted. This was fine with Marietta. Earlier, it had crossed her mind to call Macon, but she'd been stopped by a curious new feeling of loyalty toward Glinda. Whatever the problem was between them, Marietta knew immediately that she would be on her sister-in-law's side. This should have made her sad, she knew, but she felt sad only that she wasn't.

For so long, Macon had seemed to Marietta like a leaf from another limb of the family tree. A relative, someone bound to her by blood, but never as close as a brother. He was nine years older, and they'd never played together, never listened to records or gone to the movies; he was certainly no one she'd ever confided in. She couldn't remember Macon in the days when there wasn't the taut, inaudible tension stretched out between him and their father, a tension that seemed, to her, to have coagulated into indifference by the time Logan died. While Logan was enduring his final illness, she'd found her mother in tears after Macon's stilted, formal visits enough times to know that Caroline had been just as hurt by him as Marietta had been confused. She supposed she loved her brother in the way you love family, but she didn't like him very much, and she resented the pain this caused her.

A movement outside made her turn toward the window just in time to see a crow light down on the crest of the cupola adorning Butter's roof. Large, and black as obsidian, the bird stood out against the sky like a hole in a white blanket. It stared down at Marietta with something akin to sentience, as if it somehow recognized her face. She wiped her breath from the window to get a better look. Suddenly the veil between what's real and imagined seemed threadbare, and Marietta realized with a chill that she had no one to tell. She leaned back into her seat.

Then Glinda, her eyes still closed, said softly, "Marietta, I want to hear about Harry. Please. Tell me the whole story."

Marietta was normally so private that had this been a normal day she might have seen the question as something akin to intrusion, but on this strange, frozen afternoon she was surprised to suddenly find herself wanting nothing more than to tell the sister-in-law with whom she'd never had a meaningful conversation the now precious story of how her life began with Harry. She told it like a fairy tale, staring out the window, and spoke, unguarded, in a whisper . . .

He collected feathers, I learned that the first day I met him . . .

It had rained and rained the summer after she came back from Atlanta. When it finally stopped, humidity continued to jelly the air for weeks. The wooden seats of the benches lining the courthouse felt spongy and soft, like wet cardboard boxes, well into August. It had been late on one such miserable afternoon and she'd decided to go for a walk, pulling her long red hair up into a ponytail and donning a white linen dress, the least amount of clothing one could get away with without inviting unwanted stares.

She'd been standing on the sidewalk waiting to cross the street when Gerald Pinckney cut the corner too close in his new maroon Pacer, driving right through the middle of a puddle too deep to have dried in the sun. Unbeknownst to Gerald, he drove off leaving the bottom half of Marietta's dress doused in brown water, which stank to high heaven of material whose origin she didn't wish to know, and whose removal instantly became her immediate concern.

After ducking quickly into Mama's Way Cafe, hoping that most of its chairs would be empty at that time of day, she was ushered toward the ladies' room by Myrna, the afternoon waitress. Marietta rinsed off her bare legs and the hem of her white dress as best she could, finally reentering the restaurant holding her sandals in her hand, looking as though she'd been wading in the creek, and took a seat at the bar.

Myrna had mixed up the orders, giving the whiskey to the bearded man with his head in a book and the lemonade to Marietta, probably a natural mistake. And their conversation, being handed such an easy start, was only ten minutes old when they moved to a booth and ordered lunch. They were still sitting there hours later, talking and laughing, as the dinner crowd swelled then thinned back down to no one but them.

He wore a rust-red feather in the pocket of his crisp white shirt, and she had asked him why. "It's a pheasant feather," he'd said, bending his chin toward his chest to look at it closely. "I just got back from England, up in the Lake District, and I swear they're all over the road in some places. Seems like pheasants always choose the worst possible moment to charge out in front of a car, poor guys. Kinda like possums down here. But they're such pretty things, pheasants, that is. Actually, I pick up all kinds of feathers whenever I see them. They sort of remind me . . . well . . . I guess they remind me of grace. And oh . . . I don't know, that sometimes the lightest, most beautiful things are the most powerful? Know what I mean? You see these tiny little birds, weighing hardly anything, and they can lift right off the ground without even thinking about it, right up into the air as easy as song. Keeps me in my place, I guess. When you think what all it takes for man to fly, birds seem to know so much we don't. Anyway, I collect them. Feathers, that is, not birds."

She fell in love before he finished that last five-word sentence.

Cline's Antiques had for years been owned by Nina and Ivanhoe Cline, Harry's great-aunt and great-uncle. Though his family lived in Asheville, as a kid he'd spent every summer with Nina and Ivan, helping them dig through dusty barns and spider-webbed attics all over England and France, ferreting out long-forgotten treasures and art to bring home to Georgia and restore to their former, often historical, glory. Only when they were pristine would the pieces make their way onto the shop floor, and Harry soon discovered he had no small amount of talent in making that possible. Though surprised by his enthusiasm, his mother, who had his four older brothers to keep out of trouble all summer long, was grateful he wanted to go to his aunt and uncle's each and every year.

Harry learned early on that you couldn't make a fortune from this sort of life, but you could make a living, and more importantly, you could be happy. He loved the whole process: the travel, the hunt, the smell of the polish, the feel of the wood. Most of all he loved the reclamation of beauty. Whenever he delivered a dining table or bookcase to a client and saw it ensconced in its new home, he couldn't help but see it as it had been when they'd found it: languishing in some farmer's barn where it would have no doubt remained, were it not for his aunt's eagle eye. Harry found he was susceptible to that sort of satisfaction.

Years later, after he'd come to the realization that his newly minted degree in structural engineering was destined to provide him with a life he'd probably hate, Nina and Ivan up and decided to retire and move to Greece, surprising everyone but themselves. They asked Harry if he wanted the shop for his own, and he moved down to Wesleyan without one second thought. He'd been there only three months when Marietta was served his lemonade by mistake.

She began to work in Harry's shop that summer; he needed the help, and she needed to get her mind off Atlanta. While cataloging and labeling the antiques, she listened as he talked about the beautiful things with mysterious histories that filled the corners of the store, watched his eyes light up whenever a new shipment arrived, more bounty from his most recent trips to Europe. She began to feel lighter without actually realizing it, began to find enormous pleasure in things she'd barely noticed before: that particular slant of the light that signals summer's departure on an otherwise sweltering September morning, the way a weed can look like a flower when it pushes its face up through a concrete sidewalk, the colorful variations of feathers. Flycatchers, robins, seagulls, and rooks. He kept them in glass boxes all over the shop.

It had always surprised Marietta to look back and realize how little thought she gave to her answer when Harry asked her to go with him that fall on a buying trip to the Scottish Northern Isles in search of authentic Orkney chairs for a client eager to furnish her North Carolina home with the furniture of her ancestors. He'd been shy when he asked her. "This lady wants old chairs, not reproductions, and I've heard you can still find some up near Stromness. I won't sugarcoat it. It's a long way, and this time of year the weather will be less than salubrious. But I don't know, you seem like the kind of person who might need a trip like this."

Marietta said yes right then, and it was during that journey to and from Orkney that the two of them discovered four hooded chairs in perfect condition along with a desire to never be apart. She came home with an engagement ring on her hand, a silver band of Celtic knots and tiny emeralds . . .

Glinda had taken Marietta's hand halfway through the story. Now as silence filled the car once again, she gave it a squeeze and said, "Thank you."

Two minutes later they heard Gordon and Butter coming back down the walk. It had begun to snow slightly, swirling flakes so tiny they looked like grains of salt. Butter was holding her pillow close to her chest, and Gordon was carrying two overstuffed grocery sacks, one that clanged with wine bottles. As they opened their doors and climbed in, Butter said, "I had some fresh salmon in there, and I don't know about you all, but I don't want any of those casserole things people have brought, so I'm doing the cooking tonight. Something good. I brought my very best champagne, the stuff they gave me when my billboard went up."

" 'Once more unto the breach,' " said Gordon as he scrambled back into the driver's seat, steeling himself for the ride home. As he haltingly pulled out into the drive, Marietta glanced back up to the cupola. The bird was still there, staring down at the Hummer with an unrelenting focus. Quietly, she turned in her seat as they pulled away, in no way surprised to see the great black wings unfurl as the bird lifted up from the roofline to follow her home.

19

JOCELYN, MACON, MAYOR BAKER, AND ERNEST

Ernest Adcock should never have called his mother to tell her about the brick. Worried, Betsy Adcock called her friend Henrietta Pierce. Henrietta called her cousin Libby, and that call was interrupted by Libby's daughter in Savannah, who later told her aunt up in Metter, who ended up talking to her son in Locust Grove, and so, more rapid than eagles, the story inched closer and closer to a cold and rainy Atlanta, where Jocelyn Shaw sat at her desk at home working on what she knew was a fairly trivial story for the nightly news, and one she feared hadn't a prayer of making it to air. When she got the call from her photographer, Kevin, telling her what he'd just heard when he'd phoned his mother down in Flippen, all about some Confederate statue that'd been pulled down in the middle of an ice storm in a little town called Wesleyan, her nose went up like a hound dog's smelling steak, and in less than an hour she and Kevin were on Highway 75 headed south, Jocelyn putting on her makeup as they went.

When they passed the city limits sign, they found a silent Wes-leyan, every window and door shut tighter than a coffin lid. Joc-elyn had done her research on the drive down and knew where she wanted to start, so at three-thirty that afternoon they pulled up in front of the office of MRED, with its big letter "Z" on the roof and a jagged round hole in the plate-glass front window.

Ernest was struggling to cover the hole with a blue tarp he'd hurried down to Harlan's Hardware and bought for that purpose. He knew he'd need to get some boards nailed up for the job to be done properly, but he wanted to stop the cold wind from get-ting in as fast as he could, before his fingers froze off and he had to pick them up from the floor one by one. His volunteers had stayed home, and he could hardly fault them for that decision; not wanting any more trouble, he hadn't even called the police. His head shot up like a meerkat's the second he heard the car. One more brick through the window, and Ernest was done.

Jocelyn strode in, stepping over the shards of glass as though it was something she did every day. She stuck a red-gloved hand out from the arm of a navy wool coat and introduced herself. Ernest rubbed his right palm on his trouser leg and shook her hand.

"This is terrible, Mr. Adcock. I'm just so glad you weren't injured." Jocelyn tilted her head and stared him straight in the eyes. "We'd like to do a story for the Channel 46 News in Atlanta on what's happened. The persecution you've received here this morning." She kicked some of the glass away with her foot. "I'm assuming you believe it's because of the statue being removed in the night? People blame you for that, do you think?"

Ernest broke her gaze with difficulty and returned to his work. "Well, I suppose they do, or if they don't right now, they will before the day's over." He tore a piece of masking tape off the roll with his teeth. "Right now, Ms. Shaw, they're on their phones, hashing and rehashing what's happened. The statue's owner died this morning, you know. People are still processing these two things. One coming right on the heels of the other, as it were. They'll get around to blame soon enough." He looked over to Kevin and nodded in the direction of the blue tarp hanging slack at the other end of the hole in the window. "Would you mind holding that up so I can tape it?" Kevin set his camera down and picked up the tarp.

"To be honest," Ernest continued, "I don't want to talk on camera right now." He leaned around Kevin and taped up the blue tarp, immediately changing the light and the mood of the room to something strange and aquatic. "It'll be better if I just stay quiet. I'm sorry."

Jocelyn knew all the best interviews started like this. It was always the people who didn't want to talk who had the best things to say. She had many cards to play in situations such as this, and she reached for the one most reliable. "Oh, but, *Ernest*—may I call you Ernest?—just think of all the people who've experienced this kind of bigotry. And it's rising all over the country right now. Stop and consider how many people you can *help* by speaking out, not only about what you've been attempting to accomplish here in Wesleyan—working to get that Confederate statue re-moved? . . . why surely you know there are many people just like you, all over *this* part of the country especially, who are trying to do the same thing—but people also need to hear about the *conse-quences* of this kind of work, the dangers, if you will. They need to know what's still out there. They need an example of courage, of *commitment* in these times. And *you* can give them that. This could be the one good thing to come out of all this." She gestured around the glassy mess that covered the black-and-white floor without ever allowing her gaze to slip from the centers of Ernest Adcock's eyes.

Macon had driven straight to his office, his silver Audi fishtailing twice on the slick roads. The fragments of memory that had flashed through his mind in Porter Griffin's kitchen had begun to link together, forming something he recognized, and by the time he'd opened the old man's file he pretty much knew what he'd find. He couldn't believe he'd forgotten.

It had been a gallbladder attack thirty years ago that had given

Old Man Griffin the first real indication that mortality was an ecumenical concept. He'd doubled over in the middle of his Sunday lunch, convinced his heart was about to explode, certain that he wouldn't live to see the sun set. The relief when he'd found out differently had been tempered with the now inescapable realization that he wasn't going to be the first man allowed a pass but was, in fact, going to die like everyone else.

For Porter, knowing he had no relatives left on the planet, the possibility of everything he owned, especially Griffin Park—his father's pride and joy—going to the *state,* of all places, triggered an apoplexy impossible to bear. He ran to plop his bottom in the chair across from Macon's desk the minute he was released from the hospital.

"Hell, just put *your* name down," Porter had told his lawyer. "I'll figure out where I want it all to go later, and we'll redo it then. But I don't want to live one more second thinking everything I have might go to the government."

After being well and truly convinced there were no relatives available to receive all the man's worldly goods, Macon had tried to convince him to leave it to a charity. "Or, you know, some individual you deem worthy," he'd said.

"Dammit, Macon. I deem *you* worthy. I've watched your career, son. You're smart, and I think we share the same values, you know, deep down. You won't do anything stupid with it all. And it's just for now. Until I decide something different."

Old Man Griffin—the proud owner of that appellation even then—had left Macon's office that rainy morning promising to look into deserving charities that might benefit from his largesse upon death, and Macon, fully expecting him to do that, had stuck the will into the file drawer, never anticipating his eventual ownership of what he knew to be a fortune. The will had dropped deeper and deeper in his mind, each year landing like a shovelful of soil, until now as he bent over it the words before him seemed as unlikely as snow in the month of July.

Macon sat down, hard. The news of the morning was the shiny object he'd needed to make people look the other way. If he'd prayed for something to erase the memory of his humiliation at Micheline's yesterday, he couldn't have been blessed any better. But the ramifications of Porter's will were tricky; any one of them could push Macon into corners he might be reluctant to go.

He swiveled his chair toward the door and away from the window. Old Man Griffin would have insisted on prosecution for whoever was responsible for destroying the statue of Henry Benning, even if it'd been one of the nuns over at Mercy Convent. Macon knew this in the marrow of his bones as well as he knew he'd have acted on his client's wishes with all the focus of a cobra, never questioning, never disagreeing. But now the statue was his. (Hell, the whole *park* was his.) If he chose the route his client would've taken, he'd be speaking for himself alone. What *he* wanted. What *he* believed.

The cards he now held in his hands were hot ones and he knew it. Make a wrong play and he could get burned so badly he'd be even worse off than he'd been last night, lying alone and awake in his bed, playing the restaurant scene over and over in his mind, concerned he'd finally met a mountain he couldn't scale. Macon had been given a second chance, and he had to get it right.

It was supposed to be so easy. After twenty-eight years this was his final term—a swan song, a victory lap. Mayor Mac Baker had won the last election with a fat majority of every demographic in Wesleyan, something no other mayor had done since before the blacks got the vote. Everybody loved him, even if they couldn't have told you one of his policies, and nobody wanted him to retire. But after seven terms they had to admit, Mayor Baker had earned his rest.

It was that two-week vacation in Montana that finally did it for Mac. A landscape he'd never dreamed possible had turned his head right around on his shoulders and caused him to wonder just what else he'd been missing. When he came back home to Wesleyan everything he saw looked smaller. Suddenly his office seemed so airless he could barely breathe; he felt crowded and pinched in the grocery store aisle. On his daily walk to city hall the moss-draped trees hanging over the sidewalk blocked out the sky, making him feel claustrophobic and blue. The town of his birth seemed to him now as confining as the glass of a snow globe, and in less than three months after coming home from Montana he told the city council that he wouldn't run again. He only wished now he'd done it sooner.

It had been wishful thinking to expect the venom spewing out from the nation's capital to sidestep his city, but the mayor had managed to keep the taps on low these past couple of years. He was traditional enough to believe it was his job to represent everyone, whether he agreed with—or even liked—them at all. He really tried to make every decision for the good of the city, no matter what people said or how hard they tried to pull him in the direction they wanted him to go. He genuinely loved Wesleyan and figured most of its citizens were just doing the best they could to make it through life with as little trouble as possible. But he wasn't a fool. Mac Baker had grown up here, and he was well aware of what still ran beneath the streets of his hometown. There were those, and he knew most of them by name, who'd been itching for years to crawl out, put their hands around the neck of time, and drag it backward. For over a quarter of a century, he'd worked hard to deny them that chance, and for the most part he'd been successful. If it hadn't been for that damn statue in that damn park, the last year wouldn't have been so hard. And now, just when he had only ten months to go, all hell was about to break loose.

Mac slipped on the sidewalk for the third time and let out a string of profanity that should have melted whatever ice remained in his path. He grabbed hold of a stop sign and caught his breath. An ice storm, and a Sunday, to boot. By rights he should be tucked up by his own fire with his first Irish coffee of the afternoon. Goddamn the late Porter Griffin, and goddamn his statue. Well, at least the office would be warm. Bless Lucy-Jewel's heart. He'd hated to ask her to come in today.

Mayor Baker tried not to curse in front of his staff, especially his young secretary, but when she stuck her head into his office a couple of hours later to tell him that a reporter and her photographer from Atlanta were outside requesting a statement, he broke that rule in such spectacular fashion that Lucy-Jewel's face turned scarlet and the mayor had to add embarrassment to the list of disagreeable emotions he'd experienced since first waking up to the news of the morning. When Jocelyn Shaw was shown in she wasn't greeted with a smile.

If he'd had it to do over again, Ernest would never have said what he said. He wouldn't have mentioned the phrase "white privilege," would never have brought up the president, or the Baptist church. He certainly wouldn't have accused Porter Griffin's daddy of being in the Klan. But he'd been mad, and there wasn't a thing he could do about it now. It didn't do him any good to blame Jocelyn Shaw, even if, as he honestly thought, with all those sympathetic questions and commiserating nods, she'd led him into the weeds as sure as if she'd had a bit in his mouth.

As he drove home, he thought . . . Maybe it'll be all right. Maybe people will understand how easy it is to be coaxed into saying things out loud that you only ever say in your head. I'm only human. And I could have been killed with that brick, so it's not like I didn't have cause to be angry. Surely people will understand that. Maybe nobody will see it. Maybe most of the power's still out . . .

20

BUTTER, WILL, BRADY, AND IVY

Seeing her house in the light of day had been thoroughly dispiriting for Butter. It looked even worse than she'd thought. She'd called the insurance company before she called Christo, pleased with herself for being able to let her son know that she had everything under control and didn't need his help in the slightest. "What? Oh no, I don't need a place to stay. I'm over at Marietta's."

She set the alarm on her phone, giving herself an hour and a half to nap. She was exhausted, and having promised to cook dinner for everyone, she didn't trust herself to wake up in time. She pulled the white sheets up to her chin, grateful to Marietta for insisting they all lie down for a while and rest. Butter wasn't even conscious of falling asleep.

It was a dream she'd had before. Like magic, it had years ago lifted up off the pages of a book she'd been required to read for Mrs. Traylor's tenth-grade English class; she hadn't even realized the story had made an impression, couldn't even remember the title. But the words of the author had melted inside her, and the dream they'd created was always clear, never fading. It was as fickle as fair weather; she couldn't count on it—it came when it chose to, sometimes skipping years between visits, but always leaving her wistful and breathless when it did come.

. . . She is lying on her back in an orchard, a thousand apple trees in full bloom. The breeze blows pale petals over her face. She is being lifted up, lifted up bodily and carried, by someone very strong. She's sure it's a man, but like no one she knows; he's much larger and swifter, and he carries her as lightly as if she were a sheaf of wheat. She never sees him, but even with her eyes closed, she can tell he's like sunlight; there's a smell of ripe corn-fields about him. She always feels him approach, bend over, and lift her up in his arms to carry her silently away . . . always the same, always the same . . .

The ringer on Butter's phone was turned down so the notes of the familiar song sounded a long way off. It took two full cho-ruses to wake her. She recognized the deep voice the moment she heard it, and just as the dream broke apart into slivers of color, Butter saw Will Cochran's face receding into nothingness amid the falling white blossoms of a thousand apple trees.

Will told himself it was just part of the job. Having seen Macon Hargis's Hummer being driven out of town with those four peo-ple inside it, he'd known Macon's wife would've had to pass by the park on her way to The Glade to pick them up right around the time Porter Griffin died. He was just being thorough to ask the woman if she'd seen anything, and since Butter was obvi-ously with her now, and he had Butter's number here at the ready, it just made sense to call her. It wasn't until the moment he heard Butter's slightly sleepy voice that he knew his excuse was nothing less than a lie.

"Hello, Mrs. Swann. It's Detective Cochran. W . . . Will

Cochran." He couldn't believe his voice really cracked. How long had it been since he'd done this? "Did I, I mean, I didn't wake you, did I?"

"Well, to be perfectly honest, you did." He heard Butter yawn. "But it's all right. I promised everybody I'd cook dinner, so I shouldn't really be sleeping at all. I would ask if you're calling about my house, but I'm not going to be fooled by you again, *Detective.*" She drew that word out the same way she'd done when she called him Freddie, and Will grinned on the other end of the line.

So absorbed in his work he'd forgotten his breakfast and lunch, Brady finished the charcoal sketch around four, then made himself an omelet and poured a glass of wine. These he enjoyed while sitting in front of the easel, trying to determine if this was actually the start of something worthwhile, or merely a momentary infatuation with an idea that would lose its attraction as the days went on and end up making him wish he'd never started.

It was hard to paint portraits, he hardly ever enjoyed it, but it was something like sorcery when it worked, and as such, nearly always worth the trouble. With the meager tools of brush and paint he knew he could create an image more veridical than any mirror, but success required something as unreliable as it was essential: a connection with the subject that could never be studied or planned, a silent intimacy that existed far beyond love or friendship, or sometimes, even basic respect. He still remembered the best one he'd ever done, of a man that he'd truly hated. Brady often wondered if the fellow ever noticed his own noxious personality so accurately caught in the strokes of the brush.

Painting from memory was more difficult, of course, but this wasn't a commission, it didn't have to be accurate. And he usually knew from the first sketch if it was going to work. So often the eyes would tell him. Get those right and the rest of the painting would rise up around him and breathe. But if at the end of this one initial sketch, the eyes held no hope of light—no inchoate scrutiny thrown back toward him to keep him on his toes, no embryonic bit of judgment, or sadness, or joy . . . well, he'd rather paint a blue jay.

These particular eyes held promise. Already he could feel them staring out at him, questioning, sizing him up, so as the day dimmed and the ground outside began to refreeze, Brady took up his oil paints hoping for that magic reciprocity, and began to bring the face of Glinda Hargis to life.

Ivy sat in her window seat, a pair of binoculars beside her, an open book in her lap. Her finger rested on the color photograph of a black bird, while her eyes were trained on an identical creature sitting on Marietta's windowsill. When Thea came in, Ivy didn't turn around.

"Mom sent me to bring you down for dinner. She made mac and cheese. Isn't it cold in that window?" Thea asked, hugging herself for warmth.

"It's not so bad. I've stuffed a rolled-up towel on the sill to stop the draft. Come over here a minute. I want you to see something."

Thea crossed the room and Ivy scooted over so she could sit beside her. She handed her sister the binoculars. "Look over there, on Marietta's window. See that big bird? What do you suppose that is?"

Thea held the binoculars up to her eyes and stared for a good minute before saying, "Well, it's a . . . a crow, I guess. A big one."

"Yeah, but it's not. See, look here." Ivy pointed down to the picture in the book she was holding. "See how his feathers are all shaggy underneath his beak? And see how the beak is kinda hooked-like, on top? And his back feathers aren't right for a crow, either. I think that's a raven. And he's been right out there since early this morning, except for when Marietta went off with those people who're staying at her house. I've been watching. When Marietta came home, it came back. It's a raven."

"Oh, come on, Ivy. You've been reading too many fairy tales. We don't have ravens in Georgia. It's just an old crow."

Just then the bird stretched out its black wings and rose up into the milky air. The girls watched as it circled the Clines' garden a few times, painting the white ground with a graceful black shadow. Finally, it swooped down into the empty arms of the tallest poplar tree and assumed its position of watching the house.

"See? You've never seen a crow with wings that big. Have you?" Ivy said to Thea, eyes wide.

"Well, I don't know, Ivy. I guess not." Thea turned from the window and rose. "But so what? What does it matter?" Sticking a bookmark between the pages of her book, Ivy followed her sister. As the two girls went downstairs, Ivy said, "You know, in Cornwall they say that King Arthur didn't really die but was magically transformed into a raven."

"King Arthur wasn't real, Ivy."

"Oh, yes, he was. I'll lend you the book."

Thea pushed her sister into the kitchen with a laugh.

21

BUTTER, MARIETTA, GORDON, GLINDA, AND JOCELYN

Butter was listening to Bobby Darin sing "Beyond the Sea," a song that always cheered her. She'd kept the radio down low so as not to wake the others, but every now and then a pan clattered, or the oven door slammed a bit louder than she intended and she silently cursed herself. It was hard to cook dinner quietly.

She'd found a white cloth and blue napkins in the cabinet next to the refrigerator, pretty pale green glass plates in the one beside the sink, and had even braved the spitting snow to cut a few nandina branches full of red berries for the center of the table. The salad was made, the potatoes in the oven, the wine was chilled. Now she was waiting before she put the salmon in the pan, hoping the others would come in without her having to wake them. She looked forward to seeing the looks on their faces when she told them Porter Griffin had died.

"You're kidding," she'd said when Will gave her the news on the phone.

He'd heard that response at least a half dozen times already today. "I am not," he replied.

"But what a *coincidence,* don't you think? To drop dead on the very same morning, and from what you say, almost at the very same *time* he saw that thing was gone. Gives me goosebumps to think about it. Do they know what killed him yet?"

"No. But I mean, you know, he was pretty old."

"Yeah." Butter paused. "Kinda sad when you think about it."

If she were being honest, though, Butter didn't have a whole lot of sympathy on reserve for Old Man Griffin. For years she'd thought the way he clung to that statue like a drowning man was almost silly. It was all so long ago. What on earth did it matter?

But that night last August when she'd sat across her dinner table from her grandson and his new girlfriend, listening as they talked about Henry Benning—who he'd been, the things he'd said—looking at the passion on Peter's face and the slight embarrassment on Thea's, Butter had felt her throat constrict and found it difficult to talk. From then on, to her, the statue was far from benign. She could feel the thing staring at her every time she drove past.

There were many things she'd change about her life, given the opportunity. She would have finished college, for instance. She wouldn't have married as young as she had. But taken as a whole, Butter knew her life had been easy. She'd never worried about the things Thea's family had worried about. She'd never had to. She was used to talking her way out of traffic tickets with a smile and a joke, used to being welcomed in every church or fancy store, used to people meeting her eye and nodding whenever she passed them on the street. She'd never once seriously worried that Christo might be in danger walking down any street in America.

Her mother had always said nothing good came from talking about race. Over the past six months, Butter had begun to wonder if any good could ever come without talking about it.

.   .   .

There are some things you just don't understand until grief learns your name. Marietta had always wondered why mirrors are some-times covered in houses of mourning, but catching a glimpse of her reflection as she left her bedroom gave her one secular reason, at least. Her hair was a mess, her clothes were wrinkled, and the expression on her ashen face said she had neither the desire nor the capacity to fix them. It was better just not to look. Followed like a shadow by Smudge, she was the first one to enter the kitchen.

Butter jumped up, got her a glass of wine, and pulled out a chair, which Marietta ignored. "Let's sit in here instead," she said, nodding into the library, where the fire was still simmering. Mar-ietta coiled herself into the corner of the sofa; Smudge hopped up beside her. Butter poured a glass and followed, sitting back in a wide-shouldered chair and staring out at what remained of the day as the sun slipped underneath the white earth.

Marietta watched her, unnoticed. You never really know when a childhood friendship begins, she thought. Unlike the ones we forge as adults, there isn't that one particular moment you remember meeting the other for the first time. Butter had just always been. She was so interwoven in Marietta's memories of childhood, pull out her threads and the tapestry might just fall apart.

Marietta remembered the day it ended, though. The day she couldn't listen to Butter's nonsense any longer and snapped at her in a way disallowed by friendship. She hadn't meant to end it, though, had she? To need Butter as much as she did now made Marietta feel ashamed, almost dishonest. Had she truly thought Harry was the only person she'd ever really need in her life? Without preamble, she surprised herself by blurting out, "I'm so sorry, Butter."

Butter looked up, and Marietta saw a blush creep up Butter's neck and onto her face. "What?" she asked. "Sorry? For what? I'm the one who should be sorry. Crashing into your house when I know you probably just want to be by yourself. I'm sure I'll be able to be out of here by the end of the week, and I—"

"No, Butter," Marietta interrupted. "Let me say this, okay? I'm sorry about what happened between us. That awful lunch five years ago. I shouldn't have snapped at you in public like that. But . . ." She pinched the tip of her nose to stop from tearing up. "But, worse than that . . . I should never have just let you slip out of my life like I did. I think, well, I was just arrogant enough to believe Harry was the only person I'd ever really need in my life. But that's just not true. I'm really glad you're here, Butter. Glad you all are here."

Gordon came in from the sunroom just then and Marietta saw Butter smile in a way she'd not seen since they were twelve.

They were about to go up and wake Glinda when she came downstairs on her own, still halfway lost in the pages of her book. The faces arranging themselves around the dining table seemed like those of people she only halfway knew. Gordon, energized by his nap, pulled out her chair, and she sat.

Without her usual armor of perfect hair, perfect dress, and perfect makeup, Glinda was so different none of them was sure how to relate to her. It was as though in breaking apart as she'd apparently done, she'd revealed a person they didn't know. Her hair hung loose around her shoulders—it was longer than they'd thought, thick and white as a dove's wing—and it made her seem, inexplicably, younger. The other three tried not to stare.

"Okay, I'm just going to put this out here," said Gordon as he scurried around the table placing heaping mounds of salad onto everybody's plate. "You three have obviously been through a lot, well, two of you have, at least . . ." He gave Butter a warning look that she pretended not to see. "I just want to say that it would do us all good, I think, if we considered this to be a safe place, so to speak. If anybody needs to talk, they can, without anybody else being shocked and appalled, or judgy." He sat down and flicked his napkin onto his lap. No one said a word until Butter remembered her news.

"Oh, guess what? You know that fellow that brought me to your house? That detective?"

"Oh, yes?" Gordon said, grinning maliciously. "Your new grizzly bear boyfriend?"

Butter continued as though Gordon were mute. "Well, he called this afternoon, and—"

"Oh, *really*?" said Gordon, his grin even bigger, as he slipped a carrot to Trilby, sitting expectantly beneath his chair.

Butter picked up the platter of fish and handed it to Gordon. "Here, have some salmon, Gordon," she said with a sugary smile. "And please shut up." She continued, "Anyway, the big news of the day is . . . Old Man Griffin dropped dead this morning when he saw his statue was gone. God, that sounds like a line in a country song, but it's completely true." She looked from face to face, waiting for a response. "Oh, and he asked you to call him, Glinda." She took a bite of salad. "He wants to know if you saw anything on your way to The Glade. He said they think Porter must have died around dawn."

"So, they think *I* might have killed him?" Glinda laughed and reached for the cold bottle of Chardonnay, filling her glass with the pale gold liquid.

"No. *No!* Nothing like *that*," said Butter. "I mean the old coot died of natural causes, they're sure. He was, what? A hundred and three or something? I guess Will just wonders if you saw anybody in the park or anything. Anyway, I've got his number."

It said something about Gordon's ability to resist temptation that he left Butter's last sentence alone. Instead, he looked over at Glinda and asked, "You want to talk about what happened yesterday? It might do you good. Like I said, no judgment."

Glinda put down her fork and stared at the food on her plate as though unsure exactly how it had gotten there. Gordon, who had never been one to pull a bandage off slowly, went on. "Look, we all know what occurred at the restaurant, Glinda. Practically everybody in Wesleyan was there."

Glinda winced, visibly.

"It's not the end of the world," said Gordon. "It'll all blow over in a few days. Mark my words."

And it was as if that assurance, so simple and succinct, released Glinda from the debilitating panic she'd felt for hours. She looked around the table. "God, I don't know why I did it," she said, quickly. "I didn't think. It was like when the doctor hits your knee with that little mallet and your leg flies straight out without you having any control over it. A reflex, right?" She twisted the napkin in her lap, tighter and tighter. "And now I don't know how I'll ever be able to face Macon again, or what I'll say to him. I don't even know if I want to ever *see* him again.

"I guess . . . I guess it was Harry's funeral. I knew then. For the very first time. How one minute we all are going to just disappear, and it'll all be over. Our whole *life,* you know? It'll all be finished." She snapped her fingers and took a large gulp of wine. "Harry was always so . . . so alive, so happy . . . I didn't even know he was sick. And well, I don't know, I just looked at Macon in that restaurant, he was making fun of those people who've been trying to get that statue removed, and they're good, sincere people—I've met some of them, and they're not the sort of hateful idiots he'd told me they were—and he was *laughing* at them, ridiculing them. He looked so smug, so damn contemptuous, and I . . . I saw my future in his face. Right there. It just flew all over me. I mean, Harry's gone. *Gone.* Who knows how much longer *I've* got? All of a sudden. The loss of my *life,* you know? What it could have been, what *I* could have been, *might* have been. And now it's almost over. I just want . . . to . . . to settle some things, not just push them aside. I want to know what *matters,* and act like I know it. I want to be responsible for my own life, not just follow along behind his. I . . . I sound ridiculous, I can tell. I can't articulate it." She sighed. "Maybe I've just been mad at Macon for a very long time and didn't realize it. All I can say for certain is that in that moment, when I did what I did, I couldn't stand the sight of him." She downed her glass of wine, reached out for the bottle, and filled it up again.

Their forks suspended in the air, the other three stared, frozen in her torrent of words, the rawness of emotion silencing them all. None of them had expected this. It was Gordon who finally spoke, clearing his throat first to buy a few seconds. "Well. Now. I think you can safely say you have been. Mad at him, that is." He folded his arms on the table and stared straight at Glinda. "But hell, you've still got time to do anything you want to do. Well, I mean, *obviously* you can't be a *ballerina,* or an *astronaut.* And probably not president of the United States, though God knows we could use you right about now. But my Lord, Glinda. You could visit Machu Picchu, you could write a book, you could paint, you could go off and join the damn Peace Corps, like Jimmy Carter's mother did. Your life is far from over. You're very wrong about that."

"I'm almost sixty-eight, Gordon. You're much too optimistic."

"Ha! Exact same age Lillian Carter was when she took off to India. Proves my point." He took a bite of salmon. "You're just too depressed to know I'm right. Listen, honey, the first time I got dirt on my shoes from the road you're walking was almost forty years ago. Back then the young were closer to death than the old; we went to so many funerals the smell of lilies still makes me sick." He reached for the bowl of new potatoes and put three on his plate. "*I'll* never wear black again. You talk about seeing your future in somebody's face? Well, let me tell you, the future I saw, every day for years, was the ugliest one you could ever imagine.

"I was going to take Broadway by storm, and the closest I ever got was a walk-on part in a show that closed in previews. Like I said, my life looks nothing like I planned, but I like it just fine. So, I'm here to tell you, dear, the future is an unpredictable abstraction. And we are fools to believe it's anything else. You can do whatever you want to do."

"Gordon's a fatalist," said Marietta, patting her friend on his arm.

"And Marietta's an idealist," he countered, without looking up from his food. "Three guesses which one of us has an easier time of it?"

Glinda sighed. "I guess I must be . . . oh, I don't know . . . a traditionalist, I guess? Whatever that means. Always doing what's expected? Following the correct path?" She looked over at Butter, who shrugged her shoulders and took a bite of salad.

"But what do I do now? This is not Macon's fault. I humiliated him in front of everybody and laughed at him like a hyena. How can I walk that back?" She rubbed her forehead like it ached. "It was just sort of, oh I don't know, like winding a watch too far, really slowly, till all of a sudden it snaps and won't keep time anymore. Do you know what I mean?" The other three nodded and Glinda topped up her glass. The bottle of Chardonnay was emptying fast. "I've never even complained before. He'll never understand why I did what I did." She rested her cheek on her palm and Marietta noticed her wedding rings, the diamond as big as her knuckle. It looked too heavy for Glinda's hand.

"I still remember the very first time I saw him. Macon. It was at my debut, you know?"

Gordon said up straighter. "Debut? What did you—?"

"Debutante, Gordon. Not acting." Marietta talked over him, not taking her eyes off Glinda. She'd never heard this story.

"Right," said Glinda, pointedly nodding at Marietta and taking another large drink of wine. Butter looked across the table at Gordon, who raised his eyebrows in response.

Glinda hiccupped a little and continued, "Right. Deb-U-Tante. *Big* deal when I was eighteen. *Big* ball at the Piedmont Driving Club, one of the whitest places in America. And in keeping with the theme, all us girls *wore* white, too, like wedding dresses." She sniggered. "Well, that was what it was all about, right? Putting us officially on the market? Showing off our wares for prospective husbands? I still remember how my heart thumped as I stood on the side of that room waiting to hear my name called . . . Glinda Cahoon Rhodes."

"*Cahoon?*" whispered Gordon.

"Family name," said Marietta, transfixed.

"Right again!" said Glinda, raising her glass to her sister-in-law. "I'm telling you, I still see it, *clearly,* you know?" Glinda looked at Butter before cutting her eyes back toward Marietta, the main person to whom she was speaking. "I walked to the front of the ballroom and Daddy met me there. He held out his arm to take my hand, very gallant—he was in a full tux, of course, and I had on white gloves that went all the way past my elbows— and I *curtsied,* can you imagine?" Asleep in the corner of the room, both Trilby and Smudge woke and cocked their heads at the sound of Glinda's loud laughter. "Daddy led me out into the middle of that big room, and that was the precise moment I spotted Macon, standing against the wall at the back in a white jacket. Most of the men were in black.

"Well, of course he stood out. I'd grown up with practically all of the boys there, so it was easy to pick out an unfamiliar face. And that red hair helped of course." She pointed a fork toward Marietta's own auburn hair for emphasis before taking a large bite of fish, still talking as she chewed. "Just by being outside my family's circle of acquaintance, Macon was more interesting than all the other boys on offer. I thought I was defining my own independence when I agreed to that marriage proposal." She shook her head, taking another long drink. "I didn't even finish college. Well, why should I, I thought. Mama dropped out when she married Daddy. Of course, sometime between Mama and me, the rules got changed. It just took us longer to find that out where I was.

"You know, if I'm being honest . . . and I *am* being honest, why not?" She grinned at Gordon, who was smiling nervously back. "To be honest, I think it was *Logan* I really thought I was marrying. I still remember that first day Macon brought me down here to meet you all." She nodded toward Marietta and waved her wineglass in a circle around her head, splashing drops onto her navy blue shirt. "Right here in this very house, this very room, in fact. Lord, your father made such an impression on me. So smart, so funny. I still remember how he laughed with you over something you said . . ." Glinda closed her eyes. "Can't remember what it was, though I wish I could." She opened her eyes back up and grinned. "But I said to myself that day, Glinda, *this* is what you want your life to be like. And it helped that Macon and Logan looked so much alike." Taking another long drink, she gave a rueful chuckle. "Turns out the joke was on me. I ended up marrying my *own* father, not yours. Well, that's what they say usually happens to us girls, right? Whether we know it at the time or not."

Darkness had crept into the house, settling in the corners where the lamplight didn't reach. Marietta coughed a little, saying, "Well, now," in an attempt to jolt Glinda onto a different track, but her sister-in-law didn't seem to notice. She picked up the wine bottle, exaggerated a sad face when she saw it was empty, and reached across Gordon for the other. Taking a large gulp, she continued, slightly slurring her words as she spoke.

"You know, I always thought he'd cheat on me. Macon. All the other men around him cheated. I heard all about it, from the wives, you know." Glinda leaned forward, looking at Butter, conspiratorially. "But he never did. Macon, I mean. Never cheated. Not even once. I would've known. He just couldn't be bothered, I guess." She sat up straighter and brushed an unseen hair from her face. "Well, I mean, it wasn't like our sex life was ever all that thrilling, maybe he just wasn't interested in all that." Her laugh sounded more like a sneer. "He did it like it was another item on his to-do list anyway. One final chore to check off for the day, you know? I mean, he never even noticed what it was like for me, not from the very first time. Not sure he would have cared if he had. Noticed, I mean." She pushed her half-eaten dinner away, leaned forward, and grinned at her three silent companions. "Now, this is funny . . . never told anyone this . . . I started memorizing poetry while we did it, years ago, you know, to take my mind off how little I enjoyed it all, I guess. It kind of became a game, and I almost, perversely I guess, looked forward to it. I started small, you know, with 'I think that I shall never see a poem lovely as a tree.' You all know that one. But it wasn't much of a challenge, so I kept stepping it up. It got to where I could recite the whole 'Casey at the Bat' without missing a word. All thirteen stanzas!" Glinda threw back her head and howled. "I can still do it, too. Wanna hear?"

In unison, the other three demurred with various degrees of emphasis, embarrassment hanging heavy in the air as they braced for what might be coming next, but ladling out her innermost, wine-drenched thoughts in such dramatic fashion suddenly seemed to have exhausted Glinda, and after that final explosion of laughter she appeared to evaporate before their eyes. Sweat broke out on her forehead, and she slumped in her chair. Refusing dessert, she left the table as Butter rose to put the coffee on. They watched, craning their necks to see, as Glinda took the stairs slowly, one by one, disappearing incrementally out of sight on her way up to bed.

"No joy in Mudville, then," whispered Gordon. He caught Butter's eye, and the two of them tried not to laugh.

The canned tomato soup tasted just as good as the real thing, and she took another spoonful. Jocelyn Shaw was chilled to the bone. Curled like a cat under the afghan her mother had crocheted her for Christmas, she was keeping one eye on the screen of her muted TV. The weather was the main story tonight, of course. Ice storms in Georgia were rare. Layla Collier, the weekend meteorologist, had been living for something like this for months. Lead story on prime-time news; you could see the joy on her face. Jocelyn would turn the volume up when she saw her own introduction.

They'd taped her part on the steps of the Wesleyan courthouse, and she'd known it was good as she did it. That Ernest Adcock had been a godsend, she thought, crumbling crackers into her soup. Straight out of central casting. Tall as a stick insect, with a sincerity that his first name practically guaranteed. When he'd said that dead old man's daddy had been in the Klan, she'd almost choked. And she'd especially loved getting a rise out of that mayor. She'd just let him talk, let him play down the whole thing the best he could, and then she'd hit him with the question that set a vein to pulsing on the side of his head. "Do you consider the city of Wesleyan to be racist, Mayor Baker?" She had asked it as innocently as a child; he'd never seen it coming.

"*Hell* no, I don't," he'd responded immediately, his face turning enough of a satisfying red to be visible on the smallest screen. The mayor had then proceeded to bluster out so many laudatory statements about Wesleyan it would have made even the city's most ardent fans a bit skeptical, finally throwing up his hands and blurting, "Look, lady, we're all just doing the best we can down here, okay?" Jocelyn couldn't have scripted it any better.

She knew the station had sent the piece down to Wesleyan, and Jocelyn would have bet her best shoes it would run not only tonight but again in the morning, and depending on the response it engendered, she just might find herself sitting alongside the lead anchors before all was said and done. This is how it happens, she thought, wiping soup from the front of her nightgown. When you least expect it, gold can land right in your lap.

22

———

MARIETTA, BUTTER, GLINDA, AND BRADY

She was still awake at 2:00 A.M. There were sleeping pills in the bathroom cabinet, but Marietta hadn't taken any yet, and didn't want to now. Dr. Mackey had prescribed them for her on the day of Harry's diagnosis, but every night since then she'd fallen into bed as exhausted as a bricklayer, deep sleep coming so fast it felt like falling. She'd even been asleep when Harry died, his final words spoken just as they both drifted off: "See you in the morning." For some reason those words gave her comfort, as though this week without him was just some extended version of night that would sooner or later give over to a reunion with Harry at dawn.

But tonight was different. She rolled over and picked up her phone, discouraged to see the time. Marietta sat up and laced her fingers together around her knees, breathing in and out slowly the way the yoga teacher on the Internet had shown. She'd learned the breathing part but could never manage any of the poses without laughing. But maybe that did just as much good.

Finally giving up, she threw back the duvet and walked to the window, her bare feet cold on the floor. Behind her Smudge jumped down from the bed to follow, pushing against her right leg as he sat at her side.

The garden glowed like noontime, the result of a fat, full moon that hung out over the trees like a lost balloon. The Wolf Moon. Harry had taught her the names. Unable to stop herself, Marietta searched the dark net of bare limbs, in hopes of finding the bird she'd seen at Butter's, before audibly sighing at the absurdity.

It was freezing out there, she knew, but she didn't think she could stay inside any longer. She needed to be alone, to breathe in the cold air and clear her head. Pulling on whatever looked warmest, she wrapped one of Harry's scarves around her neck and jammed her feet into socks and heavy boots. She crept out of her room onto the landing, paused silently at Glinda's closed door, then crossed the floor on tiptoe with Smudge close behind.

She was almost to the stairs when she heard voices—whispers and giggles—coming from behind the door to Butter's room. She stopped, curious, but too ashamed to actually listen. When she took a step to move on, a floorboard creaked loudly underneath her right foot, and the voices immediately stopped. She heard a soft plop, then little footsteps coming closer. The door opened and an obnoxious bright light shone straight in her face. Blinking and caught like a mouse, Marietta froze.

"What are you doing out here in the dark?" said Butter. "What's the matter? Are you okay?"

"I'm fine. Turn that light out." Butter switched off the flashlight and they stood looking at each other, Marietta waiting for her eyes to refocus. "I'm just going out for a walk," she said.

"A *walk*? You're nuts. It's freezing out there."

"Yes, and as you can see"—Marietta pointed to her mismatched outfit—"I'm dressed for it."

"Well, hang on. I'll go with you." Butter turned around and scurried over to her suitcase, which lay open on the floor.

Marietta stuck her head in. "No. Now, Butter, I don't need you to go with me. It's two o'clock in the morning."

"All the more reason," said Butter, from inside her room. Marietta stepped back into the hall and leaned against the door-frame, attempting the yogi's deep breaths once again. To her right, another door opened. Glinda peered out, her hair twisted into a messy bun on the top of her head. She'd been sleeping in her shirt.

"Where're y'all going?" she whispered.

"Are you sleeping in your clothes?" Butter's head had popped out like a prairie dog from inside the hot pink turtleneck sweater she'd been struggling to put on.

"I didn't feel so good," said Glinda, flatly. "I, I threw up, and fell asleep." She kept her bottom half in the room to avoid reveal-ing her aging legs to the two women, who'd never before seen them and most likely wouldn't wish to tonight. "I should . . . I don't remember what exactly I said, but I think I might need to apologize for—"

"Oh, don't be silly," Butter interrupted. "Nobody cared, Glinda. You were upset. Don't think any more about it."

"She's right," said Marietta. "You go back to bed. You both go back to bed. I'm just going outside for some air. I'll be fine."

The three women looked at one another, and in the end, as Marietta fully expected, they both went with her. Glinda seemed to want to get outside every bit as much as Marietta did, and But-ter wasn't about to be left behind. Downstairs in the sunroom, Gordon slept as soundly as a well-fed child, with his flannel paja-mas buttoned up to his throat, and Trilby loudly snoring across his feet. He never heard a thing.

It was just as cold as Butter had feared, without a breath of wind. Hanging high in the black sky, the moon looked almost blue, its light lending an aura of unreality to the landscape; with-out even a whisper of a witch's spell the row of topiary elephants seemed ready and able to stomp around the bird feeder in their perfect circle. The three women paused at the edge of the stone back porch, then walked single file out into the garden like kids on a field trip, not one of them saying a word. Darkness never welcomes human voices.

When they reached the back of the garden, Marietta pushed between rows of cleyera bushes, opened a gate, and the other two followed her through it. Smudge ran ahead at a gallop, thrilled at this strange nighttime jaunt. They were in the woods now, a shady cathedral normally inhabited exclusively by the children of The Glade, along with a few shy deer, some armored armadillos, and a score of misunderstood possums. The tops of the trees glowed silver above them; the pine-needled floor was dark. The deep, soft scent of woodsmoke mingled with the piquancy of ice and pine, creating the fragrance of winter itself. The three breathed it in as they began to walk.

After a good twenty minutes, during which, besides their own footsteps, all they heard was the occasional cracking and snapping of ice in the trees, Glinda spoke, her voice startling in the still, silent air. "Can I ask you a question, Marietta?"

"Of course." Marietta kept walking, her eyes on the ground.

"That dark spot in the front yard, where the cross was burned that night. Why did your father keep it? Macon never said. I would've thought Logan would've wanted it gone the very next morning, something that awful."

"Oh, no," said Marietta, ducking under a low-hanging branch and holding it back for Butter. "It was because it was so awful that he wanted people to see it. I always thought it was sort of like Jackie Kennedy's Chanel suit, the pink one, you know? How she wouldn't change out of it that day in Dallas, even though it was covered in blood. She said she wanted to keep it on to show people what they'd done. I think it was that way for Dad. He wanted people to be shocked, I think." Marietta stepped over a fallen pine and waited for the other two to follow. "It's a funny thing, and I didn't realize it at the time, but I know now that's why Harry made it his business to plant such a pretty garden out back. All those roses? Those elephants? He was making a point—

to me, I suppose. That life has two sides. The ugly is always tempered by the beautiful, the dark with the light."

Butter and Glinda exchanged glances as they walked. Butter said, "Well, maybe they'll just plant a tree or something where that statue was. I mean if—" She suddenly stopped and pointed off to the left, back toward the houses. All three of them saw it: a light playing hide-and-seek through the thick stand of trees. "What's that?" Butter asked, poking Marietta in the arm.

Marietta turned, looking backward and forward, the moonlit ground so abnormally white, she found it difficult to gauge how far they'd gone. "We've obviously been walking longer than I figured. I think that must be coming from Brady's place. He hardly ever sleeps when he's painting. We should probably turn back now."

"Oh, no. Let's go see," said Butter, still whispering.

"See what? We can't knock on the man's door in the middle of the night."

"I didn't mean *that*. I just want to have a peek. You can always see inside places really well in the dark. It's one of my favorite things."

"You mean, go spy on him? How *old* are you, Butter?"

"No, not *spy* on him. Good Lord. You know me; I just want to see his *house*. I love the old houses in here. Always have. They never come up for sale, so I never get to see inside them. C'mon. We'll stay in the trees. He'll never see us." Butter stepped up her pace, clearly eager to take a look, and the other two reluctantly followed.

The ice was worse here; it took more effort not to slip, and they grabbed on to the trees as they walked. It was slow going. They were panting and warm when they stopped outside the small gate at the edge of Brady's yard, and Marietta loosened the scarf at her neck.

From where they were they could see the glass-walled studio glowing like a movie screen. There was music traveling through the frozen trees, so faint it seemed almost hallucinatory, and they looked to one another for tacit confirmation of its presence. The three women stood, side by side, like members of the same team waiting for the start of a game. There was no question that they would move closer.

Butter saw it first. Little by little, she'd crept closer to Brady's old cottage in her desire to get a glimpse inside, only to be frustrated that the studio was the sole room lighted. The rest of the house was as dark as the ground beneath her shoes. Not that the studio wasn't interesting. It looked like someplace an old sea captain would live, she thought, with turtle shells and snakeskins hanging on the walls, books in disordered stacks across the floor, and that big easel standing down at the other end of the room. She could see a cat as big as a panther sprawled across the back of a chair, and Brady himself, obviously working, on the other side of the easel. She inched her way through the trees to see what he was doing, careful to stay hidden behind their pleated gray trunks.

At first, she didn't recognize Glinda; the painting only looked familiar, the way seeing someone you know in a place you don't expect sometimes makes you pause. The realization came on slowly, but when the penny dropped, Butter gasped.

Marietta had had enough. "Come on, Butter. Let's go," she hissed, and Butter heard footsteps on the frozen ferns, moving away from her.

"Wait," she whispered back. "Y'all have to see this!" But the two other women were already back at the gate, clearly preferring to leave her where she was over getting caught out by Brady Goode. "Dammit," Butter muttered under her breath as she made her way back out to the woods.

When she caught up with the other two and told them what she'd seen, neither woman believed her. "You've seen his paintings in my bedroom, Butter," said Marietta. "They're sort of impressionistic. There might have been a resemblance or something, but how could it possibly have been Glinda? He doesn't even know her."

"I swear! If you'll just come back with me . . . he'll never know . . . you'll see for yourself. You'll be able to tell it's her in a second. There's no question." Butter was almost bouncing with frustration.

"I am not going back there," said Glinda. "Your eyes were playing tricks on you, Butter. The only place I'm returning to is bed." There was a definite edge to her voice that put an end to the matter. Marietta clicked her tongue for Smudge, and he bounded out of the woods. The three women returned to Marietta's garden in silence, Butter fighting the temptation to argue but realizing the futility and letting it go.

They left their muddy shoes on the porch, and Marietta wiped Smudge's feet with a towel she'd left by the door. Slipping inside as quietly as possible, they said good night to one another before retreating to their respective rooms. Butter and Marietta fell asleep almost instantly, but Glinda lay still in the dark with her eyes open, listening to the cracking sound of pine limbs, those too weak to stand up to the weight of the ice any longer.

Though she kept telling herself not to, Glinda couldn't stop considering the faint chance that Butter had been right, and the possibility that her likeness might be on that canvas made her feel singled out somehow, set apart, and exposed. If what Butter said was actually true then without right or permission a stranger had reached into her life and taken something he had no right to take.

Four hours later, in an effort to keep his favored routine, Gordon made himself a cup of coffee and took it back to the quilt-covered sofa. He opened the curtains a fraction to watch the morning lighten, and was propped up on his pillows, mug in hand, when he saw Glinda outside the window, leaning against one of the porch's stone columns, putting on her shoes. He watched as she straightened up, pulled her coat close around her, and set off toward the back of the garden.

Rummy's yellow eyes were tightly closed. He lay in his favorite position, curled up like a decorative black rosette at the end of Brady's bed. The snores emanating from his owner told the cat that breakfast was still a good bit away, which was more than fine by him. At this cold and early hour, warmth was more important than food. Rummy heard the woman approaching long before she knocked on the door but chose to pretend that he hadn't.

It took a good two minutes of knocking to pull Brady out of his sleep. He'd painted till five without notice of time. This usually meant that the painting was good, but he planned to reserve judgment till later in the day, after he'd been away from the thing for a while. The raps on the door were loud and insistent, and when they finally reached him, their effect was tantamount to an air raid. As was his preference, Brady had very few visitors to the house, and one at this early hour on an icy Monday morning, especially one so determined, had to mean trouble.

Without bothering to put on a shirt, he ran from the bedroom, straight to the door, and flung it open to an angrier version of the same face he'd been staring into for hours.

Glinda had come by way of the woods again, fully expecting Butter's report to be wrong, but unable to quench the need to confirm this for herself. The studio was dark now. No movement could be seen inside so she felt comfortable getting close enough to peer into the tall windows. Her eyes swept over the room, taking in all the physical evidence of an artist's life, so different from her orderly house of antiques and silk lampshades. Though music no longer seeped through the glass and out into the trees, Glinda felt it must be continuing inside; it was impossible to imagine this room without it.

The large easel was just where Butter had said it was, down at the end of the studio, and like Butter, Glinda had to edge around the glass windows to see the painting that rested there. Crouching slightly, keenly aware that she lacked the cloak of darkness Butter had worn, Glinda moved through the fern-covered tree limbs that drooped and swerved all around her, finally lifting a boa of thick Spanish moss that obscured her view, and she saw what Butter had seen.

There was no doubting the resemblance. Far from exact, its variations only seemed to add to a truth that was more revelatory than a mirror, more eloquent than an ode. Some part of her had been snared right within the most minimal of lines and shading, and Glinda felt she was looking at that part of her soul she'd kept carefully hidden, even from herself. Tears, unexpected and maddening, stung her eyes, and she blinked them back along with the urge to feel flattered, for there was no denying that this woman, this oblique version of herself she only halfway recognized, was idealized to the point of flattery. For some reason she could never have explained, this made the tears spill over. She waited until every emotion reached a boil, then simmered down only to anger. Then she went to find the front door.

Now, standing face-to-face, Glinda and Brady stared at each other, the subject every bit as flustered as the artist. It was Brady who spoke first.

"Lord, woman. You scared me half to death. Is something the matter up at Marietta's?"

Embarrassment, her least favorite feeling, drenched Glinda in hesitancy, and when she spoke it was, to her distress, in a voice even she found high-pitched and priggish. "No, Mr. Goode. Everything is fine at Mrs. Cline's. I have come to ask you a question."

"Yeah?" Brady ran his fingers through his hair, his confusion melting into an amusement he was trying hard to conceal. "Well, I'm standing here freezing, so ask it."

"I . . . well, I . . . I would like to know what gave you the right, I mean . . . who gave you liberty, exactly . . . to paint my picture . . . without asking me." Glinda gained a bit of confidence as she reached the end of her sentence but was still avoiding looking Brady straight in the eyes. She wished he'd put on a shirt.

"I see." Brady's expression was not dissimilar to the one Rummy wore when presented with a new ball of yarn. "Well, I'd like to ask *you* how you happen to know that any such picture exists?"

Glinda reddened, she could feel it all over her face like the first sip of whiskey, and the small amount of courage indignation had bestowed on her slipped away and fled. "I . . . I mean, we . . . we were walking in the woods last night . . . and we saw . . . we saw it." This explanation, stammered out apologetically, put her squarely on the defense, and she knew it. To make matters worse, it suddenly occurred to her that Brady Goode might very well have witnessed her performance at the reception on Saturday, and the inerasable sound of her own shrill laughter flooded her head like a siren.

"I see," said Brady, smiling. "Well, to answer your urgent question, no one gave me permission. I might add, however, that people are usually quite happy to have me paint their portraits. Believe it or not, they even pay me good money to do so." He rubbed his unshaven chin. "But I take your point. Perhaps I should have asked. I tell you what, why don't you decide whether or not to have me arrested *after* you see it?" He stood back and motioned to Glinda to enter.

Everything inside of her balked at the invitation, and she wheeled around to go. But the pink light of the sun was just seeping out over the horizon, giving every crystal of ice its own interior light, and causing the whole world, it seemed, to glow. When she looked up, she saw tiny lacerations in the low gray sky, slivers of light breaking through. Glinda paused, then turned back toward Brady, and noticed his eyes were green.

She would always find it strange that she didn't think of Macon. Instead, she heard Gordon's voice from last night, saying, "You can do whatever you want to do."

Glinda stepped inside the warm house.

23

MACON, WILL, LURLENE, AND THE ADCOCKS

At the very moment his wife walked into Brady Goode's studio, Macon snapped awake with the same unsettling symptoms that had sent him to the emergency room twice in the past year, certain he was having a widow-maker, the name of the sudden heart attack that had killed Clifford Dobbs last September as the man sat across from Macon at lunch, eating a chicken-fried steak in his very own restaurant. This was one of three high-priced steak houses Clifford had built up across the area, each one named for a John Wayne movie that ended with the star spanking a woman on the behind or dragging her by the arm across a field: Clifford's little private joke for his ex-wife, Tillie. There was Mc-Clintock's over in Seabrook, The Quiet Man down in Jefferson, and Donovan's Reef, Macon's favorite, in Wesleyan, just on the edge of town.

Macon had gone to high school with Clifford, played football alongside him, and now had watched him die right there on the herringbone carpet at Donovan's Reef, a good three minutes before the EMTs arrived, and barely five after telling Macon he didn't feel right, and though Macon had maintained a certain dignified detachment from the experience as it was happening, the whole thing had obviously lodged somewhere in his psyche, lying in wait for his most vulnerable nights. He'd been tested and told that his heart was just fine but whenever he woke to a pounding pulse and swimmy head Macon wasn't sure he believed it.

He sat up and reached for the glass of buttermilk he kept sitting by his bed. He took a sip along with a deep breath, then checked his phone for the time. Too early to get up, too late to go back to sleep.

He arranged his pillow to better support his neck and lay on his back in the dark. *It's always darkest before dawn.* He could still hear his mother's voice, telling him that whenever he got in a foul mood. Another bit of nonsense you learn as a child, he thought.

Macon didn't want to think about his parents, but for the past two days they'd been walking around in his head as though they remembered the way. Lying there in the cold of his bedroom, high up in his four-poster bed, he could almost hear their voices and would have willingly placed his palms over his ears like a child if he thought it would help block them out.

He'd been happy as a little kid. Macon knew this whenever he stopped to remember, which was as infrequently as he could manage. Long before he started measuring his life against others, everything about it was perfect. He remembered summer vacations at Daytona Beach, when, having packed the car before bed, they'd crept out of the house before dawn, each of them waiting till they were well out of the drive to slam their car doors so as not to wake old Mr. and Mrs. Seagraves, who lived next door and were light sleepers.

He remembered going Christmas shopping with Logan, just the two of them out to find the perfect gift for Caroline, and Macon feeling grown-up whenever his father asked him to help choose between a bracelet and a brooch. He could recall sitting in front of the black-and-white television, his dad loudly laughing at Ralph Kramden or listening intently to Senator Kennedy, whom he frequently called "our best hope for the future." Macon started dabbing Jockey Club aftershave onto his cheeks long before he had need of such a product.

The nicknames and taunts didn't begin till first grade. It was in May of that year that the *Brown v. Board of Education* decision came down, and Macon found out for the first time just what it was his father did for a living. Logan had written an editorial in approval of the Supreme Court's decision, and with all the eloquence of children parroting their parents, Macon's classmates had happily informed him of his father's many cultural failings in language he knew to be ugly and wrong. When Macon had tearfully related what he'd heard at school, Logan didn't apologize. Instead, he told his son to always be proud of doing the right thing. But Macon wasn't proud; he was humiliated. When he looked around at his friends it seemed to him that the ones who had it easier were the ones who fit in.

When President Kennedy was killed in a Texas street, Macon took that as just another confirmation of what he was already beginning to believe: that the things his father worried and wrote about were all best left alone. Macon wasn't responsible for things he couldn't control. He had no cause to feel guilty. If everybody just took care of themselves, everything would run more smoothly. By the night the cross was burned in his family's front yard, Macon almost felt it was deserved.

And now he was going to be mayor. He could feel it in his bones, the same feeling he'd had when he ran for student body president in twelfth grade. He'd known he was going to win then, too. But this was almost like God himself had arranged it. Old Man Griffin falling down dead had practically placed the election in Macon's hands, wrapped up and tied with a bow. After a long afternoon of thought, he had decided what to do, and if he knew the people of Wesleyan the way he thought he did, his plan would make it nigh on impossible for the majority of them to vote for anyone else.

He wasn't too worried about Glinda. Marietta had finally texted him to say Glinda was with her, but he had yet to text his sister back. Better if Glinda stayed away right now anyway, he thought. If he knew his wife—and who knew her better?—she was afraid to face him, and rightfully so. He imagined her at this moment, lying awake in that tiny guest room at the old house, terrified to explain herself. Well, he'd let her stew awhile. Might just do her good. If she was in some sort of hormonal mood, he really didn't want her around when he spoke to the press. But that wasn't until this afternoon. He could still catch an hour or so of sleep. And it might just do him good.

Almost without him realizing it, Will's habits had changed in the five years since his wife died. He'd turned into an early riser, something Ellen would find hard to believe, he knew. He'd always enjoyed staying up late—watching the credits roll at the end of every *Late Show with David Letterman,* finishing the last of his book, talking on the phone to his brother in California—and was almost impossible to rouse in the morning. Alarms were useless; he turned them off in his sleep, no matter how loud and discordant their sound. Ellen had thrown a glass of water in his face to wake him once when their son was a baby. He could still see her standing over him, laughing as she balanced a squalling Freddie on her hip, with that empty water glass in her hand.

There'd been no warning. One minute she'd been sitting beside him in one of those new plush seats at the Eagle Cinema 8, and they'd been watching the afternoon showing of the latest James Bond. Then, just as Judi Dench was reciting those final lines of his favorite Tennyson poem up there on the screen, he'd felt Ellen's head drop down on his shoulder, and just like that, she was gone. An aneurysm, they said. She never felt a thing, they said. He'd walked out of that theater a different man than the one who'd gone in, amazed to find that the sun had set, and the parking lot was dark. "That which we are, we are." Those familiar words of Tennyson had new meaning to him now.

He'd come home that evening to find Ellen's coffee cup on the counter where she'd left it sitting, her lipstick still bright on its edge, and he'd kept that cup right where it was for three months. When Freddie's wife, thinking she was helping, finally washed it, he'd gotten angry with her for the very first time, and told her to get out of his house.

He started taking extra shifts soon after, and before the year was out, he'd been promoted to detective. When he was offered a position in Wesleyan, he grabbed at it like a lifeline, knowing it would do him good to live in the same city as his grandkids. With an empathy honed by loss, he was good at his job, respected by his officers as well as the public, and work soon began to be something he looked forward to as he went to sleep earlier and earlier each night. Will rarely saw midnight anymore, which was why he was finding it harder than usual to rub the sleep from his eyes this morning. He was on his third cup of black coffee.

If he'd ever talked on the phone for two hours, he couldn't remember when or why.

He'd told Butter to call when her dinner was over, and she'd warned him that it would be late. "That's okay," he said. "I'll just turn the ringer off if I get sleepy." But he hadn't gotten sleepy. He hadn't turned it off. He'd sat there in his big chair by the fireplace and waited, putting another log on the fire whenever it got low, and reading the same Harlan Coben paragraph over and over and over. It was eleven-fifteen when he heard crickets, his preferred ringtone for personal calls, and he answered in a whisper, even though no one else was there.

It was no use pretending that talking to Butter had anything to do with the case. In truth, there wasn't a case at all, not yet anyway, and even if there had been, Glinda was the one who might have seen something, not Butter. Will really didn't have any professional reason to contact the woman at all.

It was so difficult for him to admit, even to himself, that he found Butter almost irresistible. It nearly hurt to do it. Still. Even after a half decade. He wanted to hide his feelings from Ellen, and he knew that was at least as ridiculous as his long-ago plan to keep her coffee cup, lipstick and all, just as it was, forever. Besides, he didn't like to think Ellen spent her time, wherever she was, worrying about what he was getting up to. He'd rather she enjoy her eternity.

"Oh God, I'm too old for this," he said out loud, and he laughed at himself as he opened the door to the pantry to see if there was anything different for breakfast. He'd reached up for a nearly empty box of Special K when the telephone rang.

"Hello?"

"Is this Detective Cochran?" Having recently heard the voice, Will guessed correctly who it was.

"Yes, Mrs. Pearson. It's me. What can I do for you?"

"Well first, you can call me Lurlene. And second, I wondered if you'd heard anything about a funeral for Porter Griffin? He's got no family that I know of."

Will told her he didn't know anything about a funeral. "Usually, the church takes care of stuff like that, don't they?"

"Yes, well . . . maybe. But I have no idea what Porter was. All I know is that he wasn't an Episcopalian. Probably a Baptist. I'll make a few calls and see what I can find out."

"Why do you want to know?"

"Why? Well, I'd want some sort of funeral when I died. Wouldn't you? Don't mistake me, I know nobody liked the old man. I didn't like him either. He led a small, angry little life in my opinion. But he was human. He was my neighbor, though God knows I never asked for him. And so, as *I* wouldn't want to go out of this world unremarked, I won't let it happen to that old goat either."

Feeling oddly chastised, Will couldn't think of anything to say.

"Look," said Lurlene. "If you'd like to get a jump start on this Griffin thing, why don't you come over here for breakfast. I can tell you everything I saw. I don't know if we told you, but Reese and I live right across from that old statue, on the other side of the park. Old Henry Benning stared straight in our windows every day of his illustrious life. Like Reese said, we could've heard the thing come down and never even known it. Thought it was all the trees falling under the ice. Anyhoo . . . I'm cooking cheese grits over here, so if you want to come talk, I'll set you a place."

Will looked down at the cereal box and said, "Well, Mrs. . . . uh . . . Lurlene. I'll be happy to have breakfast with you. I've just got to make one stop first. Take me about forty-five minutes. That okay?"

"It's fine," said Lurlene. "Just make sure you come to the back door. The front stairs are slicker than glass."

The segment of the 11:00 P.M. newscast that affected the majority of Wesleyans was the weather forecast, so the viewership had been up last night, everyone knowing the ice would be the top story, and everyone hopeful they'd seen the last blast of it for the rest of the foreseeable future.

Betsy Adcock had been tucked up in bed with the latest Louise Penny open on her lap and Ernest's father sound asleep beside her, his snoring having not yet reached the decibel level that would necessitate the insertion of the industrial-strength earplugs Ernest had ordered for her off the Internet. She'd had the television on mute but grabbed the remote the minute her son's flustered face popped up on the screen, a mere thirty seconds after the program began.

She turned up the volume just in time to hear him say, "Well, I can't say we've had tons of support here in Wesleyan. Quite the contrary, actually. There're just too many people still out there who want to take the South back to where we were in the fifties. They didn't want that statue to come down because, well, you'd have to ask them why not, I suppose."

"So do you think racism plays a part in all this, Mr. Adcock?" Jocelyn Shaw's red-gloved hand swept over the jagged pieces of glass littering the checkerboard floor, and the camera followed.

"Well, I mean, yeah. I mean, what do *you* think?" Betsy Adcock had gripped the edges of her blankets. "I mean, Porter Griffin? The man who owned the thing, well, I mean, he was really old and all, but everybody in Wesleyan knew his daddy was in the Klan."

"What?" Even from across the room, Betsy could see the

barely suppressed excitement in the reporter's wide-eyed expression. Ernest's face turned red, but still, inexplicably, he continued to talk, his lips forming words his mother had ceased to hear. A buzzing had risen up from somewhere inside Betsy Adcock's head, increasing in volume until it reverberated through her body like a hive of angry bees. There hadn't been an earplug invented that could silence the sound.

She'd turned off the TV while Ernest was still speaking and thrown the remote under the bed. Then she'd opened her night table drawer and rummaged around till she found the bottle of Ambien that had been there since those months when she'd been going through the change and couldn't sleep. The pills were two years out of date, and had probably lost some of their potency, so she'd taken three just to be safe.

His parents were still asleep at eight-thirty, which was unusual. Ernest sat in his father's old recliner by the window, waiting on a visit from Will. He liked the detective, especially after Will had helped him clean up the Zabbo's front window that August morning Ernest had found it slathered with rotten eggs. He'd never told anyone about that. It had taken him three hot showers to smell normal again. Lord only knows how long it had taken for Will.

He sometimes wondered about people like Will Cochran, those whose job it was to stay neutral. Will was just the same with Ernest as he was with anybody else. You could never tell whose side he was on. Sometimes Ernest thought that looked like the most comfortable way to live your life. But then people always assumed you agreed with them even if their opinion was repugnant to you, and Ernest had been born with a conscience that just couldn't abide that. He didn't understand how anybody could.

He saw Will's car ease its nose into the drive and answered the door before the detective even knocked. "Come on in," Ernest whispered, motioning Will into his family's dining room and pulling out a chair. "My folks are still asleep. You want a cup of coffee or something?"

"No, I'm good," said Will, matching his voice to Ernest's. "Thanks. I'm sorry to bother you. But you know I've got to ask about this."

Ernest pushed a blue file folder across the table toward Will and sat down. "I'm already ahead of you. Here's all the names of everybody who's worked with MRED since we started up. Plus every donor who's sent us money. I swear to God, Will, there's not a single person in that file who would've done something like this." He fingered the fringe on his mother's place mat, carefully choosing his words.

"You have to understand, the *reasons* we all wanted that statue gone are just as important as—maybe more important than—the actual fact of the thing. Sure, I'm happy—I guess we all are—that it's been pulled down, but we would've much rather it had happened out in the open, with some kind of agreement, or acquiescence, from both sides, you know? Knocking it over in an ice storm with nobody around? It's just not something any of us would've ever done. You're more than welcome to talk to any person in that folder you want to. But I guarantee you they'll all say the same thing."

Will had always respected the boy, even if he found him a frustrating blend of credulity and idealism. "Thanks, Ernest. I'll take a look. I'm pretty much like you, not inclined to think any of your people had something to do with what happened yesterday morning. This just doesn't seem to be anything that was too well thought out. With Mr. Griffin dead now, nobody's filed a formal complaint, and frankly, I doubt anybody will. But I don't want something worse to happen." He flipped through the folder, noticing names that he expected and a few that he did not.

"Well, thanks. I guess I'll leave you to it," Will said, picking up the blue folder and sticking it under his arm. He hesitated at the door, then turned around to face Ernest. "Look, if you don't mind some advice, I think it might be a good idea if you took a little vacation." Ernest looked up. "Yeah," Will continued, "just for a few days. You know how it is, son, people'll be all wound up about this for a little while, then the news will start to peter out. It'll disappear altogether when something else happens to steal everybody's focus, and that doesn't take too long these days. But like I said, you might be better off out of the spotlight. Especially after that interview that's running on TV. You know, just for a few days."

While Ernest stood alone at the window, watching the detective's car get smaller and smaller as it went back down the street, he could hear his own voice strangely magnified in his head, all the unfortunate words he'd said to Jocelyn Shaw, words that, considering Will Cochran's advice, were suddenly enough to make Ernest tiptoe to the closet for his suitcase. He was out the door long before his mother finally woke up.

24

IVY, GLINDA, AND ENID

There was something about the way the light lay across her room. Ivy knew it was late before she even opened her eyes and saw the clock. Nine A.M. School had been canceled; it was the only explanation for her mother letting her sleep in. Ivy threw back the covers and ran to the window. Marietta's porch light was on, she could see it shining under the eaves. Ice was still everywhere but it looked vulnerable now, more watery than it had last night. She glanced up to Marietta's bedroom window, knowing what she'd see. Yes, the bird was still there, its head tucked neatly beneath a blue-black wing. Ivy grinned.

Pulling on her clothes, she slipped out of her bedroom and down the back stairs. An ice storm was too good to waste, especially if it didn't have long to last. She slipped quietly out the door and wove her way through the backyard to the gate in the middle of the tall wooden fence that separated the Harpers' place from the woods. She could hear the ice melting all around her, egg-size drops of water hitting the pine-needled ground with sounds like footsteps. Ivy loved being in the woods, especially by herself. She increased her pace till she was running full out. Her lungs felt full of peppermint.

She was almost to the creek when she heard voices and turned to see the lady she'd met at Marietta's yesterday morning, coming out of Brady Goode's cottage. A bit of morning sunlight had woven its way down through the trees, and it grazed the lady's white hair, making it shine like a light. When she heard the door close, Ivy saw the woman heading her way and for some reason she couldn't explain, she ducked behind an oak so as not to be seen. She held her breath and watched as the woman opened Brady's gate and walked past her, back the way that she'd come. When she was out of sight, Ivy went through the same gate, past Brady's house and out toward the street, hitting the sidewalk with enough speed to arrive at Marietta's long before Glinda reached her door.

"You must be mistaken, Ivy." Marietta poured the little girl a glass of apple juice and pulled out a kitchen chair. Ivy, who was sitting on the floor with Trilby and Smudge, barely looked up. "Oh, it was her. I recognized her by her hair. Can I take the dogs outside?"

Marietta nodded, vaguely aware of Ivy leaving and Butter turning to race up the stairs. She came straight back down, a look of amazement on her face. "She's right. Glinda's not there."

"Did either of you hear anything this morning?" Marietta asked.

"I did," said Gordon, lazily turning a page in an old issue of *Vogue*. "I saw her putting on her shoes out there in the yard and heading off toward the woods. Around . . . oh, I guess, six? Six-thirty? It was just starting to get light."

"Well, why didn't you say so?" Marietta shook her head. "Honestly, Gordon."

"I just figured she needed some air. Besides, you all want to tell *me* anything?" He looked from Butter to Marietta and back again. "I heard you coming back in this morning."

"You were sound asleep when we left. We went for a walk. I couldn't sleep, and I just wanted to get out in the cold for some air. They heard me and insisted on going, too. We ended up way down at Brady's place, and Butter was convinced she saw him inside working on a portrait of Glinda. Which, I highly doubt, but maybe Glinda . . ."

Butter's eyes widened dramatically. "You don't think . . . she's been gone for hours . . . you know, her and Brady . . . Well, I mean, she's definitely not acting like herself, is she? All that talk about a watch breaking when it's wound too tight?"

"Don't be silly," said Marietta. "That's the very last thing in the world that would happen. I mean, even if Ivy is right, and Glinda was there . . . I just can't think there's anything, you know, un-toward . . ." She heard Gordon snort from behind his magazine. "No matter what kind of state Glinda was in, it takes two to tango. And I don't think Brady . . . I cannot imagine . . . well, I've never thought he was that type, exactly. I mean somebody he doesn't even know?"

"But he's a *man,* isn't he?" asked Butter.

"Here we go again," said Gordon.

"We can ask her, I guess," said Butter. "Here she comes."

They turned to see Glinda returning through the garden, pausing to say hello to Ivy before she climbed the stone stairs. She opened the door, and a rush of cold air flew past her into the room. They all waited to see what she'd say.

"Whew. It's even colder than it looks out there!" She took off her coat and threw it over the back of a chair. "I've been wander-ing. This is really a lovely little neighborhood, Marietta. I can see why you've stayed." Talking fast, and at a pitch that was a little too high, Glinda walked past where they were sitting at the kitchen table and took a glass from the cabinet. She opened the refrigera-tor, bending over to peer inside. "Any more of the San Pellegrino left from last night?" No one said anything, and Glinda stood up to look at them over the open refrigerator door. "What?" she asked.

"Nothing," said Butter and Marietta, in unison.

"They want to know what you were doing at Brady's," said Gordon, lifting his eyes from his magazine.

Glinda, whose posture had been unnaturally straight, slumped a little. "Oh. I don't know how you know, but okay. Right." She let the door close. "I just couldn't rest till I found out for myself if Butter had been right."

"And was I?" asked Butter, sitting up straight, and looking remarkably like a hungry baby bird. "Was I right? I was, wasn't I?"

"You were." Glinda pulled out a chair and sat down. "I saw it from outside. It was me. And, I don't know . . . it just made me so mad. That that man would just paint my picture without even asking me. So, I went up and knocked on his door."

"I'd be tickled pink if some man wanted to paint my picture, whether he got my permission or not." Butter popped a grape into her mouth.

"Well, I wasn't," said Glinda. "But after I saw it . . . anyway, I told him I'd sit for him. So he can finish it, you know. He said it'd only take a couple of days. That's all right with you all, isn't it?"

Everyone looked from one to the other. Marietta finally spoke. "Uh, of course it's all right. I tell you what, I promised Brady a dinner this week. Why don't I get him to come over here Thursday night? If the painting is finished, he can show it to us then. I can't wait to see it. That is, if you think you'll all still want to be here then."

"Well, if it's okay with you, I'd love to stay here a few more days, at least. Just till I decide what to do next. I'm not ready to see Macon. Not yet." Glinda looked down at her hands.

Gordon poured another cup of coffee. "I've closed the shop till Saturday, because of Harry. And I called the power company this morning—power won't be on till Friday, so I'm here till then. That is, unless you choose to hoist me to the street." He looked at Marietta, who shook her head.

"And God only knows when I'll be able to get back in the house," said Butter. "I'm going to call over there in a minute, but it'd take a miracle for it to be cleaned up already."

"Well then, it looks like it'll be dinner on Thursday night." Marietta rose and began to take the plates off the table, successfully concealing her disappointment.

Glinda gave them all a shy smile, picked up the book she'd left on the counter, and went to curl up in one of the big chairs by the window.

The other three looked one to another and Gordon gave his shoulders the slightest shrug, before looking over at Glinda and asking, "Um, what's that you're reading?"

Glinda closed the book and stared down at its cover. "*White Teeth,*" she replied. "It reminds me a lot of Dickens."

The soup wouldn't be the same without Worcestershire sauce. Enid cursed herself for not realizing she'd been out of the stuff. She stared through the kitchen window while the pot simmered on the stove, hoping the ice would melt enough for her to run to the store. When cars finally began to pass by the house around eleven, she knew it was safe to be out on the roads. She hurriedly pulled on her coat and picked up her keys, responding with a hearty "Okay" when John called from the den to remind her he was out of ginger snaps.

The Piggly Wiggly was more crowded than she would have expected. Being short on time, Enid kept her head down as she wove her way through the store, hoping not to be spotted by anyone she knew. She'd just turned in to the cookie aisle when she saw two mothers from Ivy's school, deep in conversation by the saltine crackers. She couldn't help but overhear.

"D'you see the news this morning?"

"Our power's still out. I heard about that statue coming down, though. I expect that old man who owned it is on the war path. What's he doing?"

"He's dead, that's what he's doing. Saw the thing pulled down and dropped dead right in front of his bedroom window."

"You're kidding."

"I am not. I've been saying for months something like this was going to happen. And I tell you what, it all started when Betsy Adcock's youngest son graduated. Came back down here and started up about wanting to take down that statue. It's been trouble ever since. You should have heard him last night on the news. Makes you wonder what they're teaching kids in college these days. I mean, that thing's been there for years and nobody's ever had a problem with it. And now look what's happened."

"A lot of people agree with him, though. I know for a fact Melanie Abernathy's got a sign up in her yard. And I've seen Butter Swann's own grandson out in this very parking lot, him and little Ivy Harper's older sister, sticking some of Ernest's flyers on cars. Saw them again at the library just last week. What's that boy's name? Peter? I wonder if Butter knows about that."

Enid felt her face get hot. She backed out of the aisle and hurried off to check out, leaving John's ginger snaps for another day.

25

GORDON, MARIETTA, WILL, AND MACON

The heavy gray clouds evaporated completely around noon, and by two o'clock the melting ice was running down both sides of the street like the coda of a hard rain. It sluiced noisily through the trees on the square, slid off the rooftops like sheets of cellophane. A few adventurous drivers were out, though the older folks wouldn't trust the streets until a full two days of sun had baked them dry, which suited Gordon just fine. He pulled the Fiat into a parallel parking spot, nose first, right in front of his store.

Epiphanies Bookshop sat two doors down from Cline's Antiques and right next door to McClatchey's Flowers, where Gordon stopped every morning to retrieve his standing order of a single yellow rose. No patron of Epiphanies could ever remember seeing him without that rose in his lapel. In the early years Fletcher McClatchey had tried to gussy up the boutonniere with baby's breath and fern, but Gordon always stripped those off before he left the store, so Fletcher had long ago given up on any embellishments. Just one yellow rose and a straight pin, five days a week. Gordon never worked on the weekends.

"I'm just saying, you're going to have to ask her what she intends to do before much longer. She's got to deal with Macon pretty soon, don't you think?" Gordon fiddled with his keys, finally choosing the biggest one. The bell above the wooden door jangled loudly as he opened it, waving Marietta inside. Pallid light drifted through the half-open shutters, so feeble it barely made it to the old plank floors. Gordon switched on a lamp but kept the Closed sign in the window.

Marietta threw her purse into an old leather chair and walked to the New Fiction display, running her hand along the brightly colored covers. "I don't know. I suppose. I swear, Gordon, it's like she's completely lost her mind. One more example of the fact that I don't know anything about people anymore."

"I doubt you ever did. Who does? Just give me a minute. I'm going to check in the back and see if Brady's books are here."

A forest fragrance laced the air, like the inside of an old cedar chest. Marietta's eyes drifted around the shop. She loved this place, and probably would have even if she hadn't been best friends with the owner. Ever since Gordon's first week, she and Harry had made it a point of picking out a new book for themselves every other Wednesday, a lunchtime activity that quickly became routine, and then ritual—something to celebrate, like biweekly birthdays. They'd always finish their visits with coffee and cake in the little café in the back. The last time they'd been in had been in November. Harry had chosen the latest Tana French. Marietta had picked a new edition of *The Wind in the Willows*.

Gordon watched her from the back of the store. No one alive knew better than he did that, given the chance, the horrors of the world could seep into his old friend's body like a noxious gas and poison her as surely as hemlock, calcifying concern into a dark brooding worry that could render her incapable of differentiation, gradation, or context, one that saw every awful thing as equal, allowing it all to enter her soul as one creature, almost corporeal, a monster that could, and would, eat her alive from the inside out if she didn't stay vigilant. He'd seen it happen to her once before and didn't intend to let it happen again.

"Nobody escapes them, you know," he said, dropping the box into another chair and taking out books one by one. "What you're going through. Those awful moments when your life suddenly sharpens down to a point and the space you're standing on becomes too small for your feet. You feel like you have to decide, right then, which way to jump. But that's a lie—you don't. If you wait awhile, surprising things start growing up all around you, and before you know it, you just step off into soft grass and walk on. Just 'be patient, for the world is broad and wide.'"

"Shakespeare?" she asked, grinning.

"Right you are," he said. "Ah, here's Brady's order. The McCarthy trilogy. Good."

For a moment Marietta considered telling Gordon about the little bottle of pills now hiding like something stolen in the table by her bed, but she decided against it. Some things are unmentionable, even, sometimes especially, between friends. Instead, she got up and walked to the window, lifting one of the little horizontal slats on a shutter to peer outside. A group of people were beginning to gather down the street near the courthouse. "Something's going on," she said, squinting to see if there was anyone she knew.

Gordon pulled the shade back on the door and stuck his head around it. "Let's get going," he said, turning back and picking up Brady's books. "That Closed sign in the window won't mean a damn thing if somebody spots me in here."

Marietta followed him out the door and waited while he locked it again. As the small crowd continued to gather a block and a half down the street, they both got back into the Fiat and pulled out of the square, never noticing the strange black bird with the dark, wide wingspan that followed behind them, floating like mist in the January sky.

.   .   .

At three o'clock sharp the sun let loose one anemic ray straight down on the roof of city hall, providing neither warmth nor illumination. Having gotten a tip from Cole Frost, a reporter at the *Wesleyan Journal,* Will now stood at the back of a crowd of about fifteen people, leaning against a No Parking sign and waiting for Macon Hargis to walk out the double doors of his office for a press conference.

"God only knows what he'll say, Will. You might want to be there," whispered Cole, anxious not to be overheard. "Mark my words, Hargis is planning to ride this Griffin thing right into the mayor's office. The rumor he's planning to run has been floating around the paper for weeks. And he won't care how ugly it gets, as long as it helps him win."

Of course, it was already getting ugly. Ernest Adcock's interview, and Mayor Baker's uncomfortable on-camera response, had leapt onto the front page of the *Wesleyan Journal* this morning like a creature with claws, knocking the ice storm down below the fold. Ernest had acted on Will's advice and packed up the offices of MRED, thanked what volunteers he could get hold of for a job that had apparently succeeded without any of their help, and gone to Sandestin to rest and reassess. His parents had turned off their phones.

The town wore edginess like an itchy sweater. When Will stepped through the door of Mama's Way Cafe at one, the windows were steamy, with a voluble lunch crowd even larger than normal, warming their hands around cups of hot coffee and their ears with news that didn't need to be exaggerated to enthrall. Outrage bounced around the tables in whispers louder than the sizzling bacon for the BLTs.

"Whoever did it should be tried for murder, sure as I'm sitting here, I believe that."

"You're crazy. Nobody *murdered* anybody. The old man just died, Janey."

"Yes, but *why* did he die? He looked out, saw that statue down, and *died.* They found him right in front of the window. Now, you

can't tell me the shock of that didn't kill him. As outright as murder, if you ask me."

"Nobody's asking you."

"Who do you think did it? I'm telling you: it was one of those
kids with that Mr. Ed group. I'll bet you anything."

"It wouldn't have been anybody from around here. I'm sure of
that. Couldn't have been. Could it?"

Things quietened down when news filtered in about the brick
that'd been hurled through the MRED window. If anybody felt
that was justified, they weren't going to say so out loud.

Will left Mama's Way Cafe, put on his sunglasses, and looked
around. With the Good Lord seeing fit to snatch Porter Griffin
from the earth, he had indulged in a bit of hope that they'd all
been given a way out of this mess, that what remained of the tension that statue had caused would be swept up and carted off right
along with what remained of the thing itself. Of course, the
situation could always get worse. Will hoped to see that it didn't.

Almost unconsciously, he took the measure of the crowd. A
few reporters from the paper, a couple of clerks from Hargis's office, several curious strollers grateful to be out of the house now
that the ice was beginning to melt. And there was the mayor's
secretary, Lucy-Jewel, wasn't that her name? Over behind the
trunk of that tree. So, Mac had received a tip-off as well. Then
the rumors were probably true. But Will could tell him, Macon
wasn't going to announce his candidacy today. He'd want a bigger
splash, some cameras. Above all, he'd want his wife standing beside him, and Will was one of the few people who knew she
wouldn't be.

At five after three the big oak doors of Hargis Law seemed to
shudder a little, then open wide. Out stepped Macon, grinning
like the politician he was planning to become, followed by three
familiar members of Wesleyan's hierarchy, their presence a clear
indication of Macon's plans. Will recognized Leonard Pennington
of the Historical Society, Mae Jordan of the United Daughters of
the Confederacy, and Noah Broussard of the First Baptist Church.

Macon rearranged his features into a grave expression and, nodding at no one in particular, pulled out a sheet of paper and began to read:

"I want to say that I am heartbroken by the death of my long-term client Mr. Porter Griffin. Heartbroken and horrified by the way in which he died yesterday, prostrate right in front of the window overlooking the destruction of the statue he fought so valiantly to defend. Some could say that sight caused his death, and nobody could prove they were wrong.

"As the sole beneficiary of his estate, I will continue to act on Mr. Griffin's behalf for as long as I can. You all know how much Griffin Park meant to Porter, how much the statue of Henry Benning meant to him, in particular. His own father, Lucius, had that statue erected before Porter was born, to commemorate our Southern heritage and honor the brave boys, *our* brave boys, who fought for it. It is our history, and to those who say it should be removed, well, I say we erase that history at our peril. I believe we are doomed to repeat what we do not remember.

"Therefore, I support the Wesleyan Police Department in their efforts to apprehend the culprit or culprits who destroyed Porter Griffin's statue, and when they are found, I will be pressing charges for criminal trespass immediately. That's the least I can legally do. But when that is done, I will personally be funding an identical replacement of the Henry Benning statue to be reerected in Griffin Park. Thank you all so much."

The muttering started like the flip of a switch.

"What'd he say?"

"Did he say *he'd* inherited Old Man Griffin's estate?"

"Griffin left everything to *Macon*?"

"That sounds about right."

"What? He's gonna put the thing back *up*?"

From the back of the crowd a few people heard Detective Will Cochran say, "*Shit*."

26

———

LUCY-JEWEL, THE MAYOR, CHRISSY, AND REVEREND BROUSSARD

Lucy-Jewel Whitmore lost twenty-six pounds in the summer between her freshman and sophomore years at Auburn, and she'd kept them off all the three long years since, which is the hardest part, as anyone, particularly Lucy-Jewel, can tell you. So, it wasn't for lack of willpower that she couldn't keep from crying whenever she got good and mad. No matter what she did to stop it—from biting the inside of her lip to digging her nails into the palms of her hands—if something really made her angry she'd start bawling before she could think of a single thing to say. She'd teared up just listening to Macon Hargis, and by the time she got back to her desk just outside the mayor's office door, her bottom lip was trembling like tomato aspic. She didn't even bother to hang up her coat but went straight to Mac Baker's door and knocked.

"Come on in."

Mac was standing at the window, chewing on the end of a

pencil. He whirled around when he heard Lucy-Jewel open the door.

"Hey, Lucy-Jewel! What'd you find out?" Then, after taking one look at her face, "Oh, Lord, is it that bad?"

The mayor sat down at his desk and listened as Lucy-Jewel recounted—nearly verbatim, for she had an excellent memory—everything Macon Hargis had told the people on the sidewalk in front of his office. She'd collected herself by the time she was done, grateful to have handed her hot, angry knowledge over to someone who actually might be able to do something about it.

Mac Baker sat silent for a long minute before rising slowly and going back to the window. Lucy-Jewel heard him swear under his breath.

"What are you going to do about it?" she asked.

Her impertinence was noted, but not questioned. "What *can* I do?" he replied. "If Porter Griffin really did leave everything to Macon Hargis, well then, we're in the same fix as we always were. That land belongs to him. And if he wants to rebuild the damn thing, I'm not sure there's anything we can do to stop him."

Having already crossed one invisible line, Lucy-Jewel found it easier to leap over another. "What?" She took a step closer to him. "What do you *mean* you can't do anything about it? You're the mayor, for God's sake. I mean, I understand you couldn't make that old man tear the thing down, but surely, *surely,* you can pass some kind of ordinance or something to prevent somebody else from building another one!"

Mac turned to look at her, almost amused. "And just what do you think a lawyer like Hargis would do if I suddenly passed 'some kind of ordinance or something'? You think he'd just accept that and say, 'Okey dokey then, I'll just change my mind'?"

He could almost see the girl begin to deflate, like a balloon with a slow leak. "Here's the deal, Lucy-Jewel. With Macon Hargis, none of this is about that statue. He couldn't care less about that thing. No, what he's got on his mind is running for mayor."

He almost laughed out loud at the look of shock on her face as she whispered, "No way."

"Yes, ma'am. Sit here, Lucy-Jewel, and take off your coat." Mac turned one of his maroon leather chairs toward her, and he sat down in the other, folding his hands, thinking it out as he talked. "Yeah, I bet you anything that before the filing deadline on August fourteenth, Macon Hargis will be a candidate for mayor of our city. Rumors like that don't start on their own, and I've been hearing them in certain circles since before Thanksgiving. Now, Harrison Gray might well beat him. People like Gray, they like him a lot, and Macon knows it. And I guess you might have heard about the little spot of embarrassment Macon got all over his pants after poor Harry Cline's funeral the other day?" He cut his eyes toward her, and Lucy-Jewel nodded, fighting a grin. "Well, an old peacock like Macon would have taken that pretty hard. Might've caused him to reconsider the whole thing. He could have thought all the attention that comes with running for office just might not be worth it after all. Put his family troubles on a platter for everybody to pick at. But he knows one thing for sure: if he's going to continue with his plans then he's got to make sure everybody forgets what his wife did to him, right there in front of God and everybody, and how's he going to do that?"

Lucy-Jewel sat as wide-eyed as a kid being told a bedtime story. "I don't know," she said.

"Well, you understand I can't say for *certain,* but here's what I'm betting." Mac was tapping his fingers against one another in a speedy rhythm. "Macon Hargis figures pretty much every race is going to be near fifty-fifty, no matter who's running these days. So, if he can just nudge his part of fifty percent up a little tiny bit, then he'll be the one sitting in this office come January, and Harrison Gray will be back at his desk at the high school. It's not as if he's short of blueprints to follow. All he has to do is make a big stink about putting the general back up on his horse, make folks afraid that other people are trying to take something important away from them, hell, that they *took* something away already . . . and he just might stand a chance."

"Damn." Lucy-Jewel blinked at the mayor, who grinned and nodded back.

"My thoughts exactly," he said.

Lucy-Jewel's lips trembled in spite of herself. Sensing the meeting was over, she stood and headed for the door. "But I don't get it," she said, turning around. "Ernest told me that Macon Hargis's father was some big champion of civil rights, that he won awards for it and things. Is that right?"

"Completely right," said Mac. "Logan Hargis was a great man, in my estimation. A courageous man, on the right side of history. But you know, Lucy-Jewel, sometimes the nut falls a long way from the tree."

With her hand on the doorknob, she looked at the mayor. "You, of course, know the one thing that would stop him from ever sitting behind that desk."

The mayor looked up. "What's that?"

"If you were to run one more time."

Lucy-Jewel lowered her eyes and fixed him with a level stare, one that seemed to come from a face much older than her own. Mac was reminded of his late wife, or maybe even his mother, and he felt, for one hot pulse of a moment, that he'd like to throw Macon Hargis in the lake.

She'd been going out with Ernest Adcock for only a few weeks, hadn't even kissed him yet, so she really shouldn't have been so peeved when he called her from the car on his way to the beach. "Maybe you care for this one," her mother had annoyingly observed, never even looking up from her book, when Lucy-Jewel had tossed her phone across the breakfast table in irritation.

"Well, he's not going to get a chance to find out if he runs off and hides like this at the first little bit of trouble."

"Lucy-Jewel, you've got no idea what that boy's probably dealt with since he started this Mr. Ed thing. First bit of trouble, my foot. I cannot begin to imagine all the ugly letters and phone calls, probably even threats, he's received. Just because he hasn't told *you* about every one of them, don't think they haven't happened. Have a little understanding, hon."

"In the first place, *please* don't call it 'Mr. Ed,' Mother. Good *grief*, I wish he hadn't named it that. And in the second, I do know about some of that stuff you're talking about. I'm not naïve. I just think he should've held his head up a little longer. Especially now that somebody's had the good sense to put us all out of our misery and get rid of the thing once and for all."

"I don't blame him a bit for getting out of town right now, Lucy-Jewel. People would think he was gloating if he stayed, and Lord knows what they'd do then." Trudy Whitmore turned a page in her book, never noticing that her daughter had left the room.

Now Lucy-Jewel sat at her desk, staring down at her phone, and wondering if she should call Ernest to tell him about Macon's plans. Her mother had been right: he had been through a lot. She knew this. On their first date somebody in a silver Camry had thrown a tomato at his car while they sat at the red light on Marshland Road, taking off so fast afterward that neither of them could get a tag number. Ernest had just said he was grateful it wasn't a summer tomato. "An old winter one isn't juicy enough to make too much of a mess," he'd said, wiping off the car when they got to the restaurant. But she'd seen the weariness written all over his face, and a bit of humiliation, too.

Lucy-Jewel put the phone back inside her purse and, angry again, this time at herself, wiped a fat tear from her cheek.

Reverend Broussard followed Macon back to his office after the press conference, his new Lands' End parka making a squishing sound every time he swung his arms. Macon hadn't invited him up but the Reverend didn't care; he was used to insinuating himself into other people's company, often without them ever quite figuring out exactly how he'd managed it. He joined people for lunch whenever he saw an empty seat, turned up at parties to which no one remembered inviting him. He considered this natural geniality—for him it could never be labeled anything else—as a useful and necessary tool for evangelism, a calling particularly prized by his Baptist faith, and one that solemnized every daily encounter he had. Macon just thought he was rude.

Chrissy Cantrell felt guilty the minute the preacher walked in, an infuriating holdover from her days in the church. In spite of the fact that she had watched *CBS News Sunday Morning* instead of sitting in a pew since the days when Charles Kuralt was the host, every time Reverend Broussard came in the front door of Hargis Law she still felt like running out the back.

He'd been her pastor when she was a child. From her place in one of those hard wooden pews at First Baptist, she'd sat soaking up a fear of God that remained with her no matter how many times she walked down the aisle to be saved; six trips by the time she was twelve, and none ever seemed to take. It wasn't until she married Jack that she'd felt safe enough to admit that fear, a confession that finally freed her. She'd now come to believe that Noah Broussard didn't really know squat about his chosen subject but found she still looked around for an exit every time she heard the Reverend on the stairs.

From the looks of things, she was going to be fighting flight a lot more over the next few months. Chrissy knew, come hell or high water, on the first Tuesday in November, Noah Broussard planned to see Macon Hargis elected mayor. She expected him to be in and out of this office at least once a week until then.

"All I'm saying is, I think it would do us good for you to start coming over to our church, Macon." The Reverend gave Chrissy a cursory smile as he handed her his coat and followed Macon through to his office. She hung the puffy parka on the rack by the bookcase, grateful that Macon closed his door even though she could still hear every word that was said.

"I don't see any reason for that," said Macon. Chrissy heard the familiar exhalation of his favorite chair. "I've been going to

St. Cyprian's since I was a boy. They might think it strange if I left now."

"I'm going to be frank with you, Macon. Now you know as well as I do, the people in that church are too liberal to ever vote for you. Especially since you're going to be leading the charge to get that statue put back up. It's a noble cause, I do believe that, and I'm proud to stand beside you on this. Like I've always said, history is something to preserve, not erase. And I want you to do what you feel like God is telling you to do. Of course, I want you to do that. I'm just saying there's more people over at First Baptist who'll vote for you. More people on the straight and narrow there if you know what I mean. And some of them just might start wondering why you're choosing to stay in such a liberal congregation. That's all I'm saying."

Chrissy made a face. Oh, I know exactly what you're saying, she thought.

Macon sat staring at the Reverend, comparatively calculating the congregants of the two Wesleyan churches. There was no doubt First Baptist had more people in its pews. "I'll give it some thought, Noah," he said. Chrissy shook her head.

"And now, this little matter about what happened over at Micheline's Saturday, the . . . you know . . . uh, incident with your wife, Macon. With Glindy."

"Glinda," said Macon, looking at the preacher over steepled fingers.

"Right, right. Well now, all of us have little tiffs every now and then. I tell you, my bride, Karen, can get right peevish with me on occasion. And sometimes she forgets to hide it. But now, we need Glindy to, you know, straighten up before this campaign gets under way, and . . ."

"Glinda," said Macon.

"Huh? Oh, yes. Sorry. But I mean, she'll be all right, won't she? She's on board, right? That'll be important to people, you know. You've got you a beautiful family, Macon. People'll need to see them. So, uh, Glin . . . Glinda . . . she's with us, isn't she? You two are okay, aren't you?"

Macon stared straight into the blue eyes of Noah Broussard just long enough to make him uncomfortable and gain the upper hand, then waited a moment longer.

"You won't need to worry about my wife," he said, with a finality that told the Reverend the road to this topic was closed for the rest of the day. On the other side of the door, Chrissy Cantrell made a gagging noise successfully disguised as a cough.

27

MARIETTA, IVY, AND JEN

The laughter they heard from the porch only increased in volume when Marietta opened the door. Following the sound into the kitchen, she and Gordon found Butter and Glinda leaning on the counter, each doubled over with the sorts of sniggers and snorts that generally afflict the tipsy. Butter nudged Glinda when she caught sight of the other two in the doorway, and both women stood up a bit straighter. The bottle of gin sitting between them was nearly empty.

"Oh, hey there," said Butter, a little louder than was necessary. "We thought it'd be good to eat early, since Glinda has to be at Brady's this evening to sit for her picture." She gave Glinda a one-armed hug, and grinned. "And neither of us ate lunch. Did y'all? Is it all right with you two if we eat dinner now?" She turned and pointed to a long dish, still steaming from the oven. "Despite Glinda's recent unfortunate association with this particular concoction, we are having lasagna." Both Butter and Glinda laughed.

"We found Becky Kyle's in the fridge. Figured we could trust her to make a decent one. Jen's is in there, too, but I wouldn't touch that with a ten-foot pole, even if she is my daughter-in-law." She screwed up her face, then laughed again. "She puts eggplant in it." Butter picked up a large glass bowl and held it aloft as though it was an award she'd just won. "Glinda made a salad." Glinda beamed, her long hair draped over one shoulder.

"They are *drunk*," Gordon whispered behind Marietta's back. She pinched his arm, fighting a laugh.

"Uh, sure. That's fine," said Marietta. "Just, um, just let us get out of these heavy coats. We'll be right with you." The two of them backed out of the kitchen, retracing their steps to the foyer.

"Well. Is this going to be a repeat of last night?" asked Gordon, hanging his coat on the rack and removing his gloves. "Who knows what else we might find out?" He looked at Marietta, who swallowed a laugh and shook her head.

Butter was taking the bread out of the oven when they returned to the kitchen. "I thought we'd just eat on trays in the library," she said. "By the fire? Keep from messing up the table, you know. The dogs are next door with Ivy. She said it'd be all right." She sliced the bread into four large pieces and placed one on each plate. "Here you go. One for each of us. Y'all get settled and I'll pour some of this champagne I brought over from the house. I've been saving it for a special occasion."

Butter's last two words were slurred just enough to tempt Gordon into saying, "I don't know, Fluffy. You think you might have already had enough?"

She wheeled around to face Gordon, pointing the bread knife in his face. "Little man, would you please, for God's sake, stop calling me that ridiculous name. I hate it, I always have, and what's more, you know I hate it. It took me years to shake it off, and still . . . even now . . . every time another one of Mary Ann Barber's umpteen cousins up and dies, she comes back to town calling me *Fluffy*, and won't let me get away with acting like I don't know what she's talking about. Nicknames stick to you like tar on a hot highway. Look at Christopher! I gave my *own son* a beautiful name, but that little McGee boy started calling him Christo the first week in kindergarten, and that was that. *Christo.* Sounds like a clown's name."

Surprised at the outburst he attributed, rightly, to too much gin, Gordon's eyes widened, then narrowed. "All this from a woman named *Butter*? The woman doth protest too much. You've gone by a nickname the whole of your life."

"You little weasel. Butter is right there on my birth certificate. Tell him, Marietta! She knows."

Gordon turned to Marietta, who nodded and picked up her tray. "She's telling the truth. That's her real name."

"Yes, and it's not my fault I was saddled with it. I *should* have been called Cassandra, after Mother. Now, that's beautiful. But no. Mama and Daddy thought 'Butter' was sweet, God help them. And speaking of God"—she looked pointedly at Marietta—"if he was interested in evening things out, you would have been named Zenobia, like your great-grandmother, and you"—she turned back to Gordon—"you'd be named . . . oh, what now? . . . 'Tiny,' or 'Knothead.' Something like that."

"Your wit simply devastates me." Gordon's smile, though wicked, held amusement that didn't escape Marietta's notice, but she was surprised when he said, "Okay, Fluffy. I won't call you that again. Ever."

"You, you promise?" said Butter, her shoulders falling a little in disbelief.

"All you had to do was ask me." Gordon settled into the sofa beside Marietta, his dinner tray on his lap.

Butter paused, unsure now about what she'd just done. "Uh, well, good. That's that, then. Good." She picked up the bottle of cold Veuve Clicquot, filled the four glasses, and handed them out. "Okay then, Glinda's got some news. *Big* news." She looked over at Glinda, who'd just taken a bite of lasagna. "Are you going to tell them, or am I?"

Every eye turned to Glinda, and she swallowed hard. "I . . . Butter got a phone call a little while ago . . . from Will, the detective, you know, and . . ." She swallowed again and reached for her glass. Taking a large sip, she looked over at Butter. "You tell it. He talked to you, anyway."

Butter was sitting on ready. "You won't believe it. Will called and told us that Macon held a press conference today. Just a little while ago, in fact. In front of his office. Will was there. He said Macon told everybody there that *he* inherits Porter Griffin's *whole* estate. Lock, stock, and barrel. Can you believe it? I mean, that old coot was worth a fortune. And that house! My God, do you all know how much that thing is worth on today's market? I swear, Glinda went whiter than a boiled egg when I told her. She didn't have any idea. I had to make her a vesper to calm her down. Well, several vespers, actually. I owe you a bottle of gin, Marietta."

Glinda looked up. "You're burying the lede, Butter." They all heard the vein of sarcasm running through the sentence.

"Huh? I am? Oh. Yeah, right. And Macon told everybody he plans to put that old statue back up." There was a long pause. "I really can't believe he'll actually do it, though."

"I can," said Glinda, finishing the last of her wine, glass straight up with her head back.

It was a good fifteen seconds before the wineglass flew past Gordon's nose, so close it made his eyes cross. It hit the door to the garden and shattered, painting the hardwood floor with tiny slivers of clear glass that resembled the ice outside. When they turned to look at Marietta, she was already on her way out of the room.

Through the frost-stenciled window, Ivy had seen the bird light atop Marietta's roof, and known immediately that her friend was back home. This unquestioned knowledge should have struck her as strange, but Ivy was still at an age where she could accept magic as ordinary.

She had hoped some of the ice would remain, but the temperature had risen this afternoon, just like that skinny woman on Channel 12 had said it would, and though Ivy hoped things might refreeze in the night, she'd bet anything school would be open tomorrow. After being outside all day she was now lying on her bed sandwiched between Trilby and Smudge and had just gotten to her favorite part of *Jane Eyre,* the chapter where the mad-woman almost burns Mr. Rochester up in his bed, when she heard the row start downstairs. She slowly stroked Smudge's white fur as she listened, happy not to be the one under the glare of disapproval. It was Thea's turn.

"It's not that we don't think it's a worthy cause, God knows. You know we feel the same as you about that statue. It's just that you should have *told* us, baby." Her mother sounded calm, which usually meant her father would be angrier.

"These people can get violent, Thea," he said, and sure enough, Ivy heard his irritation loud and clear. "I mean, you watch the news, don't you? You've seen what can happen. Do you think I want my baby girl in the middle of something ugly?"

"We just handed out some pamphlets and stuff, Daddy. In the middle of the *day.* Nobody bothered us. I mean, well, we got called a few names and stuff, but that's nothing compared to what John Lewis did in Selma." Thea sounded a little defiant, which Ivy knew would do her no good.

"John Lewis?" There it was: her dad was angry now. "Do you think I want your skull bashed in the way his was? And for your information, that happened in '*the middle of the day,*' too." Ivy heard him take a deep breath like he did when he was trying not to get mad. "Honey, I admire your passion, I really do. But you are sixteen years old. I want you to live to be an old, old woman. I don't want you to get hurt. I suppose you went to that rally in the park back in September? Right? Yeah? I figured. Do you realize that thing could have turned on a dime? All it would've taken was for some of these rednecks to have shown up ready for a fight—or *armed,* for God's sake—and there you'd've been, right in the middle of hell. I know what I'm talking about, Thea, don't you think I don't. Now, I don't blame Peter, he's been just as sheltered as you have. But I think you two should stay away from each other for a few weeks. Until all this settles down. We're going to have to call his parents. No, I'm serious. I'll bet you anything there's some people who aren't going to let this statue thing go anytime soon, and I want you two to stay well out of it. I know Peter's folks will want the same thing. Don't you look at me like that, Thea."

Ivy sat up, listening hard, but Thea didn't reply. She heard her sister come out of the kitchen, go to her room, and slam the door. Having idolized Thea, agreed with her, wanted to be just like her, for as long as she could remember, Ivy felt a bit traitorous and confused now. Maybe it was another sign she was growing up that she could see her father's point. Because, like him, Ivy wanted Thea to stay well out of it, and they both knew it would take a lot more than a talking-to to ensure that she would.

Cellphones announce who's calling, in big block letters right on their screens, so as Marietta heard the ring buzz in her ear for the third time, she knew Macon was holding his phone in his hand, staring down at her name, and deciding whether or not he wanted to talk to his sister. He finally answered, halfway through the fifth ring.

"Marietta. I . . . uh . . . I've been meaning to call you. See how you were. Since the funeral." His formality would have been almost humorous if it hadn't been so painful.

"I'm fine, Macon. I had a migraine, as I'm sure you heard from Butter. You know the drill with those for me—not much I can do but sleep. But that's not why I'm calling."

"Oh?" The defensiveness that pierced that one syllable was sharper than a blade, and Marietta felt her face get hot.

She probably should have waited to make this call until later, when she'd calmed down—she knew that now—but hearing his voice, so equally her brother's and that of a stranger, she couldn't seem to stop herself blurting out, "Macon, what are you doing? How can you possibly put that horrible statue back up? What is *wrong* with you these days? I don't even know you anymore."

"I beg your pardon?" he snapped. "How many times over the

years have I called you, baby sister, to voice my disapproval over your actions? Huh? None, that's how many. You have absolutely no right to tell me anything, and you know why? Because it's none of your damn business. Just like Harry being ill was obviously none of mine."

Marietta sat down heavily on the side of her bed, shocked into a whisper by his anger. "That was how Harry wanted it," she said, her voice as small as a child's. "We didn't tell anybody."

"Oh, I doubt that. I'm sure you told Gordo." The sneer in his voice made Marietta mad. She sat up straighter, holding the phone in a grip so tight her fingers went numb. She could see herself, almost as though she were standing across the room watching, not wanting to say what she was about to say, but powerless to stop the words from leaving her mouth, knowing, even as they did so, they would only make things worse.

"Macon, you have a chance to do something that would benefit the whole town here. By deciding to put that statue back up in the park, you're lighting a fire that can only get hotter till it ends up burning all of us in one way or another, including you. Please don't do it. Think of what Dad stood for here in Wesleyan, don't . . ."

"Oh, and there it is! Throw that up in my face." She heard him take a deep, exaggerated sigh, then pause in what she knew was an attempt to control his anger. "Listen, Marietta," he continued, "I don't want to get into all this with you, I really don't. Not with Harry having just died. So, let's just leave all this alone. Lots of families don't see eye to eye. I know how you feel about everything. Believe me, I've read enough of your 'letters to the editor' to last me a lifetime. I just don't happen to agree with you, and contrary to what you've always thought, about everybody, disagreeing with you doesn't make me a bad person. So, let's just leave all this alone. And you can tell my wife it's fine with me if she stays with you as long as she wants. I'll talk to you soon."

Marietta heard the phone go silent. When she saw Butter's worried face appear at the door, she burst into tears. "I should be able to handle these things better. God." Standing up, she began to pace the room, tears rolling down her cheeks while Butter stood in the doorway, stunned.

"Why do I continually expect him to be different than he is? He's like . . . like . . . gum on my shoe. I want to ignore him completely, but I never can, can I? He'll always be my brother." She pointed toward the door, causing Butter to turn around. "I mean, look at that photo of him on the landing. The one at the top of the stairs. He looks just like Logan. Every time I see him, I think of Dad. I can't help it, and it only makes things worse." She wiped her face roughly with the back of her hand. "What on earth do you do when you no longer like the people you love?"

"Come over here and sit down. You'll make yourself sick." Butter steered Marietta by the shoulders toward the chairs at the window. They both sat, but Marietta hopped right back up, resuming her back-and-forth across the bedroom floor, rubbing her forehead as she paced.

"I should've been stronger, you know? I've never been able to understand why I wasn't. I never told you. Didn't you ever wonder why I quit my job in Atlanta? My dream job, all those years ago? I was going to be like Dad, remember? Some kind of warrior for good, right? Oh, I know I said I didn't enjoy it, that it just wasn't for me, and then three months after I came back home, I met Harry, and well, everything changed. But it turned out I couldn't handle it. The reality of what people are capable of. I covered the Atlanta child murders for the paper, you know, back in 1980? And it broke me right in two, everything just went dark for me, bleak. I didn't have any answers for all I saw. Couldn't even get out of bed, not for weeks. Had to go into a hospital, scared Mother and Dad to death. And I, I've always been afraid it would happen again."

She went to look out the window. "I don't know how to explain it. It's like I'm always walking along the top of this really narrow wall, and on one side is a beautiful sunny meadow and on the other is nothing but quicksand and bones, and I'm up there trying to keep my balance and not fall off on either side. Harry, well, Harry kept me balanced."

"Well, honey, why don't you just drop down on the pretty side and stay there? People do, you know. You can."

"Oh, Butter, I could never pretend the other side's not there. I need to see it all as clearly as I can. How can I help make it better if I don't? And if I don't try to make things better, what good am I?" Marietta let the curtain drop and began to pace the room again. "Macon never knew any of this, never knew what happened to me in Atlanta. I know he thinks I'm rigid, unforgiving, that I demand people see things the way I see them. But I just can't give ugliness an inch, not one inch, or I'm afraid it'll take me over again. Does that make any sense?"

Butter nodded, trying to follow. "Of course it does, sweetheart."

"I know I did the same thing to you, and I'm sorry, Butter. I sat back and assumed I knew how you felt about things, without ever giving you the courtesy of asking. And then, well, because I thought I knew, I just went quiet. I had Harry, and Gordon, and figured they were all that I needed. I walled myself off from everyone else. I know most people probably can't tell, but that's really what I've done. And now, Harry's gone."

"Well, I'm still here," said Butter. "And so's Gordon. And we're not going anywhere."

Outside on the windowsill, the black bird tucked his beak beneath his dark-feathered wing, settling himself in for the night.

Jen had just poured her nightly cup of Lady Grey tea and was on her way to join Christo on the sofa for episode eight of *The Crown* when she heard her phone ring from the bedroom. She almost didn't answer it, but curiosity pushed her up the stairs.

"Hello."

"Is this Jen Swann?"

"It is."

"Jen, this is John Harper. Thea's father?"

"Thea?"

"Yes. You know, Peter's friend? I thought we ought to talk

about what happened in Griffin Park over the weekend. My wife, Enid, and I don't really think the kids should see each other for a while. Just until all this is over. Don't mistake me, I know they didn't have anything to do with it, but you know how people are. The two of them have been seen around town together, working with this MRED group, handing out flyers and things, and we just don't want them to be caught up in something they won't be prepared for."

Jen's cup of tea tilted, splashing hot Lady Grey on her fleece pants. "Ow!" She banged the cup down on her dresser and pulled the wet fleece away from her leg.

"Uh, you all right over there, Mrs. Swann?"

"Huh? Oh, yes, I . . . I just spilled some . . . Mr. Harper, I have absolutely no idea what you're talking about. I don't know anyone named Thea. You must have the wrong number."

"This is Peter Swann's mother, right?"

"Well, yes. I'm Peter's mother, but I'm quite certain he doesn't have a friend named Thea." As fast as she could Jen was mentally examining every Facebook page she'd seen connected with her son. There were just so many of them, and more every day; she couldn't have possibly looked at them all.

"Mrs. Swann, I don't know what to say here. I'm sorry if I'm telling you something you were unaware of, but Thea and Peter have been, uh, well . . . friends, since the summer. We just assumed you both knew. Peter's been to our house on numerous occasions. He's a great kid and we're all really fond of him over here. And I want you to know that Enid and I didn't have a clue the two of them were helping out down at that MRED organization, or we would have made sure to talk that over with you and your husband. Anyway, I guess you'll need to speak with Peter. Just be assured that we're making Thea stay away from any protests or anything that might start up again over the plans to put that statue back up, and we've told her that we think she and Peter should maybe not see each other, for a few weeks at least. Just until all this blows over. And hopefully it will, without any trouble."

"Yes, well . . . thank you, Mr. . . . Harper, was it?"

"Yes. John Harper."

"Right, well. Thank you for calling. I appreciate it."

Her phone still in her hand, Jen sat down on the bed and pulled up Peter's Facebook page, typed in the password he didn't know she had, and looked at his list of friends. My God, he had more than three thousand now. She entered Thea Harper's name in the search box and her rapid breathing stopped cold.

28

HARRISON GRAY, REVEREND BROUSSARD, AND THE MAYOR

Harrison Gray brought his lunch to work most days. Maybe this was because he worked in the same high school he'd gone to as a boy and couldn't imagine doing anything other than what he'd done back then. It still felt like he was out of bounds if he left school in the middle of the day, even if he was now, strange as it sometimes seemed, the principal of Wesleyan High. More likely it was due to the fact that hardly a lunch hour went by without something or somebody needing his attention. Friday it had been a fight in the cafeteria between the Callahan brothers, a nearly weekly event easily anticipated and dealt with. The day before that a freshman girl had passed out cold standing in front of her class reading a poem. An ambulance had to be called. For some reason Harrison had asked who the poet had been. Sylvia Plath, he'd been told. Well, no wonder, he'd thought.

Having once roamed these halls as both a basketball star and a scholar, a rarity even back then, he had the credentials to be one of those men for whom high school remained the pinnacle, the glory days, the Eden. But it was wrong to think he'd gone into education as a way to relive his past. He'd loved the classroom since childhood; teaching had never been his fallback position.

For Harrison there was nothing better than watching the light change in a kid's eyes—from dull jadedness to clear curiosity—and feeling like he'd somehow made it happen. It was better than a full-court buzzer beater with your girlfriend in the stands. And you never knew exactly what might do it; for some kids it took nothing more than the unique arrangement of words in a particular sentence that seemed to have been written for them alone, or a devious arrangement of numbers and symbols, once incomprehensible, then suddenly, miraculously, as decipherable as a name. To think that he could make a difference in the way a person sees, the way a life might turn out, even for one kid, well . . . you could get addicted to that feeling.

He'd run for school board five years ago, not long after being promoted to principal, never expecting to win. But he had won, big. He'd been a classmate, a teammate, a teacher, a coach, to just about everybody in town; not a soul had anything bad to say about Harrison Gray. He'd already been reelected once and would've been again if he hadn't decided to run for mayor.

It was something he'd never have thought of doing if Mac Baker hadn't planned to retire. Mac had always been a claws-out champion for public schools. But last year when he'd made it known that this would be his last term, Harrison had begun to worry. He'd watched the new secretary of education at her confirmation hearings, been stunned by her lack of experience, appalled at some of her proposals. He'd gone around the house fuming for weeks. Finally, his daughter, home from college and never willing to let her father off the hook, pushed him to run. "Think globally, act locally, Daddy," she'd said. "It's not full-time, anyway; you can still keep your day job. And just think what an advocate for teachers and kids you'd be if you were mayor."

Mac had been thrilled when Harrison told him he was planning to run. He'd thrown an arm around Harrison's shoulder and said, "I can feel like Wesleyan's being left in good hands now," evidence of his proprietorial view of the city as well as the prick-ling guilt he felt over leaving his post. So far Harrison was run-ning unopposed, something both he and Mac fully expected to change as the days got closer to the filing deadline in August. Harrison was relieved the race was nonpartisan. He had no stom-ach for the sort of politics he saw being played out on the national stage.

Peering into the little Smeg refrigerator he'd installed in his of-fice, he pulled out a tuna fish sandwich and a Coke. He'd just taken a bite when his door opened and a student aide—one of the twins, Meghan or Melissa, he never could keep them straight—told him the mayor was on the phone. "I told him you were eat-ing lunch," the girl said, shyly, "and he told me to tell you he didn't care." She blushed as though the words had been her own.

"It's okay," he mumbled, tuna salad stuck to the roof of his mouth. "I'll talk to him." Meghan or Melissa closed the door, and Harrison swallowed. He took a quick swig of Coke and picked up his phone. "Hey, Mayor. What can I do for you?"

"Well, Harrison. We've got us a problem."

Lurlene had known Noah Broussard long before the days when his name was on the sign at the First Baptist Church, so she never treated him with the same vaguely uncomfortable deference he was used to inspiring in most of the people around town. This bothered the Reverend more than he ever let on. He always felt a nagging need to put Lurlene in her place, but given her quick wit and reputation for not suffering fools, he never seemed to work up the nerve to try. It was, he thought, one of the more regrettable aspects of the ministry that he couldn't ask his secre-tary to lie and say he wasn't in whenever someone like Lurlene happened to call. He picked up the phone now, feigning delight.

"Lurlene! How wonderful to hear from you. What can I help you with today, my dear?"

"Don't spread it so thick, Noah. I'm not 'your dear,' and you know it. I sat behind you in civics class, back when they used to teach such things, and I'm one of the few people who know there's a bald spot the size of Texas under that store-bought hair of yours. I'm calling about my neighbor. Porter Griffin. Was he a member of First Baptist? I'm wondering about his funeral. I gather he has no family. What have you heard?"

Noah, whose hand had flown protectively to his head, now reached for the little yellow rubber ball his wife had given him to squeeze whenever he got upset. "I don't know if he's on the rolls, Lurlene. But he was here every Easter. I would assume he was a Baptist." He cringed when he heard his own voice; it sounded whiny, even to him.

"Yes, well, I would assume so, too. But could you get Constance to look and see for me? If he is on your rolls, we need to think about some sort of service for him. I don't know if anybody in town will come, but the man deserves a funeral, no matter how much of an old tyrant he was. I figure you agree with me about that?"

A thicket of ideas had started sprouting in the Reverend's head. Disagreeable though he was, Old Man Griffin seemed to be the gift that kept on giving. "Don't you worry about a thing, Lurlene. We'll make sure your neighbor gets an adequate send-off. I'll set it up for Friday. We'll put it in the paper."

"Good. Thank you, Noah. You'll earn your pay this week. I'll see you soon."

Reverend Broussard put the phone down and gave the yellow ball a few enthusiastic squeezes. Thoughts were pinging around his head, bouncing off one another, doubling and tripling into ideas. He called out for his secretary. "Constance? Could you do me a favor and check our rolls? See if Old Man . . . uh . . . Porter Griffin is on them?"

"Give me just a minute, Pastor. We keep those down in Laura's office. I'll go see."

Noah waited until he heard the outer office door close, then picked up the phone.

Macon was at the corner table at Donovan's Reef, waiting on a steak. He usually went to Micheline's for lunch, but after Glinda's display on Saturday, he wasn't sure he'd ever darken that door again.

It was a new waiter who placed his salad on the table, some sort of foreigner, he thought. Macon could tell the man had no idea who he was, and this fact erased any obligatory need for politeness. When his phone rang, he didn't bother to silence it.

"Macon Hargis."

"Hello there, Macon," said Noah Broussard. "I've got a proposition for you."

The bottle of bourbon was old. Mac kept it in the back of his closet, behind some old census reports and the rolled-up plats of once contentious, now defunct, development proposals. He held it up to the afternoon light, amazed it was still half full—or half empty, he supposed, depending on the person looking. The bottle being, as it was, exclusively reserved for particularly detestable days, Mac was surprised to see so much of the cherry brown liquid remained.

He dug around in his desk for two glasses and polished them up on his shirt. The irony of having summoned the high school principal to his office wasn't lost on him, but he knew this was a meeting that had to be had face-to-face. For all the confidence he had in Harrison Gray, he was doubtful the man had any idea of what a successful campaign against Macon Hargis might entail. It wasn't that he thought Harrison weak—quite the opposite, really—he just worried a little that he might be sending a pure-bred into the ring with the neighborhood junkyard dog. Hargis would fight dirty, had already started, and Mac wasn't clear just how Harrison Gray would respond. He intended to find out.

At three-thirty on the dot, Mac heard the outer door open, some polite greetings, then a soft knock on his door. Lucy-Jewel ushered Harrison into the office with the sort of bashfulness adults nearly always retain for their favorite teachers, and Mac told her to go ahead and take off for the day. He'd lock up after his meeting.

He always forgot how tall Harrison really was. Watching the man arrange his long legs in the proffered chair, Mac thought Harrison seemed to be somehow ill-designed for mortal life, almost as though he were royal. Always alert for qualities on which to capitalize, Mac was pleased to note that handsome Harrison Gray was a good five inches taller than his potential opponent, which was something that would irritate Macon Hargis as much as it delighted the man whose job he intended to acquire. The mayor handed the principal a glass of bourbon, and sat down in the opposite chair.

"As I said on the phone, Harrison, I wish like crazy I had better news. There're not too many people I'd hate to see run for this job more than Macon Hargis, for many reasons, the least of which is that he hasn't an idiot's idea what being mayor is all about. If there was some legal way I could stop him, I'd do it in a heartbeat. Might even consider a few *il*legal ways, if I was foxy enough to come up with some. But from what he said yesterday at that jackleg press conference of his, I bet he's planning to run, and run on a platform that just might rip the city in two if we're not careful. We're going to have to come up with some strategies that can tamp down some of this stuff, without making too many people too mad."

Harrison wasn't used to hard liquor, and it burned his throat. The pain was almost welcome. When Mac had told him over the phone what he knew of Macon Hargis's plans, Harrison had lost the appetite for the rest of his sandwich. He hadn't bargained on this. The possibility of his campaign for Wesleyan's mayor being hijacked by the sort of discordance Macon Hargis had in mind made him feel sick. Like a lot of people he knew, he'd been pleased when he heard that statue had been knocked down with so little fanfare, hopeful the whole business was over for good. Now it looked like he was going to be thrown face-first into a fire he'd hoped had just been extinguished.

"Can't I just run on the issues, like I planned, education being the primary one? I mean, everybody knows Tillman Elementary needs a new roof, and the high school is almost out of classrooms.

We've ordered three new trailers for next year already. I don't have any desire whatsoever to see this campaign turn into some kind of right-versus-left circus. Hell, this is a nonpartisan race, Mac. Always has been."

"Well, it ain't nonpartisan anymore, my friend. Macon Hargis plans to line up every Confederate-flag-waving, red-hat-wearing person he can find, you can bet your boots he does. If we let him, he'll turn you into a weak-wristed, bleeding-heart liberal before you can say 'wait a minute.' And it don't matter how important the issues are; you won't be able to do a blame thing about any of 'em if you don't get elected."

Mac, taking Harrison's silence for comprehension if not agreement, continued. "Now, the way I see it, we've got two choices. We can head off Macon at the pass, and you can decry the loss of Porter Griffin's bit of Wesleyan's history even louder than he does, or . . ." He held his palm out toward Harrison, who'd started to sputter complaint. "Or . . . we can simply play his own game on the opposite side of the fence, get the other side riled, come out and say that the removal of that statue was the best thing for the city and you're glad that it's gone. Hit Hargis head-on. Raise your chin and say that taking it down was the right thing to do, in the long run, you know. I mean, I can tell you for a fact, those Mr. Ed folks were right when they said ole Benning was becoming something that discouraged new development. Hell, I was on the phone just last week with Wally Chandler, you know, of Wally's Wings and Wavy Fries? They're all over Florida, and Wally's been thinking about putting one out on Marshland Road—it'd be the first one in the state—but he was curious as to what we planned to do about that damn statue. Said a lot of his people didn't want to come up here if we didn't get rid of the thing. Said their board was nervous about the publicity they'd get. All this social media stuff? You know, it can shut a business down in an afternoon if something bad somebody twitters or something goes septic."

"Viral," said Harrison.

"Oh. Okay. Well so, between you and me, Harrison, whoever

knocked that thing over did Wesleyan a favor. 'Course, it *was* a crime . . . I mean, technically . . . so we'll have to be careful how we put it. But I think we can come up with a way to play it so as not to sound like we're applauding the *way* it came down. Frankly, I wish we actually knew who did it. Would help if we did." Mac was, as usual, figuring things out as he talked.

"But here's the deal," he continued. "The very thing we don't want to do is run from the issue. That's exactly what Macon expects. I've heard people say you can't judge the past with the morals of today, but how do we move forward if we don't? I tell you what, it's one thing for that statue to have gone up in 1918, and it's quite another for somebody to put it back up a hundred years later. We need to illustrate this miscalculation for Macon and cut that bastard off at the knees. If he wants a debate, then we'll debate. If he goes all holier-than-thou on our asses, well . . . your family's churchgoers, aren't they?"

Harrison looked stunned. "Uh, yeah, we are, I guess. First Methodist."

"Good, good. Well, make sure you don't miss a Sunday between now and Election Day. Hell, sing in the choir if you have to. Become a deacon. Do Methodists have deacons? The point is, Harrison, we can't let Macon paint you as some reprobate lefty, and God knows, he'll try. That pie-faced Broussard from over at First Baptist was standing at his elbow yesterday, pious as a priest." The mayor took a long gulp of bourbon. "Now, Harrison, don't look so worried. People really *like* you, even more than they like me, and I'll have you know, I'm beloved. We'll be all right. I guarantee it, you'll be sitting in this office come next year. I just wanted to look right at you and ask if you're up for it. What about it, man? You ready for a fight?"

When he was asked the same question later that night while lying in bed beside Carly, his wife, Harrison said the same thing. "I guess I better be."

29

BRADY, WILL, CONSTANCE, ERNEST, AND PETER

Since the statue had met its ignominious end, speculation about the identity of the culprit had moved through the fecund world of Facebook pages, tweets, and texts like a living thing, each careless comment hastily typed with no concern for consequence or cause, and left out in that fertile, windowless world to spawn so many others of similar nature that by now suspicion had at least grazed everyone in town who'd ever as much as intimated the slightest aversion to the stone memorial of General Henry Benning. No one was prepared to accuse anyone else to their face, however, and when they got right down to it, not a soul in Wesleyan actually believed anybody they knew personally would have done such a destructive thing, no matter how worked up they might have been over an issue that had bloomed into controversy only several years ago. Now that everyone's attention had been so successfully snared by Macon's plan to put the statue back up, the collective view was that whoever knocked it down must have been from out of town.

As news of Benning's imminent rebirth continued to travel across town, cleaving the population of Wesleyan as cleanly as an ax, as was its purpose, homemade signs began to sprout up, most of them equating the resurrection of the statue with the South rising again itself, a trope whose burial ground had always been pretty shallow. Some of these signs were a bit cruder than others. On his way into town, Brady had sat at the traffic light in front of the post office and watched with amusement as Mac Baker made Bob Carroll pull up the one he'd been hammering into the jonquil bed that ran along the sidewalk, the frustration clear in the mayor's voice. "What's gotten *into* you, Bob? You want your grandsons to know this is your handiwork?"

Brady recognized the reporters as he drove past them into the parking lot outside Isbell's Art Supplies. Their forced nonchalance was an act he remembered all too well from the weeks others of their kind had waited outside his ad agency, morning till night, until the afternoon they finally perked up and charged, microphones aimed toward him as he left his office in the handcuffs he still saw as overkill. On this quiet, cold corner in Wesleyan, furtively gazing around for someone deemed most likely to make a sensational interview, they stood out like a troop of kangaroos.

He knew why they were here. As she'd sat on that tall chair in his studio, as still and serene as glass, Glinda had told him a lot. So much, in fact, that he'd been grateful to hide his face behind the canvas on which he painted her likeness. Among other things, he now knew of her husband's plans to reinstall that Confederate statue—something the Californian in Brady saw as nonsensical—and that Macon and Glinda had inherited the fortune that had belonged to Porter Griffin. He'd never seen a woman more embarrassed to be suddenly rich. All this was catnip to news crews hungry for ratings. He knew they'd love nothing more than to stick one of those microphones in Glinda's pale face and was surprised at how protective he felt toward a woman he'd only recently met.

Brady stood for a minute outside the door to Isbell's, watching as one of the reporters—a toothy young man in a peacoat and scarf—approached Bella Davis and her sister, Gail, whom Brady had met at Breakfast at Epiphanies the month they'd read *Prince of Tides*. Although they were normally two of the most agreeable old ladies in town, as soon as the reporter asked them their opinions on the statue, they began to argue like cats. The delight on the interviewer's face was shamefully evident.

"You can't be serious, Gail. I mean"—Bella turned to face the reporter—"personally, I've never had much of a problem with the thing. It's been there since before we were born, so I never thought anything about it and"—turning back to her sister—"neither did you, don't pretend you did. But now that it's been pulled down, I say just let it go. It was all so long ago, none of us need to hold on to it anymore. I'd a whole lot rather everybody gets along. The town's just not the same as it was when that thing went up. Maybe whoever got rid of it did us all a favor."

The microphone immediately swerved to Gail, who sputtered, "Daddy wouldn't have thought that way and you know it." Gail turned to lean in, anxious to be heard. "I mean, we never once thought about *race* when we saw that thing. Mama taught us to say 'horsey' by pointing up at it whenever we went past. I say put it right back up, even shinier than before."

Brady shook his head, and pushed open the door of Isbell's, letting it slam shut behind him.

Will had spent the morning interviewing most of the MRED volunteers, at least those who weren't in school, and found each one of them to be believably shocked, though none could admit they weren't pleased that the object of their righteous passion had been so efficiently dispatched. A few even mentioned "God's will" before Will reminded them that there were those who wanted the statue to stay who'd also claimed messianic support.

Around two o'clock he pulled up alongside Griffin Park and parked the car. This was his third visit, and as he buttoned up his coat and went back through the gates, Will hoped there was something he'd missed.

Lurlene was crossing the street in front of her house, having called Good Neighbors Fencing first thing this morning to see how soon they could come and secure her backyard. Taking Spot for a walk several times a day, especially with patches of ice still lurking here and there, was rapidly losing its charm.

Spot pulled on his leash like a mastiff, and Lurlene grabbed hold of the iron fence for support, yanking the dog to a sliding stop. She almost wished she'd taken that rabbit-head cane Reese had ordered for her, "all the way from Italy," as he so often repeated. It still sat unused by the back door. If she fell today, he'd never let her leave the house without it.

As they rounded the corner, Spot squared his stout little shoulders and propelled Lurlene forward, causing her to bleat out a phrase from her rarely used, but remarkably extensive, lexicon of curses. The detective's head popped up through the bushes, not six feet away. "Whoa! You need some help over there?" he called.

"Oh, hey, Will. No, thanks. We're good. He's just a . . ."—the beagle was tugging again—"a . . . vibrant . . . little creature." Lurlene jerked Spot back and pushed her knitted cap farther up her forehead. She was beginning to break a sweat.

"Hey, by the way . . . ," she said. "I spoke with Noah Broussard, you know, down at First Baptist? And it turns out Porter was a member of that church so Noah's going to make sure there's a proper funeral. It's supposed to be Friday morning. Thought you might like to know."

Will pushed aside the holly branches and came toward the fence. "Huh. Well, that's good. Thanks for telling me. Don't know if I'll make it. I didn't know the old man, except by reputation, you know."

Lurlene snorted. "Well then, you knew him as well as anyone. He fit his reputation pretty perfectly. You take care now."

"You, too."

Will watched her continue on, her newly acquired pet pulling her forward as if she were a feather in a windstorm. As he headed back to his car, he considered what she'd said. If Reverend Broussard was in charge of Griffin's funeral as well as helping Macon Hargis get elected . . . Maybe he should find out a little more. Will pulled out his phone when he got in the car.

Constance Farrell had been the secretary at First Baptist for many years. She'd already been through three different pastors by the time Noah Broussard put his brass nameplate on the desk and had adapted to each of them as neatly as a well-tailored suit, even though none had stayed longer than a couple of years. Only one had left under ignominious circumstances, though, and that had been something Constance considered to be at least as much the fault of that divorcée who'd moved here from Charleston as it was of the former Reverend Smith. Constance's loyalty to each one of her bosses was unwavering, but in Noah Broussard she felt she'd finally found a man worthy of that devotion, fully and completely. Constance was the lion at the gate that every pastor prays for. In her eyes, the current reverend could quite simply do no wrong.

When Will phoned to ask about the funeral, she was pleased to tell him that Reverend Broussard was planning a lovely service for the man that nobody particularly liked. Of course, she didn't say that last part out loud, but she thought it, as she knew most of Wesleyan probably would. This funeral was only more proof that Reverend Broussard was a wonderful man, in case there was anybody who needed it.

"Let me see here," Constance said, pushing her reading glasses higher up her nose. "I'm just typing up the program now. Yvonne Little is going to sing. She's got a beautiful voice. Lead soprano in the choir. Sings the national anthem at our Values and Votes conferences every year. She's singing "How Great Thou Art." And . . . Leonard Pennington is to read from Ephesians, and Mae Jordan is doing a poem by Henry Timrod. Of course, Reverend Broussard will give the sermon. Oh, and Macon Hargis is doing the eulogy, right before the Reverend speaks. Like I said, it should be a lovely service."

Will thanked Constance and ended the call. He sat in his car, tapping his fingers on the steering wheel.

Ernest Adcock always figured the people who called this the Redneck Riviera either had never been here, or just had no appreciation for beauty. Particularly now, when there was hardly another soul around, this was his favorite beach. He dug his bare feet deeper into the sand and pulled his sweater up tighter around his neck. January wasn't the best month to visit, but he'd needed to get away to a place where all his memories were good. Sandestin had been where his family had taken every summer vacation when he was little, and the halcyon glow it had acquired during those years had never faded for Ernest.

He'd sat on the beach for the last day and a half, considering what to do next. His main goal had been accomplished. The statue had come down. He should have been pleased, and he was, down deep. But his victory seemed clouded by the fact that he'd had nothing to do with it. No real statement had been made, no good triumphing over evil and all that. It had just suddenly disappeared with no one to thank, or to blame.

He told himself that shouldn't matter. Getting rid of the thing was the point. But as ashamed as he was to admit it, Ernest would have liked to have had a bit of pomp, something to underline the event and claim it for history. After all the embarrassment he'd endured over naming his committee MRED—and pretending that didn't bother him, which was much harder than it had looked—not to mention having had a brick thrown through his window as well as several perfectly aimed insults, some eggs, and at least one tomato hurled in his direction, it just seemed like he should have been in a place to claim a victory of sorts, even if it was a bit pyrrhic. Ernest closed his eyes and listened to the waves.

He'd turned the ringer off but could still feel his phone vibrating in his front shirt pocket. He let it buzz on for a few seconds before pulling it out. He'd expected to see Lucy-Jewel's number, or maybe his mother's, and was surprised when the name of one of MRED's younger volunteers popped up on the screen.

Peter Swann was grounded for eternity. It wasn't because of Thea; his parents had stressed that point so heavily anyone with half a brain would've doubted it was true, as Peter most certainly did. Nor was it because he'd been working with the group trying to remove the only Confederate statue in Wesleyan. "Not in the slightest," they'd said. No, he was grounded because he hadn't told them, which was, in their eyes, infinitely worse. "You can lie just as much by not telling us something as by telling us," his father had said, while his mother had stood behind him, her eyes red from crying or fuming, Peter couldn't tell which.

He'd heard by accident about Old Man Griffin's lawyer's plans to rebuild the statue, not meaning to eavesdrop when their neighbor stopped by to let them know the estimate for removing the big oak tree the ice had brought down on the swimming pool fence. Lemuel Pratt, the president of the homeowners' association, had been in city hall to pay his water bill and had heard people discussing the Hargis press conference.

"Yes, I tell you, it pays to have rich clients," Lemuel said. "That Porter Griffin left everything he owned to Macon Hargis. I mean, the whole enchilada, and he owned quite a lot. And now Hargis is saying he's going to put that statue back up to honor the old man's wishes."

Peter had crept away from the kitchen and up to his room to call Ernest.

"You're absolutely sure about this?" Ernest was having trouble hearing in the seaside wind.

"That's what Mr. Pratt said. And he heard it from some people who'd been there when the lawyer was talking. So, I guess it's right. Whatcha going to do, Ernest?"

"I'm coming home," Ernest said.

30

MARIETTA, GORDON, GLINDA, AND BUTTER

As girls, she and Butter used to ride down the sidewalks of The Glade on their bicycles, all the way to the end of the neighborhood, where scores of other children on similar conveyances had worn a narrow path between the two houses that sat in the palm of the very last cul-de-sac, all on their way to the creek. Too insignificant to be named, the creek wound its way around the border of The Glade, its water clear as glass, its bed full of moss-slick stones and chocolate-pudding mud, home to tadpoles and turtles and the occasional heron who had taken a detour on its way to the marsh. Some of the older boys had once said they'd seen a water moccasin curled up on a rock, its triangular head resting atop a tightly coiled body that had to be at least five feet long, but believing them would have meant staying away from the creek, so nobody really did.

Butter always kept a radio in the basket of her bike, turned up loud so she and Marietta could pedal along to the music, their own personal soundtrack to the journey they took almost every summer morning, speeding up when a fast song played, slowing down to a ballad. Once the bikes were laid on their sides in the tall grass, and the girls had made themselves comfortable on one of the cool, flat rocks that lined that part of the creek, they'd unwrap the sandwiches Caroline had made them, lean back against a tree, and talk. Who knows what they talked about? It's never the words one remembers. Rather, it's the feeling that remains, that indefinable closeness that ties childhood friends together, no matter how far they travel apart. Butter had never lost that feeling for Marietta, and if Marietta had forgotten its comfort, her long confession to Butter had returned it to her.

For the past four nights Marietta and Butter had closed all the curtains against the cold and curled up by the fire while they watched a series of old movies. They'd eaten popcorn, talked trivialities, teased Gordon, and as she sat dozing on the porch beside Gordon this morning, Marietta felt as far removed from grief as she'd been since before Harry had gotten sick last April. The distraction was a gift the ice storm had given her, she knew this. Sequestered here in the house with the people who'd known her the longest and best, it had been easy to forget about Macon, easy to believe nothing was wrong in the world. Until they went home, it was all Marietta wanted. She couldn't think any further than that.

This morning the sharp edge of the ice storm no longer honed the air. Every hour since dawn had lightened and lifted until now as she sat looking out the sunroom windows, lost in lazy memory, Marietta could almost believe in spring. In Wesleyan it seemed, once entertained, the simple idea of that season was enough to set it moving across the fields and out to the marshes, turning everything green. Soon, she knew, it would be hot enough to glue the breezes together.

Beside her in a straight-backed chair, Gordon sat shucking corn and wondering where it had come from. January corn. He fully expected it to be as flavorless as cardboard. Still, Brady had brought over a load of fresh shrimp for dinner tonight, and it was an unwritten rule in this part of the world that corn on the cob would have to be part of that menu. The sun sidled away from his bare feet, and Gordon felt the temperature fall in response. He scooted his chair forward, out of the shade.

Although he was keeping it to himself, Gordon was ready to go home. Being the solitary creature he was, he longed for a private night, alone with a good book, a cup of coffee, and Trilby by the fire. He'd never lived with anyone else after Alan and wasn't the least bit ashamed to be set in his ways. Here with this trio of disparate women—one who'd lost her husband, one who'd lost her house, and the other who'd, apparently, lost her mind—he was beginning to feel a bit twitchy.

The sudden appearance of Butter made him jump, a half-shucked ear of corn falling from his fingers and rolling across the floor. Marietta stopped it with her foot, brushed it off, and tossed it into the large china bowl wedged between Gordon's knees.

"Sorry. Didn't mean to scare you." Butter stood in the doorway with one leg pulled up behind her, stretching, and staring outside. "I'm going for a run."

"You should go with her," said Marietta, grinning over at Gordon.

"Only if I can bring my corn."

The two of them watched Butter as she went down the side stairs, breaking into an easy lope on her way to the sidewalk. "How many times a day does that woman run?" asked Gordon, squinting as the sunlight hit his eyes.

"Several. Between you and me, I think she's been using it as an excuse to talk to her detective. I hear her on the phone to him a couple of times a day. There's a big crush happening there, I do believe. And it seems to be mutual. I told her to invite him to dinner tonight. She seems really happy. Hasn't moaned about her house at all."

"Well, thank God for that. I couldn't take any more drama. I mean . . ." Gordon looked around dramatically. "Glinda? Seriously? What's she doing over there at Brady's every night? Now that it's just the two of us, you can't tell me you don't think that isn't weird. I mean, *Glinda*. Straitlaced, perfectly coiffed, clear-nail-polish Glinda? I don't suppose she's said anything to you?"

"No. And I don't know. I really don't."

"It's like I've always said, the ones who are wound up the tightest eventually blow up the biggest. A few little sins along the way might have helped ease her along. Kept her from saving them all up for one week, you know? I mean, if things were going to be awkward with Macon before, when he just had a little lunch on his britches, I hate to think what's going to happen when he finds out his wife has been playing patty fingers with an artist."

"No. *No!* I can't believe that. You don't really think so? Like you say, it's *Glinda,* for Pete's sake, Gordon. I'm not sure about Brady, but I just can't bring myself to think Glinda's been doing anything other than sitting for a painting, just like she's told us." They looked at each other, and Gordon shook his head.

" 'The fittest time to corrupt a man's wife is when she's fallen out with her husband.' Besides, you heard her the other night. She might not remember everything she told us—she was sloshed, after all—but I'm telling you, I haven't seen somebody more liable to take a walk on the wild side since the night I got lost in the French Quarter during Mardi Gras, 1978, which is a story best left to another time."

"Maybe we'll be able to tell tonight," Marietta said, closing her eyes as the warm sun crept over her face. "Brady's supposed to unveil that painting at dinner. We'll get to see them both together."

"And you really don't think she had any idea they would inherit all of Old Man Griffin's estate? I know she went and got drunk again when Butter told her what Macon had said in that stupid press conference of his, but I couldn't tell if it was because of that statue or because of the fact that she's now a bona fide heiress. I mean, that old guy was worth a fortune, wasn't he?"

"I think he was. But I really don't believe Glinda knew. And I don't think we should ask her. Not right now, anyway."

"Honey, I'm not saying anything to anybody." The next to last
ear of corn fell into the bowl as an exclamation point.

The house was so quiet. Glinda could hear them talking, their
voices carried along on a current of central heating that wafted
up to her little guest room under the eaves, where she lay on her
back in the bed. Their words were a reminder of all she'd pushed
to the corners of her mind these past several days, these past forty
years, and they didn't bother her in the slightest, which she saw
as more evidence of how far out she'd flown since Harry's funeral. If she hadn't left home the morning of the ice storm, if
she'd faced Macon that very day, would things have been different? Would it have been possible to turn away once again from
the truth she'd denied all these years? She'd said it all aloud now,
told everything to a man she barely knew, and the spoken word
always makes things real.

She'd lied to her friends when she married. Told everyone she
felt the same fluttery feelings her roommates described when
they returned to the dorm rooms late at night after finally meeting "the one." She'd shown them the huge solitaire on her finger,
nodded and grinned, and said, yes, she too knew what it felt like
to lose the ability to eat, or sleep, to be so consumed by thoughts
of that one special person that you could honestly stand on a
street corner you'd known all your life and not have a clue where
you were, which is what actually happened to her friend Vickie
Butler when she got engaged. The girl froze stock-still one hot
afternoon on the corner of Peachtree Street and Brighton Road,
lost as a goose, one half mile from where she grew up. Later on,
Glinda just lied to herself.

She turned over on her side, pulling her knees to her chest. It
was when the children were little, and they'd gone on that trip to
see the redwoods; that's when she'd known it for sure. Standing
beneath those ancient trees she'd felt so insignificant, so small, a
wonderful feeling. She'd bent her head back as far as it would go
and still couldn't see the top of Hyperion, the tallest one. Her

eyes had followed the great tree down, down, down, to where
Macon stood at its wide base, impatiently calling for her to take
his picture, and that, hardly an epochal moment, was when she'd
known for certain she had never been in love.

It terrified her to admit it. Looking at him standing there with
his picture smile on his face, it had just hit her like a spray of cold
water, the horrible fact that she'd never thrilled to Macon's touch
the way women did in books, never caught her breath at the sight
of him coming toward her in a crowd or lain awake in the middle
of the night just to listen to him breathing. By the time she realized it, her girlfriends had lost all those gleaming emotions themselves and begun to divorce, or at least complain about, the men
they had married—those same men who'd once elicited such
passion and lust—so Glinda figured that even if she'd never had
the feelings she'd expected, and hoped for, they obviously weren't
designed to last. She'd just been spared the pain of disillusionment
when they gradually slipped away. You never miss what you didn't
have, she'd thought.

The hardest part was that nothing changed after the redwoods.
She buried the knowledge so carefully, so completely, she thought
she'd never be able to find it again. But she could now see that it
had been like swallowing an explosive, a tiny bomb of truth guaranteed to rip everything apart one day without warning, and
now that day was here.

The hours she'd spent, sitting on a tall, high-backed chair,
under the laser-sharp gaze of a man she didn't know while he attempted to document this moment in her life, had felt like the
most intimate experience she'd known. She wanted this painting,
wanted—no, *needed*—to see what Brady Goode was seeing, because she knew it had never been there before. She could lie to
herself in a mirror, Lord knows she'd done it for years, quickly
rearranging her face into something more serenely benign whenever she caught even a glimpse of disquiet. But a painting always
told the truth. Having this record of who she was now, she
thought, just might give her the courage she'd need to never lose
this person again.

The painting had felt like a violation when she first saw it through his window, her expression so naked and revealing she could have slapped Brady Goode in the face. She'd stomped into his house, tracking ice on his floor, fully prepared to demand that he tear the thing up. Then he'd turned the canvas around to face her and her legs had suddenly felt like they were full of wet sand. She'd leaned back against a table and stared into the face of the woman she'd always wanted to be. Brady hadn't even noticed. He'd stood there behind her, arms crossed, analyzing her image with all the detached precision of a surgeon. He was proud of his work. She could hear it in his voice.

"I tell you what," he'd said. "I'll cook your lunch if you'll just sit for me today. Maybe tomorrow, too. You could really help me get this right. I'm a good cook, so it's not a disingenuous invitation."

And she'd turned around to face him, saying, "I can't sit for a *portrait*. Look at me. I'm a mess. I've hardly had any sleep at all, and my clothes are all wrinkled. This sweater is a hundred years old, and my hair . . ." She'd run her fingers through her hair, so unused to it being down around her shoulders.

Brady had smiled when he said, "Ma'am, I can't compare how you regularly look with the woman standing in front of me, because I don't really know you at all. But anything you added to yourself would be, in my humble opinion, merely gilding the lily. You are perfect just as you are."

And that had been the first time in Glinda's whole life she'd known a fluttery feeling for herself.

She'd told him he could do it only if he'd give her the portrait when he was through, and he'd reluctantly agreed. So, there she'd sat, for hours in his studio, while the winter sunlight fell through the tall glass windows and her heart kept time with the icicles dripping from the eaves, and she'd talked. With Brady's face hidden behind the canvas the studio had been for her what Glinda imagined a confessional was to a Catholic, and she'd told him things she'd never told a soul, not even herself. It was in that forced stillness, so far from the troubles of home, that she began to listen to her own words, and began, bit by bit, to put herself back together again.

It had happened last night, just as she was leaving, the painting finished, the talking all done. She'd taken steps she could never retrace when she reached for the doorknob, and he placed a hand on her shoulder. She could smell the paint and turpentine on his old flannel shirt, and when she'd turned to face him, he'd slipped his hand around her neck, lifted up her hair, and kissed her softly, just below her ear. Glinda had felt her insides turn liquid and had backed into the door for support. By the time he reached her lips she no longer cared about anything but how it felt to be wanted by someone who was a stranger to her only four days before.

She knew she should feel ashamed and probably would in time, but right now, at this moment as she lay in bed listening to Marietta and Gordon talking about her as though she were some- one else, Glinda could honestly say she felt more at peace with herself than she had in years. Brady had, quite unwittingly, she supposed, given her the courage she needed to do what she had to, and she'd always be grateful to the man for that, even as she knew neither of them would ever mention last night again.

Butter had avoided looking at Gordon when she stood in the sunroom doorway. She hoped he hadn't noticed, but he probably had. The man rarely missed anything; from a wink to a nod his eyes caught it all, and after last night, who knew that better than she?

It had been after dinner, and the three of them sitting in those same sunroom chairs, hardly talking, while the sun sank lower and lower behind the bare trees, like the closing of a sleepy eye. With the darkness came the cold. Marietta was wrapped up in one of Harry's old robes; Gordon had a blanket over his lap. When she'd shivered, he'd offered to run upstairs and get her a sweater, and Butter had been grateful, only a few moments later realizing what he might find when he opened her suitcase, sitting there on the floor of her room.

She'd jumped up and followed him but had been too late. When she'd gotten there, he was standing by her bed, Marietta's little silver box with the engraved "H" on its top, shining in the center of his hand, fallen from its hiding place in the sleeve of Butter's sweater, which was now draped over his arm.

His face wouldn't tell if he was quizzical or amused, and it was the mile-wide difference between those two reactions that made Butter so mad. She would have gotten around to anger eventually, of course, if only to sidestep the embarrassment that crawled up her spine like a rash. She'd snatched the box from him and stuck it back in her suitcase before saying, more nonchalantly than she knew was appropriate, "It was just a silly impulse, a whim. I'll apologize to her. She'll forgive me."

"You will not apologize," he'd said, narrowing his hazel eyes to olive green slits. "Marietta doesn't need to make *you* feel better. She doesn't even know the thing is missing. Just put it back the first chance you get. Besides, my dear, you don't get to ask the person you're jealous of to forgive *you*." And with that, he'd dropped the sweater onto her bed and walked from the room, leaving Butter's feeble "Jealous? Who said anything about being jealous?" evaporating in the air like a bad smell.

He was waiting for an explanation, she could feel it, like a smug little priest in a robe. And so now she ran, faster and faster down the sidewalks of The Glade, away from the knowledge that he had been right. But no one was that good a runner, and when she finally reached the creek, out of breath and sweating, Butter slumped down on one of the same cold rocks she and Marietta had so frequently visited as girls.

Gordon had done what she'd never had the courage to do. He'd spoken the truth out loud. And he'd known the truth for years, of course he had; he'd watched her watch Marietta since the days when they were kids. He'd seen how much she'd always craved Marietta's approval, attention, and maybe, sometimes, just a bit of her own jealousy back. And now he had proof. She shuddered to think what he'd say about all the others. But nothing of any value, Butter thought desperately, as she sat alone, staring down at her reflection in the clear waters of the creek. Probably nothing Marietta had ever even missed.

She could see them all now, huddled together in that old shoebox she kept under her bed. A barrette shaped like a butter-fly. She'd taken that from the top of Marietta's desk in third grade. A hardback copy of *Matilda,* signed to Marietta from her aunt Kathleen, loaned to Butter and purposely never returned. A handkerchief embroidered with pink flowers that . . . oh, God . . . had probably belonged to her mother. Butter had lifted that right out of Marietta's purse the weekend she married Joe. And . . . well . . . a few other things—all small, though, nothing big . . . nothing of value, not really.

She'd known he needed no tangible proof. The knowledge had always been there on Gordon's face, every time they hap-pened to be in the same place at the same time, that little wicked flash of mirth in the center of his eye, that tiny bit of laughter in the corner of his mouth. Butter had hated him for it, too. He'd always seen straight through her to the secret she'd tried to keep hidden: that for so long she'd been so jealous of Marietta that it had sometimes made her sick.

What made this all so much worse was that something had changed when Marietta opened up to Butter the other night: a spell had broken, a curtain had torn, the shimmering bubble in which Butter had encased Marietta since childhood had suddenly burst, allowing Butter to see her old friend as the lovely, fright-ened, kind, unforgiving human she was. She could never have guessed Marietta was that breakable.

She'd grabbed that silver box as she had all the other things, without thought, almost as though it were hers, as if hoping that a tangible piece of Marietta, though stolen, could bridge the space that gaped between them. But that space had never existed. Despite the impression she gave, Marietta had always been just the same as anybody else, susceptible to anger and confusion, sor-row and love. Butter had felt a return of their friendship of child-hood, before assumptions and expectations muddied the water.

But that silver box could ruin everything. Butter couldn't

shake the fear that Marietta would find this admission so bewildering that their friendship, which had faded to pale these past few years, might easily dissolve right into nothingness. She leaned back against a tree with her arms crossed over her eyes, the laughter of the creek in her ears.

She stayed like that for a good fifteen minutes, till her phone sang out from inside the pocket of her jacket. When she pulled it out, her heart somersaulted over Will Cochran's name shining there in the dappled winter light. "Hi, there," she answered.

"So, what time do you want me tonight?" he asked. Butter grinned, and the little pilfered box drifted down to the basement of her mind.

31

LUCY-JEWEL, THE MAYOR, ERNEST, AND MACON

Lucy-Jewel was typing the minutes of the last city council meeting in between bites of strawberry yogurt. She'd just gotten to the citizens' input section, always the most tedious part, and she rested her head on her hand, wondering whether anyone would notice if she paraphrased Alex Bailey's routine rant. The man spent the entire two weeks between meetings scouring the city for something new to complain about, but this time he was covering old ground. That he found the stop sign in front of his house woefully inadequate, especially every afternoon around three-thirty, when the high school kids were let loose, was already a well-documented fact. There was no reason to type it all up again, and not just because at this particular meeting he'd called his own councilman a jackass. Lucy-Jewel was disinclined to type that into the official record and had just decided to skip Alex Bailey's comments completely when somebody knocked on the door.

"Come on in," she called, standing up and shoving the carton of yogurt into her drawer. She sat right back down again when Ernest walked in.

"What are you doing here? I thought you were at the beach."

"Your boss called me this morning. Wants to talk to me about something. Got any idea what?" Ernest sat down across from Lucy-Jewel and crossed his legs.

"The mayor called *you*? Well, gee, that can't be good, can it?" Ernest shrugged. "Anyway, why aren't you still in Florida? I thought you were staying the whole week."

"I was. But then I heard about the new plans to do . . . you know . . . try and revive that damn statue, and I wondered if I should come back. Don't know exactly what I can do about it. I mean, if Old Man Griffin was a fierce opponent, then Macon Hargis will eat us alive. But I figured I owed it to everybody to at least talk to them about it. See what they think we should do. So, I came on home."

"Well, if y'all decide to fight this at all, do yourself a favor and change that name. And check all the possible acronyms before you do."

A pained expression washed over Ernest's thin face, and she was almost sad to have said it. She got up and bent her head toward the mayor's door. "If he wants to see you, I guess I better show you in." Ernest stood behind her as she knocked.

"Come in," called Mac, and his cheerful tone, Lucy-Jewel knew, signified nothing. He could be mad as a demon, and he'd still sound like that. She stood aside, Ernest walked past her, and she quietly closed the door, fighting, and losing, the battle to stand there and listen.

Mac gave the boy a long, hard look, fully mindful of the intimidating weight of his stare. It came with the office, and he used it judiciously, cross-referencing those who withered beneath it with the ones who sent the thing back to him with one of their own. It was useful information. Ernest Adcock merely returned the stare with a half-bemused smile. Mac thought he might like the boy.

"So. Mr. Adcock. Take a seat." Mac gestured to the chair in

front of his desk, and Ernest sat down. The mayor folded his hands. "I've been watching you for a while now, Ernest," he said, squinting ever so slightly.

"Why?" This was not the response Mac expected.

"Why? Well . . . you've been making a few waves in town since you came back from school. You seem to be a man of convictions. Convictions that you know how to act on. People listen to what you say; they follow you. That's a big responsibility, son, and you seem to have weathered it well."

"If by 'listen to what you say' you mean throwing bricks and tomatoes at me, well then, yeah, I've been a huge success. The very thing I was working for did happen, though, even if I had nothing to do with it. So, I'm feeling pretty good about that. At least I was, until the old man's lawyer decided to put the thing back up."

"Yeah, well. That's unfortunate. But maybe we can help each other out on that." The mayor saw a flicker of suspicion cross Ernest's face and couldn't say he really blamed the kid. People his age had been raised to distrust politicians, and probably for good reason. Mac decided to get straight to the point. "Look, Ernest, here's the deal. Not too many people know this yet, but good money's on Macon Hargis running for my job. This is my last term, you know." Mac paused for a second to allow for the usual exclamations of regret but could instantly see none were forthcoming. He continued, "And I'll tell anyone who'll listen that Hargis is not the man for the job. Especially as I can see that he's going to use this issue to whip up support and split the city even more than the thing's already done."

Ernest nodded, still confused about why he was being made privy to this information.

"You graduated from Wesleyan High, didn't you?" Mac asked.

"Uh . . . yes, sir. Class of 2013."

"So Harrison Gray was your principal."

"Oh yeah. Mr. Gray was great. Used to come play pickup games in the gym with us after school. I dunked on him once, not an easy thing to do. He seemed to love it, too. Made my day. I lived off that for weeks."

"Yes, Harrison's a great fellow. A good man. And he'll be a terrific mayor if I have anything to do about it."

"Is he running?" asked Ernest, and Mac was pleased to see excitement in his eyes. This was how he wanted everybody to feel when they heard Harrison Gray was throwing his hat into the ring.

"He is indeed. And he's going to be looking for a well-organized, passionate, intelligent campaign manager. You see where I'm going with this, Ernest? I'm of the opinion that that man should be you."

Finally, thought Mac. I've said something that rattled the boy. Ernest gaped at him now, unable to formulate a cogent response. "Me?" he asked. "You want *me*?"

"I do," said Mac. "You've already got some good volunteers working with you. I've seen them putting flyers on all the cars at the Piggly Wiggly every afternoon since Thanksgiving. A dedicated bunch. You call 'em up and get 'em to help us out. Let everybody know that Principal Gray needs to be our next mayor. What do you think, Ernest? You in?"

Always a sitting duck for a pep talk, Ernest nodded vigorously before he even gave it a good thought, but even if he'd done so, the answer would have been the same.

"Good deal, son. Good deal." The mayor slapped his hand down on his desk and grinned. "And your first act of business is going to be attending Porter Griffin's funeral tomorrow, right along with me and Harrison. Confuse the hell out of the opposition. Bring Lucy-Jewel with you but tell her if during the proceedings she happens to get mad, I do not want to see her start crying."

The trail that began just outside Red Rascal's paddock coiled through a patch of piney woods unknown to most of the citizens of Wesleyan. It continued up and over the gentle ridge that bordered Highway 4, and slid down alongside the azalea-studded gardens at the Jessamine Country Club, where Macon Hargis had been a member since the year he turned thirty-five. That was also the year he won the largest divorce settlement in the county's history for Miriam Longstreet, who'd been the only daughter of the country club president, and whose disastrous marriage the man had been anxious to eradicate in the most lucrative way. Macon's rapid admission to Jessamine was something he'd chosen to see as coincidental rather than compensatory.

This ride was one he took every day, or at least tried to, even in the thickest hours of summer, when humidity cloaked both horse and man, making them damp and choleric long before the final gallop toward the barn. It was the one time of day Macon felt truly himself, and if he ever questioned why he was closer to Red Rascal than to any other creature on earth he'd look to these rides for the answer.

Today was turning into a battle of wills. Invigorated by a temperature that refused to climb above fifty degrees, Red Rascal wanted to run, tossing his head, and kicking in frustration whenever Macon pulled him back to a walk from a canter. Macon needed to think, and a slow walk along this trail was the best place to do it. Old Man Griffin's funeral had made the news, thereby garnering more attention than Macon had expected when he agreed to do the eulogy, and this was putting him deep in second thoughts. He'd never given a eulogy before. It required a certain kind of sincerity that Macon found difficult to feel, much less express in public, and the more he thought about what to say, the more he regretted having agreed to say anything at all, particularly when he had so much at stake.

So far, the idea for putting the statue back up had achieved what Macon had hoped it would. He'd been clapped on the back for two days by those in town who, he knew, were best placed to support his campaign. People were talking, people were taking sides, and he hadn't been asked about his humiliating exit from

Micheline's last Saturday afternoon, not even once. As long as he played it carefully, got the right kind of publicity, Macon figured the wave of sentiment that old statue engendered would bear him straight into Mac Baker's office without a wrinkle in his shirt.

If only he hadn't seen those letters this morning. Remembering Chrissy's censorious tone when she'd flung them onto his desk made him only more unsettled. "Here you go," she'd said, before turning on her heel. "You might want to take a look at *these* before that funeral tomorrow." She'd slammed his office door on her way out, something deference, he assumed, had never permitted before.

He had to admit he'd blanched when he read them. Some were ugly, all were angry, and each clearly implied that Macon was in full agreement with every word. If any of these letter writers came to the funeral and caused a ruckus, Macon wasn't sure what he'd do.

He knew the people of his hometown. After forty years in the courtroom, he could choose a Wesleyan jury with an accuracy that was almost mechanical. Pull any one of them out of a crowd and Macon could tell you what books they read, what movies they went to, what bumper stickers they were most likely to put on their cars, and what those cars would be. The postmarks on those letters represented people unknown, and unpredictable, and Lord knows, if the slightest unpleasantness were to erupt tomorrow it would fly back onto him in an instant, which was something that didn't bear thinking about for any length of time.

Macon pulled Red Rascal up at the end of the country club's gardens and sat there under the oaks looking out over the green hill to the sprawling brick structure on whose ivy-swathed patio he'd enjoyed so many summer parties and Sunday dinners. The trail forked here, the left path leading back up toward the club, the right continuing on—pine-needled, wide, and shady—as it wove its way through the woods to end up at Bobbin Lake. Macon usually turned right, letting Red Rascal run full out till they hit that dirt road encircling the lake like it was Churchill

Downs itself. It was what the big horse expected, and he pawed the dirt beneath his hoof, snorting in impatience, anxious to go, but Macon held him back while he worried.

He'd considered phoning Will Cochran to tell him about the letters but had almost instantaneously rejected the idea, not wanting to aggravate a situation that was probably—yes, more likely than not, Macon thought—destined to be as peaceful as a picnic. You couldn't talk about Porter Griffin without mentioning that statue, of course; he'd just have to parse his words carefully so as not to inflame anybody who might have more on their mind than paying respects to the dead. Sometimes he ran things by Glinda. He could do that tonight, he thought, in that one ragged flash before he remembered.

She was circling his mind like a hawk, but Macon kept pushing her out. Even after his terse conversation with Marietta, Glinda still hadn't phoned him, still hadn't apologized, or explained, and if he was surprised by how much he'd missed her presence these past few nights, as usual, he had no intention of admitting that, even to himself.

It was cold under the oak trees. He reached into his coat pocket and took out his riding gloves, pulling them on no easy task with Red Rascal poised to take flight. For one brief moment Macon considered heading back for a whiskey at the club, then, looking off down the sun-dappled path through the woods, he yanked his cap down tight, gave Red Rascal his head, and the two of them galloped off toward the lake like they were being chased.

32

BRADY, WILL, GLINDA, BUTTER, AND MARIETTA

This had always been his favorite time of day. Both moon and sun vying for control of the sky, yellow, pink, and navy working it out over a pale blue canvas stretched tight above the trees, not quite night, but no longer afternoon. With Glinda's portrait tucked under his arm, Brady strolled up Pinehurst Street as slowly as an unconscious thought, taking no notice of the clouds beginning to gather just on the edges of night. Rain was coming.

It had been while he was wrapping up the painting, pulling the last bit of brown paper across her bright eyes, masking that unsettling stare, that he realized it was going to take him a while to get past this one. He'd never even seen it coming. And to think he'd thought he was through with all that. Too old now, all over. What an idiot he was.

·   ·   ·

Will had been sitting at the red light on the corner of the square, his eyes on the front of Cline's Antiques—the bronze stags in their black bows, the wreath of white roses still fresh on the door—when he'd heard Butter's message inviting him to dinner at Marietta's house. Without intending to, he turned right instead of left, heading out across the railroad tracks, toward Butter's billboard. On arriving, he had stopped the car and sat there for ten whole minutes staring up at her face, too beguiled to feel like a fool. When he'd finally called her back it was like a decision had been made, and Will felt free as a bird.

Wearing a freshly ironed shirt, he pulled up to 17 Pinehurst Street around dusk, a good fifteen minutes early. Hargis's Hummer sat in front of the house, as alien in that spot as a duck. Will got out of his car and walked around the thing slowly, pausing to stare at its back end as though something were written there.

Glinda watched him from a window on the landing, one hand holding back the curtain, the other up to her throat. So that's what a detective looks like, she thought. She'd imagined someone wiry and hard. This fellow was large and twinkly, and she suddenly felt happy for Butter. She saw him stoop down to examine the back bumper, then pull out his phone to take a picture. Movement distracted her, and when she looked down the street to the right, she could see another man walking toward the house; she didn't know him well enough to name him by his gait.

As Brady came closer, piercing a hole in the twilight and growing more distinct every second, Glinda could clearly see the large rectangular package he carried. She knew who he was now, knew what he carried; the brown paper wrapping disguised nothing for her. Her heart pounding, she checked in her pocket for her keys, then headed downstairs before either man knocked on the door.

As everyone milled around the house, exchanging perfunctory observations on the weather and the traffic, Marietta lit the candles on the table, pausing to smooth out a shallow wrinkle in the old embroidered tablecloth she and Harry had brought back from Ireland only last year. She called them all to the table, letting them choose their own seats, and dinner began, conversations starting up slowly, then breaking off into pairs of similar interest between Brady and Gordon, Butter and Will. Only Glinda sat silent.

Marietta heard their conversations as though she was watching a play. She felt no need to contribute; in fact she desperately hoped no one would wish her to do so. This was more than enough for now.

"Freddie tells me it's pretty much livable now," Will was saying. "I mean, well, you can imagine there's still some damage to some of your furniture, but the house is all dried out. The ceiling's fixed, and you can move back in whenever you want. I kinda made sure the fellows at Windward saw it as a priority."

Butter beamed up at him, forgetting, or perhaps not wishing, to hide her growing affection. "I'm so grateful, Will. Really. It was just such a shock to wake up and see it all like that. I'm kinda ashamed now, you know, about how I acted. You must have thought I was crazy."

"No, of course I didn't. I mean, hell, I'd've been upset if it had happened to me. You had every right to, well, cry and all." He grinned down at her, Butter grinned back, and Marietta could see in an instant where this was going to go.

Brady and Gordon were intently discussing the Cormac Mc-Carthy novels and whether any of them should have been made into movies, and still, Glinda sat silent at the end of the table, her eyes frequently drifting out the window to where the darkness had smothered the waning light with the sorts of clouds that held lightning and thunder. Marietta had noticed that Glinda and Brady weren't talking much to each other, and when they were, they seemed formal and stiff, indications of what she had feared: something had happened between them, something unexpected, ill-advised, and now probably regretted. She watched them over her wineglass, astonished at the transformation in her sister-in-law, and irritated at Brady for quite possibly taking advantage of a woman so clearly at sea. Her gaze drifted over to the painting, still hidden from view, leaning against the kitchen wall. One look at that and she'd know for sure.

Marietta's eyes floated around the table. These people were connected to her in ways she couldn't ignore, no matter how badly she often wanted to, no matter how hard she sometimes tried. Whatever the impulse was that had pulled Butter out into the aisle at St. Cyprian's and pushed her toward that dingy yellow bathroom where Marietta had been hiding, had placed her here at this table, back into Marietta's life. Even Macon, as much as she wished to turn from him and pretend that the things he said and did had nothing to do with her, even he couldn't be cast aside completely. He was her brother, that would always be so, and as such, wouldn't she always be tied to him? Shouldn't she be there for him when he needed her? She didn't know for certain, but looking over at Glinda now she would bet Macon was going to need somebody, sooner than he realized, and his ignorance of this vulnerability succeeded in doing what the mere ties of family could not: it humanized him, making him seem almost pitiable, even though Marietta knew he'd prefer indifference over pity any day of the week.

Suddenly, without preamble, Glinda's voice rose up over the others' as she directed a question toward Will that silenced everyone. "Detective Cochran? I think we'd all like to hear if you've reached a plausible theory concerning that statue in the park. Any ideas yet what happened?"

Will looked at her, rising to the surface of his focus on Butter with obvious difficulty. "Oh, nobody wants to talk about that right now, Mrs. Hargis."

"Call me Glinda, please. Just Glinda." She placed her knife on her plate and folded her arms across her chest, leveling a stare at Will. "That's where you're wrong, Detective. I think we'd all love to know what you think. I have a hunch someone like you must have figured it all out by now. It's almost been a week."

Will cleared his throat and leaned back in his chair. "Well, I've got a few ideas about what happened. Nothing I'd want to lay out here on the table for everyone to see." He smiled, looking from face to face till his eyes rested on Glinda. "Since your husband announced his plans to put that thing back up, seems like every-body's madder than they were before. You can feel it on the street. Signs are already going up." He looked over at Marietta. "You've seen a few here in The Glade already, I bet. I saw some as I drove in. KEEP IT DOWN, in big red letters. That's apparently going to be the new slogan." He chuckled. "I have to admit, that has a little more wit than some of the ones I've seen downtown.

"I've heard the Sons of Confederate Veterans has put the word out, and a lot of their chapters around the Southeast are planning to be at Old Man Griffin's funeral tomorrow, as well as a few other, more obscure, groups of similar persuasion. Some sort of show of solidarity. That's fine, they've got a right to be there. And I guess it's possible that you haven't heard, but your husband, ma'am"—he inclined his head toward Glinda—"well, he's doing the eulogy. Some news crews are already setting up, I believe. I saw their trucks parked at the church. Maybe you see where I'm going with this? In the current climate, as they say, this funeral could easily get out of hand, and I just don't want that to happen. Nobody does. I'm sure you, most of all." Glinda raised her eye-brows at him and smiled.

Will continued, still directing his words to her: "You know, your husband has pretty much equated the loss of that statue with Porter Griffin's death, implied right out in front of his office the other day that whoever knocked it down practically killed the old man . . . and I've just been thinking, as it's Macon himself who's turned out to be the one who's inherited all that Griffin had . . . well, I don't know, I bet he'd hate for people to ever even imag-ine he had something to do with its coming down. What do you think, Glinda?"

Confusion had frozen every face; only Glinda looked relaxed. She smiled slowly, then took a sip of wine. "I think you want me to blackmail my husband," she said, her eyes on her glass.

"Not at all. I prefer to think of it as just making him aware of some things he probably hasn't considered," Will said, folding his napkin and running his thumbnail along the crease. "Who knows, it might not even work. But then again, it just might help shut all this mess down. Let the town get back to normal."

"Normal?" Glinda laughed. "Don't you think the horse is already out of the barn on that, so to speak? Have you even listened to people lately? There's a new *normal,* Mr. Cochran. And people seem to have taken to it with enthusiasm. They're proud of their bigotry now. It's the new patriotism. The new religion, too. I heard some of them at Harry's reception down at Micheline's last Saturday. That old statue was only a focal point. Take it away and they'll just find something else to distract them from what we've all become."

The house was so quiet the rain that had started up outside sounded as though it was right in the room. "Maybe so, but I doubt they're in the majority," Will said, softly. "And you can't sit there and honestly tell me it won't help a little to keep that particular 'focal point,' as you call it, out of Griffin Park for good. Hell, maybe we are just kicking the ball down the road, not dealing with the reasons why some people wanted to keep the thing up there. I don't know. I just take it a day at a time. You see, I'm not one of these people who say you've got to accept the world as it is. I don't. I so often *object* to the world as it is. But I do think you've got to *begin* with the world as it is. And that's a very different sort of a thing. We just have to do what we can. Every day. And on *this* day, I think you might be able to do something nobody else can do. That's all I'm saying. And I wouldn't have said anything at all if your husband hadn't vowed to put the thing back up where it was. But I know the trouble that's going to cause, and just thought maybe you, Mrs. Hargis, could help put an end to it before it all got started good, you know. Of everyone in town, I'm thinking you're in the best position to talk some sense into the man."

Glinda smiled a slow, calm smile. "I asked you to call me Glinda. And I can assure you, Detective, that statue will never again stand on the grounds of Griffin Park."

.   •   •

The others tried to pick up the scattered pieces of their original conversations after Will and Glinda came to the end of theirs, but with unsatisfactory results. After dessert was over, and the night was starting to fray around the edges, they all took their coffee into the dimly lit library. Brady brought the painting into the room, set it on a table against the bookshelves, and ceremoniously cleared his throat.

"The moment has come, my friends," he said, the many glasses of wine he'd had evident in the timbre of his voice. "I gotta tell you, if you'd sworn to me a week ago that I'd have completed what was probably the best portrait of my career by tonight, I'd have laughed at you right in your face. Portraits are hard. I've never really liked doing them." He glanced over at Glinda, standing back in the doorway, and smiled a soft smile. "I sort of rely on kismet to show me my subjects these days, and kismet is never a fool.

"A few days ago I saw a face I couldn't get out of my head. You know, kismet." He snapped his fingers, then started to untie the twine. "I'll always be grateful to Glinda for this"—he turned to look at her now, and Marietta could see his eyes shining—"this chance to create something I'm so very proud of." He laughed a little, rubbing the back of his neck. "You know, I tried to tell the woman that most people pay me to paint their portraits, but this one"—he pointed at her—"this one acted as though it should be the other way around. Said she'd sit for it only if I gave it to her when I was done, and God help me, I took that bargain. But I don't regret it. Just the experience of creating something like this has been enough payment for me. Best take a good look now, though. I'll never exhibit it. It's hers alone, and I hope through the years when she looks at it, she'll know I truly believe it's the best thing that I've ever done."

The last knot loosened, and the brown paper fell from the painting, slipping to the floor with a harsh crackle. Once again, silence filled the room as everyone stared. It was undeniably Glinda up there, but a Glinda so defenseless, so beautiful, that she stole all the available words from their heads. Her face seemed unmasked, as though something no one had ever taken notice of before had been removed, leaving behind the essence of a woman no one had yet met. It wasn't just the absence of makeup that gave this impression, it was the look in her eyes; you couldn't quite tell if they were questioning, accusing, or sad, but you couldn't seem to look away from them. A full minute passed before anybody said a word.

It was Marietta who spoke first. "I feel like I'm meeting you for the first time, Glinda." And everybody nodded. They turned to look at Glinda, but she kept her eyes on the painting, saying nothing. As they watched, she calmly walked across the room and picked her portrait up in her arms. She moved toward Brady and kissed him full on the mouth, then turned on her heel and left.

They all stared at one another when they heard the front door open and close, then ran toward the sitting room window like children. They were just in time to see the Hummer turn around in the driveway, heading up the street in the pouring rain, exceeding the speed limit by a good fifteen miles.

33

MACON AND GLINDA

Red Rascal's stone barn had been photographed for the Style section of *The Atlanta Journal–Constitution* in the winter of 2013, prompting many in Wesleyan to remark that the big Hanoverian bay resided in fancier quarters than they did. Macon had laughed off those comments as nothing more than palaver even as he relished the undeniable whiff of envy that accompanied every one. He'd designed the barn himself, without the slightest input from Glinda or his children, and it was the one place on the whole of their property that the family saw as exclusively his, which was enough to make it his favorite place on earth. He visited Red Rascal every night at this time.

He had an office in the house, of course, behind a tall door off the main hall, where the lighting was low and the requisite prints of mallards and deer were hung on the oak-paneled walls, but it was the one in the barn where he consistently could be found, even if most of what he accomplished there was of a more trivial nature: reading back issues of *The Chronicle of the Horse* while drinking his best whiskey, and listening to classic country music. You couldn't even see the house from here.

Tonight, the cold rain was slapping the barn windows as Macon sat with his legs propped up on his old rolltop desk and a long yellow legal pad in his lap, his lips moving slightly in a whisper unheard by anyone save the horse, who was at this moment contentedly consuming his nightly bucket of grain. Macon had gone over the eulogy three times in the past hour and felt he'd finally gotten it right. Just enough emotion to honor the old man, but not enough to inflame either side, though privately Macon thought there'd be only one side attending this particular funeral. The images of all those letters he'd thrown into his office trash can—then retrieved to put in a folder, just in case—came into his mind, and he shooed them away.

This anticipated company of like minds should have made the writing a bit easier, of course, but Macon was aware he was walking the edge of a razor. His words needed to seem egalitarian— and, not to put too fine a point on it, mayoral—while at the same time remaining irreproachable to all in the crowd who had revered Porter Griffin as one of the last champions of a cause that, to them, was neither lost nor forgotten.

A loud clap of thunder seemed to confirm he was done; this was as good as he was going to get it tonight. Decades of courtroom oration had taught him to always leave room for spontaneous thought. Tomorrow he'd size up the congregants and let his wits lead the way. They rarely steered him wrong.

Macon turned off the light on the desk and strode the few feet down to Red Rascal's stall. "All tucked in, boy?" he said, as usual, to the horse, who never replied but always seemed to understand. He let his forehead fall against Red Rascal's and left it there for a long minute, breathing in the familiar fragrance of sunshine, grass, and leather like a tonic concocted only for him. It was a nightly ritual unknown by anyone but horse and man, more habitual to Macon than prayer.

Finally turning to leave, he stood at the door of the barn watching the rain pummel his pathway home, tiny bits of pea gravel bouncing up and down. Sighing heavily, he buttoned his tweed coat and turned the collar up. His cap was pulled down almost to his eyes, but still the water hit his face. With his hands deep in his pockets, he walked toward the house, head bent low, thinking you get just as wet whether you run or you walk. Macon never ran in the rain.

Glinda pulled the Hummer into the garage and switched it off, listening to the echoing pops and clicks as the big engine began to cool itself down. Outside the rain fell like a white metal curtain; she could hear it hitting hard on the roof. She sat there as she listened, looking down at her hands folded tight in her lap, her posture like that of a penitent. How different she felt from the woman who'd backed this thing out and driven away on the icy roads, not even a week ago. How quickly things can change.

What was it she'd overheard Gordon say this morning? Something about the people wound the tightest always blowing up the biggest? Something like that. She'd wanted to run downstairs to the sunroom and ask him to his face why he hadn't warned her. Surely if you see someone heading for such a reckoning you should urge them to alter their ways. But people don't confront one another, do they? Glinda rested her head on the steering wheel. Why hadn't she, at least once in their marriage, asked her own husband what he truly believed, who he really was? Why hadn't she ever made him answer for his actions and his words, made him say if they were merely part of an act, representations of who he really was, or if, as she most feared, he couldn't even tell the difference between those equally troubling definitions of his character?

He'd always mistaken her silence for agreement, and why wouldn't he? She'd snuggled so deep inside the comfort of blind acquiescence for so many years, carefully avoiding the drafts slipping beneath the closed doors of her mind, afraid she'd be blown right away if those doors ever opened a hair. Thinking about what Macon was going to do with the information she was about to deliver seemed only to make her stronger. Moving quickly, Glinda got out of the Hummer, pulled the painting from the seat beside her, and closed the door.

She let herself into the kitchen through the garage, unsurprised at the neatness inside. Macon had always been one to clean up after himself, his coffee mug washed and dried the second he drained the last drop. The room, as she had suspected, bore no traces of a man in the least disturbed by the near-weeklong disappearance of his wife. Even the dish towel was folded. He was so sure of her, she thought. So certain she'd return.

The silence told her Macon was still at the barn, which was what she'd expected when she saw his car in the garage. He was usually down there this time of the evening, no matter the weather. Leaving the kitchen, Glinda walked down the long hallway to Macon's office, went inside, and slipped the painting behind the door. Then she went straight over to the liquor cabinet. She knew he kept all the best whiskey down there in the barn, but there was some good stuff here, too, and right now she couldn't think of anything she needed more. Pouring herself a glass of Glenfiddich, she walked over to the stereo and ran a finger down the row of old records till she found the one she was searching for. Dropping the needle onto the vinyl, she sank into the long leather sofa and crossed her legs. She would wait for him here.

The path from the barn led up to the front porch, and Macon was soaked by the time he reached that white-columned shelter. He leaned against the wall and took off his riding boots, leaving them to dry on the mat, then removed his hat, beating the excess rainwater out against his thigh. He heard the music as soon as he opened the door.

It had been his mother's favorite. It took only a note or two before Macon could see her as clear as day, sitting on the stone porch overlooking the back garden on Pinehurst Street with her eyes closed, listening to the music drifting out through the open window from the stereo inside. Dvořák's "Song to the Moon." It was like a backsliding Baptist hearing "Just as I Am" years after leaving the church. Macon slammed the door as he went inside.

He tromped down the hall in his sock feet. She was easy to find—he just followed the music, reaching his office long before the song was done. Without a nod to Glinda, sitting in the corner of the sofa, Macon strode toward the stereo and lifted the tone-arm roughly. The scratch across the vinyl was audible; it would always remain.

"So," he said, stuffing the record back in its sleeve, "you've decided to once again grace us with your presence. You'll be happy to know I didn't call the children. Didn't particularly see the need to worry them over what was so obviously a tedious bit of hormonal drama."

Glinda laughed, a sound so unexpected to Macon's ears that he turned around and stared. "I called them myself the other night," she said. "We had a lot to talk over. I know now why Josh left last year, and why he doesn't yet plan to come back. Why did you never tell me, Macon? Perhaps *you'll* be happy to know I'm going to visit him and Lizzie in France. I'm leaving right after Porter Griffin's funeral tomorrow." She got up and walked slowly to the bar to pour a bit more whiskey into her half-full glass. It was a long minute before she turned around to face him, and when she did, it was with a confidence she hadn't expected. She switched on the lamp and saw the shock in her husband's eyes.

"Good God, woman. What have you done to yourself?" he asked, taking in her loose hair and clean face. This time her laughter angered as well as surprised him. "I'm serious here, Glinda. What is wrong with you? You need a doctor or some-thing?"

"No, Macon. I don't need a doctor. I feel better than I have in years. But I've come here to tell you a few things before I go. I'm not sure when I'll be back. Or *if*, for that matter. You might want to sit down. And take off that wet coat."

"I'll sit down when I want to, Glinda. And my coat's fine."

"Suit yourself. You always do." She walked back over to sit on the arm of the sofa, casually taking a sip of her drink. "I hear you're planning to speak at Griffin's funeral," she said, calmly, looking up at him over the rim of her glass.

"I don't know how you heard that, but yes, yes I am."

"I heard it from a detective tonight. At your sister's dinner table. I just left there. Will Cochran? He said he spoke with you after Griffin died."

In spite of himself, Macon looked confused. He took off his coat and hung it across the back of his chair. "What was he doing at Marietta's?"

Glinda smiled. "I told you. We were all having dinner." She ran her finger slowly around the top of her glass. "You know, he's a pretty smart man, Will is. He didn't come right out and say it, but I think he's figured out something that nobody else has, at least not yet. But we'll get to that. First, I want to give you something." She rose and walked to the door, then pulled out the painting from behind it, holding its face toward her. She leaned it against the cold hearth, and left it there, blank side out. Turning to face him, she said, "I think you should be the one to have this, Macon."

"What in God's name are you talking about, Glinda? I'm getting tired of this. Do you intend to apologize to me for last Saturday or not?"

Glinda smiled again, which only irritated him further. "I do need to apologize to you, Macon. But not for last Saturday. I need to apologize for not being honest with you all these years. For letting you think I approved of the way you lived your life, for letting your life become *our* life.

"I'm not who you always thought I was, you see. I'm not somebody who believes more is always better, who thinks other people are here only to abet our successes, who thinks anyone is in any way less than I am. For a long time now, I've hated so many of the words that have come from your mouth, and the casual way you've spoken them. For years, in fact. I hated the way you started defending that stupid Confederate statue down in the park. It's wrong, Macon. And I'm sorry I never told you how I felt. I should have."

"Oh, good God, Glinda. Don't start up with that statue to me. I've already heard from that sister of mine about this. It's just a big chunk of marble that a lot of old folks around here happen to love. It's been standing up in that park longer than anybody can remember, and it reminds people of their childhoods, when people got along, and everything was a bit simpler. What's wrong with that?"

"There's only one kind of people who love that statue, Macon. White people. You have to know that." Glinda shook her head. "You know, there's so much stuff in this world that we can't do one thing about. I don't think that bothers you much, at least from what I can tell—certainly it doesn't bother you as much as it does 'that sister of yours.' But when that old man left that park to you, he gave you the power to shut down a bunch of heartache about one thing . . . just one . . . that stupid statue, that monument to the Confederacy that was put up to make sure every dark face in this town knew just where they stood."

"Hell, Glinda. You're not going to make me feel guilty for that. And don't start up telling me I'm racist, either. You know better. Just because I don't keep a burned scar in my front yard like my father did, like *my sister still* does, to remind everybody in town how I feel about racists, doesn't mean I am one."

"I'm not calling you anything, Macon. But I've lived with you long enough to know there's something, something deep down in your soul, that tells you some people, people like us, are better than others. I'm not sure if it started out as an act, something to make you feel accepted, or something that you long ago figured out could get you what you want. Or if it's who you really are. I've never been able to tell, and that scares me to death. But it's not for me to say, or even worry about, anymore. All I know tonight, Macon, is that you vowed to put that statue back up again, and I'm here to tell you that's not going to happen."

"Is that so?"

Glinda looked him in the eye. "It was me, Macon. I'm the one who pulled down the statue of General Henry Benning."

Macon stared at her for a moment, his arms crossed over his chest. Then he started to laugh. "You? You pulled down a fifteen-foot marble statue? Right. Mind telling me how you did that all by yourself? Just who helped you?"

"Nobody helped me. Well, I take that back. I suppose you helped me really. At least that ridiculous vehicle you had to buy helped me. Turns out it was good for something. See, I discovered that if you take a sturdy rope—like the kind you use on the boat—and you manage to tie a pretty good knot—like the kind you taught me to tie when we've been sailing—around two of that horse's legs, then tie the other end of that big rope to the bumper of a 2006 Hummer, and then you get back in the thing and gun it, well, all I can say is that old statue came down in spectacular fashion. Didn't even have to drive thirty feet. It was almost like the thing was tired and ready to go. Made an almighty crash, I can tell you. It's a pity, really, that nobody was around to see it. But I've got that ice storm to thank for that. Not a soul was out that morning. You know us Southerners don't drive in the ice, not if we can help it." Glinda smiled over at Macon, who'd finally sat down in his chair.

"Only trouble was, I couldn't get the other end of that rope back through the fence. The knot was too big. So, I sort of clipped it with some nail scissors I had in my purse. That was my one mistake, leaving that bit behind, still tied on to what was left of that horse's leg. I'm sure Will Cochran found it. That's how he managed to figure out more than I would have thought anybody could. I mean, who would expect *me,* of all people? But then again, I couldn't have done it without that Hummer, so, like I said, I guess you kind of helped, too. I know you've always seen that thing as some sort of extension of yourself." She grinned and took a sip of whiskey, holding up the glass to watch the amber liquid sparkle in the lamplight.

"I don't have to tell you, I was pretty out of my mind the morning after I had my little . . . oh, I guess you'd call it a nervous breakdown. I remember it being called that in my mother's day, though I'm not exactly sure what the accurate term is now. Anyway, whatever it was, I was pretty much on the edge. Harry's funeral hit me harder than even I realized at the time. Sweet Harry. Gone, just like that." She snapped her fingers and took a deep drink.

"What I did at Micheline's was pure impulse, you know. I heard you talking with your—what are they exactly? Friends? Well . . . you can be such an arrogant son of a bitch, Macon, that I just pushed that lasagna under your butt without thinking. It felt like taking off a tight skirt. It's felt like that ever since. And well, when I left here driving your Hummer, and I saw that statue up ahead, standing there in the park, just passive—innocent like, you know—as if it had no idea about all the trouble it was causing by just existing, well . . . it just seemed like the right thing to do."

"I don't believe it." Macon was staring up at his wife like she was a stranger.

"Well, sugar, Will Cochran certainly does. He's been able to match the rope I left behind with some serious scratches on the bumper, I know he has. I saw him taking a picture of the thing not three hours ago, and I'll bet my life he found the other end of that rope the very morning it happened." She laughed again, stared at Macon's face, and shook her head. "This is so funny. How many times have I heard you say that the truth doesn't matter, the only thing that matters is what people believe? But here's the thing about truth: it doesn't care what you *believe*. Your belief might make you feel better, but it doesn't change the facts one iota, and the fact is, Macon, I did it. I am the one who sent Old Man Griffin's statue flying across his park the morning of the ice storm. Therefore, as you yourself have said, I am also, at least laterally, responsible for killing him. Imagine. Your own wife. And lo and behold, who inherits everything Porter has when he dies? The only person alive who actually knew what the old man's will specifies? Oh, I can hear them all down at Donovan's Reef right now. *'Did Macon put her up to it?' 'He would've known just how badly the old man would take it.' 'So, what, he gets rid of Porter, and then puts the statue back up to make it look all hunky-dory?'* You must admit, Macon, it doesn't look good."

Macon could think of nothing to say.

"So, here's the bottom line: if you don't get up at that old man's funeral tomorrow, and you don't make this right, I swear to God I'm going to tell everybody you told me to do it for the money, and my conscience won't let me stay quiet. I'll tell them you knew Porter Griffin better than anybody in this town, and you knew just what was likely to happen if he saw the destruction of his beloved statue with his very own eyes. You knew his heart was weak, so weak he could go at any moment. You knew the shock might kill him, if not that very morning, then pretty soon after. How do you think the court of public opinion will take that one? If you think getting a mess of lasagna all over your britches was humiliating, I can assure you this will be a whole lot worse."

"I didn't know anything about a weak heart!"

"Doesn't matter whether you did or not. Remember, it only matters what people believe. So, like I said, you are to let everybody know you're not going to put that thing back up in Griffin Park, and you're going to tell them you think it's wrong to have ever even considered it. I'll be sitting right there in the front of that church, Macon, and if you don't do it, I swear to God I'll walk straight out and over to the *Wesleyan Journal* and give them an exclusive they'll remember for years. Don't you think I won't."

Glinda drained her glass in one gulp and walked back over to the fireplace. She lifted the painting, turned it around, and placed it high up on the mantel, where it covered the Audubon print that hung there the way reality covers myth. She stepped back to give Macon a clear view. There was a long silence.

"What . . . who . . . who did this?" he asked, never taking his eyes off the painting.

Glinda cocked her head, staring up to the mantel. "It's something, isn't it? Brady Goode did it. You've met him, he had a show at Jessamine a couple of years ago. Fundraiser for the Historical Society. And you've seen his picture in the paper. Pretty famous artist. All I know is that he gave me something I'll never be able to repay him for."

Macon turned sharply and looked at his wife. "Did you have an affair with this man?"

"What on earth makes you think that, Macon?"

"Because . . . well . . . I mean . . . look at you." He pointed up to the mantel. "You look, you look like somebody who's just rolled out of bed."

Glinda laughed. "Is that all you see, Macon? Look at that woman! Look at her hard. You've never even met her before, have you? You've never even wondered if she existed." She shrugged, her nonchalance like a slap. "Maybe I did have an affair. Maybe I didn't. I guess you'll always have to speculate on that. Every time you look at this, you won't know just what to believe. What the truth really is. Maybe you'll think there might have been other things about me you never knew, never even guessed at. You'll have plenty of time to study it. The painting is yours now. I don't need it anymore."

"But why? Why did you do this, Glinda? All of this?"

Glinda ran her fingers through her long white hair. "I don't know, Macon. Like I told you, I just sort of cracked up. It must have been Harry's funeral. Or maybe it was going to happen no matter where I was. But thank God it did happen, while there was still time for me to change." Placing her hands on his shoulders, she gripped him hard. "We don't have long, Macon. That truth fell down on me, sitting in St. Cyprian's with Harry up front in that urn. We're here for such a short time. I mean, people always tell you that, but you never really believe them, not deep down in your bones. But you and me, Macon? We're on the last lap. We don't have many more chances. And I don't know, maybe I just needed to do something to be forgiven for. More than just sins of omission."

"And you expect *me* to forgive you?" He twisted out of her grasp; the well-practiced sneer of the courtroom, though diluted, was still there.

"Oh, Macon," she sighed. "I'm not talking about *you*." She walked to the door and turned. "I'm going upstairs to pack. I'll be spending one more night at Marietta's, then I'm catching the nine o'clock flight out of Atlanta tomorrow night. Josh and Lizzie are expecting me Saturday. I'll see you tomorrow at First Baptist for the funeral. Goodbye, Macon."

34

RONNIE

While it was still dark Ronnie Childers made some French toast for breakfast, even though that was a tough task on a hot plate. The insides ended up soggy and the edges were burned, but a lot of maple syrup could pretty much make anything palatable. He could have used the big kitchen upstairs, of course. It still sat just like she'd left it, as spotless as an operating room, each shiny fork stacked one on top of the other in the silverware drawer, not one curved edge out of line.

She'd been dead for three months now, as long as summer vacation used to be when he was little, and he still couldn't go upstairs. He came and went as he'd done before, through the narrow back door to the basement that led to the tiny apartment she'd fixed up for him when he lost his last job. She'd embroidered daisies on his bedroom curtains, so he knew he'd never change them.

They hadn't been right, the people who'd told him it would get better with time. It had gotten only worse. At her lay by himself in his twin bed, imagining those rooms up above him in the dark, rooms that still smelled like her. He could almost see her toothbrush getting stiffer and stiffer in that glass by the sink, the indentation of her body still there in that old yellow chair. Some nights he wondered if she ever drifted back to look around when nobody was watching, if her hand ever reached for his door. It took him hours to get to sleep these days.

He'd dug the old photo out of the drawer right after he saw Jocelyn Shaw's first report on the Sunday night news, laid it on his little kitchen table and stared at it, marveling at the sight of his daddy, younger than he himself was now. They'd toured the South together when Ronnie was seven, visiting all the Confederate monuments, but this was the one he remembered because this was the only picture they had from the whole trip. His daddy had asked an old lady to take it for them. She'd set her red purse on a bench while she did it.

When he'd heard about the statue being privately owned by that old man who died when he saw what they'd done to it, all the anger he'd been trying to ignore for so long almost knocked him to the ground. He'd spent the past several days on the Internet reading about the monuments being taken down all over the South, each one a memory of him and his dad, and his anger turned slowly to rage. He didn't care that he'd have to drive six hours to get there. The least he could do was pay his respects.

35

LURLENE, HARRISON, LUCY-JEWEL, WILL, MACON, AND MARIETTA

The inaugural service of the Wesleyan First Baptist Church took place seven months after the start of Prohibition and two days after women won the right to vote, so there was plenty of brimstone lying around for the Reverend Gideon Moss to throw into his very first sermon at his very first church. Reverend Moss remained at First Baptist till the Allies won the Second World War. He wouldn't recognize the place today.

The steeple bells went first, replaced in the sixties by the jaunty sound of electronic carillons. These could be turned on by a switch in the vestibule, their sound less like a summons to worship than an invitation to the traveling carnival that used to camp out in the field by Tillman Elementary every summer in June. The graceful brick chapel of 1920 was sacrificed in the late seventies to the inferior gods of modernity, and in its place a long white building of dubious design was stretched across the hill above Meridian Street, a low-ceilinged structure that looked far too much like a government building to foster much reverence in the casual observer. It was dwarfed in the eighties by a gym that was built to entice younger people to God, but which was today mostly used by the Tiny Tumblers Gymnastics Club and Golden Agers Yoga Class.

On this bleak, gray morning the straight-down winter rain that had washed away the last vestiges of ice showed no intention of ceasing, not even to accommodate a funeral, which only made the already colorless building more unwelcoming and bleak. Despite this, the parking lot was full, and Lurlene pointed Reese to the bank next door, where an overflow crowd was rapidly claiming the empty slots of a rain-soaked morning.

"I never in my life," she said, vigorously rubbing the condensation from the car window to get a better look. "Look at these cars, Reese. They can't all be here for *Porter*. There's a place over there." She pointed to the end of the first row at the parking spot closest to the drive-thru ATM.

"All I'm seeing is a lot of cars from out of town. Look, Leeny . . . that one is from Oklahoma. Alabama . . . Tennessee." Reese turned around in his seat, taking in the different license plates. "I don't know about this. All the press this thing has gotten since Macon opened his trap . . . Did you see those news crews out front? That Shaw woman's back from up in Atlanta, under a tent right by the church sign. Obviously, they all think something might be newsworthy. How would you feel about just going back home and skipping this thing?"

Lurlene snorted. "I am not about to let a bunch of yahoos from out of town change my plans. The Birthright Boys. The Gray Ghosts. My foot, Reese. I'm probably one of the only people here who actually even knew the man. The old goat, I'm going in there and help send him off like I intended." She picked up her handbag, peered out at the pouring rain, and sighed. "And yes, I'll use the damn cane today, since you'll have the umbrella."

Harrison sat on the third row of the church, between his wife and Lucy-Jewel. Ernest Adcock, his newly minted campaign manager, sat on the girl's other side, flanked by the mayor, who was reading the order of service for what seemed like the fifth time. None of them wanted to be here. Harrison knew that as well as he knew his own name. He could still hear Carly when she asked him this morning to explain to her why they were going to a funeral for a man he'd never even spoken to. "It's kind of sad," she'd said as she stood on her tiptoes to tie his tie. "Don't you think? I mean, is anybody going to be at this thing for the old man himself? Seems to me like everyone's going just to make some sort of statement or something. To represent their *side,* you know. I just wonder if there's anybody who'll be there just because they're sorry a sad old man passed away." Harrison resettled himself in the pew, knowing the hardness of the wood had little to do with how uncomfortable he felt.

Beside him, Lucy-Jewel was thinking the very same thoughts, though from a divergent angle. She was wearing a dress her mother had bought while on a trip to New York City with her cousin, a good five years ago, one the lady had never even worn; she'd had to cut the tags off when she brought it to Lucy-Jewel this morning. Black wool crepe and elegant, it was something Lucy-Jewel might have worn on a date. Even though Ernest had asked her to come, she wasn't sure if this *was* a date, or if they both were just here at the request of her boss. The one thing she knew for certain was that she wasn't here for the right purpose; she couldn't stand Porter Griffin, despite having never met him in the flesh.

Glancing around behind her, Lucy-Jewel saw very few people she knew, and most of them, she was sure, weren't here for Porter Griffin either. Not really. She nodded over at Macon Hargis's secretary, Chrissy, and the woman pulled a face, which made Lucy-Jewel want to laugh even as it confirmed what she already figured: the only reason Chrissy had come was to see what her own boss was up to. Macon Hargis was supposed to give the eulogy. This set Lucy-Jewel's teeth on edge. Him she *had* met, and she liked him almost less than the man she hadn't, the one now lying in the coffin up front.

Will had spoken to Lurlene and Reese, he'd nodded at the mayor and Lucy-Jewel, and said hello to Principal Gray and Ernest Adcock, but as he'd expected, he didn't recognize most of the other people assembled in the pews. From his place on the back row, his eyes passed over the crowd with more than a casual interest, picking out the plainclothes officers he'd strategically placed here and there, and coming back to Butter with every three-quarter sweep. He didn't like her sitting so close to the front; in fact he would've much preferred it if she hadn't come at all but, like Marietta, she had been determined to support Glinda, and he admired them both for that.

He watched as another couple of men he'd never seen before came down the center aisle. Will would be willing to bet if he ran a number of these folks through the database they'd set a whole lot of red buttons flashing. Even more worrisome, he'd noticed a few suit jackets fitting less than perfectly around a few men's waists, which he knew from experience meant there were at least several firearms present. He found Butter again, in her blue dress, sitting between Marietta and Glinda on the second row, and wished once again that all three women had seen fit to stay home. His eyes flew to the front of the church then, as a young woman entered and made her way to the baby grand. Here we go, he thought, sitting up a bit straighter and setting his jaw.

Lydia Clayton normally played the piano for First Baptist funerals, but she'd come down with a head cold last night and so had enlisted the services of her daughter, Candy, assuring her that the crowd would be small and the songs fairly basic. Candy was a tall, angular creature whose sharply attenuated limbs seemed wholly unsuited to the piano bench and whose morose expression, Lurlene knew, had much more to do with the dread of her impending performance than it did with any funereal feelings she might have had for the deceased. From where she and Reese sat in the middle of the church, Lurlene could tell the girl was nervous. Clinker notes were liberally sprinkled through the first verse of "Rock of Ages."

The murmuring of the crowd of strangers simmered down to silence as Candy ran through the list of preservice music, all songs she knew by heart and could play with her eyes closed, which,

Lurlene noticed, she was mostly doing. "The Old Rugged Cross." "Sweet Hour of Prayer." By the time she got to "In the Garden," Candy had loosened up and was playing most of the notes as written.

The rain seemed to be gathering strength the closer it came to the funeral's start, and Candy's last line of "Amazing Grace" had a postlude of thunder that made Butter jump and caused Mayor Baker to drop the hat he had resting on top of his knee. Harrison Gray picked it up and handed it back just as a black-robed Reverend Broussard came out the side door and walked up the red carpeted stairs to the throne-like chair that sat just to the right of the pulpit.

The Reverend nodded, and Yvonne Little rose from her spot on the front row, walking up onto the podium with all the confidence of someone who'd made this short journey many times before. As the one soprano in the First Baptist choir who could consistently be counted on to soar up the scale and hit the high notes without making anyone flinch, she was often tapped for occasions like this. Being not only capable but loud, Yvonne was the linchpin that held the choir's rendition of the Hallelujah Chorus together at every single Christmas cantata. The year she came down with the flu, they wisely switched to "Away in a Manger."

Yvonne started "How Great Thou Art" off low, so there'd be enough room to sail into the chorus without any trouble, and by the time she got there, every eye in the room was on her, urging her forward to a finish that disappointed no one, and even made a few people cry. When she was done, Yvonne smiled, gave a little nod, then walked back down to her seat, passing Wesleyan's Historical Society president, Leonard Pennington, as he made his way up.

Leonard made a show of opening his Bible and putting on his reading glasses, a performance Lurlene was expecting and one that made her poke her husband in the ribs. She'd thought about joining the Historical Society once, had even attended two of its meetings, though the second time was simply to satisfy her conscience by giving Leonard one more chance not to be, as she described to Reese later, "too much of a patronizing old know-it-all for somebody who hadn't even been born in the South." Reese pushed her arm away now, determined not to let her make him laugh.

Leonard sniffed, lifted his eyes to the heavens, then began to read from Ephesians, the catch in his voice something Lurlene wasn't alone in finding more than a little bit fake. Her mind began to wander. When she focused again on the service, Mae Jordan was already halfway through her reading of Henry Timrod's "The Unknown Dead," its long vivid stanza so stuffed with rain, death, battle plains, and pride, it seemed almost to have been written with Porter Griffin in mind. The crowd murmured appreciatively when Mae finished.

Marietta's nervousness continued to increase with every minute that passed. Glinda sat beside her, her eyes fixed, her back straight, her hands folded so tight they looked bloodless. It was a posture she'd maintained throughout the service. Marietta doubted the woman had blinked. Now, as Reverend Broussard introduced Macon, she could almost feel Glinda's breath still, as though by holding it inside her she could somehow control what might happen next.

Marietta looked toward the other side of the church, to the front row where Macon was sitting. She saw him bend his head toward his right shoulder, cracking his neck, an unconscious habit held over from high school. He hesitated for a moment before finally rising and making his way the few feet from his seat and up the stairs to the podium. Noah Broussard gave him an encouraging nod.

The yellow piece of paper was moist in his hands. Macon slowly flattened it out on the slanted top of the old oak pulpit, looking down at it for a good ten seconds before nervously clearing his throat. When he finally spoke, he sounded to Marietta more like her older brother than the infamous lawyer he'd become.

"Ah . . . Good morning. I . . . uh . . ." Macon chanced a look at Glinda, but she sat facing forward, her eyes on a vase of lilies, her back as rigid as an ironing board. Macon stared back down at his notes and continued. "I was asked here today to eulogize my client, and friend, Porter Griffin." A smattering of applause arose from the crowd, but Macon didn't stop to give it room to grow. "Truth is, I really couldn't call Porter a friend. Not really. I'm not sure anybody in this town could. From what I could see . . . thinking about it now . . . I guess you might say he was a bit of a loner." A few people chuckled and Macon cleared his throat. "But I saw him fairly often, at least probably more than anyone else here, and I . . . I tried to do the best by him.

"Last year, um, when some people in town approached Porter and asked him to take down the statue of Confederate General Henry Benning, well, he became very upset." Will could feel a wave of concurrence roll over the crowd and sat up a little closer to the edge of his pew. Macon took a deep breath and continued.

"Now, as a lawyer it's my job to serve my client, no matter what my personal feelings might be, and I have endeavored to do just that for the past year. And the truth is, well, there was no legal reason for the man to have taken the statue down. I told him that. But of course, as . . . uh, as you all know . . . the issue grew a little bigger than it probably should have." The sanctuary was so quiet Marietta could hear her own heartbeat. She stared up at her brother, unable to imagine what he was about to say.

"Now . . . I realize that I . . . um . . . that, well, earlier this week I told you I was going to put the statue of Henry Benning back up. Because at the time I thought that, well, you know, I thought that would have been what Mr. Griffin would have wanted and all. But now that some time has passed, I . . . well . . . I wonder now, that is, now that I've thought about it . . . if maybe he might have rather had some peace here in town instead." Will heard a low rumble, like the faint start of an engine, the bass notes of a confused crowd. Macon's mouth was getting dry.

"You know, we all get old, and sometimes, I mean, some of us, we start to look for ways to smooth things out a bit, make it a little bit easier for ourselves . . . um, and, well . . . for everybody.

So maybe, I mean, when I think about what Porter might tell us now that he's dead, if he could come back, you know . . . then I'm thinking he might not have wanted the thing back up again after all. He might tell us to put it all to rest. So, I . . . I think the best way to honor him might just be to leave things as they are, you know, and not resurrect something that obviously causes us all so much—"

"*Traitor!*"

The shout flew out over the congregation, rebounding off the stained-glass windows and clapping back in the center aisle with a crack louder than the thunder outside. Ronnie Childers leapt up from the pew in front of Lurlene, his right arm outstretched toward Macon. He yelled the word once more and a shot rang out on the first syllable. The bullet would have hit Macon right between the eyes had he not leaned to the side to take a sip of the water that Constance always left on the pulpit for Reverend Broussard. Instead, it ricocheted off the choir loft railing, shattering the vase of white lilies that sat on the pedestal next to the organ. Chaos rained down on the congregants.

The piano bench fell over as Candy Clayton jumped up, clearing the distance between herself and Reverend Broussard in a couple of inelegant lunges, and landing atop the preacher like a Tupperware lid. People screamed, a few making a run for the door, but most were frozen where they sat, staring at the man standing in the middle of the church who was still pointing a gun straight at Macon Hargis.

Macon was frozen, looking bewildered, hands flat on the pulpit, eyes locked on the gun. In the interminable moment it took for the second bullet to travel the distance to where he stood, Macon turned to look at his sister as Marietta flew out into the aisle, arms raised to protect him. Then people heard a crack like a watermelon breaking open as Lurlene Pearson brought her rabbit-head cane down on top of Ronnie Childers's head, dropping him to the ground in one blow.

36

———

Sometimes it happens with a sound. The slamming of a door, the closing of a coffin lid. Far too often we are denied the luxury of seeing the car drive slowly away, getting smaller and smaller until it slides over the last hill, and is gone. Rarely are we allowed to prepare for the thing that turns us around in our tracks, that sharpens our life to a point.

The sound of the gunshots that morning—those two short, sharp, metallic snaps that at first seemed to everyone in the First Baptist Church like some sort of joke—struck the town of Wesleyan like a cold slap across the face. Those scalding metal bullets, no bigger than thumbnails, pierced the wall that divided everybody, causing the tallest parts to crumble and fall at everyone's feet. A quiet shame now seemed to nestle in those cracks and crevices where zealotry and anger had only recently worked so hard to take root. Nobody wanted to talk about the statue anymore. Nobody wanted to admit they'd ever had the slightest opinion on the thing. People still heard those shots in their sleep.

Most of the strangers that filled the pews that rainy morning at Old Man Griffin's funeral had run from the church when the bedlam broke out; nobody knew who they were. If Ronnie Childers had intended his actions to be the catalyst for something much worse, he'd hardly had long to feel disappointed. Lurlene Pearson had seen to that.

Sergeant Larry Crowder had once again been on duty when Will's urgent call for backup came in. "Mrs. Pearson. Yes, that's what I said, Larry. Lurlene. She just raised that cane of hers and bashed him right on top of his head. Cracked his skull clean in two. Hell no, we won't charge her! I don't care who this guy is or what his family might say. God knows how many lives Lurlene Pearson may have saved here today."

Larry had put down the phone and placed his head in his hands. From kitchen tables and den recliners, from movie theaters to Mama's Way Cafe, all over town every officer on the Wesleyan police force was called to the First Baptist Church. "You read about these things," Larry had said to Jocelyn Shaw when she stuck a microphone in his face later that afternoon, "almost like you're reading some kind of story, something too far-fetched to ever be true, too far out there to ever happen in the town you grew up in."

Spring had come earlier than ever, one more new definition of normal but such a welcome sight that if they'd even noticed it arrived before it should, people wouldn't have been able to make themselves care. Folks swore they'd never seen the azaleas so scarlet or known the gardenias to smell quite so sweet. A heavenly white fragrance drifted up from every backyard garden, wafting out over fences, around corners, and down the newly green streets, an invisible elixir that seemed to soothe the tired soul like forgiveness itself.

May had apparently held back extra beauty as a gift for this, its last Saturday afternoon. The sky was cloudless. It appeared to have been painted with the same blue as the hydrangeas that nodded and bobbed down below. The large bird stretched out and circled the garden, high in the air, riding the breeze like a kite.

Back on the ground he could see her, surrounded by friends. Right now, she was laughing.

He dipped his black wings lower, sailing down closer to watch, to make certain. He was grateful he'd been allowed this chance. As he settled in the shelter of a sweetgum tree, he heard a pinging sound ring out from the back of the garden, getting louder and louder until it reached every ear.

The guests turned to see Gordon Lovett standing beside the punch bowl, waving his arm in the air, back and forth, as though saying goodbye from the deck of a ship. "Ladies and gentlemen," he said, with the loudest voice in his repertoire, "may I please have your attention? Yes? Thank you. Peter Swann? A little quiet please? You can talk to Thea later." Christo gave his son a playful smack, a few people tittered, and Peter's face went bright red.

"A good three weeks ago, when Butter started begging and pleading with me to give this toast . . ." Gordon grinned and held up his hand. "Just kidding, just kidding, she didn't ask me to do this at all. In fact, she's probably petrified about what I might say." He shielded his eyes from the sun and looked around for Butter, who was sitting in the shade at the side of the garden, shaking her head. "I like to tease her. Always have. It's not fun unless you get a rise out of somebody, and Butter has always been *so* reliable about that, the perfect audience. Thank you, Butter, dear. For always letting me hone my rapier wit at your expense. You made me what I am today." He gave a little bow in Butter's direction and continued.

"If you had told me, even six months ago, that I would be standing here in Harry's lovely garden, giving an engagement toast to Butter Swann . . . and that I'd be doing it as her friend and confidant, God help me . . . well, I would have said you were a man of infinite jest." More laughter from the crowd took Gordon's voice to a slightly higher decibel. "Just goes to show you, you're never too old to be surprised. For as the poet said, 'Once in a while the odd thing happens, once in a while the dream comes true, and the whole pattern of life is altered, once in a while the moon turns blue.'

"An ice storm in Wesleyan. As rare as Auden's blue moon, so rare an occurrence in this part of the world, Butter could be forgiven for thinking it was a miracle created just for her and Will. For, 'tis true: if Butter's pipes hadn't frozen and burst in that storm then these two might never have met." Everybody laughed as they strained to get a good look at Butter and Will.

"Yes, yes, thank God for weather," said Gordon, who paused now, staring straight at Butter. "You see, Butter and me, well . . . she won't mind me telling you . . . we were never the best of friends. But what's past is prologue, and happily so. When that ice fell down on Wesleyan, it knocked a lot of things out of place, and we were but two of the many. And as you all doubtless know, before that cold week was out, well, let's just say a lot of us discovered just how much we're all connected to one another, whether we especially want to be or not.

"And now here we all are, four short months later, with a brand-new couple about to walk down the aisle, throwing caution to the proverbial wind, and embracing hope in the future. And there's just not one thing wrong with that." Everybody applauded as Will leaned over to give Butter a kiss.

Gordon lifted his arm high in the air. "So, I raise my glass on this gorgeous afternoon, in my best linen trousers and my pair of pink shoes, to wish my two friends—Butter and her big, handsome policeman, Will—a long and happy marriage. May the course of your true love run smoothly, all the rest of your days."

From her place on the old green glider, Marietta smiled as cheers flooded the air. She had wanted to tease Butter over the swiftness of the engagement but didn't really have the heart. Butter's happiness ran before her like a carpet of flowers; everyone who came near her found themselves standing knee-deep in it. Marietta felt almost privileged to have been witness to it all, from that grim, icy morning after Harry's funeral when she'd looked out the window and seen Will holding Butter's arm as he led her up to the door, all the way to the night she heard Butter close that same door and run up the stairs like a girl, flapping her left hand in Marietta's face, an antique diamond shining from her finger.

They'd both squealed and then smiled, listening as the echoes of their own girlhood voices stirred and danced about the room. Marietta had promised her friend this engagement party that very night.

She doubted she could have stopped Butter from moving in to take care of her if she'd had the strength to try. Two and a half long months. Well, the doctors said her depression made the recovery take a bit longer, and she supposed they were right. They also stressed, over and over—and she was so tired of hearing it— how incredibly lucky she'd been. Marietta sometimes wondered if God gives us a spleen just to lose, that one organ you can afford to have ripped from your body without too much consequence.

She'd ended up taking the full force of the second bullet for both herself and her brother, flying right out of that pew when she saw the gun pointed directly at Macon, propelled by instinct rather than thought. It had passed through her, altered its lethal direction, and hit Macon in the knee instead of the heart, which had been its mission. Marietta didn't remember anything else.

She didn't see Ernest Adcock push Lucy-Jewel Whitmore to the floor with such force it broke the clasp on her pearls, sending them rolling all over the beet-red carpet, and causing Leonard Pennington's feet to fly out from under him as he attempted to sprint from the room. Nor did she see Mayor Baker and Principal Gray running toward the shooter in what turned out to be a redundant attempt to render him harmless. Lurlene, bless her heart, had seen to that by herself.

And she'd missed what folks told her was the strangest sight of all: the huge black crow that had flown in through the open doors as people frantically pushed their way out of the church. The thing had swooped low over the crowd, shrieking and screeching and scaring them all, and though everyone agreed it had been an unsettling sight, it depended on who was telling the story whether the bird was seen as some sort of feathered form of judgment or deliverance. The bird had soared to the top of the cross that hung high over the baptistry, and there it had sat, its brown eyes glaring down over the frightened crowd, until Marietta was borne from the church. Then it had sailed out the front doors into the dense wall of rain, leaving most people reluctant to admit that they'd seen it at all.

From her spot on the porch, Marietta let her eyes slowly wander over the crowd. Christo and Jen with Enid and John, brought together by their children, now talking like old friends. Ernest Adcock, his brief association with Harrison Gray prompting him into not politics but education; word had it he was starting at Auburn in the fall on his way to becoming a teacher. Harrison Gray would run unopposed, as Mayor Baker had hoped all along. Marietta almost turned to mention this last bit of news to Harry, before realizing, once again, that he wasn't sitting beside her. The pain hit her, a fresh wave that hadn't dulled in the slightest.

She still expected Harry to be in the garden whenever she gazed out the window, still looked for him to come up the drive around dinnertime or to already be in bed when she got there at night, warming the covers for her the way he used to do. She waited for him to ask about the book she was reading, listened for him talking to Smudge, could have sworn she'd heard his footsteps on the stairs just last night. She hadn't seen the raven since the shooting.

She distrusted the fabled seven stages of grief. The denial and the guilt, the anger and bargaining, she could run through them all before noon. She'd occasionally manage acceptance and hope before bedtime, only to have depression come roaring back with a vengeance just as she turned out the light. It was a tricky and tiring process.

"Moving from one 'stage' of grief to another like a tenth grader moves between classes is just ludicrous," Gordon had authoritatively told her the sunny afternoon in March when he'd found her still in bed with no apparent intention of rising. "Hell," he'd grumbled, "if that method's accurate, then I've been stuck in the netherworld between anger and depression since 1984. 'Every man can master a grief but he that has it,' Marietta."

"Eliot?"

"Shakespeare," he sighed. "Listen, a few days ago I thought I saw Alan in the produce aisle, looking at tomatoes—which, strangely, he never even liked—and that same old heartbreak hit me again, as fresh as a breath of sea air. He's been gone thirty years and sometimes it feels like last week.

"Try and tame it and it only gets worse. Best thing I've found to do is make friends with it. Let it walk right beside you. It's a vile creature, but it comes wrapped up in memories that you'll never want to lose, and the longer you welcome it into the room with you, the stronger those memories get." Gordon had gotten up from the side of her bed to put more water in the vase of tuberoses he ordered for her every week, talking all the while. "And you'd think the memories would be painful, right, all tangled up in grief like they are, but instead, they become the very thing that heals you. They'll never be so strong as to squelch the grief altogether, of course, but they're much more powerful than you'd think, and eventually they manage to hold it at arm's length long enough for you to start to see a future. Those memories become the weapons you fight grief with, and eventually, they start to win some big battles. You can trust my word on this." He'd set the flowers back down on her night table with a look of shy triumph in his eyes.

The sun kept on rising, and this afternoon as she sat here in the shade with Smudge close beside her, she was hopeful. In the midst of such joy, it was difficult not to be. Looking over the crowd she saw Macon sitting alone under the oak tree by the fence, hidden from most of the others. Marietta got up and walked toward him.

"That seat empty?" she asked, pointing to the wicker chair beside her brother. He pushed it forward and motioned for her to sit down. They sat beside each other in silence.

"Nice party," he said, after a minute or two.

"I'm glad you came. Lurlene and Reese bring you over?"

"Yeah. I don't guess I'll ever be able to say no to Lurlene Pearson again. Or you, either, for that matter." They both looked over to the dessert table, where Lurlene was pointing out a piece of coconut cake with the end of her cane. She was never without that cane now.

"She's been bringing me dinner every night, and I don't know how to get her to stop," said Macon.

"Why would you want her to? She's one of the best cooks in the county. And she's right across the street from you now."

Macon sighed, an invitation for the question Marietta really wanted to ask. "Have you heard from her, Macon?"

Her brother kept his eyes straight ahead. "We've talked a couple of times. She says she can't change her mind. I'm still not sure why she puts it that way. But I think she will, though, eventually. I still haven't signed the papers."

Marietta thought of the last time she'd seen Glinda, sitting on the side of her hospital bed, twisting a pair of brown leather gloves in her hands while Marietta kept trying to convince her what had happened was in no way her fault.

"But if I hadn't forced Macon into doing what he did . . . I'm just so sorry, Marietta."

"Glinda, you did the right thing. And you stopped Macon from doing the wrong thing. None of us could have predicted what happened. And the finger of blame points in too many directions to count. You did what you knew was right, and that's all any of us can do at any given moment."

Glinda had taken Marietta's hand in her own. "I feel like I've missed out on a friendship that would have meant the world to me. Please tell me you'll come visit this summer. Josh lives in a lovely part of France, and he swears he has plenty of room. Bring Gordon, too, if he wants to come."

Marietta had smiled. "You know, we just might. There's room in my life for another good friend." She glanced over at Macon now, wondering whether to tell him that she and Gordon already had their tickets to France.

Instead, she asked, "And you didn't want to stay in the house?"

"Well, no. After Glinda left and Maggie came in to take care of me, well, I mean, Maggie's a good girl, but she stayed too long as it was. I was fine by myself. But after she was gone I, well, I just thought a change might do me some good." His voice took on a brittle edge. "Every time I looked out the front window, down toward the barn, all I could think about is how long it's going to be before I'm able to ride again. Hell, it was taking me half an hour just to get down to the mailbox." Macon shifted his weight to lessen the pressure on his knee just as Ivy ran past with Trilby and Smudge fast on her heels. "Besides, I might have given the city the park, but the Griffin house is mine. I might as well use it."

Marietta sat in silence, watching the little girl and the dog. "But, you know, it's getting better, the knee," said Macon, making a stab at the positivity he thought she probably wanted. "Dr. Jarrett says I should be able to drive again before the end of June. We'll see." He cleared his throat. "I, uh, I do appreciate you sending that girl over to exercise Red Rascal. Been meaning to tell you. I see her from the window sometimes. She's a good little rider."

"Oh, yeah. Thea's been winning ribbons since she was barely old enough to walk. I knew she could handle that horse. But you didn't need to pay her, Macon. Enid told me you offered her a hundred a ride. That's ridiculous."

"Well, her parents wouldn't let her take it. *That* was ridiculous. I finally got them to agree to thirty. Told them I wouldn't go any lower, take it or leave it. The kid deserves to be paid for her work, even if it doesn't feel like work to her. Thirty bucks still doesn't seem to be enough to me, but she seems happy, and Red Rascal looks good."

The afternoon light was beginning to sharpen, drawing black shadows across the green grass. Several people began to say their goodbyes to Butter and Will. Then, almost as though he was talking to himself, Macon asked, "Did you hear what he said?"

"What? What who said?"

"That guy. The one who shot us."

"No, Macon. I don't think I heard anything."

Macon stayed quiet, long enough for Marietta to think he'd

chosen not to say any more. When he spoke again, it was almost in a whisper. "I did. I heard him. Right before he did it, he yelled out that word: 'traitor.' Didn't you hear him? That's the last word I heard. He yelled it at me, right at me, and I can't get it out of my head."

"I didn't hear him, Macon."

"That's what the boys used to call Daddy when I was in school, you know. I used to see it, all over town. Somebody always wrote it across his picture somewhere, whenever another of his articles came out back when we were little. You know, those civil rights things he used to put in the paper? I got hell for those every time he published one."

"I never knew that."

"Oh, yeah. All the time. I got beat up more times than I can count." Macon lifted his knee with both hands, moving it into another position. The silence between them this time was longer.

"I know our dad was a good man," Macon finally said, squinting up at the sun, so much brighter now that it was beginning to set. "And I know he loved me; I do. I loved him, too."

Marietta reached across and put her hand on top of her brother's. "Time only moves one way, Macon. I guess we all have to decide for ourselves what to do with the past before we can move on to something better."

"Yeah, well. I hope I can."

"I think sometimes hope's a good enough place to start. I'm counting on that myself."

Lurlene and Reese were making their way across the garden, the rabbit-head cane pointing at the boxwood elephants as they passed them. "I swear, Marietta, I cannot believe how these things have grown," Lurlene called out. She continued when they got closer. "Between you and me, I thought that idea of Harry's was the silliest thing I'd ever heard, but Lord, did he prove *me* wrong. You have to be on the garden tour next year, hon. Everybody needs to see these. You ready to go, Macon? I got you a big plate of dessert for later. Enough cake to have you all fixed for the week."

Standing in front of him, Lurlene blocked the sun completely, her face nothing more than shadow when Macon looked up. "It's good to be all fixed up, Lurlene. Thank you." Then, turning to Marietta, he said, "Looks like my ride's here, sis. I'll be seeing you."

As he stepped through the gate, Marietta called out, "Want to go to dinner one night this week, Macon? I've had my driving privileges back for a while now. I could pick you up."

Macon turned, then slowly grinned at his sister. "Sure," he said. "That'd be nice."

Most of the guests had gone home now. Enid and Thea were almost done with the cleaning up, having flatly refused to let Marietta lift a finger to help. Not that she argued. Truth be told, her side was beginning to hurt. She left Butter and Gordon on the porch, where they'd all been sitting, and went back into the house and up the stairs to her room to find the pain pills the doctor had given her for just this purpose.

Rummaging in her bedside drawer, her fingers closed around a small bottle, and she pulled it out. It wasn't the one she expected. In her hand was something she'd thought she'd never forget but had. Harry's pills, the ones she'd saved, just in case. Marietta stared down at them now as if they were something odd, something macabre. Then she went straight to the toilet and flushed them. The empty bottle clattered down to the bottom of the trash can, the noise both affirmation and rebuke.

Suddenly the wind began to blow. The bedroom curtain reached out for her and from the open window she could see the leaves of the maple trees making fists of lime green. From down in the garden, she heard Ivy calling, "Marietta! Look, Marietta! Oh, come here and look."

She hurried down the stairs and out onto the porch just in time to see a massive flock of birds landing high in the trees, densely gathering on the edge of her roof like a ruffle of black lace. The birds stared down on the people in the garden, nodding

silently as if in comment on the pitiful limits of earthbound existence. And then, almost as though they'd decided to give the
poor people a gift, they lifted as one, into the glowing light of the
dying day.

For the next few minutes, they floated through the air, their
movements more intricate than any kaleidoscope, a feathered
ballet that swirled and twirled in time to a music none of the
people could hear. Tilting her head back to watch them, Marietta
felt her spirit rise up and float among the dark wings, backward
and forward, reaching up to the rising moon, falling back toward
the tired earth, a longing that made her soul ache.

"It's a murmuration," whispered Thea. "We learned about
them in school. Nobody knows why they do it."

Thea's voice pulled Marietta's eyes away from the birds. She
turned to look at the faces around her, each one staring up to the
sky, lost in the beauty above, and her mind flew back to all those
recent afternoons spent lying in bed, listening as Thea read her
Alice Munro stories with an understanding far beyond her years.
She thought of Enid, bringing her Sunday lunch, complete with
linen napkins and a vase of white peonies balancing atop the
wicker tray. Of Ivy presenting her with the first batch of choco-
late chip cookies she'd ever made all by herself, wrapped up and
tied with a bow. The afternoon Gordon hauled a card table up
the stairs to her bedroom so he could work on a huge puzzle of
cats that she knew he detested, all so she wouldn't be alone while
she dozed. She remembered the comfort it gave her to know
Butter was sleeping next door, in the same twin bed she'd slept in
when they were girls, alert to any sound that might signal Marietta needed something in the night. Of Will changing her porch
light when it went out, of Butter turning it on for Ivy on those
evenings when Marietta didn't feel like coming downstairs.

Every person here was holding tight to one of those ropes that
tethered her fast to the ground, just like her father had told her.
She could no more decide to leave now than she could yet fly.
Maybe Gordon had been right when he told her all any of us can

ever really manage is to love our crooked neighbors with our crooked hearts. It was no small thing to try.

Without a backward glance, the birds suddenly turned to go. Like the smoke from a candle, the dark, joyous cloud rose toward the heavens, leaving the people alone in the garden once more. Marietta watched them evaporate into the approaching night, and as the very last one disappeared, she saw it, lying at her feet. A feather. Long and glossy black, still warm from the breast of the bird.

Butter said her goodbyes in the garden, promising to call Marietta tomorrow. When she reached the stone porch she looked back at her old friend, standing there with her hand on Smudge's white head, both of them looking up toward the sky. At Marietta's feet Harry's magical row of boxwood elephants moved round and round in their constant circle. We've come full circle, too, Butter thought. She stared at Marietta for a moment, then reluctantly turned to go back inside. She had a wedding to plan.

Will was loading presents into the car as Butter came through the shadowy house, stopping at the open front door. He saw her standing there and he smiled, holding on to her eyes for a long second before turning back to the car. Butter paused, then opened her handbag. Removing the small silver box, she placed it carefully on the entry table, where it belonged. Her eyes swept over the darkened rooms where, if she listened hard enough, she was sure she could hear those long-ago voices she remembered so well. Brushing a lone tear from her cheek, Butter closed the door behind her with a soft click.

ACKNOWLEDGMENTS

This book would be so much less without the kind attention of my editor, Shauna Summers. She makes this process pure pleasure and I trust her completely, which is such a gift.

All my gratitude to the team of wizards at Ballantine. They all are simply the best, and working with them is nothing but joy from beginning to end. Thank you, Kara Welsh, Jennifer Hershey, Kim Hovey, Karen Fink, Taylor Noel, Quinne Rogers, Mae Martinez, Belina Huey, Ella Laytham, Cindy Berman, and Susan Brown.

And I'll never know how I got so lucky to call Kimberly Whalen both my agent and my friend. I can't imagine all this without her.

My special thanks to:

Peggy Green, for your honesty and kindness, and those long lunches during which we always put the world to rights.

Vickie Mabry, for being my honest, faithful first reader.

Allison Adams, for Mama's Way Cafe, and for making me learn the Laurel and Hardy dance well enough to perform it in public.

Jayne Parker and Beckie Yon for your graciousness, enthusiasm, and friendship. How happy I am you two are in my life.

Brian McCarthy, Joey Pitts, and Natalie Spalding for sharing your specialized knowledge so willingly in aid of this book.

Ruby Drake Lodge in Twin Bridges, Montana, for providing me with a serenely beautiful place to jump-start this story when a pandemic and an insurrection tried to snatch it away.

And always, to Pat, for giving me such a soft place to land for lo, these many years.

Finally, since childhood, I have been lucky to count some older women among my friends. It was a pleasure to sprinkle this book with women like them, women for whom chronological age is no impediment to curiosity, or change, or great good humor, even in a mercurial world like our own. I hope I made Nina Young, Mary Ellen Parker, Malvina Carman, and Ruth Vaught proud.

The inspiration for the character of Logan Hargis in this book was Ralph McGill, editor and publisher of *The Atlanta Constitution* from the 1940s through the 1960s. McGill was known at the time as "the conscience of the South"; his writings held the magnifying glass so close to the Southern shame of segregation and inequality, emotions often caught fire. He was labeled a traitor even as he won the Pulitzer Prize for his transformative work.

For those perhaps unfamiliar with Ralph McGill, I would recommend his 1963 book, *The South and the Southerner,* as well as the excellent overview article in *The New Georgia Encyclopedia* by Leonard Teel, entitled "Ralph McGill."

A lifelong Southerner, Pamela Terry learned the power of storytelling at a very early age. Terry is the author of *The Sweet Taste of Muscadines* and the internationally popular blog *From the House of Edward,* which was named one of the top ten home blogs of the year by London's *The Telegraph.* She lives in Georgia with her songwriter husband, Pat, and their two big dogs, Andrew and George. She travels to the Scottish Highlands as frequently as possible.

ABOUT THE TYPE

This book was set in Bembo, a typeface based on an old-style Roman face that was used for Cardinal Pietro Bembo's tract *De Aetna* in 1495. Bembo was cut by Francesco Griffo (1450–1518) in the early sixteenth century for Italian Renaissance printer and publisher Aldus Manutius (1449–1515). The Lanston Monotype Company of Philadelphia brought the well-proportioned letterforms of Bembo to the United States in the 1930s.